Born in the Kingdom of Fife in 1960, Ian Rankin graduated from the University of Edinburgh in 1982, and then spent three years writing novels when he was supposed to be working towards a PhD in Scottish Literature. His first Rebus novel was published in 1987, and the Rebus books are now translated into thirty-six languages and are bestsellers worldwide. He is the recipient of four Crime Writers' Association Dagger Awards, including the prestigious Diamond Dagger in 2005, and in 2004 he won America's celebrated Edgar Award. A contributor to BBC2's *Newsnight Review*, he has also presented his own TV series, *Ian Rankin's Evil Thoughts*. Ian is a number-one bestselling author in the UK and has received the OBE for services to literature, opting to receive the prize in his home city of Edinburgh, where he lives with his partner and two sons.

You can discover more about the author at www.ianrankin.net

EVEN DOGS IN THE WILD

Retirement doesn't suit John Rebus. He wasn't made for hobbies, holidays or home improvements. Being a cop is in his blood. So when DI Siobhan Clarke asks for his help on a case, Rebus doesn't need long to consider his options. Clarke's been investigating the death of a senior lawyer whose body was found along with a threatening note. On the other side of Edinburgh, Big Ger Cafferty — Rebus's long-time nemesis — has received an identical note and a bullet through his window. Now it's up to Clarke and Rebus to connect the dots and stop a killer . . . Meanwhile, DI Malcolm Fox joins forces with a covert team from Glasgow who are tailing a notorious crime family. There's something they want, and they'll stop at nothing to get it . . .

IAN RANKIN

EVEN DOGS
IN THE WILD

Complete and Unabridged

CHARNWOOD
Leicester

First published in Great Britain in 2015 by
Orion Books
an imprint of
The Orion Publishing Group Ltd
London

First Charnwood Edition
published 2017
by arrangement with
The Orion Publishing Group Limited
An Hachette UK Company
London

A catalogue record for this book is available
from the British Library.

ISBN 978–1–4448–3143–6

Published by
F. A. Thorpe (Publishing)
Anstey, Leicestershire

Set by Words & Graphics Ltd.
Anstey, Leicestershire
Printed and bound in Great Britain by
T. J. International Ltd., Padstow, Cornwall

This book is printed on acid-free paper

Prologue

Eventually the passenger ejected the tape and tossed it on to the back seat.

'That was the Associates,' the driver complained.

'Well they can go associate somewhere else. Singer sounds like his balls have been trapped in a vice.'

The driver thought about this for a moment, then smiled. 'Remember we did that to . . . what was his name again?'

The passenger shrugged. 'He owed the boss money — that's what mattered.'

'Wasn't a lot of money, was it?'

'How much further?' The passenger peered through the windscreen.

'Half a mile. These woods have seen some action, eh?'

The passenger made no comment. It was dark out there and they'd not encountered another car for the last five or so miles. Fife countryside, inland from the coast, the fields shorn and awaiting winter. A pig farm not too far away, one they'd used before.

'What's the plan?' the driver asked.

'Just the one shovel, so we toss to see who breaks sweat. Strip off his clothes, burn them later.'

'He's only wearing pants and a vest.'

'No tattoos or rings that I saw. Nothing we need to cut off.'

'This is us here.' The driver stopped the car, got out and opened a gate. A churned track led into the forest. 'Hope we don't get stuck,' he said, getting back in. Then, seeing the look on the other man's face: 'Joke.'

'Better be.'

They drove slowly for a few hundred yards. 'There's a space here where I can turn,' the driver said.

'This'll do, then.'

'Recognise it?'

The passenger shook his head. 'It's been a while.'

'I think there's one buried somewhere in front of us, and another over to the left.'

'Maybe try the other side of the track, in that case. Torch in the glove box?'

'Fresh batteries, like you said.'

The passenger checked. 'Right then.'

The two men got out and stood for the best part of a minute, their eyes adjusting to the gloom, ears alert for unusual sounds.

'I'll pick the spot,' the passenger said, taking the torch with him as he headed off. The driver got a cigarette lit and opened the back door of the Mercedes. It was an old model, and the hinges creaked. He lifted the Associates cassette from the seat and slipped it into his jacket pocket, where it hit some coins. He'd be needing one of those for the heads-or-tails. Slamming the door shut, he moved to the boot and opened it. The body was wrapped in a plain blue bedsheet. Or it had been. The trip had loosened the makeshift shroud. Bare feet, pale skinny legs,

2

ribcage visible. The driver rested the shovel against one of the tail lights, but it slid to the ground. Cursing, he bent over to retrieve it.

Which was when the corpse burst into life, emerging from sheet and boot both, almost vaulting the driver as its feet hit the ground. The driver gasped, the cigarette flying from his mouth. He had one hand on the shovel's handle while he tried to haul himself upright with the other. The sheet was hanging over the lip of the boot, its occupant disappearing into the trees.

'Paul!' the driver yelled. 'Paul!'

Torchlight preceded the man called Paul.

'Hell's going on, Dave?' he shouted. The driver could only stretch out a shaking hand to point.

'He's done a runner!'

Paul scanned the empty boot. A hissing sound from between his gritted teeth.

'After him then,' he said in a growl. 'Or it'll be someone else's turn to dig a hole for us.'

'He came back from the dead,' Dave said, voice trembling.

'Then we kill him again,' Paul stated, producing a knife from his inside pocket. 'Even slower than before . . .'

Day One

1

Malcolm Fox woke from another of his bad dreams.

He reckoned he knew why he'd started having them — uncertainty about his job. He wasn't entirely sure he wanted it any more, and feared he was surplus to requirements anyway. Yesterday, he'd been told he had to travel to Dundee to fill a vacant post for a couple of shifts. When he asked why, he was told the officer he'd be replacing had been ordered to cover for someone else in Glasgow.

'Isn't it easier just to send me to Glasgow, then?' Fox had enquired.

'You could always ask, I suppose.'

So he'd picked up the phone and done exactly that, only to find that the officer in Glasgow was coming to Edinburgh to fill a temporary gap — at which point he'd given up the fight and driven to Dundee. And today? Who knew. His boss at St Leonard's didn't seem to know what to do with him. He was just one detective inspector too many.

'It's the time-servers,' DCI Doug Maxtone had apologised. 'They're bunging up the system. Need a few of them to take the gold watch . . . '

'Understood,' Fox had said. He wasn't in the first idealistic flush of youth himself — another three years and he could retire with a solid pension and plenty of life left in him.

Standing under the shower, he considered his options. The bungalow in Oxgangs that he called home would fetch a fair price, enough to allow him to relocate. But then there was his dad to consider — Fox couldn't move too far away, not while Mitch still had breath in his body. And then there was Siobhan. They weren't lovers, but they'd been spending more time together. If either of them was bored, they knew they could always call. Maybe there'd be a film or a restaurant, or just snacks and a DVD. She'd bought him half a dozen titles for Christmas and they'd watched three before the old year was done. As he got dressed, he thought of her. She loved the job more than he did. Whenever they met up, she was always ready to share news and gossip. Then she would ask him, and he would shrug, maybe offer a few morsels. She gulped them down like delicacies, while all he saw was plain white bread. She worked at Gayfield Square, with James Page for a boss. The structure there seemed better than at St Leonard's. Fox had wondered about a transfer, but knew it would never happen — he would be creating the self-same problem. One DI too many.

Forty minutes after finishing breakfast, he was parking at St Leonard's. He sat in his car for an extra few moments, gathering himself, hands running around the steering wheel. It was at times like this he wished he smoked — something to occupy him, to take him out of himself. Instead of which, he placed a piece of chewing gum on his tongue and closed his mouth. A uniform had emerged from the station's back door into the car park and was opening a packet of cigarettes. Their eyes met as Fox walked towards him, and the other man gave the curtest of nods. The uniform knew that Fox used to work for Professional Standards — everyone in the station knew. Some didn't seem to mind; others made their distaste obvious. They scowled, answered grudgingly, let doors swing shut into his face rather than holding them open.

'You're a good cop,' Siobhan had told him on more than one occasion. 'I wish you could see that . . .'

When he reached the CID suite, Fox gleaned that something was happening. Chairs and equipment were being moved. His eyes met those of a thunderous Doug Maxtone.

'We've to make room for a new team,' Maxtone explained.

'New team?'

'From Gartcosh, which means they'll mostly be Glasgow — and you know how I feel about *them.*'

'What's the occasion?'

'Nobody's saying.'

Fox chewed on his gum. Gartcosh, an old steelworks, was now home to the Scottish Crime Campus. It had been up and running since the previous summer, and Fox had never had occasion to cross its threshold. The place was a mix of police, prosecutors, forensics and Customs, and its remit took in organised crime and counterterrorism. 'How many are we expecting to welcome?'

Maxtone glared at him. 'Frankly, Malcolm, I'm not expecting to *welcome* a single one of

9

them. But we need desks and chairs for half a dozen.'

'And computers and phones?'

'They're bringing their own. They do, however, request . . . ' Maxtone produced a sheet of paper from his pocket and made show of consulting it, ' "ancillary support, subject to vetting".'

'And this came from on high?'

'The Chief Constable himself.' Maxtone crumpled the paper and tossed it in the general direction of a bin. 'They're arriving in about an hour.'

'Should I do a bit of dusting?'

'Might as well — it's not as if there's going to be anywhere for you to sit.'

'I'm losing my chair?'

'And your desk.' Maxtone inhaled and exhaled noisily. 'So if there's anything in the drawers you'd rather not share . . . ' He managed a grim smile. 'Bet you're wishing you'd stayed in bed, eh?'

'Worse than that, sir — I'm beginning to wish I'd stayed in Dundee.'

★　★　★

Siobhan Clarke had parked on a yellow line on St Bernard's Crescent. It was about as grand a street as could be found in Edinburgh's New Town, all pillared facades and floor-to-ceiling windows. Two bow-shaped Georgian terraces facing one another across a small private garden containing trees and benches. Raeburn Place, with its emporia and eateries, was a two-minute walk away, as was the Water of Leith. She'd

10

brought Malcolm to the Saturday food market a couple of times, and joked that he should trade in his bungalow for one of Stockbridge's colony flats.

Her phone buzzed: speak of the devil. She answered the call.

'You off up north again?'

'Not at the moment,' he said. 'Big shake-up happening here, though.'

'I've got news too — I've been seconded to the Minton enquiry.'

'Since when?'

'First thing this morning. I was going to tell you at lunchtime. James has been put in charge and he wanted me.'

'Makes sense.'

She locked her car and walked towards a gloss-black front door boasting a gleaming brass knocker and letter box. A uniformed officer stood guard; she gave a half-bow of recognition, which Clarke rewarded with a smile.

'Any room for a little one?' Fox was asking, trying to make it sound like a joke, though she could tell he was serious.

'I've got to go, Malcolm. Talk to you later.' Clarke ended the call and waited for the officer to unlock the door. There were no media — they'd been and gone. A couple of small posies had been left at the front step, probably by neighbours. There was an old-style bell pull by the pillar to the right of the door, and above it a nameplate bearing the single capitalised word MINTON.

As the door swung open, Clarke thanked the

11

officer and went inside. There was some mail on the parquet floor. She scooped it up and saw that more was sitting on an occasional table. The letters on the table had been opened and checked — presumably by the major incident team. There were the usual flyers too, including one for a curry house she knew on the south side of the city. She didn't see Lord Minton as the takeaway type, but you never could tell. The scene of crime unit had been through the hall, dusting for prints. Lord Minton — David Menzies Minton, to give him his full name — had been killed two evenings back. No one in the vicinity had heard the break-in or the attack. Whoever had done it had scaled a couple of back walls in the darkness to reach the small window of the garden-level laundry room, adjacent to the locked and bolted rear door. They had broken the window and climbed in. Minton had been in his study on the ground floor. According to the post-mortem examination, he had been beaten around the head, then throttled, after which his lifeless body had been beaten some more.

Clarke stood in the still, silent hall, getting her bearings. Then she lifted a file from her shoulder bag and began to reread its contents. Victim had been seventy-eight years old, never married, resident at this address for thirty-five years. Educated at George Heriot's School and the universities of St Andrews and Edinburgh. Rising through the city's teeming ranks of lawyers until he reached the position of Lord Advocate, prosecuting some of Scotland's most high-profile criminal trials. Enemies? He would have had plenty in his heyday, but for the past decade he had lived out of the limelight. Occasional trips to London to sit in the House of Lords. Visited his club on Princes Street most days to read the newspapers and do as many crosswords as he could find.

'Housebreaking gone wrong,' Clarke's boss, DCI James Page, had stated. 'Perpetrator doesn't expect anyone home. Panics. Game over.'

'But why strangle him, then start beating him again once the victim's deceased?'

'Like I say: panic. Explains why the attacker fled without taking anything. Probably high on something and needing money for more. Looking for the usual — phones and iPads, easily sold on. But not the sort of thing someone like the noble lord would have in his possession. Maybe that annoyed our man and he took out his frustration then and there.'

'Sounds reasonable.'

'But you'd like to see for yourself?' Page had nodded slowly. 'Off you go then.'

Living room, formal dining room and kitchen on the ground floor, unused servants' quarters and laundry room below. The window frame of the laundry room had been boarded up, the window panel itself removed, along with all the shards of glass, to be taken away and examined by forensics. Clarke unlocked the back door and studied the small, well-tended private garden. Lord Minton employed a gardener, but he only visited one day each month in winter. He had been interviewed and had expressed his sadness, along with his concern that he hadn't been paid

13

for the previous month.

Climbing the noiseless stone staircase to the ground floor, Clarke realised that, apart from a toilet, there was only one further room to check. The study was dark, its thick red velvet curtains closed. From the photographs in her file, she could see that Lord Minton's body had been found in front of his desk, on a Persian rug that had now also been taken away to be tested. Hair, saliva, fibres — everyone left traces of some kind. The thinking was: the victim was seated at his desk, writing out cheques to pay his gas and electricity bills. Hears a noise and gets up to investigate. Hasn't got far when the attacker bursts in and smacks him on the head with a tool of some kind — no weapon recovered yet; the pathologist's best guess, a hammer.

The chequebook lay open on the antique desk next to an expensive-looking pen. There were family photos — black and white, the victim's parents, maybe — in silver frames. Small enough to be slipped into a thief's pocket, yet untouched. She knew that Lord Minton's wallet had been found in a jacket over the back of the chair, cash and credit cards intact. The gold watch on his wrist had been left too.

'You weren't that desperate, were you?' Clarke muttered.

A woman called Jean Marischal came in twice a week to clean. She had her own key and had found the body the following morning. In her statement she said the place didn't really need that much attention; she just thought 'his lordship' liked a bit of company.

14

Upstairs there were too many rooms. A drawing room and sitting room that looked as though they'd never seen a visitor; four bedrooms, where only one was needed. Mrs Marischal could not recall a single overnight guest, or a dinner party, or any other kind of gathering, come to that. The bathroom didn't detain Clarke, so she headed downstairs to the hall again and stood there with arms folded. No fingerprints had been found other than those belonging to the victim and his cleaner. No reports of prowlers or out-of-place visitors.

Nothing.

Mrs Marischal had been persuaded to revisit the scene later on today. If anything *had* been taken, she was their best hope. Meanwhile, the team would have to look busy — it was expected that they would *be* busy. The current Lord Advocate wanted twice-daily updates, as did the First Minister. There would be media briefings at midday and four, briefings at which DCI James Page had to have something to share.

The problem was: what?

As she left, Clarke told the uniform outside to keep her wits about her.

'It's not true that the guilty always come back, but we might get lucky one time . . . '

On her way to Fettes, she stopped at a shop and bought a couple of newspapers, checking at the counter that they contained decent-sized obituaries of the deceased. She doubted she would learn anything she hadn't already read on a half-hour trawl of the internet, but they would bulk out the file.

Because Lord Minton was who he was, it had been decided to locate the major incident team at Fettes rather than Gayfield Square. Fettes — aka 'the Big House' — had been the headquarters of Lothian and Borders Police right up to April Fools' Day 2013, when Scotland's eight police regions vanished to be replaced by a single organisation called Police Scotland. In place of a Chief Constable, Edinburgh now had a chief superintendent called Jack Scoular, who was only a few years older than Clarke. Fettes was Scoular's domain, a place where admin took precedence and meetings were held. No CID officers were stationed there, but it did boast half a corridor of vacated offices, which James Page had been offered. Two detective constables, Christine Esson and Ronnie Ogilvie, were busy pinning photos and maps to one bare wall.

'We thought you'd like the desk by the window,' Esson said. 'It's got the view if nothing else.'

Yes, a view of two very different schools: Fettes College and Broughton High. Clarke took it in for all of three seconds before draping her coat over the back of her chair and sitting down. She placed the newspapers on the desk and concentrated on the reporting of Lord Minton's demise. There was background stuff, and a few photographs dusted off from the archives. Cases he had prosecuted; royal garden parties; his first appearance in ermine.

'Confirmed bachelor,' Esson called out as she pushed another drawing pin home.

'From which we deduce nothing,' Clarke warned her. 'And that photo's squint.'

'Not if you do this.' Esson angled her head twenty degrees, then adjusted the photo anyway. It showed the body *in situ*, crumpled on the carpet as if drunkenly asleep.

'Where's the boss?' Clarke asked.

'Howden Hall,' Ogilvie answered.

'Oh?' Howden Hall was home to the city's forensic lab.

'He said if he wasn't back in time, the press briefing's all yours.'

Clarke checked the time: she had another hour. 'Typically generous of the man,' she muttered, turning to the first of the obituaries.

She had just finished them, and was offering them to Esson to be added to the wall, when Page arrived. He was with a detective sergeant called Charlie Sykes. Sykes was normally based at Leith CID. He was a year shy of his pension and about the same from a heart attack, the former rather than the latter informing practically every conversation Clarke had ever had with the man.

'Quick update,' Page began breathlessly, gathering his squad. 'House-to-house is continuing and we've got a couple of officers checking any CCTV in the vicinity. Someone's busy on a computer somewhere to see if there are any other cases, within the city and beyond, that match this one. We'll need to keep interviewing the deceased's network of friends and acquaintances, and someone is going to have to head to the vaults to look at Lord Minton's professional life in detail . . . '

Clarke glanced in Sykes's direction. Sykes

17

winked back, which meant something had happened at Howden Hall. *Of course* something had happened at Howden Hall.

'We also need to put the house and its contents under a microscope,' Page was continuing. Clarke cleared her throat loudly, bringing him to a stop.

'Any time you want to share the news, sir,' she nudged him. 'Because I'm just about ready to assume you no longer think this was a panicked housebreaker.'

He wagged a finger at her. 'We can't afford to rule that possibility out. But on the other hand, we also now have this.' He took a sheet of paper from the inside pocket of his suit. It was a photocopy of something. Clarke, Esson and Ogilvie converged on him the better to see it.

'Folded up in the victim's wallet, tucked behind a credit card. Shame it wasn't noticed earlier, but all the same . . . '

The photocopy showed a note written in capital letters on a piece of plain paper measuring about five inches by three.

I'M GOING TO KILL YOU FOR WHAT YOU DID.

There was an audible intake of breath, followed by a few beats of complete silence, broken by a belch from Charlie Sykes.

'We're keeping this to ourselves for now,' Page warned the room. 'Any journalist gets hold of it, I'll be sharpening my axe. Is that understood?'

'Game-changer, though,' Ronnie Ogilvie offered.

'Game-changer,' Page acknowledged with a slow, steady nod.

2

'Why Fettes?' Fox asked that evening as he sat across from Clarke at a restaurant on Broughton Street. 'No, let me guess — it's to reflect Minton's status?'

Clarke chewed and nodded. 'If you've got brass or politicians coming for a look-see, Fettes trumps Gayfield Square. No grubby little neds for the suits to bump into.'

'And a more congenial setting for press conferences. I watched Page on the news channel. Didn't manage to spot you, though.'

'He did okay, I thought.'

'Except in a case like this, no news isn't exactly good news. First forty-eight hours being crucial, et cetera.' Fox lifted his glass of water to his lips. 'Whoever did it has to be on our books, right? Or is he a first-timer — might explain why he bolloxed it up.'

Clarke nodded slowly, avoiding eye contact and saying nothing. Fox put his glass down.

'There's something you're not telling me, Siobhan.'

'We're keeping it under wraps.'

'Keeping what under wraps?'

'The thing I'm not telling you.' Fox waited, his stare fixed on her. Clarke put down her fork and looked to left and right. The restaurant was two thirds empty, no one close enough to overhear. Nevertheless, she lowered her voice and leaned

19

across her plate until only inches separated their faces.

'There was a note.'

'Left by the killer?'

'It was in Lord Minton's wallet, hidden away. Might have been there for days or weeks.'

'So you can't say for sure it was from the attacker?' Fox mulled this over. 'All the same . . . '

Clarke nodded again. 'If Page ever finds out I told you . . . '

'Understood.' Fox leaned back again and stabbed at a chunk of carrot with his fork. 'Does complicate things, though.'

'Tell me about it. Actually, don't — tell me about your day instead.'

'Crew from Gartcosh have arrived out of nowhere. Set up shop this afternoon and Doug Maxtone's incandescent.'

'Anyone we know?'

'I've not been introduced yet. Boss hasn't been told why they're here, though apparently he's going to be briefed in the morning.'

'Could it be a terrorist thing?' Fox shrugged. 'How big a team?'

'Six at the last count. They're installed in the CID suite, meaning we've had to relocate to a shoebox along the corridor. How's your hake?'

'It's fine.' But she had barely touched it, concentrating instead on the carafe of house white. Fox poured himself more water from the jug. Clarke's water glass, he noted, was still full.

'What did the note say?' he asked.

'Whoever wrote it was promising to kill Lord

Minton for something he'd done.'

'And it wasn't in Minton's handwriting?'

'Letters were all capitalised, but I don't think so. Cheap black ballpoint rather than a fountain pen.'

'All very mysterious. Just the one note, do you think?'

'Search team will be in the house at first light. They'd already be there if Page could have organised it — budget's in place for seven-day weeks and as much overtime as we need.'

'Happy days.' Fox toasted her with his water. Clarke's phone started vibrating. She had placed it on the table next to her wine glass. She checked the screen and decided to answer.

'It's Christine Esson,' she explained to Fox, lifting the phone to her ear. 'Shouldn't you be at home with your feet up, Christine?' But as she listened, her eyes narrowed a little. Her free hand reached for the wine glass as if on instinct, but the glass was still empty, as was the carafe. 'Okay,' she announced eventually. 'Thanks for letting me know.' She ended the call and tapped the phone against her lips.

'Well?' Fox prompted.

'Reports of a gunshot in Merchiston. Christine just heard from a pal of hers at the control room. Someone who lives on the street called it in. A patrol car's on its way to the scene.'

'Some old banger backfiring?'

'Caller heard breaking glass — living-room window, apparently.' She paused. 'The window of a house belonging to a Mr Cafferty.'

'Big Ger Cafferty?'

21

'The very same.'

'Well, that's interesting, isn't it?'

'Thank God we're off duty.'

'Absolutely. Perish the thought we'd want to take a look.'

'Quite right.' Clarke cut off a chunk of hake with the side of her fork. Fox was studying her over the rim of his glass.

'Whose turn to pay?' he asked.

'Mine,' Clarke replied, dropping the fork on the plate and signalling for a waiter.

★   ★   ★

The patrol car sat kerbside with its roof lights flashing. It was a wide street of detached late-Victorian houses. The gates to Cafferty's driveway were open and a white van was parked there. A couple of neighbours had come out to spectate. They looked cold, and would probably head in again soon. The two uniformed officers — one male, one female — were known to Clarke. She introduced Fox, then asked what had happened.

'Lady across the street heard a bang. There was a flash too, apparently, and the sound of glass shattering. She went to her window but couldn't see any sign of life. The living room lights went off, but she could see the window was smashed. Curtains were open, she says.'

'He's been quick enough getting a glazier.' Fox nodded towards Cafferty's house, where a man was busy fitting a plywood covering over the window.

'What does the occupant say?' Clarke asked the uniforms.

'He's not opening his door. Tells us it was an accident. Denies there was anything like a shot.'

'And he told you this by . . . ?'

'Shouting at us through his letter box when we were trying to get him to open up.'

'You know who he is, right?'

'He's Big Ger Cafferty. Gangster sort of character, or at least used to be.'

Clarke nodded slowly and noticed that a dog — some kind of terrier — was standing next to her and giving one of her legs an exploratory sniff. She shooed it, but it sat back on its haunches, staring up at her quizzically.

'Must belong to a neighbour,' one of the uniforms surmised. 'It was padding up and down the pavement when we got here.' He bent down to scratch the dog behind one ear.

'Check the rest of the street,' Clarke said. 'See if there are any more witnesses.'

She headed up the path towards the front door, taking a detour to where the glazier was nailing the panelling into the window frame.

'Everything okay here?' she asked him. As far as she could tell, the living-room curtains were now closed, the room behind them in darkness.

'Just about finished.'

'We're police officers. Can you tell us what happened?'

'Accidental breakage. I've measured up and it'll be good as new tomorrow.'

'You know neighbours are saying a bullet did this?'

'In Edinburgh?' The man shook his head.

'You'll need to give your details to my colleagues before you leave.'

'Fine by me.'

'Have you done work for Mr Cafferty before?'
The man shook his head again.

'But you know who he is? So it's not beyond the realms of fantasy that there was a gunshot of some kind?'

'Tells me he tripped and fell against the pane. I've seen it happen plenty times.'

'I'm guessing,' Fox interrupted, 'he made it worth your while to come out straight away.'

'It says 'Emergency' on my van because that's what I do — emergency repairs. Immediate response whenever possible.' The man hammered the final nail into place and checked his handiwork. There was a toolbox on the ground next to him, along with a portable workbench where he had sawn the plywood to size. The shards of glass had been swept up into a dustpan, larger pieces placed one on top of the other. Fox had crouched down to examine them, but when he stood up, the look he gave Clarke told her he hadn't gleaned anything. She turned towards the solid-looking door, pressing the bell half a dozen times. When there was no response, she bent down and pushed open the letter box.

'It's DI Clarke,' she called out. 'Siobhan Clarke. Any chance of a word, Mr Cafferty?'

'Come back with a warrant!' a voice from within yelled. She put her eyes to the letter box and could see his shadowy bulk in the darkened hall.

'It's good you've turned the lights off,' she said. 'Makes you less of a target. Do you reckon they'll come back?'

'What are you on about? You been on the sauce again? I hear you're getting too fond of it.'

Clarke could feel the blood rising to her cheeks. She managed to stop herself checking Fox's reaction. 'You could be endangering your neighbours' lives as well as your own — please think about that.'

'You're dreaming, woman. I knocked against the glass and it broke. End of story.'

'If it's a warrant you want, I can fetch one.'

'Bugger off and do that then, and leave me in peace!'

She let the flap of the letter box clack shut and straightened up, fixing her eyes on Fox.

'You reckon you've got something better than a warrant, don't you?' he said. 'Go on then.' He motioned towards the phone she was clutching in her right hand. 'Give him a bell . . . '

3

The Oxford Bar was almost empty, and John Rebus had the back room to himself. He sat in the corner with a view of the doorway. It was something you learned to do as a cop — anyone coming in who might mean trouble, you wanted as much warning as you could get. Not that Rebus was expecting trouble, not here.

And besides, he was no longer a cop.

A month since his retirement. He had gone quietly in the end, demanding no fanfare, and turning down the offer of a drink with Clarke and Fox. Siobhan had phoned him a few times since, on various pretexts. He'd always managed to find some excuse not to meet up. Even Fox had got in touch — Fox! Ex-Professional Standards, a man who had tried snaring Rebus many a time — calling in an awkward attempt to share gossip before getting to the point.

How was Rebus doing?

Was he coping?

Did he want to hook up some time?

'Bugger that,' Rebus muttered to himself, finishing the dregs of his fourth IPA. Time to call it a night. Four was plenty. His doctor had told him: best cut it out altogether. Rebus had asked for a second opinion.

'Here it is then,' the doctor had said: 'You should stop smoking too.'

Rebus smiled at the memory and rose from his

pew, taking the empty glass with him to the bar.

'One for the road?' he was asked.

'That's me done.' But as he stepped outside, he paused to get a cigarette lit. Maybe one more, eh? Freezing outside, and a wind that could slice bacon. Quick cigarette and back inside. There was a coal fire burning. He could see it through the window, sharing its warmth with no one now he was out here. He looked at his watch. What else was he going to do? Walk the streets? Take a taxi home and sit in his living room, failing to pick up any of the books he'd promised himself he would read? Bit of music and maybe a bath and then bed. His life was turning into a track on a CD with the repeat function engaged, each new day the same as the one before.

He'd made a little list at the kitchen table: join the library, explore the city, take a holiday, see films, start going to concerts. There was a coffee ring on the list, and soon he would crumple it into the bin. One thing he had done was sort out his record collection, finding a few dozen albums he hadn't played in years. But there was a problem with one of the speakers — the treble kept coming and going. So he'd have to add that to the list, or else start a new one.

Redecorate.

Replace rotting windows.

New bathroom suite.

New bed.

Hall carpet.

'Easier just to move,' he said to the empty street. No need to flick ash from his cigarette — the wind was doing that for him. Back indoors or taxi home? Toss a coin?

Phone.

He dug it out and peered at the screen. *Caller: Shiv.* Short for Siobhan. Not that she would countenance being called Shiv to her face. He considered not answering, but then tapped the screen and pressed the device to his ear.

'You're interrupting my training,' he complained.

'What training?'

'I'm planning on doing the Edinburgh Marathon.'

'Twenty-six pubs, is that? Sorry to break into your schedule.'

'I'm going to have to stop you there, caller. There's someone on line two with a less smart mouth.'

'Fine then — I just thought you might like to know.'

'Know what? That Police Scotland is falling to pieces without me?'

'It's your old friend Cafferty.'

Rebus paused, his brain switching gears. 'Keep talking.'

'Someone might just have taken a potshot at him.'

'Is he all right?'

'Hard to say — he's not letting us in.'

'Where are you?'

'His house.'

'Give me fifteen minutes.'

'We can come fetch you . . . '

A taxi had turned into Young Street, its orange light on. Rebus walked into the road and waved for it to stop.

'Fifteen minutes tops,' he told Clarke, before ending the call.

★   ★   ★

'Want me to try the bell for you?' Fox asked. He was on the doorstep in front of Cafferty's home, flanked by Rebus and Clarke. The glazier had gone, and the officers from the patrol car were still collecting information from neighbours. The blue flashing light had been turned off, replaced by the orange sodium glow of the nearby street lamps.

'He seems to want to communicate by shouting through the letter box,' Clarke added.

'I think we can do better than that,' Rebus said. He found Cafferty's number on his phone and waited.

'It's me,' he said when the call was picked up. 'I'm standing right outside and I'm about to come in. So you can either open the door, or wait for me to put in another of your windows and climb in through the wreckage.' He listened for a moment, eyes on Clarke. 'Just me — understood.' Clarke opened her mouth to protest, but Rebus shook his head. 'It's baltic out here, so quick as you can and we can all go home.'

He put the phone back in his pocket and offered a shrug. 'It's okay for me to go in because I'm not a cop these days.'

'He said that?'

'He didn't need to.'

'Have you spoken to him recently?' Fox added.

'Contrary to received opinion, I don't spend

my days fraternising with people like Big Ger.'

'There was a time.'

'Maybe he's just more interesting than others I could name,' Rebus bristled.

Fox looked ready to respond, but the door was being opened. Cafferty stood behind it, mostly hidden in shadow. Without another word, Rebus stepped inside and the door closed behind him. He followed Cafferty from outer hall to inner. Cafferty walked past the closed door to the living room, turning into the kitchen instead. Rebus wasn't about to play that game, so entered the living room, turning on the light. He'd been in the room before, but there had been changes. A black leather suite. A vast flat-screen TV above the fireplace. The curtains in the bay window had been pulled shut; he was drawing them open when Cafferty walked in.

'You've tidied most of the glass,' Rebus commented. 'Still wouldn't risk it in bare feet, mind. But at least floorboards are better than carpet — the splinters are easier to spot.'

Hands in pockets, he turned to face Cafferty. They were old men now, similar build, similar background. Sat together in a pub, they might be mistaken by a casual onlooker for pals who'd known one another since school. But their history told a different story: fights and near-deaths, chases and prosecutions. Cafferty's last stint in jail had been cut short after a cancer diagnosis, the patient making a miraculous recovery once free.

'Congratulations on your retirement,' Cafferty drawled. 'You didn't think to invite me to the party. Hang on, though — I hear there *was* no party. Not enough friends left to even fill the back room at the Ox?' He made a show of shaking his head in sympathy.

'The bullet didn't hit you, then?' Rebus retorted. 'More's the pity.'

'Everyone seems to be talking about this mysterious bullet.'

'I just wish we still had a tap on your phone. I'm betting that in the minutes after, you were shouting the odds at every villain in the city.'

'Look around you, Rebus. Do you see bodyguards? Do you see protection? I'm too long out of the game to have enemies.'

'It's true plenty of people you hate have predeceased you — one way or another. But I still reckon there are enough to make a decent-sized list.'

Cafferty smiled eventually and gestured towards the doorway. 'Come into the kitchen. I'll pour us a drink.'

'I'll take mine in here, thanks.'

Cafferty sighed and shrugged, turning to leave. Rebus did a quick circuit of the room and was by the fireplace when Cafferty returned. It was not an overly generous helping, but Rebus's nose told him it was malt. He took a sip and rolled it around his mouth before swallowing, Cafferty opting to knock his back in one gulp.

'Nerves still jangling?' Rebus guessed. 'Don't blame you for that. So you didn't have the curtains closed. Probably reckon you don't need them — nice big hedge between house and pavement. But that means he was standing on

31

the lawn, directly outside. What were you doing? Crossing the room to find the TV remote, maybe? At which point he's not more than eight or ten feet away. You still can't see him, though — lights on in here, darkness out there. Yet somehow he misses. Meaning it's either a warning or he's some kind of rookie.' Rebus paused. 'Which would you guess? Maybe you don't need to — could be you already know.' He took another sip of whisky and watched Cafferty ease himself on to the leather sofa.

'Say someone *was* trying to kill me, would I be daft enough to stay put? Wouldn't I be heading for the hills?'

'You might. But if you've no idea who's behind it, that isn't going to help you find them. Maybe you get tooled up, call in some favours and bide your time until he tries again. Morris Gerald Cafferty prepared is a very different creature from one who's been caught on the hop.'

'So when I tell you that I'd had a nip too many and tripped over my own feet, smacking the window . . . '

'You've every right to stick to your story. I'm not a detective these days; nothing I can do one way or the other. But if you did feel you needed some help, Siobhan's right outside and I'd trust her with your life. I'd probably even trust her with mine.'

'I'll bear that in mind. Meantime, I hope I've not taken you away from whatever it is cops like you do when they're put out to pasture.'

'We tend to spend our days reminiscing about

the scum we've put in jail.'

'And the ones who got away too, no doubt.' Cafferty pulled himself back to his feet. He acted like an old man, but Rebus felt sure he could be dangerous when cornered or threatened. The eyes were still hard and cold, mirroring the calculating intelligence behind them. 'Tell Siobhan to go home,' Cafferty was saying. 'And the door-to-door is wasting time and effort. It's just one broken window, easily fixed.'

'It's not, though, is it?' Rebus had followed Cafferty for a few steps but then stopped by the wall opposite the bay window. There was a framed painting there, and as Cafferty turned towards him, he dabbed at it with the tip of one finger. 'This painting used to be over there.' He nodded towards another wall. 'And the wee painting hanging there used to be here. You can tell from where the emulsion has faded — means they've been swapped over recently.'

'I like them better this way.' Cafferty's jaw had tightened. Rebus gave a thin smile as he reached out with both hands and lifted the larger painting from its hook. It had been covering a small, near-circular indentation in the plaster. He shut one eye and took a closer look.

'You've prised out the bullet,' he commented. 'Nine mil, was it?' He dug in his pocket for his phone. 'Mind if I take a snap for my scrapbook?'

But Cafferty's hand had gripped him by the forearm.

'John,' he said. 'Just leave it, okay? I know what I'm doing.'

'Then tell me. Tell me what's going on here.'

But Cafferty shook his head and relaxed his vice-like grip.

'Just go,' he said, his voice softening. 'Enjoy the days and the hours. None of this is yours any more.'

'Then why let me in?'

'I'm wishing I hadn't.' Cafferty gestured towards the hole. 'I thought I was being clever.'

'We're both clever, it's why we've lasted as long as we have.'

'You going to tell Clarke about this?' Meaning the bullet hole.

'Maybe. And maybe she'll go get that warrant.'

'None of which will get her any further forward.'

'At least the hole rules out one theory.'

'Oh aye?'

'That you fired the gun yourself from in here.' Rebus nodded towards the window. 'At someone out there.'

'That's some imagination you've got.'

The two men stared at one another until Rebus exhaled loudly. 'I might as well head off then. You know where to find me if you need me.' He got the painting back on its hook and accepted the handshake that Cafferty was offering.

Outside, Clarke and Fox were waiting in Fox's car. Rebus climbed into the back.

'Well?' Clarke asked.

'There's a bullet hole in the far wall. He's got the bullet out and won't be handing it over to us any time soon.'

'You think he knows who did it?'

34

'I'd say he hasn't a clue — that's what's got him spooked.'

'So what now?'

'Now,' Rebus said, reaching forward to pat Fox on the shoulder, 'I get a lift home.'

'Are we invited in for coffee?'

'It's a flat, not a fucking Costa. Once you've dropped me, you young things can finish the evening doing whatever takes your fancy.' Rebus looked towards where the terrier was sitting on the pavement, watching the occupants of the car, its head cocked. 'Whose is the mutt?'

'Not sure. The uniforms asked around, but nobody's missing a pet. Couldn't be Cafferty's, could it?'

'Unlikely. Pets need looking after, and that's not the man's style.' Rebus had dug his cigarettes out of his pocket. 'Mind if I smoke in here?'

'Yes,' came the chorus from the front.

The dog was still watching as the car moved off. Rebus feared it was about to try following them. Clarke swivelled around so she was facing the rear seat.

'I'm fine,' Rebus told her. 'Thanks for asking.'

'I hadn't quite got round to it.'

'No, but you were going to.'

'It's good to see you.'

'Aye, you too,' Rebus conceded. 'Now, is there any chance you can get Jackie Stewart here to put the foot down? There's a cigarette with my name on it waiting at the other end . . . '

★   ★   ★

In his kitchen, Cafferty poured another whisky, adding a drop of water from the cold tap and finishing it in two swallows. He expelled air through his teeth and slammed the empty glass on to the table before running his hands down his face. The house was locked, all doors and windows checked. From his pocket he took the bullet, compressed from impact. Nine mil, just as Rebus had surmised. Once upon a time, Cafferty had kept a nine-mil pistol in the safe in his den, but he'd had to ditch it after having had recourse to use it. He placed the misshapen bullet next to the empty whisky glass, then opened a drawer and found what he was looking for, tucked away near the back. The note that had been shoved through his letter box a few days before. He unfolded it and examined the words again:

I'M GOING TO KILL YOU FOR WHAT YOU DID.

But what *had* Cafferty done? He pulled out a chair, sat down, and began to consider.

Day Two

4

Next morning, Doug Maxtone gestured for Fox to follow him out of the cramped office into the empty corridor of St Leonard's police station.

'I've just been briefed,' Maxtone said, 'by our friends from the west.'

'Anything you can share?'

'We discussed their request for that 'ancillary support' I mentioned yesterday . . . ' Maxtone broke off and waited.

Fox tapped a finger against his own chest and watched his boss nod slowly.

'You worked Professional Standards, Malcolm, so you know all about keeping your mouth shut.' Maxtone paused. 'But you also know about spying. You're going to be my eyes and ears in there, understood? I'll want regular updates.' He checked his watch. 'In a minute, you're going to go knock on the door. By then they'll have decided how much they need to tell you and how much they think they can get away with *not* sharing.'

'I seem to remember they wanted to vet potential candidates.'

Maxtone shook his head. 'I've made it pretty clear you're what's on offer.'

'Do they know I used to work Complaints?'

'Yes.'

'In which case I expect I'll be welcomed with open arms. Any other advice?'

'The boss is called Ricky Compston. Big wide bastard with a shaved head. Typical Glasgow — thinks he's seen it all while we spend our days directing tourists to the castle.' Maxtone paused. 'None of the others bothered with introductions.'

'But they did tell you why they're here?'

'It's to do with a — ' Maxtone broke off as the door to the CID suite swung open. A face appeared, glowering.

'That him?' a voice barked. 'When you're ready . . .'

The head disappeared, the door remaining ajar.

'I better go say hello,' Fox told his boss.

'We'll talk at the end of the day.'

Fox nodded and moved off, standing in front of the door, giving himself a moment before pushing it all the way open. There were five of them, all standing, mostly with arms folded.

'Shut the door then,' the man who had originally opened it said. Fox reckoned this must be Compston. He had the rough dimensions and general demeanour of a prize bull. No handshakes, just down to business.

'For the record,' Compston said, 'we know this is shite, yes?'

He seemed to require an answer, so Fox gave something that could have been construed as a nod of agreement.

'But in the spirit of cooperation, here we all are.' Compston stretched out an arm, taking in the room. The desks were sparsely furnished — just laptops and mobile phones, plugged into chargers. Almost no paperwork and nothing pinned to the walls. Compston took a step forward, filling Fox's field of vision, so he knew who was in charge. 'Now I know what *your* boss is thinking: he's thinking you're going to run straight back to him every five minutes with the latest gossip. But that wouldn't be very wise, Detective Inspector Fox. Because if anything leaks, I know for a fact as hard as my last shit that it won't have come from my team. Is that clear?'

'I think I've some lactulose in my drawer, if that would help.'

One of the detectives gave a snort of laughter, and even Compston eventually broke into a brief smile.

'You know I used to be Professional Standards,' Fox ploughed on. 'That means I've got a fan club here with precisely no members. Probably explains why Maxtone chose me — keeps me out of his hair. Besides which, I don't expect he thinks this is going to be a laugh a minute. You might need me and you might not. I'm happy to sit on my arse playing Angry Birds for the duration — salary still goes into my bank.'

Compston studied the man in front of him, then turned his head towards his team.

'Initial assessment?'

'Standard Complaints wanker,' a man in a light blue shirt said, seeming to act as the voice of the group.

Compston raised an eyebrow. 'Alec isn't usually so effusive. On the other hand, he seldom

41

gets people wrong. Standard Complaints wanker it is. So let's all sit down and get uncomfortable.'

They did, and introductions were finally made. The blue shirt was Alec Bell. He was probably in his early fifties, a good five or six years older than Compston. A taller, younger, undernourished-looking officer went by the name of Jake Emerson. The only woman present was called Beth Hastie. She reminded Fox a little of the First Minister — similar age, haircut and facial shape. Finally there was Peter Hughes, probably the youngest of the team, dressed for the street in a padded denim jacket and black jeans.

'I thought there were six of you,' Fox commented.

'Bob Selway's otherwise engaged,' Compston explained. Fox waited for more.

'That makes five,' he said.

The group shared a look. Compston sniffed and shifted a little in his chair.

'Five it is,' he stated.

Fox noted that no ranks had been mentioned. It was clear Compston was in charge, with Bell as his trusted lieutenant. The others seemed like foot soldiers. If he had to guess, he'd say they hadn't known each other for any great length of time.

'Whatever it is you're up to, there's a surveillance element,' Fox said. 'You'll appreciate that surveillance used to be a big part of my job, so that might be the one skill I have that'd be useful to you.'

'Okay, smart-arse, how did you work that out?'

Fox's eyes met Compston's and stayed there. 'Selway is 'otherwise engaged'. Meantime Hughes is dressed so he doesn't stand out in certain situations. He looks fairly comfortable, too, which means he's done it before.' Fox paused. 'How am I doing?'

'Maxtone really didn't tell you?'

Fox shook his head, and Compston took a deep breath.

'You'll have heard of Joseph Stark?'

'Let's pretend I haven't.'

'Your boss hadn't heard of him either. Unbelievable.' Compston made show of shaking his head. 'Joe Stark is a Glasgow gangster of long and ugly standing. He's sixty-three years old and not quite ready to pass the baton to his son — '

'Dennis,' Alec Bell interrupted. 'Otherwise known as a nasty little turd.'

'With you so far,' Fox said.

'Joe and Dennis, along with some of their crew, have been enjoying a wee road trip of late. Inverness first, then Aberdeen and Dundee.'

'And now they're in Edinburgh?'

'Been here a couple of days and don't look like budging.'

'And you've had them under surveillance throughout?' Fox surmised.

'We want to know what they're doing.'

'You don't know?'

'We've got an inkling.'

'Do I get to hear it?'

'They might be looking for a guy called Hamish Wright. He's based in Inverness but has friends in Aberdeen, Dundee . . . '

'And here.'

'I say 'friends', but contacts might be a better description. Wright runs a haulage business, which means he has lorries crossing to the Western Isles, Orkney and Shetland, even Ireland and the Continent.'

'Could be useful if there was something illegal that needed distributing.' A head-and-shoulders shot of Wright had been handed to Fox. He studied the face. It was chubby and freckled and topped by curly red hair. 'Looks like a Hamish,' he commented.

'Right.'

'Would it be drugs he's moving?'

'Oh yes.'

'For the Starks?' Fox watched Compston nod. 'So why haven't you busted him?'

'We were about to.'

'And we reckoned we'd take down Stark and his son too,' Bell added. 'But then Wright went AWOL.'

'And Stark's your best chance of finding him?' Fox nodded his understanding. 'But why's Stark so interested?'

'There'll be reasons,' Compston said.

'To do with money?'

'Money and goods, yes.'

'So where are Stark and his men? Who are they talking to?'

'Right now, they're in a café in Leith. They're staying at a bed and breakfast nearby.'

'Bob Selway's watching them?'

'Until I relieve him in forty minutes,' Peter Hughes broke in.

'Reckon young Peter will blend in?' Compston asked Fox. 'We did wonder if these days he'd need one of those hipster beards, seeing how Leith is going up in the world.'

'Like he's old enough to grow a beard,' Alec Bell snorted.

Hughes made a single-digit gesture but looked as though he'd heard all the jokes before. Fox could sense the team softening a little. He wasn't being accepted, but they were ceasing to see him as an immediate threat.

'So that's where we are and why we're here,' Compston said with a shrug. 'And if you'll let us get on with it, we'll leave you to your Angry Birds.'

But Fox had a question. 'Stark and his men were in town last night? What did they get up to?'

'Dinner and a few drinks.'

'You had eyes on them all evening?'

'Pretty much. Why?'

Fox gave a twitch of the mouth. 'You'll have heard of Morris Gerald Cafferty, known as Big Ger?'

'Let's pretend I haven't.'

'Unbelievable,' Fox echoed. 'He was a major player on the east coast until recently. Similar age to your Joe Stark.'

'And?'

'Someone decided to take a potshot at him yesterday evening around eight o'clock.'

'Whereabouts?'

'At his home. Shooter was outside, Cafferty was inside, meaning it might have been a

45

warning of some kind.'

Compston ran a hand across his jaw. 'Interesting.' He looked to Alec Bell, who offered a shrug.

'Seven till nine they were in the Abbotsford,' Bell recited. 'Drink at the bar, meal in the upstairs restaurant.'

'And where were we?'

'Peter was at the bar throughout.'

Hughes nodded his agreement. 'Apart from a quick break for a slash. But Beth was posted outside.'

'At the end of Rose Street, not more than twenty yards away,' Beth Hastie confirmed.

'Probably nothing to it then,' Compston said, not quite managing to sound as if he meant it. Then, to Fox: 'Would your man Cafferty have had dealings with the Starks?'

'I can try to find out.' Fox paused. 'Always supposing you're willing to trust me that far.'

'You know Cafferty to talk to?'

'Yes.' Fox managed not to blink.

'You can bring up the Starks without him getting wind of the surveillance?'

'Absolutely.'

Compston looked at the other members of his team. 'What do we think?'

'Risky,' Hastie offered.

'Agreed,' Alec Bell muttered.

'Fox is right about one thing, though,' Compston said, rising to his feet. 'Starks hit town and almost immediately someone fires a shot across the bows of the competition. Could well be a message.' His eyes were boring into

46

Fox's. 'You reckon you're up to this?'

'Yes.'

'How will you do it?'

Fox shrugged. 'We just chat. I'm pretty good at reading people. If he suspects the Starks, he may let something slip.' He paused. 'I'm assuming they'd have access to a gun?'

Alec Bell snorted.

'I'll take that as a yes.' Then, to Compston: 'So do I talk to him or not?'

'You don't so much as hint at the surveillance.'

Fox nodded, then gestured towards the silent, cadaverous figure of Jake Emerson. 'Doesn't say much, does he?'

'Not in front of Complaints he doesn't,' Emerson sneered. 'Scumbuckets, the lot of you.'

'See?' Compston said with a smile. 'Jake keeps his counsel mostly, but when he *does* speak, it's always worth hearing.' He held out a hand for Fox to take. 'You're on probation, but for what it's worth — welcome to Operation Junior.'

'Junior?'

Compston gave a cold smile. 'If you're any kind of detective, you'll work it out,' he said, releasing his grip.

5

Fox stood on the pavement outside the four-storey tenement on Arden Street and made the call, his eyes fixed on one of the second-floor windows.

'What do you want?' Rebus's voice asked.

'You at home?'

'Bowls game doesn't start for another hour.'

'Using your bus pass to get there?'

'You're sharper than you used to be — that's what a spell in CID does for you.'

'Can I come up?'

Rebus's face appeared at the window. 'I was just nipping out to the shop.'

'I'll walk with you. I thought we could talk about Cafferty.'

'Why would we want to do that?'

'I'll tell you when you come down.' Fox ended the call, holding the phone away from him for effect. Rebus remained at the window for a moment, then disappeared. Two minutes later, wrapped in a three-quarter-length black woollen coat, he emerged into the street, turning left and heading uphill, Fox at his heels.

'Before you ask, I've cut back,' he informed Fox as he lifted a cigarette from a near-empty packet.

'Have you tried vaping?'

'I hate that word.'

'Have you, though?'

'A couple of times. It's just not the same.' Rebus stopped briefly to get the cigarette lit. 'There's some news on Cafferty?'

'Not exactly.'

Rebus looked at Fox for the first time since coming out of the tenement. 'So I'm here under false pretences?' He started walking again.

'Do the names Joe and Dennis Stark mean anything to you?'

'Joe's an old-time Glasgow thug. His son didn't fall far from the tree.'

'Ever had dealings with either of them?'

'No.'

'Might Cafferty?'

'Almost certainly. You couldn't have one city tramping on the other's turf, not without war breaking out.'

'So there'd have been powwows between the two?'

'And their equivalents in Aberdeen, maybe Dundee . . . '

'That's interesting.'

'Why?'

'Because the Starks visited both those places recently.'

'What's your thinking, Malcolm?' Rebus glanced in Fox's direction. 'And by the way, are you and Siobhan sleeping together?'

'Would it bother you if we were?'

'I'll always look out for her. Anyone hurts her, it'll be me they answer to.'

'She's an adult, John. She might even be tougher than either you or me.'

'Maybe, but just so you know.'

'We're friends — that's as far as it goes.'

They had turned the corner at the top of the street. There was a Sainsbury's across the road, and Rebus stopped by its door, taking a final couple of drags on his cigarette before stubbing it out.

'Didn't even smoke the whole thing,' he said. 'Be sure and tell her that. You never did answer my question.'

Fox followed him into the shop. 'What question?'

'Why do you want to know about the Starks?'

'They arrived in town a couple of days back. Just wondered if there might be a reason for them to target Cafferty.'

Rebus's eyes narrowed as he picked up a basket. He was silent while they perused the first aisle. Instant coffee, a small loaf, a litre of milk, packets of link sausages and bacon. As they passed by the wine and beer, Rebus gestured with his free hand.

'Tell her I didn't buy a single can or bottle.'

At the counter, however, he added a fresh pack of cigarettes to his purchases, along with a sausage roll from the hotplate.

'A man has to have some vices,' he said as they made for the exit. Outside, he slid the first inch from its paper bag and took a bite. Flecks of pastry broke off and peppered the lapels of his coat.

'What do you want me to do?' he asked.

Fox slipped his hands into his pockets, hunching his shoulders against the stiff breeze. 'Would Cafferty talk to me about the Starks?'

'You think Joe Stark is responsible for last night?'

'Maybe the son. Revenge for some grievance.'

'I'm not sure Dennis would have missed. He'll have had a bit of practice down the years.'

'So it was a warning of some kind, somebody trying to put the wind up Cafferty. You have to admit, it's odd how this happens the day after the Starks hit town.'

'There is that,' Rebus conceded. 'But say we mention as much to Cafferty . . . '

'Yes?'

'Well, he might want to explore the possibility.'

'He might,' Fox agreed.

'And that could get ugly.'

Fox was nodding slowly as Rebus chewed on another mouthful of food. When the chewing stopped, replaced by a widening smile, Fox knew he'd done his job.

* * *

Lunchtime, and the Golden Rule was almost empty. The main bar was connected by a set of steps to a larger seated area that boasted another bar, only open when the place got busy. They had this room to themselves. Cafferty looked comfortable, seated at a corner table well away from the window. He had a double whisky in front of him. Rebus carried a pint through, while Fox, a couple of steps behind him, brought nothing at all.

'Malcolm Fox, isn't it?' Cafferty reached out a hand, which Fox shook. 'Out of the Complaints these days, I hear. I suppose with John heading into the wilderness, you felt the job had lost any sense of challenge.' He toasted both men and took a sip from his glass.

'Thanks for agreeing to meet me,' Fox said.

'It's not you I'm meeting, son — it's your ex-colleague. Always worth finding out what's going on in that head of his.'

'Be that as it may . . . '

Cafferty was flapping one hand, signalling for Fox to stop. There was silence around the table, broken only by the sounds of the TV from the distant bar. Eventually Rebus put down his glass and spoke.

'A shot was fired at you last night — we all know it. Most of your obvious enemies are long gone — '

'Present company excepted,' Cafferty interrupted, making another toast.

'But then DI Fox discovers that Joe Stark is in town, along with his son.'

'They've not sectioned Dennis yet?' Cafferty feigned surprise.

'We're wondering if there's any possible connection,' Rebus continued. 'I've spent half the night turning it over, and I'm not coming up with more than two or three names.'

'Ah, now you've got me interested. What names?'

'Billy Jones.'

'Living in Florida, as far as I know.'

'Eck Hendry.'

'Went to stay with his daughter in Australia. I think he suffered a stroke a couple of months back.'

'Darryl Christie.'

Cafferty's lips formed an O. 'Ah, young Darryl.'

'Your protégé back in the day.'

'Never that. Darryl's always been his own man. Doing well too, I hear. Business expanding, never a blemish on his character.' His eyes met Rebus's. 'Almost as if he had the law on his side.'

'Maybe he's just always been that bit cannier than you.'

'That must be it,' Cafferty pretended to agree. 'But I doubt he sees me as any sort of threat to his various interests, not these days.'

'You don't sound a hundred per cent sure,' Fox couldn't help interrupting.

'We live in uncertain times. Not six months ago, we thought we were soon going to be an independent country.'

'We still might be.'

'And wouldn't that be a grand scheme?' Cafferty smiled behind his glass and tipped it to his mouth.

'Thing you need to know about Big Ger,' Rebus began for Fox's benefit, 'is that if he seems to be offering you something, there's a game being played. He doesn't rule out Darryl Christie, maybe in the hope we'll go looking at Darryl and turn up something — something advantageous to Big Ger himself.'

Cafferty winked at Fox. 'It's like he knows me better than I know myself — saves me a fortune in therapy.' Then, turning his attention back to Rebus: 'But you've got me intrigued — why *is* Joe Stark here?'

'Whatever it is, he's obviously not sharing it with you.'

'That son of his will be in charge of things soon. Maybe Joe's introducing him to society.'

'It's a theory,' Rebus acknowledged.

'Everything is, until there's proof. Will you go ask Darryl?'

Rebus met Cafferty's stare. 'You forgetting I'm retired?'

'What do you think, DI Fox? Does Rebus here act like someone on the scrapheap? He *will* talk to Darryl, you know. Him and Darryl are old pals — didn't you do one another a favour not so long back?'

'Don't believe all the stories,' Rebus advised. He got to his feet, pulling his coat around him.

'Not finishing your drink?' Cafferty gestured towards the half-full pint. 'I suppose there's a first time for everything.' Then, stretching out his hand again, 'Nice to see you, DI Fox. Say hello to the fragrant Siobhan for me. And be sure to tell her you're hanging on to Rebus's coat-tails. She might well have some sage advice on the subject.' He gave a little chuckle, which only intensified when Fox snubbed the handshake and instead began following Rebus towards the exit.

6

Clarke pinched the bridge of her nose, screwing her eyes shut. For almost three hours she had been reading about David Minton — his upbringing, education, career in the law, failed attempt to become a Conservative MP, and eventual peerage. As Lord Advocate, he had been able to speak in the Scottish Parliament, though the current administration had changed the role so that Lords Advocate no longer attended cabinet meetings. Minton's closest colleague had been the Crown Agent, Kathryn Young. Young was putting pressure on Page and his team, phoning four times and turning up unannounced twice. Same went for the Solicitor General, who at least had one of her flunkeys act as inquisitor — easier to dismiss than the actual Crown Agent.

Clarke had thought she knew a bit about the legal profession — in her line of work, she spent a good deal of time with lawyers from the Procurator Fiscal's department. But this was above her pay-scale and she was having trouble clarifying the role of the Lord Advocate. He was of the government but not in the government. He was in charge of the prosecution service, but his role as chief legal adviser to the government of the day made for complications in the form of potential conflicts of interest. Post-devolution, the position of Lord Advocate no longer came with the sinecure of a life peerage, but Minton's appointment had pre-dated the opening of the Scottish Parliament. He was unusual in one respect, having decided against becoming a judge after his role as Lord Advocate ended, something he shared with only one other colleague, Lord Fraser of Carmyllie.

And hang on, what did the Solicitor General
• do again?

Then there was the Advocate General for Scotland, who advised the UK government on matters of Scots law. He was based in London but had an office in Edinburgh — and there had been phone calls from both to add to the mix. The procurator fiscal (actually a fiscal depute) attached to the Minton case was called Shona MacBryer. Clarke had worked with her before and liked her a lot. She was sharp, thorough, but relaxed enough so you could joke with her. She'd been in to see Page several times, but Clarke hadn't as yet slumped to her knees and begged for a two-line explanation of the Scottish legal hierarchy. No detective wanted a lawyer to think they were more stupid than most lawyers already considered them to be.

With nothing better to do, Clarke wandered along to the cafeteria — one thing about Fettes, it at least had a cafeteria — and settled at a table with a mug of tea and a Twix. She was remembering that Malcolm Fox had been based here throughout his time in Professional Standards. She wasn't sure he had found his feet yet in CID. He was a nice guy, maybe too nice. Visited his dad in the nursing home most weekends, and phoned his sister from time to time in failed attempts to mend fences. Clarke liked hanging out with him — it wasn't that she thought him a charity case. She'd told him as much a few weeks back. His response — 'Absolutely, and don't think I see you as one either' — had caused her to bristle, saying nothing for the rest of the DVD they'd been watching. Later that night she had stared at her reflection in her bathroom mirror.

'Cheeky sod,' she'd said out loud. 'I'm a *catch.*'

And she'd punched her pillows a few times for good measure before settling down to sleep.

'Mind if I join you?'

She looked up to see James Page standing there, coffee mug in hand.

'Of course not,' she said.

'You looked like you were thinking great things.'

'Always.'

He took a slurp from his mug. 'Are we making headway?' he asked.

'We're doing what we can. Every housebreaker in the city is under orders — if they give us a name, they'll have a friend when they next need one.'

'So far to no effect.'

'X snitches on Y, Y on Z, and Z on X.'

'In other words, you're not hopeful.'

'Hopeful, no; curious, yes.'

'Go on.' Another slurp of coffee. The few dates they'd gone on — some time back — he had done the same thing, whether the drink was hot, tepid or cold. She'd asked him to stop, but he had seemed incapable, and couldn't see the problem.

'First you have to put that mug down until I've left the table.'

He tried staring her out, then complied.

'To begin with,' Clarke went on, 'we shied away from Minton's private life. Break-in gone wrong, we thought. But the note changes that. The deceased did something to annoy someone.'

'Probably in his professional rather than private life,' Page cautioned.

'Which is why you've got Esson and Ogilvie digging back through several years' worth of cases and judgments. Thing is, it would have to have been a really big case, right? For someone to decide that the perceived injustice merited a death threat. And also, wouldn't it need to be something recent, or else why are they suddenly so riled?'

'Maybe they just got out of jail.'

'And again, you've got someone checking the files. But we may be looking at this whole thing the wrong way. From what I've discovered about Lord Minton, he's almost *too* perfect. Every-one's got secrets.'

'We've examined his house, been through the contents of his personal and work computers. No weird or accusatory emails. His office say they've received no letters out of the ordinary. I've asked — even if the mail was marked Private or Personal, they were instructed by Lord Minton to open it. No phone calls — we've checked his home number and mobile. There's nothing *there*, Siobhan.'

'What are we talking about then? A case of mistaken identity? Note sent to the wrong person, window of the wrong house's laundry room broken?' She couldn't help thinking about the previous night at Cafferty's. 'He hung on to the note, James. More than that, he kept it close to him. To my mind, he knew it meant something.'

'Why didn't he tell anyone, then?'

'I don't know.' She ran a hand through her hair. 'Maybe we need to talk to his friends again, starting with the closest.'

'That would be Kathryn Young, wouldn't it?'

'From what I hear.'

Page sat in silence for a moment. 'I'm still not convinced, Siobhan. The attacker broke in — it's not as if Minton opened the door to someone he knew.'

'Front door's dangerous, though — whole streetful of potential witnesses.'

'But to clamber over walls, sneak through back gardens . . .'

'I doubt we're looking for someone of the victim's generation, though you never can tell.'

Page gave a loud sigh. 'Can I drink my coffee now?'

Clarke smiled, rising from her seat. 'I'll see you upstairs,' she said.

★   ★   ★

There was a Starbuck's on Canongate, and Kathryn Young had agreed to meet them there.

She had a forty-minute window between meetings at the Scottish Parliament, so she placed her order with Clarke by text. The tables were small and fairly public, but Page had done his best. They were in an alcove near the back of the room, and he reckoned the regular noises of milk being frothed and beans being ground would mask their conversation from the other customers.

Young carried with her a heavy-looking satchel. It made one of Scotland's most senior lawyers resemble a teacher encumbered by a week's unmarked homework. She was well-dressed, but the wind howling down towards the Parliament had messed up her shoulder-length brown hair and put a glow in her cheeks.

'Small latte,' Clarke said, pushing the mug towards her. Young nodded her thanks and removed her coat and scarf.

'Any news?' she said.

'There's something we'd like to share with you,' Page said quietly, leaning forward with his elbows on his knees, hands pressed together as if in prayer. 'We've been debating motive.'

'I thought it was a straightforward housebreaking.'

'So did we, until we found this.' He gestured towards Clarke, who handed over a photocopy of the note. Young's brow furrowed as she read.

'Someone sent it to Lord Minton,' Clarke explained, 'and Lord Minton kept it in his wallet. To my mind, that means he didn't just dismiss it as some kind of prank. We're wondering who his enemies might have been.'

'I'm at a loss.' Young handed the note back. 'You've not made this public?'

'We didn't see how it could help — not just yet,' Page explained.

'You knew the man as well as anybody,' Clarke said, making eye contact and noting that Young's eyes were the same shade of brown as her hair. 'So we're wondering if you can shed any light. Did he ever mention anything about threats, or someone who had a grudge against him, real or perceived?'

The Crown Agent was shaking her head. 'We weren't close in that way. I'd known David maybe twelve or thirteen years. But his real friends — the ones he spoke about — they're mostly dead, I think. Other lawyers, at least one MP, businessmen . . . ' She was shaking her head again. 'I'm sorry, but I really can't think of anyone who'd want to harm him.'

'Maybe a case he'd prosecuted?' Clarke persisted.

'He was always very guarded. I mean, he would talk in general terms, or discuss matters of procedure, diligence, precedence. He had memorised famous trials of the past . . . '

'And you hadn't noticed a change in him recently? More guarded, maybe? On edge?'

Young concentrated on her coffee while she pondered this. 'No,' she said eventually. 'Nothing. Mrs Marischal would know before I did, though — she spent more time sharing a cuppa with him than dusting anything. Or else whoever works in his office these days — have you asked them?'

'We have, though we might try again.'

'You can't be sure the person who sent that note is the same one who broke in,' Young stated.

'We're aware of that.'

'You should make it public — the note, I mean. Someone out there might recognise the writing.' She glanced at her watch and took another swig of coffee. 'I'm afraid I have to get back. I'm sorry I haven't been much use.'

'Do you think it's worth our while talking to anyone at the New Club? He used to go there most days.'

Young shrugged her way back into her coat and picked up her scarf. 'I've honestly no idea.' She bent at the knees to retrieve her satchel. 'So much for the paperless office,' she said with a grim smile, making her way towards the door.

'That was time well spent,' Page said to Clarke through gritted teeth.

'Maybe she's right about the note, though. It's all we've got; be a shame not to use it.'

'The press will blow it out of all proportion,' Page cautioned. 'We'll have people scared to leave their houses because there's a killer out there and anyone could be his next target. Plus the nutters will come out of the woodwork with the usual premonitions and theories.'

'And our killer, knowing we're no longer treating it as a break-in gone wrong, has plenty of time to pack his bags and head elsewhere.' Clarke was nodding her agreement. 'All of that's true, James.'

He looked at her. 'But you still think we should do it?'

'Do you know what a soft launch is? No press conference. We give it to one outlet, someone who'll report it without the sensationalism. Social media will spread the story, but it'll be *our* version. By the time the other papers get hold of it, the fire will have died back a bit.'

'I assume you've a journalist in mind?'

Clarke nodded and lifted her phone, angling it towards him. 'Soon as you give the word.'

Page leaned back in his chair and folded his arms. The nod he gave was half-hearted at best. Clarke made the call anyway.

Laura Smith was at the café twenty minutes later, by which time Page had headed back to the office. He'd used the excuse of a meeting, but Clarke knew he was putting distance between himself and the plan. If it blew up in their faces in any way, Clarke would be the one left explaining to the Chief.

'You've grown your hair,' Clarke said, after Smith had paid for a bottle of water and seated herself in Page's chair.

'And you've had yours cut — it suits you.' Smith broke the seal on the bottle and tipped it to her mouth.

'How's the newspaper business?'

Still drinking, Smith rolled her eyes. She was just over five feet in height, but every inch of her was focused on getting ahead, which was tough when your chosen profession seemed to be in its death throes. She wiped her lips with the back of her hand and screwed the top back on the bottle.

'More redundancies in the offing,' she said.

'You should be safe though, no?'

'Well, I'm the only crime reporter they've got, and last time I looked, crime still sold papers, so . . . ' She gave a huge shrug of the shoulders and concentrated her attention on Clarke. 'Is it about Lord Minton?'

'Yes.'

'On the record?'

'Sort of. Though I'd prefer it if 'police sources' was the phrase of choice — and I'll need to see what you write before your editor does.'

Smith puffed out her cheeks. 'Is that non-negotiable?'

'Afraid so.'

Smith gave a twitch of the mouth and dug her phone out of her pocket. 'Can I record this anyway, just as a memo to myself?'

'I don't see why not. But I'm going to be showing rather than telling.'

Smith was busying herself with her phone's recording function. When she eventually looked up, Clarke was holding out the photocopied note.

'From Lord Minton's wallet,' she stated.

The noise Laura Smith made — as captured by her phone — was pitched somewhere between a squeal and a whoop.

7

'Is this where you ask me about the favour I'm supposed to have done Darryl Christie?' Rebus asked Fox. They were in the Saab, Rebus driving. Fox was gripping his seat belt with one hand and the door handle with the other.

'I'm not Complaints any more.'

'Doesn't mean you wouldn't shop a bent cop though, right?'

'As you keep reminding me, you're not a cop these days. We headed to the Gimlet?'

Rebus shook his head. 'I forgot — I took you there once to see Darryl. But he's long finished hanging out at dives like that. He owns a couple of nightclubs in the city centre, along with a casino and 'boutique' hotel, whatever that means.'

'It usually means expensive.'

'Well, we're about to find out.'

'What makes you think we'll find him there?'

Rebus glanced towards his passenger. 'People tell me things.'

'Even though you've retired from the police?'

'Even so.'

The car had made its descent from Queen Street into the heart of the New Town. Just before reaching Royal Circus, Rebus pulled over to the kerb. He applied the brake but the car crept forward.

'Keep forgetting it does that.' He shifted the

65

gearstick into first before turning off the engine.

'Ever thought about trading up to the twenty-first century?' Fox was having trouble with the seat belt. Eventually he got it unlocked and clambered out, while Rebus rubbed the Saab's roof and told it not to listen to the nasty man.

The hotel was part of a typical Georgian terrace, its signage discreet. Inside there was a hallway containing nothing as obvious as a reception desk. Rebus turned left into a plush cocktail bar. A slim young Asian man in a bright red waistcoat was ready with a smile.

'Checking in, gentlemen? Take a seat and someone will be with you in a trice.'

'We're here to see Darryl,' Rebus corrected him.

'Darryl . . . ?' The smile was hardening.

'Darryl Christie, son,' Rebus barked. 'I know he doesn't like visitors, but he'll make an exception. Just tell him it's Rebus.'

'Rebus?'

Rebus nodded and sank back into a heavily padded black velour sofa. Fox stayed on his feet, studying the furnishings. Thick velvet curtains tied back with plaited golden ropes. Odd-shaped mirrors. Jelly beans and rice crackers in little bowls on each glass-topped table. Rebus was helping himself to a scoop of each.

The barman had disappeared around the back of the gantry and was making a muffled phone call. There was music playing, but not obtrusively. Something electronic.

'Doing all right for himself, then,' Fox commented.

'And as Cafferty said, all of it looking above board to the naked eye.'

'But he's dirty nevertheless?'

'Oh yes.'

'And we've not done anything because . . . ?' Fox sat down opposite Rebus.

'Because he's been lucky. Because he's clever. Because maybe he has friends in the right places.'

'What would your guess be?'

Rebus swallowed the last of the snack and began picking between his teeth with a fingernail. 'Sometimes there's such a thing as a responsible criminal.'

'Explain.' Fox sat forward a little, ready to learn.

'Well, there's always going to be organised crime — we know that. All over the world, society's tried shutting it down and it never quite happens. As long as there are things we judge illegal, and people out there who want those things, someone will come along to provide them. In a place the size of Edinburgh — small city, crime not a huge problem for most of the residents — you might have room for one decent-sized player. And as long as that player doesn't get too greedy, too cocky or too violent . . . '

'They'll likely be tolerated? Because they do some of the policing for us?'

'It's all about control, Malcolm. That and acting responsibly.'

'What was Cafferty like when this was his playground?'

Rebus took a moment to form his answer. 'He was the school bully. It was all about muscle, and not giving a damn about the consequences.'

'And Christie?'

'Darryl's a negotiator. If he'd gone into stock-broking or flogging Bentleys to bankers, he'd have made his fortune. But he chose this instead.'

The barman had reappeared. He tried for another smile but didn't quite manage it. 'Mr Christie says he'll be with you shortly. He also said to order drinks while you're waiting.'

'Well that's very kind of him,' Rebus said. 'Do you want anything, DI Fox?'

'Maybe an Appletiser?'

'So that's an Appletiser for my colleague and a Laphroaig for me.' Rebus nodded towards the shelf of malt whiskies. 'In fact, make it a double.'

'You remembering the drink-drive limit?' Fox warned.

'It's tattooed on my forearm.'

'Water or ice on the side, sir?' the barman was asking.

'Is that question for me or him?' Rebus enquired.

Taking the hint, the barman got to work.

Their drinks had just arrived at the table when Darryl Christie appeared in the doorway. He waved away the barman and settled himself on the sofa next to Fox and facing Rebus. Rebus had known him since he was a teenager, but Christie was in his early twenties now, and all trace of acne and youth had gone. His face had hardened, his hair was professionally groomed. The suit didn't look cheap and neither did the shoes. He sported an open-necked shirt with cufflinks prominent at either wrist. The watch, at a guess, was worth more than Rebus's car, even with a few thousand miles removed from its clock.

'How's business?' Rebus asked.

'On the up. It's been a difficult few years for everyone.'

'It's certainly aged you, Darryl. Is that a bit of grey at your temples?'

'Said the man in the twilight zone.'

'You heard I've left the force?'

'Did you not see the fireworks? We had quite the celebration here, trust me.' Christie draped his arms over the back of the sofa and gestured towards Fox. 'This you training your replacement? We've met before, haven't we?'

'Briefly,' Fox said.

'I think I remember congratulating you on your manners.' Christie nodded to himself.

'We're here because of what happened to Big Ger Cafferty last night,' Rebus said.

'Namely?'

'Someone put a bullet through his living-room window.'

'Is he all right?'

'Shooter missed.'

'Dearie me.'

'Maybe deliberately, who knows?' Rebus placed his empty glass on the table with a clunk.

'Cafferty's told you it was my doing?'

'You know what he's like.'

'I know he hates my guts. It's why he's talking to the Starks.'

'Joe Stark?' Rebus asked, feigning surprise.

'Came into town a couple of days back. Booked into a B and B and the owner thought I'd be interested.'

'You're sure Joe's here to see Cafferty?'

'Not Joe so much as Dennis. Cafferty wants him put in charge.'

'Of what?' Fox asked, not quite understanding.

'Of this!' Christie was on his feet, arms outstretched. 'The city — *my* city.'

'You sure you've not watched *Scarface* one too many times?' Rebus asked.

Christie sat down again, but the agitation he had been hiding was now evident in his posture. He pumped one of his knees as he spoke. 'It's the old story — my enemy's enemy is my friend. Cafferty's not got much more than a couple of years left in him. Last thing he wants is to be on his deathbed knowing *I'm* still around. Dennis Stark is the perfect choice. Guy's crazy, for a start. Tell him to take me down and he'll make sure it's messy. And who else is there? Cafferty doesn't know the new regimes in Aberdeen and Dundee. But he knows Joe Stark. They're like two sides of the same piece of bog paper.'

'I think you might be misreading the situation,' Fox said.

'Besides,' Rebus broke in, 'if Cafferty's getting all chummy with the Starks, that gives *you* all the more reason to warn him off with a bullet.'

'I've found, contrary to appearances, that a bullet is a pretty blunt instrument,' Christie said. 'Credit me with a bit more subtlety.' He was regaining his composure. 'And if shooters are involved, I'd put the Starks in the frame every single time. Could be they want to make sure Cafferty's compliant — so he knows he can't muck about with them. World they live in, that's the way they do business.'

'Have you met with them?' Fox asked. 'Spoken to them?'

'Not yet.'

'Cafferty thinks Dennis is maybe being toured around the country so he can get to know the various people he needs to know — people just like you.'

'There's nothing in my diary, if that's what you're asking.'

'Word to the wise, Darryl,' Rebus said. 'You know yourself they're old school. You've just said as much. Subtlety isn't going to play well with them.'

'I'll bear that in mind.'

'Fox and a couple of his colleagues could maybe talk to them, let them know they're not welcome.'

'DI Fox doesn't look too sure about that.'

'No . . . it's just . . . maybe I . . . '

'Well anyway,' Christie said, slapping both his knees before rising to his feet again. 'Thanks for stopping by. We both know it was a waste of time — Cafferty playing his usual games — but all the same . . . '

'Just wish I could have put a bigger dent in your profits.' Rebus gestured towards his empty whisky glass. 'And remember what I said about the Starks. Dennis might be the mad dog, but it's Joe who controls the leash.'

71

Christie gave a slow nod and preceded them into the hallway, bounding up the staircase two steps at a time.

'A young man in a hurry,' Fox commented as they left the building.

'Taking its toll, though,' Rebus said thoughtfully. 'I don't like my gangsters jumpy.' He lit a cigarette. Fox was preparing to walk to the car, but Rebus stood his ground. 'What did you mean in there? When you said he was misreading the situation?'

'Nothing.'

'There's something you know, something you're not telling. How did you find out the Starks were in town? And that they'd stopped off in Aberdeen and Dundee? I doubt you've any grasses worth the name.'

'It was mentioned at St Leonard's.'

'Why, though? The Starks have probably been over here a dozen times this past year without a red flag being raised. And Christie was right about the look on your face when I said CID could go warn the Starks off. Why isn't that a good idea, Malcolm?'

'I'm not allowed to tell you.'

'Why not?'

'That's just the way it is.'

'We're not in a Bruce Hornsby song here — you want my help but you won't tell me anything? Well thanks a bunch, pal, but don't go thinking I'll ever be giving you my last Rolo again.'

Having said which, Rebus flicked his half-smoked cigarette at Fox's feet and stomped off towards the car.

★ ★ ★

Cafferty sat at his kitchen table. The wooden shutters had been pulled across the windows, meaning no one could see in. He'd phoned a guy he knew — ex-army, ran half the city's nightclub doormen — and now there were two well-built young men stationed in a car on the driveway, just inside the gates. The car was facing the pavement, so that anyone walking past could see them. And every ten minutes, one of them would make a circuit of the property, peering over the wall at the back to make sure no one was in a neighbouring garden. It wasn't much, but it was something. In the past, Cafferty had employed a bodyguard, who slept in a room above the garage, but that had become an extravagance. Years before that, of course, he'd had half a dozen guys around him at all hours — used to drive his wife of the time demented. She'd get up in the night to go to the toilet, and find one of them watching her from the staircase. And when she went shopping or to meet friends, there would be the mandatory driver, who was under orders never to let her out of his sight.

Different these days, or so Cafferty had thought.

He had spent the past hour and a half making calls. Problem was, a lot of the people he'd known in the past were now reduced to ash, or had moved halfway across the world. Still, he'd put the word out — he was willing to pay top dollar for up-to-date information on the Starks, father and son, plus their associates, close or otherwise. He'd already learned that they had visited certain businesses in Aberdeen and Dundee in the previous week, which backed up his theory that Dennis was being introduced to people prior to taking over from his old man. The phone was lying on the table, fully charged and waiting for news. Next to it sat the squashed bullet. Cafferty pushed it around with a fingertip. Time was there'd have been someone in his pocket, someone from CID or the forensic lab. He would have handed it over and found out what he could. These days he hardly knew where to start, though again he had mentioned his interest to a few of the people he'd called. Maybe there was someone who knew someone.

There was Rebus, of course. But why would Rebus take it to the lab on the quiet rather than handing it over to CID?

What did it matter anyway? Had to be the Starks or Darryl Christie — the Starks for the sheer hell of it, Darryl Christie as a way of welcoming them to the city and showing them the new pecking order.

Whichever it was, he would find out. And they would pay.

★ ★ ★

There was nothing for Siobhan Clarke to do now but wait. The *Scotsman* would run the story online in the evening, flagging it up on its Twitter feed. Probably wouldn't be until nine or ten o'clock, though, so that when the morning edition appeared they still had the print exclusive. Smith had texted to assure her that it was a front-page splash, unless one of the royals died or was caught on camera with a line of coke.

'Perish the thought,' Clarke had muttered to herself.

Esson and Ogilvie had been busy. They'd compiled a list stretching back half a decade of deaths occurring during break-ins — not just private homes, but workplaces too: security guards hit with crowbars, elderly couples threatened with torture if they didn't say where their valuables were. Around three quarters of the cases had been solved.

'Or at least someone went to jail,' Esson had said, half joking.

There was one from the previous year — a woman attacked in her bedroom in Edinburgh. Her ex-husband was suspected, but there had never been enough evidence to satisfy the procurator fiscal that a guilty verdict would be reached. Another piqued Clarke's interest — just a fortnight back, in Linlithgow. Retired care worker who had, three years before, scooped a million pounds on the lottery. Spent half the money on a big new house with a view of Linlithgow Palace. The man lived alone, his wife having predeceased him. Found in his downstairs hall, skull caved in, hit from behind. Kitchen door forced open from the outside. The case was still active. Clarke had asked Esson and Ogilvie what they thought.

'Worth comparing notes?' Esson had asked in turn.

'It was news at the time,' Ogilvie added. 'The lottery win, I mean.'

'Someone knows he's got a few bob, so they burst in thinking it'll be piled up on the coffee table?' But Clarke had told them to make enquiries anyway, then had driven to the city mortuary, where, entering by the staff door, she surprised one of the assistants as he was removing his scrubs in the deserted corridor.

'Just here to see Professor Quant,' she explained.

'Upstairs.'

Clarke managed a smile of apology as she squeezed past. 'Nice tats, by the way,' she said, watching the young man starting to blush.

Deborah Quant was in her well-lit, tidy office. There was a shower cubicle behind one of the doors and Clarke could smell soap and shampoo.

'Not disturbing you?'

'Come in, Siobhan. Take a seat.'

Quant had pulled back her long red hair, fixing it with a band. 'Just finished up,' she explained. 'But I've a function this evening, so . . . '

Clarke had noticed the dress hanging from a hook. 'Looks lovely,' she commented.

'Better than most of the guests will deserve — academics and senior medics.'

'Taking a date?'

'Got anyone in mind?'

'I heard you'd been out a couple of times with a recent retiree.'

Quant smiled. 'Drinks and dinner only. But can you really see John sitting through a black-tie event with a load of superannuated surgeons and professors?'

'Did you ask him?'

'Actually, I did. He declined.'

'Gracefully, I'm sure.'

'The swearing was minimal. So what can I do for you, Siobhan?'

'It's the Minton inquiry. You did the autopsy.'

'I did.'

'I've looked at your report. I was just wondering if anything else had come to mind.'

'About what?'

'Lord Minton had received a threatening letter — well, just a note really.' Clarke handed over another photocopy. 'I'm wondering if that changes your thinking in any way.'

'Man died from a combination of blunt-force trauma and strangulation — either would probably have been sufficient. Attacked from the front or the side, most probably the front. Victim is on his way to the door of his study, having heard a noise, and the attacker bursts in and hits him with the same hammer he used to smash open the laundry-room window. Marks on the throat tell us the attacker had large hands, probably male.' Quant shrugged. 'This note doesn't alter any of that. Was it found in his drawer?'

'His wallet — why do you ask?'

'In the photos from the locus, the desk drawer was open a couple of inches. I thought maybe the first officers on the scene . . . '

'They would have known better than to touch anything.' Clarke narrowed her eyes, trying to remember the crime scene. The drawer had been closed by the time she'd visited. Nothing odd about that. 'I don't suppose you carried out another autopsy a couple of weeks back, on that lottery winner?'

'From Linlithgow?' Quant shook her head. 'That was blunt-force trauma too, wasn't it? During a break-in. No sign of strangulation, though, if I remember correctly.'

'I wouldn't mind seeing the report.'

'That's easily arranged. But of course there'll have to be a quid pro quo.'

'Meaning?'

Quant nodded towards the dress. 'You have to pretend to be me for the evening. I really just want to go home to bed.'

'Tell you what I *can* do,' Clarke offered. 'I can phone your mobile after the first hour or so. There's a situation and you're urgently needed . . . '

'Have you got my number?' Quant asked with a grin.

'Give it to me,' Clarke said.

8

Only Ricky Compston and Alec Bell were in the office when Fox got back. They were eating custard slices and drinking tea, their feet up on their respective desks.

'Where have you been?' Compston demanded. 'Apart from whispering sweet nothings in your boss's ear.'

'Actually, I've not seen Doug Maxtone. But I did go talk to Big Ger Cafferty.'

'Feel free to keep us waiting.'

'Where are the others?'

'The Starks have been on the move. We're using two cars so we don't get clocked. Hence the exodus. That good enough for you, DI Fox?'

Fox lowered himself on to one of the empty chairs. 'Cafferty seems to think a local criminal called Darryl Christie might have been behind the shooting, maybe to impress the Starks. He reckons the Starks are in town so Dennis can get a feel for the city prior to taking over the family business. It would also explain the stops in Aberdeen and Dundee.'

'We've already told you why the Starks are here.'

'Be that as it may, I decided to have a word with Darryl Christie. *He* already knew that the Starks are in town.'

'Did he bring them up first, or did you?'

'He didn't need any prompting.'

'So you're telling me two Edinburgh bosses just opened up to you?'

Fox offered a shrug. 'Do you want to hear what else Christie said?'

'Go on then, hotshot, impress me.' Compston brushed pastry flakes from his tie.

'Christie is of the opinion that the Starks are here to meet Cafferty. Why? So that Cafferty can help them install Dennis as the city's new boss, in place of Christie. As far as we know, that's not the case, but it's what Christie thinks.'

'How did he know they were in town?' Alec Bell asked.

'The B and B owner.'

'Well, well, well,' a voice drawled from behind Fox. The door, which he hadn't quite shut, was wide open now. Rebus stood with a hand resting against either jamb. 'This isn't quite what I expected, I have to admit.'

Fox jumped to his feet. 'How did you get in?'

'Someone forgot to tell the front desk I'm off the books.'

'John bloody Rebus,' Bell said.

'Hiya, Alec.' Rebus gave a wave. 'Not given up the good fight yet, then?'

'I've heard of you,' Compston said.

'Then you're one up on me.' Rebus stretched out a hand for Compston to shake. Compston complied, introducing himself as he did.

'Desks for five, meaning we're a few short,' Rebus was musing, studying the room. 'And barely any paperwork. Hush-hush, is it? Here to take down the Starks?'

Compston was staring hard at Fox, waiting for

an explanation. Rebus tried to rest a hand on Fox's shoulder, but Fox twisted away from him.

'Can't really blame Malcolm here,' Rebus said. 'I was the only way he was getting to Cafferty and Christie.'

'Is that right?' Compston's eyes were still on Fox, while Fox's were directed at the floor.

'Chief Constable must really have a stiffy for the Starks — team like this doesn't come cheap.' Rebus slid his backside on to a desk, feet waggling. 'I'm guessing Foxy is your local liaison, and he asked for my help because he wanted to impress you with his gung-ho, can-do attitude. How did he do?'

'This is no place for a civilian, Rebus,' Compston said.

'War breaks out in the city, it's bad for everyone, whether in a uniform or not. If you're watching the Starks, you know the score. They *might* be readying to take down Darryl Christie.'

'That's not why they're here,' Alec Bell let slip, receiving a withering look from Compston in response.

'Darryl thinks it is. He's got it into his head that they're coming for him, stoked up by Cafferty.'

'They've met neither Cafferty nor this Darryl Christie,' Compston stated.

'So Dennis isn't being introduced to low society?' Rebus scratched his cheek. 'You sure about that?'

'We've got our eyes and ears on them.'

'One of them didn't happen to mosey over to

Cafferty's neck of the woods last night and point a gun at him?'

'We don't think so.'

'There may have been gaps in the surveillance,' Fox piped up. 'Just about big enough to make it a possibility.'

'I'm wishing now I'd stuck you in a corner with that fucking Angry Birds game,' Compston snarled, jumping to his feet and pacing the room.

'For what it's worth,' Rebus said, 'Malcolm didn't tell me a single thing about the operation here, and nothing he said in front of either Cafferty or Christie will have made them any the wiser.'

'You found out, though.'

Rebus shook his head. 'He got me curious, that's all.' He glanced at the clock on the wall. 'Now, how about letting me drag you across the road for a drink? It's not the worst boozer in town, and I'm betting no one's had the decency to wet the team's head, as it were.'

'We're supposed to be waiting for the lads to report in,' Bell cautioned.

Compston thought for a moment. 'Won't do any harm, though, will it? No more than has already been wreaked by DI Fox. You can man the post here if you like, Alec.'

'Strength in numbers, Ricky — I better come with you.'

'It's unanimous, then.' Rebus eased himself off the desk. 'Lead the way, DI Fox — it's your round, after all.'

* * *

The pub was half full of workers on their way home and students playing games of chess and draughts. There being no free tables, the group made for the far end of the bar. Fox bought the drinks — three pints and a sparkling water.

'If I'd known you didn't drink,' Compston admonished him, 'you'd have been off my team from minute one.' He took the first of the proffered beers and tried a mouthful, smacking his lips.

'How have you been, John?' Bell and Rebus clinked glasses.

'Mustn't grumble, Alec. You still in Glasgow?'

'Attached to Gartcosh these days.'

'Congratulations. Bit of a step up from busting druggies and wife-beaters.'

'Aye.'

'So someone's running around your city with a firearm?' Compston interrupted. 'Doesn't seem to have made the news.'

'Cafferty's saying it was an accident. Tripped and smashed a window. Neighbours say otherwise, and there's a bullet hole in his living-room wall.'

'The two of you are cosy, then?'

'Insofar as I've spent half my life trying to put him away.'

'Any success?'

'He was released from jail on medical grounds, followed by a miracle cure.' Rebus placed his glass on the bar. 'So, are you ready to tell me a story, or do we just keep going around the houses like a taxi driver on his first trip to Livingston?'

Compston looked to Alec Bell.

'John's one of the good guys, despite all appearances,' Bell confirmed.

'The Starks,' Compston began, after a further moment's consideration, 'are looking for a man called Hamish Wright. He's a haulage contractor, used to deliver drugs around the country in his containers. We've been watching the Starks for a while, and when they left Glasgow for Inverness and visited Wright's yard there, we knew something was up. Aberdeen and Dundee after that, and now here.'

'Have you tried looking for Wright yourselves?'

'He's definitely done a flit. Wife is covering his arse, says he's in London on business, but he's not made any calls on his phone and there's nothing to show he's there.'

'What about his car?'

'Parked in the garage at his home.'

'Does the wife seem spooked?'

'I'd say so.'

'He's got something belonging to the Starks?' Rebus speculated.

'Drugs and cash, probably,' Bell offered.

Compston's phone was buzzing — incoming call. 'It's Beth,' he said, pressing the phone to one ear while covering the other with his free hand. But the noise in the bar proved too much, so he began making for the door. Once he was outside, Rebus focused on Bell.

'What's he like then, Alec?'

'He's all right.'

'Better than you?' Rebus didn't sound convinced.

84

092650066

<u>Reservation</u>

Name: WEBB · R·F·

Collect by: 3/4/21

**Thank you for using
Reserve and Collect**

**Your items are due for return
on;**

12/4/21

**Library staff are following
additional safety precautions
when selecting your library
items.**

If you wish to take extra
precautions, time is the best
disinfectant. We recommend
quarantining them for an additional
72 hours.

You can renew your items online
or over the phone if they have not
been reserved by another
customer.

**Please visit
www.worcestershire.gov.uk/
libraries for up to date library
news and information**

worcestershire
c o u n t y c o u n c i l

'Just different. It *is* drugs and cash, by the way. Plenty of both. All this stuff about muscling in on your man Christie is wrong. Or them going after Big Ger Cafferty, for that matter.'

'You got wire taps or something?' Rebus mused.

'Better than that.' Bell turned his attention towards Fox, checking that the door was still closed and stabbing a finger at him. 'This goes no further.'

Fox held up his hands in a show of appeasement.

'We've got a man on the inside. Deep cover.'

'Bob Selway?' Fox guessed, but Bell shook his head.

'No names. He's been undercover for more than three years, worming his way closer and closer to the Starks.'

'Takes a bit of stamina,' Rebus said, impressed.

'Explains why my boss thought we were welcoming a team of six,' Fox added.

'Aye, someone at Gartcosh bolloxed that up — and got Ricky Compston raging at them for their efforts.'

'Three years — is that how long the team's been together?'

Bell shook his head again. 'There've been others before us. The Starks are behind half the crime in Glasgow and beyond — so far no operation's been able to nail down their coffin.'

'Sounds like your mole's not exactly earning his keep,' Fox commented. Bell scowled at him.

'So what's the story with this haulage

contractor?' Rebus hoisted his pint to his mouth.

'Wasn't happy moving stuff for the Starks. Wanted to be more of a freelance operator, you might say. He was talking to people in Aberdeen and elsewhere.'

'Including here?' Rebus watched as Alec Bell nodded slowly. 'Meaning Darryl Christie?'

'Very possibly.'

'So the Starks *will* want a face-to-face with Darryl.'

'They might, but they'd rather find Hamish Wright first, if he's sitting on half a million in coke and eccies and the same in lovely hard cash.'

'Your man's told you this?'

'Yes.'

'You've got enough to take to trial?'

'Just about.'

'But you want more.'

Bell gave a wide smile. 'Always.'

'The longer your man is embedded, though, the more risk there is of him being rumbled.'

'He's aware of that.'

'Deserves a medal, whatever happens.'

Bell was nodding as Compston pushed open the door and strode towards the group, rubbing his hands to warm them.

'The Starks have been meeting a man called Andrew Goodman.'

'He runs a stable of nightclub bouncers,' Rebus said.

'That's right. Which means he has a say in what gets into pubs and clubs.'

'His boys do,' Rebus corrected.

'Including illegal substances,' Fox added, 'and those carrying them with intent to sell.'

'Very good,' Compston said.

'He knows Hamish Wright?' Rebus asked.

Compston shrugged. 'This is a long game we're playing. But eventually all the bits of the jigsaw will fit together.'

Rebus wrinkled his nose. 'Sometimes a bit gets lost between the floorboards, though. Or it wasn't in the box from the get-go.'

'Cheery bastard, aren't you? Whose round is it?'

'I need to be going,' Fox apologised.

'Back across the road to report to your boss? Decided yet how much you're going to spill?' When Fox didn't answer, Compston made a shooing motion, dismissing him, but Fox lingered.

'I know why it's called Operation Junior,' he stated.

Compston lifted an eyebrow. 'Go on then.'

'The *Iron Man* films — Robert Downey Junior plays a character called Stark.'

Compston was miming a round of applause as Fox made his exit.

'Same again, John?' Bell was asking. Rebus nodded, watching the retreating figure. Then he turned towards Compston.

'Malcolm's all right, but the one thing he's not is dirty. So if you start crossing the line, that may be when he sounds the alarm. Up until then, he'll be fine.'

'I'm not happy he brought you in.'

'He told me the bare minimum. Until I walked

into St Leonard's, I didn't know what I was going to find.'

'But you'd sussed there was something he was holding back.'

'Only because I'm good at this. So where are the Starks now?'

'Dennis and his boys are eating a curry somewhere on Leith Walk, and the dad's on his way back to Glasgow — got a bit of business there, apparently.'

'With one or two of your team on his tail?'

'Jake and Bob,' Compston confirmed, more for Bell's benefit than Rebus's. 'Means you and me might have to spell for Beth and Peter a bit later.'

'Fine by me,' Bell said.

Compston turned his attention back to Rebus, making a show of looking him up and down.

'So what do we do with you, Mr Rebus?'

'Apart from getting the next round in, you mean?'

'Apart from that, yes.'

'Well, I suppose I could tell you a bit about Cafferty and Christie. Just to pass the time.' Rebus gestured towards one of the tables where two students were finishing a board game and rising to leave. 'Or I could tan your arse at draughts — I'll leave it to you to choose.'

★ ★ ★

Doug Maxtone was walking down the corridor, shrugging his shoulders into his overcoat, when Fox reached the top of the stairs.

'Thought I was being stood up,' Maxtone said. 'Went to the office, but it's in darkness.'

'Sorry, sir. Some of them are on surveillance and the others went for a drink.'

Maxtone stopped walking, adjusting his scarf. 'Well then?' he said.

'How much did they share at the briefing — just so I'm not telling you what you already know?'

'Compston and his team are in town to keep tabs on a gang run by Joe and Dennis Stark.'

'And the Starks are here . . . ?'

'Because someone's done a bunk and they want to find him.' Maxtone paused. 'I thought *you* were the one making the report?'

'To be honest, there's not a lot I can add. Compston's team are keeping watch, but so far the man being sought hasn't turned up.'

'And Edinburgh's just one stop, yes?'

'That's right, sir. They've already looked for him in other cities.'

'So if they don't find him soon, they'll move on elsewhere?'

'I'd presume so.'

'Fine then.' Maxtone made to move off, but paused. 'Compston's behaving himself? No regulations being broken, no toes trampled?'

'Not that I'm aware of.'

'But *would* you be aware of it?'

'I think so.'

'Fine then,' Maxtone repeated. 'See you tomorrow, Malcolm.'

'Absolutely.'

Fox watched as his boss began to descend the

stairs. No reason the man had to know anything — about Cafferty and Christie or the missing drugs or the cop who had infiltrated the Stark gang. No reason for any of that to trouble Doug Maxtone's evening.

He walked to the door of the Operation Junior office and turned the handle. Sure enough, it wasn't locked. He switched on the lights and went in. There were two laptops, both in sleep mode. He dabbed a finger against both trackpads, waking them and confirming that they were password-protected. A few sheets of paper lay on one desk, including the photo of Hamish Wright. Beneath it was a copy of a phone bill — Wright's most recent mobile bill, to be precise. Someone had checked the numbers, the details scribbled in the margin. Fox took his own phone out and snapped a picture, then put everything back in order, padding back to the door and switching off the light once more.

It was his night to phone his sister, and he would take care of that as soon as he got home. After which he planned to fire up his computer and see what he could glean about the Starks and their cohorts.

And if that didn't take as long as he feared it well might, he'd call Siobhan just prior to bedtime to ask how her day had gone and maybe tell her a little of his.

Day Three

9

Having stopped at a newsagent's to buy a paper, Fox got back in his car and phoned Siobhan Clarke. She answered on the sixth ring.

'I was wondering why I couldn't reach you last night,' Fox said, staring at the front-page headline.

'Got a bit hectic, I admit.'

'You gave the story to your pal Laura.'

'Yes.'

'I'm guessing today will be busy too.'

'Actually, I'm happy for James to hog the limelight. I'm heading to Linlithgow with Christine. We're just about there.'

'Oh?'

'Anyway, what are you up to?'

'Those visitors I mentioned, the ones from Gartcosh? I'm acting as liaison, sort of.'

'Keeping an eye on them for Maxtone?'

'Pretty much. They're in town because a Glasgow gangster's — '

'Sorry, Malcolm, you're breaking up. And I need to start looking for the turn-off.'

'Maybe speak to you later then?'

But the signal had gone. Fox turned off the phone and skimmed the news story again, before placing the paper on the passenger seat, on top of a bulging folder. There had been a *lot* about the Stark family on the internet. He'd printed off much of it and taken everything to bed with him, along with a pad of lined A4 paper. Joe Stark's wife had died young, leaving him to bring up their only child, Dennis. Fox reckoned Joe had lacked any but the most basic parenting skills. He'd been too busy extending his empire and consolidating his reputation as one of the most ruthless thugs in Glasgow gangland — which was no mean feat, considering the competition. Dennis had been trouble from his earliest days in primary school. Bullied (and maybe worse, ignored) by his father, he'd become a bully himself. It helped that he'd grown up fast, building muscle to go with his threats. In his early teens, only a wily lawyer had stopped him doing time for an attack outside a football ground.

He had used an open razor — similar to Joe's weapon of choice in the 1970s. That interested Fox — the son imitating the father, hoping to gain his approbation. In his twenties, Dennis had served two stretches in HMP Barlinnie, which did little to curb his excesses while at the same time making him new allies. Fox hadn't been able to find out a whole lot about this coterie. Joe's men were in their fifties and sixties predominantly, and tales from the Glasgow badlands featured them regularly. But Dennis's cohorts were a generation younger and had learned the art of subterfuge. They appeared on no front pages, and in precious few court reports. Driving to St Leonard's, Fox wondered if, shown photos, he would be able to pick out the undercover cop.

The only person in the office was Alec Bell.

He yawned a greeting and stirred his coffee.

'Ricky's having a lie-in,' he explained.

'He took the dawn shift?' Fox guessed.

Bell nodded and rubbed at his eyes. 'He's not keen, though — there's half a chance old Joe could place him.'

'They know one another?'

'A couple of run-ins back in the day. But seeing how Joe is in Glasgow right now . . . '

'Compston reckons he's safe enough taking a shift?' Fox nodded his understanding. 'Anything else I need to know?' he asked, hanging up his coat.

'Not really, unless you happen to have the name of a good curry house — so far, Glasgow beats your overpriced city into a cocked hat.'

'I'll have a think. Meantime, I was wondering if you had a file on the Starks — something I can pass the time with.'

'It's mostly on computer.'

'Any surveillance pics?'

'Why would you want those?'

Fox shrugged. 'Just occurred to me last night that I've no idea what the entourage looks like.'

Bell got busy on his laptop and crooked a finger. Fox walked over to the desk and studied the screen from behind the older man's shoulder.

'That's Joe,' Bell said, using the cursor to circle Joe Stark's face. The photo showed a group of men walking down a pavement. 'To his left is Walter Grieve, and to his right Len Parker. Those three have known each other for ever — Joe probably trusts Walter and Len more than he does Dennis.'

'Bit of tension between father and son?'

'You know how Prince Charles has spent his whole life waiting to take over the family firm?'

'For Charles read Dennis.' Fox nodded his understanding. He was studying Joe Stark. Of course, he'd seen plenty of photos of the man during his previous evening's excavation of the internet, but this photo was recent. Stark's face was more heavily lined, his hair thinner, slicked back from his forehead.

'Looks a bit like Ray Reardon, no?' Alec Bell commented.

'The snooker player?' Fox considered this. 'Maybe.' Though in truth he didn't see it. There had always been a twinkle in Ray Reardon's eyes. All he could see in Joe Stark's face was cold malice.

Bell had reduced the photograph to a thumbnail and was poring over the others on his screen. He clicked on one. The inside of a busy pub. Five men seated at a table.

'Dennis and his crew,' Bell said, pointing at each man as he named them. 'Rob Simpson, Callum Andrews, Jackie Dyson, Tommy Rae, and Dennis himself.'

'Doesn't look much like his dad.'

'Takes after his mum, apparently,' Bell said.

'Big bastard, though. Does he go to the gym?'

'Addicted to the weights. Uses all the bodybuilding potions and powders.'

'Is his hair permed, or are the curls natural?'

'God-given, far as I know.'

'You ever talked with him?'

Bell shook his head. 'I wouldn't be on the team if I had. Can't have anyone from the Stark gang clocking us.'

96

'Doesn't seem to apply to your boss,' Fox mused.

'Special dispensation — Ricky pushed hard to bring Operation Junior into the world.' Bell turned his head to study Fox. 'Go on then,' he said. 'You're bursting to ask.'

'Well, if you insist — is your guy one of the four with Dennis?'

'What do you think?'

'None of them looks like a cop.'

'How far would our man get if he did? Or if he spoke or acted like one?'

'I take it he's not using his real name.'

'Course not.'

'And you've built a life story for him, just in case someone checks?'

'We have.'

'How long did you say he'd been in the gang?'

'I don't think I did say.' Bell was suddenly cagey. Rather than open any of the other photos in the album, he closed the lid of his laptop and took another slug of coffee.

Well, that was fine. Fox had names now. Given a bit of privacy, he would run another internet search, just on the off chance.

'News from Glasgow?' he asked, moving into the middle of the room.

'Joe's still there.'

'He took both his lieutenants with him when he went?'

'Yes.'

'So it's just Dennis and his gang of four left here? Any idea what they'll be doing today?'

'Looking for Hamish Wright.'

97

'Have they stuck around longer than in Aberdeen or Dundee?'

'Seems that way.'

'That might mean something — maybe they're convinced he's here.'

'Maybe,' Bell conceded.

'Your man on the inside hasn't said?'

Bell gave him a hard stare. 'He doesn't often get the chance to update us.'

'When did you last hear from him?'

'Five days ago.'

'Before you came to Edinburgh?'

'That's right. If and when the Starks get hold of Wright, that's when he'll make the call.'

'How long's he been — '

'Enough fucking questions, Fox. I wish I'd never opened my mouth in the first place.'

'Ah, but you did — I think you were trying to show off in front of Rebus. Is that a fair reading?'

'Get lost.'

'Hard to do in my own office.' Fox stretched out both arms to reinforce the point. 'And you did let slip last night that your mole's been in character for over three years.' He tapped his forehead. 'Thing about not drinking is, I tend to remember things.'

'Then you'll not have forgotten what Ricky said to you that first day — you're on probation. And after that trick you pulled, going to Rebus behind our backs . . . ' Bell shook his head slowly. 'How's your dad, by the way?'

Fox's eyes narrowed. 'My *dad*?'

'And your sister, Jude. Not too close to her, are you?' Bell gave a sly smile. 'Ricky needed

98

certain assurances that he knew the kind of man he was getting. Your boss came through with a potted biography. Now if that had been Ricky, he'd have handed over a minimum of detail with a few howlers mixed in. DCI Maxtone proved to be a lot more accommodating. Remember that when you make your next report. Some chiefs are better than others, and some teams really *are* teams. The sooner you stop acting as Maxtone's snitch, the sooner you'll find that out.'

'Is that a fact?'

'Think about it. You said yourself you're one step above pariah status here. Maybe we can offer you something better for a time.'

'Better than Angry Birds?'

'I'll let you be the judge of that,' Bell said, opening the lid of his laptop again.

★ ★ ★

'Papers called him the 'tragic lottery victim',' Christine Esson said. 'Makes it sound as if it was the lottery that did for him.'

'Which, if someone killed him for his money, is almost true,' Clarke replied. The new-build two-storey brick house was surrounded by a high wall and electric gates. These gates had been left open for them. The driveway was short and led to a paved parking circle. To the right of the house stood a three-car garage. Clarke stopped her Astra in front of it, next to a BMW 3 Series. The man who got out of the Beemer straightened his tie and did up a button on his suit.

'DS Grant?' Clarke checked. The man nodded. 'I'm DI Clarke, this is DC Esson. Thanks for meeting us.'

'No trouble at all.' Grant ducked back into his car long enough to produce a folder, which he handed over.

'Post-mortem examination, crime scene stuff and the forensic report.'

'Much appreciated. The case is still active, yes?'

'Absolutely.'

'I'm not a reporter, Jim. You can tell the truth here.'

Grant gave a thin smile. 'I suppose we've reached the treading-water stage. Team's been cut to the bare minimum. We've interviewed everyone we can think of, put feelers out, studied CCTV from the town centre and the routes in and out of Linlithgow . . . '

'Much the same as we've been doing in Edinburgh.'

'High-profile victims, that's the only solid connection that I can see.'

'And men who lived alone,' Esson chipped in.

'Michael Tolland wasn't a bachelor like your Lord Minton, though,' Grant countered. 'Married quarter of a century. Wife was already ill when they scooped the lottery. Liver cancer. Didn't live long enough to get any good from it, but her husband wrote a six-figure cheque to charity after she passed on.'

'Between that and the house, he wouldn't have had a lot left over.'

'About two hundred and seventy-five thousand.'

'Any children?'

Grant shook his head. 'His sister's kids look like getting the lot. Sister passed away eight months ago.'

'Not the luckiest of families, despite appearances.' Clarke was studying the front of the house.

'Want to go inside?' Grant jangled a key chain.

'Lead the way.'

There were still bloodstains on the beige hall carpet. Clarke took out the crime scene photos, sharing them with Esson. Beyond the hall there was a large living room, dominated by an oversized TV screen and surround-sound speakers. There were a few ornaments, but not many. A single framed photo of husband and wife at their registry office wedding. Ella Tolland had worked as an administrator for the local council. A decade younger than her husband. In the photo she was managing to smile, but her mouth was closed, in contrast to her husband's toothy grin. He gripped her upper arm as if to stop her heading for the hills.

'Happy marriage, was it?' Clarke enquired.

'No reason to think otherwise. I've stuck a DVD in the folder, a couple of interviews they did after hitting the jackpot.'

'Thanks.'

Grant led them through to the kitchen, showing them where the door had been forced. The door itself had been removed as evidence and replaced with something more basic.

'We're thinking a crowbar or similar.'

'And that's what was used to attack the victim?'

'No weapon recovered, so we can only speculate, but the pathologist reckoned it would be consistent. You said on the phone, though — you think a hammer in Edinburgh?'

'Now you've brought up the crowbar, we may revisit that.'

'No weapon found?'

'We've searched the streets nearby, back gardens, communal bins, even the Water of Leith.'

'Same here. We had a dozen men walk the road between here and the highway — fields, ditches, you name it.'

'Any thoughts, Christine?' Clarke said.

'Does DS Grant know about the note?'

Grant himself decided to answer. 'Yes, but there was nothing like that found here.'

Clarke had opened the fridge. 'Wasn't much of a cook, was he?'

'From talking to friends, he seemed to eat in the pub a lot, or else grab takeaway.' Grant opened a drawer and lifted out a pile of menus. 'Preference for Chinese and Indian — and not all local, either. Then again, if you've got money, distance is no object.'

'You've searched the house from top to bottom?' Clarke checked. 'The note would've been easy to miss.'

'I could see about giving it another go, if my boss will lend me the bodies.'

Clarke looked to Esson. 'What do you think?'

'I think the chances of the two cases being linked are slim.'

'How slim?'

'Catwalk supermodel. We've got two victims with nothing to connect them — they didn't know one another and moved in very different social circles.'

Clarke was sifting through the contents of the file. 'Mr Tolland was never in trouble with the law? No court appearances?'

'Clean as a whistle, though I dare say some of the people he looked after might not be strangers to a summons.'

'How do you mean?'

'He was a care worker — people with problems, that sort of thing.'

'Could any of them have carried a grudge?'

'Lord Minton never handled that sort of case,' Esson cautioned.

'Maybe back in the day he did,' Clarke replied.

'I don't think this was personal,' Grant stated. 'Breaking and entering gone wrong, rather than hamesucken.'

Clarke almost smiled at his use of the word — the Scots legal term for breaking into someone's house with intent to harm them.

'So what did they take?' she asked, closing the file once more. 'Not even his laptop or iPhone is missing. Credit cards, cash, Breitling watch — all still here, same as in Lord Minton's house. Why didn't the perpetrator just wait till the place was empty? Not another house for half a mile — nobody to hear anything. For some reason, the victim has to be home.' She paused. 'Who found the body, by the way?'

'An old friend. Tolland had missed a pub quiz — he was team captain and he took it seriously.

When he didn't answer his phone, the friend dropped round. Gates locked, but when he hoisted himself up on to the wall, he could see the TV was on. Eventually he wandered around the back and found the door open.'

'How old a friend?'

'Since school, I think.'

'Maybe talk to him again. If Tolland *had* received any kind of threat, he might have confided. At the very least, he'd probably have appeared anxious or out of sorts.'

'Okay,' Grant said.

'In which case, I think we're done here.' Clarke shook Grant's hand. 'And thanks again for meeting us.'

'My pleasure,' Grant said.

As the Astra turned back down the driveway, Clarke asked Esson what she thought.

'Not really my type — probably irons his underpants.'

'He did have a look of the tailor's dummy about him, didn't he? Reckon he really will talk to the friend again?'

'Yes, but only because it gives him an excuse to get back to us. When you turned away to open the fridge . . . '

'What?'

'His eyes were doing everything short of stripping the clothes off you.'

Clarke squirmed. 'I thought you were the one he liked.'

'I'd say the man's not had a woman for a while. Has he got your mobile number?'

'Yes.'

'Probably not the very next text, then, but the one after that.'

'What?'

'It won't be about work — trust me.'

Clarke made a face.

'If you're the betting type, I'll gladly take your money,' Esson teased.

'Not the next text but the one after? A text rather than an actual phone call?'

'Twenty quid says one or the other.'

'Twenty quid it is.' Clarke took her hand off the steering wheel long enough for the two women to shake on it.

10

Rebus drove past Cafferty's house and saw the car in the driveway, just inside the open gates. Two men in the front, watching him as he watched them. He parked on a meter and walked back to the house. The men didn't move as he passed them, but he felt their eyes on him as he walked up to the front door and rang the bell. The living-room window had been replaced, but the brick-coloured putty had yet to be painted. Cafferty opened the door.

'I take it you told them I was coming?' Rebus nodded towards the car. 'Wise to get a bit of security.'

'Come in.' Cafferty led the way into the living room. The painting hiding the bullet hole had been removed, the hole filled in. The plaster looked fresh, but would need repainting.

'You sounded a bit frazzled on the phone,' Rebus said. 'Has something happened?'

Cafferty had settled on the edge of an armchair. Rebus sat down opposite him.

'You seen the paper?' The *Scotsman* was on the coffee table. Cafferty turned it round so it faced Rebus. There was a photo of David Minton, and a headline about the threat on his life.

'I've seen it.'

Cafferty eased something from his trouser pocket and placed it on the coffee table. It was the bullet prised from the wall, half wrapped in a piece of paper.

'What am I supposed to do with that? I'm not a cop, remember.'

'Look at the paper.'

Rebus narrowed his eyes, then reached forward and unfolded the note.

'Christ,' he said. 'Siobhan needs to see this.'

'Is she working the Minton case?' Cafferty watched as Rebus nodded, his eyes still on the note and its bald threat:

I'M GOING TO KILL YOU FOR WHAT YOU DID.

'Where did it come from?' Rebus asked.

'It was just lying inside the front door one morning.'

'Folded like this?'

'No. It was lying flat, message-side up, like someone had pushed it under the door rather than using the letter box. Meant I'd see it straight off.'

'You don't have any cameras?'

'CCTV, you mean? Any idea how useless that is?'

Rebus looked at the note again. 'How long ago?'

'Five days back.'

Handwritten capitals in what looked like black biro.

'So who sent it?'

'The same person who took a shot at me.'

'You know that for sure, or are you just guessing?'

'I'm putting two and two together.'

'Guy who killed Lord Minton didn't use a gun.'

'And yet we both got identical notes. You saying the shooter may not be the same person?'

'I'm not saying anything . . . ' Rebus had been about to call Cafferty by his first name, but stopped himself. Big Ger? Morris? Gerald? He was Morris Gerald Cafferty. He was Big Ger. Nothing would have sounded quite right.

'John,' Cafferty said quietly. 'What the hell is this about?'

'Someone thinks you and David Minton wronged them in some way, and they're intent on making you pay.'

'I didn't know who Minton was until the news told me he was dead.'

'You never faced him across a courtroom? He never locked up any of your men?'

'No.'

'He's the law, you're a gangster — already there's a connection.' Rebus realised he had taken out his cigarettes, the pack and a lighter clutched in the same hand.

'Go ahead if you really need to,' Cafferty said.

'I can wait.' Rebus put them away again. 'The bullet will go to ballistics. It's pretty beaten up, but if the gun's been used before, we might get a match.'

'Okay.'

'And Siobhan's going to need a proper interview with you — on the record.'

'She has to promise the news won't leak. Last thing I need is reporters climbing over me.'

'You know what investigations are like.'

'I know they're about as watertight as a paper boat.'

'Meaning you'll have to take your chances. Siobhan will do what she can. But if she thinks it'll help the inquiry to go public . . . '

'Aye, fair enough.' Cafferty looked suddenly tired and old.

'Those two gorillas out front may not be enough. If I were you, I'd find somewhere with a bit more anonymity.'

'Maybe a guest house, eh? With the Starks along the corridor.'

'You know where they are?'

'I made a few calls — know thy enemy and all that.'

'You think they . . . ?'

'How the hell do I know what I think? I think *everything*. Every bastard I ever did wrong to — know how long that list is?'

'A good few of them must be dead — some, only you'll know where the bodies are.'

'You're about as funny as a coronary.'

'I'd say you're well on your way to one of those. But getting riled isn't going to help. You've really no idea why someone would send you that note?'

'No.'

'And when the shot was fired, you didn't see whoever did it?'

'I saw . . . maybe the vaguest shape. A padded coat with a hood pulled down low over the head.'

'Male?'

'Judging by the build.'

'Age?'

'No idea. Maybe six foot tall. Just a glimpse as the window smashed. But I was ducking, too, and making for the door. I wanted to get out of that bloody room.'

'Twenty years ago, you'd have been out of the house and chasing him down the street.'

Cafferty managed a smile. 'With a cleaver in my hand.'

'If we were to get to the bottom of this, I'd want it to go to trial. Wouldn't look good if the suspect died while on remand.'

'Might be a deal-breaker.'

Rebus was holding up his phone. 'Before I call Siobhan, I need you to promise.'

'That I won't whack whoever tried to whack me? I'll promise that if you promise the media won't get wind of that note.'

'Why is it such a problem?'

'Use your loaf, John. With the Starks circling the city? And Darryl Christie — I'm assuming you talked to him?'

'He said the bullet was nothing to do with him. He seemed antsy, though.'

'Because of the Starks?'

'He seems to think they might try muscling in — with your blessing.'

Cafferty shook his head slowly. 'Whatever's going on, I can't afford to look weak, or like I'm suddenly cosying up to the law and order brigade.'

'You've not completely left the game, then?'

'Neither of us has — or ever could.' Cafferty managed another smile.

'You still reckon one or the other might be behind this?'

'Everything is possible.'

'So where does Lord Minton fit in?'

'Maybe he'd taken backhanders somewhere down the line — let off the Starks' men, or Christie's. Thinking of making a clean breast of it towards the end of his life . . . ' Cafferty shrugged. 'I'm not the detective here.'

'Then maybe it's time I called one,' Rebus suggested.

'Maybe it is,' Cafferty conceded, leaning back in his chair.

⋆   ⋆   ⋆

Clarke arrived with Christine Esson. This, too, was apparently a deal-breaker, and Esson was sent to wait in the car. Both note and bullet still sat on the coffee table, and Clarke noted them immediately.

'Okay,' she said, exchanging looks with both men. 'Which one of you wants to do the talking?'

'He does,' Rebus said, nodding towards Cafferty. 'I need to feed the meter and have a smoke.'

He headed back outdoors, passing the bodyguards' car. Only one of them was inside. The other had his back to Rebus as he walked sentry-style towards the rear garden. Rebus tapped on the window and the man in the driver's seat obliged by lowering it an inch.

'Just the two of you?' Rebus enquired.

'We're working shifts with another pair. Mr Cafferty tells us you used to be a cop.' He watched as Rebus got a cigarette going.

'I was army before that — Parachute Regiment.' Rebus exhaled smoke. 'How about you?'

111

The man gave a slow nod.

'I can usually tell.'

'Same way I can usually spot a cop. Is it serious, what's happening with Mr Cafferty?'

'Might be.'

'He's a sitting target as long as he stays here.'

'Just what I've been telling him.' Rebus flicked ash on the driveway. 'Keep up the good work, eh?'

As he walked up the road, digging change from his pocket, he saw Christine Esson crouched on the pavement next to Clarke's Astra. She was patting the wire-haired terrier.

'Looks like you've made a friend,' Rebus commented.

She straightened up. 'It's nice to feel wanted.' Then, with a gesture towards Cafferty's house: 'I'm not happy about being shut out.'

'Siobhan will tell you all about it.'

'So why am I not in there?'

'Because Cafferty's hardly a major contributor to the Police Benevolent Fund.'

'Exactly — yet here we are offering our help.'

Rebus watched as the dog sniffed his shoes before returning to the more attentive Esson. 'That's what we do, Christine, sometimes whether people want it or not.'

'Are you forgetting you've retired?'

Rebus looked at her. 'You know, for a second there, it actually had slipped my mind. But being a civilian has its advantages.'

'Such as?'

'Not answering to anyone, just for starters. And at the end of the day, no forms to fill in. How's the Minton case, by the way?'

'We're just back from Linlithgow. Lottery winner got done in a couple of weeks back.'

'I remember that. Siobhan thinks there might be a connection?'

'Tenuous at best.'

'No note left at the scene?'

'Local team's going to give the house another search.'

'Your priorities may be about to change,' Rebus warned her.

'Why's that?'

But Rebus just smiled and walked on, crushing the remains of his cigarette underfoot and paying for a new parking ticket at the machine. She was playing with the dog again as he passed her on his way back to the house.

He had left the front door unlocked so he could let himself in. Clarke was seated in the chair Rebus had vacated, Cafferty across from her. She was studying the note.

'Whose is the dog?' Rebus asked Cafferty.

'What dog?'

'The one that's always outside.'

'Turned up a week or so back. I think it's a stray.'

'Looks like someone's feeding it, though.'

'A lot of soft touches on this street — present company aside.'

Rebus turned his attention to Clarke. 'What's the thinking?' he asked.

'Mr Cafferty is unwilling for this to be made public,' Clarke answered. 'I've told him that will be DCI Page's decision. Meantime, I want the bullet taken to the forensic lab for analysis

— they might want to send it elsewhere if their equipment isn't up to the job. Could be a while before we get any results.'

'And the note?'

'Looks like the same pen, probably the same hand. Again, I'd like an expert to give us an opinion.'

'Reckon it adds up?' Rebus folded his arms. 'Minton was attacked inside his home by someone who broke in. Not nearly the same MO as standing on somebody's lawn and shooting through a window.'

'You think the notes and the shooting are unconnected?'

'I'm just raising a doubt. The murder in Linlithgow has more in common with Minton than this does.'

'What murder in Linlithgow?' Cafferty interrupted.

'Not important,' Clarke told him.

'Lottery winner a few weeks back,' Rebus added, earning a glare of disapproval from Clarke for his efforts.

'I remember hearing about that,' Cafferty said.

'It's really not important,' Clarke stressed.

'So what's next?' Rebus asked.

'Mr Cafferty needs to come to HQ and give a statement.'

'No way,' Cafferty stated, raising a hand. 'I walk in there, it's going to be all over the news.'

'We could bring the recording equipment here,' Rebus suggested.

Clarke gave him another look. 'And by 'we', of course, I mean Police Scotland.'

'I'm not sure the Fiscal's office would go for it,' Clarke said.

'But you could ask?'

'I need to take this to DCI Page first.' Clarke was digging in her pocket for her phone.

'I don't want any more cops in here,' Cafferty warned her. 'You, I'll just about tolerate.'

'And John?'

Cafferty stared at Rebus. 'For now, I suppose,' he conceded.

'Well, I need to speak to Page anyway.' Clarke got to her feet and moved towards the door, making the call as she went. Cafferty stood up and found himself face to face with Rebus.

'The crew outside,' Rebus said. 'Two-by-two, twelve-hour shifts . . . '

'What about them?'

'Where did they come from?'

'How do you mean?'

'I mean, are they part of Andrew Goodman's show?'

'What does it matter?'

'Just that Goodman's been in at least one meeting with the Starks since they hit town.'

'I know — Andrew told me. He's a good guy.'

'And did Andrew happen to say what the Starks wanted from him?'

'A guy from the Highlands called Hamish Wright was mentioned, but only in passing. Seemed it wasn't him they were looking for so much as something he's got hidden away somewhere.'

'And we both know what that will be.'

'Thing is, we're talking a commodity of some considerable bulk.'

'Not easy to hide?'

'And difficult to move without someone noticing. No way Wright can use one of his own lorries.'

'So he'll be in touch with other hauliers maybe?'

'If he feels he needs to move it. Then again, it may be stowed away somewhere he reckons no one can find it.'

'Would he know people in the city?'

'I'd say so.'

'You wouldn't be one of them?'

'I'm not of a mind to get into that sort of discussion.'

'Which sort of answers my question. Do you know where Hamish Wright is?'

'I'd be surprised if he's anywhere — anywhere above ground, that is.'

Rebus's eyes narrowed. 'Then why are the Starks looking for him?'

'What makes you think they are?'

'What do you mean?' But Cafferty just shook his head and placed a hand on Rebus's shoulder, steering him towards the door. 'How much of this did you already know when Fox and I spoke to you?'

'You worried I'm not being honest with you, John?'

'I suppose there's a first time for everything.'

'To put your mind at rest, I only heard from Goodman after you and I had our little chinwag in the Golden Rule.'

'I'll get you to a safe house,' Rebus said, stopping just inside the front door. 'It's yours as soon as you tell me what's really going on.'

'Go find a dominoes game or something. If I want advice on protection, I'll consult the police rather than a pensioner.'

'I wish that bullet had done some damage to your thick fucking skull.'

Cafferty paused at the front door and thought for a moment.

'No you don't,' he said, pulling open the door and ushering Rebus outside. The terrier was at the gate, watching both men, its tail wagging.

11

Fox was in the back of the Audi A4, Bell driving and Compston in the passenger seat. Bell and Compston were readying to relieve Hastie and Hughes. They hadn't wanted to bring Fox, but he'd insisted, threatening to take it to Doug Maxtone. And he had proved useful, since the satnav seemed singularly ill-equipped to deal with traffic snarl-ups, roadworks, and prospective short cuts.

'Piece of shit,' Compston had decided, flicking a finger against its screen.

Now they were driving along a road on an industrial estate. Car dealerships, a scrapyard and a self-storage facility.

'Where are you?' Compston asked into his phone. Then he cursed. 'We just passed them,' he told Bell. Fox turned to look through the rear window. Hastie and Hughes were in the parked Vauxhall Insignia. Opposite stood CC Self Storage, an anonymous slab of a building. Dennis Stark and his team were somewhere within, presumably talking to the boss.

'We'll do a circuit and come round again,' Compston was telling his phone. 'You pull out, we pull into your space, and you give Fox a ride back to base.' Then, turning towards Fox: 'CC Self Storage belongs to Chick Carpenter. It's his Aston parked behind the fence. Pulled some information on him from the system. Bit too chummy with your pal Darryl Christie. Christ knows who's got stuff hidden away in that unit.'

'Makes sense for the Starks to be paying a visit,' Fox commented. They were approaching a T-junction, Bell signalling left.

'Plenty other storage units in the city,' Compston continued, 'not all of them owned by Carpenter. The Starks have already visited two that are, on the face of it at least, more legit than this.'

'I'd have thought this a more obvious target.'

'You and me both. Maybe they were stocking up on info from Carpenter's competitors.'

'Plus, if he's friends with Christie and the Starks know it . . . '

'Softly softly,' Compston agreed with a nod.

Left and left again . . . more industrial facilities, some with vans and lorries outside. A fast-food kiosk selling burgers and hot drinks. Kerbside was busy with parked vehicles, which was good — less chance of the surveillance being noticed.

'How long will they keep at it?' Fox asked. 'In Edinburgh, I mean?'

'They do seem to be lingering.'

'Meaning they've got a whiff of something?'

'Maybe.' Compston had an incoming call. He put it on speakerphone. 'What is it, Beth?'

'Bit of an argument in the car park. Pointed fingers getting pointier.' Alec Bell pressed his foot more firmly on the accelerator. 'Carpenter has a mate with him, but it's two against five.'

'We're just about back with you.'

'Do we intervene if things get — '

'We do nothing,' Compston stressed. 'The pair of you are bystanders. You stay in the car — understood?'

'Yes, sir.'

Compston turned towards Bell. 'Slow down. Don't want to draw attention.'

They were almost at the storage unit.

'Try not to gawp,' Compston warned. 'Eyes front.'

But Fox couldn't help himself. He watched as the argument turned suddenly physical, Dennis Stark aiming a kick and a punch at one of the men, at which point his posse made sure the second man didn't do anything stupid. The punched man had dropped to one knee. He wore a suit and tie, and Fox assumed this was Carpenter. His companion, the one being cautioned by Stark's men, was a couple of decades younger and dressed in a T-shirt and denim jacket. Jackie Dyson hauled Carpenter back to his feet and smacked his forehead into Carpenter's unprotected nose. The man's knees buckled and he was on all fours as Dennis Stark squatted in front of him, grabbing him by the hair and yelling into his bloodied face. Dyson meantime had unzipped himself and was aiming a stream of urine over the Aston Martin's driver's-side door.

'We can't just do nothing,' Fox said.

'Watch us,' Compston told him. They were past the altercation, heading for the T-junction again. 'U-turn this time, Alec,' Compston ordered. Then, into his phone: 'Everything okay there?'

120

'We're sitting tight.'

'Well done.'

'Broad daylight,' Fox offered. 'Not exactly low-profile any more.'

'Joe will be furious,' Compston agreed.

'Smacking of desperation?'

'Old man's back in Glasgow. That means two things: Dennis wants a result, so he can brag about it to his dad. But he's also off the leash, and this is the kind of thing that happens when he's given his freedom. Take it nice and easy, Alec . . . '

They were passing the altercation again, but it was winding down. The prone and blood-spattered Carpenter was being tended to by the younger man, while Dennis and crew walked nonchalantly in the direction of their people carrier. Fox was getting his first real look at them in the flesh. He still wouldn't put money on spotting the undercover cop. Simpson, Andrews, Dyson, Rae — none of them looked in the least fazed by what had just come to pass. Stark walked slightly ahead of them, clenching and unclenching his fists.

'Any idea where they'll be headed next?' Compston asked into his phone.

'We think a pub called the Gimlet.'

'I know that place,' Fox interrupted. 'Used to be owned by Darryl Christie.'

'Well,' Hastie's voice continued, 'it's now owned by a man called Davie Dunn, who used to drive long-distance lorries.'

'For Hamish Wright?'

'Back in the day.'

'Okay, Beth,' Compston said. 'Alec and me will park at the end of the road here. You come and get Fox.'

'Running surveillance needs more than just the four of us.'

'I know — hopefully the Glasgow contingent won't be much longer.' Compston ended the call.

'We could phone for an ambulance,' Fox suggested. 'There's an injured man back there.'

'Fuck him,' Compston said. 'If he needs sorting out, his stooge is there with him.'

Alec Bell's eyes met Fox's in the rear-view mirror. Bell shook his head almost imperceptibly — warning Fox to drop the subject? Or ashamed of his boss's reaction? Fox couldn't tell.

'A surveillance is just that,' Compston was saying airily. 'Don't tell me you wouldn't have said the same when you were in Complaints.'

'Never had cause to find out,' Fox replied, as Bell pulled the car over.

'So the Gimlet used to be owned by Darryl Christie, eh?' Compston mused, rubbing a hand across his chin. 'Problem with a wee town like this — everyone's connected.'

'Meaning Christie won't be happy if Dennis starts kicking off anywhere in the vicinity.'

Compston nodded slowly as the people carrier roared past. They watched it round a corner.

'Out you get then,' Compston said. Fox did as he was told, watching the Audi head off. The Vauxhall Insignia drew level with him and he climbed into the back.

'I'm not happy about what just happened back

122

there,' he commented.

'We're not in the business of keeping you happy,' Beth Hastie said from the passenger seat.

Peter Hughes gave a dry chuckle as he signalled right at the junction. Fox sat back and admired the view, wondering how long it would take Hughes to work out they were headed in the wrong direction.

★ ★ ★

Clarke had reported to James Page in person, delivering both note and bullet. Afterwards, he had folded his arms and, transfixed by the two items on his desk, told her to give him ten minutes, which was why she was back in the body of the kirk with Esson, Ogilvie and the rest of the team. There was no sign of DS Charlie Sykes, and Clarke said as much.

'The Invisible Man,' Esson commented.

'He had something he needed to do in Leith,' Ogilvie added. He had pulled his chair over to Esson's desk so she could give him the news, having been briefed by Clarke on the drive back from Cafferty's house.

'Boss is deciding the next steps,' Clarke told them now.

'Changes things a bit, doesn't it?' Ogilvie offered.

'Maybe — John Rebus isn't sure there's a solid connection. I mean, the notes, yes, but not the murder and the shooting.'

'What's Rebus got to do with it?' Ogilvie queried with a frown.

'Nothing,' Clarke conceded. 'He's just the one who persuaded Cafferty to come to us rather than start enquiries of his own.' Clarke rubbed at her eyes. 'Did Christine mention Linlithgow?'

Ogilvie nodded. 'Though again . . . '

'I know: barely any connection worth the name.'

'Tea would cheer us up,' Esson declared. 'And I'm buying.'

'That would be great,' Clarke said.

Esson grabbed her purse and headed off to the canteen, Clarke taking her seat next to Ogilvie. She asked him what he'd been working on.

'Not much. Collating various reports and interviews, looking at the crime scene stuff.'

'Anything I need to know?'

'Well . . . '

'No matter how fanciful or thin it's going to sound,' Clarke assured him.

'I was reading through the scene of crime report, plus the two interviews conducted with Lord Minton's housekeeper.'

'Jean Marischal? More of a cleaner, wasn't she?'

'If you like. But here's the thing.' Ogilvie pulled out photos from the crime scene. 'First officers to arrive state that the desk drawer was open a couple of inches.'

'Yes, Deborah Quant said the same,' Clarke remembered.

'You can see it here.' Ogilvie slid a photo towards her. 'Then later, the SOCOs pulled the drawer all the way open to get shots of the contents. Mrs Marischal tells us she cleaned in the den but that the desk drawer was seldom unlocked. Lord Minton

124

kept the key on him — and it was found in his pocket after his death. What does a locked drawer suggest to you?'

'That there was something he didn't want her to see.'

'And you'd guess that to be . . . ?'

'Well, he was seated at the desk paying bills, so maybe his chequebook?'

'That's what I thought too. But look at the contents of the drawer again.'

Clarke saw stationery, a second chequebook, correspondence, various paper clips and bulldog clips and even a bottle of Tipp-Ex.

'What is it I'm not seeing?'

'Something that isn't there. I'm guessing he was the tidy sort, and that the chequebook he'd taken out of the drawer usually sat on top of the other one.' Ogilvie traced a finger over an empty section of the drawer. 'But what was it that used to be in this space here?'

'Stuff could have shifted around when the SOCOs pulled it open.'

'Except they tell me they used extreme care.'

'You're saying the intruder took something?'

'Desk drawer was open a couple of inches. I doubt that would have been comfortable for anyone sitting there trying to do some work.'

'True,' Clarke said.

'So either the intruder took it, or Lord Minton had opened it himself and was taking something out when he heard a noise.'

Clarke was peering more closely at the photo. 'Couldn't just have been the other chequebook?'

'No way of telling for sure.'

'Did Jean Marischal ever see the drawer when it was open? Never so much as a glimpse?'

'Worth talking to her again?'

'Maybe.'

Page was standing in the doorway. He signalled for Clarke to join him. She patted Ogilvie on the shoulder as she got up.

'Close the door,' he told her once she was inside his office. 'Sit down if you like.'

Clarke remained standing.

'I've already had enough grief since we went public with the Minton note,' he began. 'Only effect it seems to have produced is more noise from upstairs. Everyone wants this thing cleared up and no one wants it getting messy.'

'So we keep the Cafferty note to ourselves?'

'For the time being. Anything that seems to link a prominent member of the legal establishment to a local thug is hardly going to please the powers above.'

'You'll talk to Shona MacBryer?'

'Fiscal's office need to know. I'll make Shona see that a quiet interview with Cafferty at his home is preferable to bringing him in.'

'How about the team here?'

'I assume word's already gone around.'

'Only Esson and Ogilvie so far. But when we interview Cafferty . . . '

'I'll brief the troops.'

'And then pray for no leaks.'

'Indeed.' He leaned back in his chair and pressed his hands together, the tips of his fingers touching his lips. 'What's your gut feeling here, Siobhan?'

'The attacks themselves are very different, but the notes look identical.'

'So we should be seeking a connection between Cafferty and Minton?'

'Cafferty says there isn't one.'

'Some sort of vigilante?'

Clarke shrugged and watched as Page pressed the palms of his hands flat on his desk.

'What about Rebus?' he asked.

'What about him?'

'He's close to Cafferty, isn't he?'

'In a manner of speaking. You think we should attach him to the case?'

'In a consultative capacity. What's the old saying about pissing out of the tent rather than in?'

'Should I talk to him then?'

'I don't suppose it can do any harm, can it?'

Clarke didn't know how to answer that, so ran her tongue across her lips instead and shifted her feet slightly, eyes on the floor.

'Very well then,' Page decided, pressing his hands together once more as if in prayer. 'Talk to the man.'

Clarke nodded and made her exit. Christine Esson was waiting with her tea. Clarke took it and moved into the corridor, taking out her phone and making the call.

'Yes, Siobhan?' Rebus said by way of answer.

'Page wants you inside the tent rather than out.'

'Is that even possible?'

'You'd be acting in a consultative capacity.'

'Like Sherlock Holmes? Would I need invoices

and stuff? And a housekeeper and a sidekick?'

'Are you interested or not?'

'He really wants me because I'm a conduit to Cafferty?'

'Yes.'

'Is Cafferty's note going to be kept out of the public domain?'

'For now.'

'Formal interview with him at his house?'

'Page thinks he can clear it with Shona MacBryer.'

'Then what's left for me to do?'

'I'm guessing you'll think of something.'

'Do I detect a lack of enthusiasm, DI Clarke?'

'Only because I know what you're like — put you in a tent, you start trying to knock the poles down.'

'Better than peeing on you from outside, though, eh?'

'Let me think about that for a moment.' She could almost hear Rebus break into a smile.

'Consultative capacity,' he echoed. 'I quite like that.'

'I thought you might. Just remember — you're still not a cop. No warrant card, no real powers.'

'Well, tell Page I'm considering his proposal, but I don't come cheap.'

'You'd do this for no pay at all, John — we both know it.'

'Maybe we should meet later to compare notes.'

'The Oxford Bar?'

'Around nine?'

'Okay.'

'And why not bring Malcolm along?'

'Malcolm's not part of this case.'

'I know that, but I'd like him there anyway. The two of you have gotten so busy, it'll be nice for you to catch up.'

'See you at nine, then.'

Clarke ended the call and took a slurp from the cardboard cup as she walked back into the incident room. Ogilvie seemed to have been sharing his theory with Esson. Esson was holding a close-up photo of the desk drawer, peering at it.

'What do you think?' Clarke asked her.

'It's interesting.'

'I think so too.' Clarke looked at Ogilvie. 'Christine's already had a bit of an away day — you ready for yours?'

'Absolutely,' Ronnie Ogilvie said.

12

There was no longer anyone keeping guard outside David Minton's house on St Bernard's Crescent. A set of keys were being held at HQ, so Clarke had brought those, along with a note of the number for the alarm system. Having unlocked the door, she punched the code in while Ogilvie stooped to pick up the waiting mail.

'Anything?' she asked.

'Mostly flyers.' He added the collection to a pile on the nearby table.

The house was beginning to smell musty, and with the heating turned off there was a pronounced chill.

'Hope the pipes don't freeze,' Ogilvie commented.

'Minton's study is this way,' Clarke said, leading him past the foot of the imposing staircase. The curtains had been drawn closed, so she yanked them open. The window gave a view down on to the small back garden. The laundry room was directly below. Would Minton have heard the glass breaking? There was a venerable transistor radio on the desk, but no evidence that he'd had it switched on that evening. Clarke settled herself in the chair and slid the drawer open a couple of inches.

'More or less right?' she asked.

'But remember, the deceased had a bit more girth to him . . . '

'A bit?' she chided him. 'So the chair would have been further out from the desk?' She pushed it back. 'About here?'

Ogilvie nodded. 'From where it's hellish uncomfortable to write cheques.'

They studied the photos they'd brought with them. The chequebook and pen sat eight inches from the edge of the desk. It would have been almost impossible for Minton to reach either with the drawer open the way it had been.

'So we're back where we started,' Clarke said. 'Either the victim opened the drawer, or his attacker did.'

The drawer itself had been emptied, everything bagged as evidence and taken away to be examined. Clarke slid it out completely and held it up to the light, then placed it on top of the desk.

'This is where the gap was?' she checked with Ogilvie. 'Where you reckon something might have been removed?'

Ogilvie looked at the area she was circling with her finger.

'Yes.'

'Something measuring — what? Nine inches by six? A book of some kind?'

'Not quite a rectangle, though, is it?' he qualified, showing Clarke the photo again.

'Not quite,' she conceded. 'And the mark on the base of the drawer?' Again she pointed to the spot where the putative item had once sat.

'Grease? Ink, maybe?'

'Worth getting forensics to take a look?'

'Maybe, yes.'

Clarke made the call to the lab at Howden Hall. Then, to Ogilvie: 'They're asking if we can drop it in, save them the trek.'

Ogilvie shrugged his acquiescence.

'Fine,' Clarke said into the phone. Then, again to Ogilvie: 'Go see if you can find a bin bag for us to carry it in.' He was heading out of the room as Clarke told the lab they'd be there in half an hour or so. But then she remembered something. 'Actually, maybe closer to an hour. I need to go back to Fettes first. Got something else I want you to take a look at — bullet, probably nine mil.'

'You go months and months without seeing a bullet,' the voice on the other end of the phone told her. 'And then you get two in one week.'

Clarke blinked twice before finding her voice. 'Say again?'

'Another bullet came in a couple of days back.'

'Came in from where?'

'Extracted from a tree in the Hermitage.'

'What happened exactly?'

'No idea.'

'So who can I talk to?'

'I can let you know that when you come in.'

'Fine. An hour then.'

'Any later and we'll have shut up shop for the day.'

'Justice never sleeps.'

'Maybe not. But it does have a darts match and a late supper with the girlfriend.'

The phone went dead in her hand just as Ogilvie returned from the kitchen with a large white bin bag.

'Brabantia,' he said. 'Only the best for his lordship.' Then he saw the look on Clarke's face.

'Same day someone took a potshot at Cafferty, a bullet was fired into a tree in The Hermitage. That's not a million miles from Cafferty's neighbourhood, is it?'

'Not a million miles, no. Actually, probably less than two.'

'That's what I thought,' Clarke said, helping Ogilvie manoeuvre the drawer into the bag.

* * *

Cafferty was in the back seat, the two bodyguards in front of him. Andrew Goodman's office was above a glazier's on a narrow street near Haymarket, the drive from Cafferty's house taking less than seven minutes.

'Wish I'd known,' Cafferty said, as Goodman met him at the door. The two men shook hands and Goodman led Cafferty inside.

'That I'm so close to yours?'

'That you're above a glazier's,' Cafferty corrected him.

'Right enough — might have been a deal to be done there. Want a coffee or anything?'

Cafferty shook his head. 'I'm here to pay what I owe you.'

Goodman raised an eyebrow as he settled himself behind his desk. He was tall and toned and shaven-headed, with piercing blue eyes. 'You're finished with my lads?'

'I've an overnight bag in the back of their car. Going to lay low for a bit.'

133

Goodman was thoughtful. 'They could still be useful, though.'

But Cafferty shook his head. He pulled a roll of banknotes from his coat and peeled off ten.

'This enough?'

'It'll do. Want a receipt?'

'That won't be necessary.' Cafferty stepped forward and placed the notes on the desk. As Goodman stretched out a hand to take them, Cafferty snatched at the man's wrist, gripping it hard.

'What did the Starks say to you, Andrew?'

'I already told you.' Goodman's gaze was steady.

'But did you tell me the truth?'

'They're looking for Hamish Wright. But they're more interested in something he has that belongs to them — wouldn't say what, but we can both guess.'

'Did they mention Darryl Christie at all?'

'Why should they?'

'It's an answer I want, rather than another fucking question.'

'They didn't. But I hear they've just roughed up Chick Carpenter.'

'The storage guy?'

Goodman nodded.

'Used him once or twice myself,' Cafferty mused. 'Before he started getting pally with young Darryl.' He released his grasp. Goodman snatched his hand back.

'Sorry about that,' Cafferty said. 'I might be just a bit more on edge than usual. Is Carpenter okay?'

'I heard he's in A and E.'

'Darryl won't be happy about that.'

'I wouldn't think.'

'Bad times on the horizon.'

'Thing is, every lowlife in town knows something's up. If the Starks were clever, they'd have been making daily trips from the west rather than hanging around like a fart under a duvet.'

'They want to be seen. They want the word out that they're after someone or something. That way, maybe the right info will come to them rather than them having to hunt it down.'

'I see that, but it means everyone's out on the chase — and most will want to keep whatever they find to themselves. It's turning into a feeding frenzy.'

'Except without any sign of the actual prey.' Cafferty dug his hands deep into his pockets and straightened his shoulders. 'I want you to be my eyes and ears, Andrew. I'll call you every day.' He paused. 'If that's all right with you.'

'Fine and dandy. So where will you — ' Goodman broke off. 'Sorry, stupid question.'

'I'm going to phone for a taxi and fetch my bag from the car.'

'Sure thing.' Goodman got up from the desk.

'And if word of my little disappearing act gets back to anyone — the Starks or Christie or *anyone* — I'll know who to blame. Okay?'

'You don't need to worry about me. And remember, I'm ex-army — in your situation, I'd be doing exactly the same. If all you know is that the enemy's out there somewhere, you keep your

135

head down until it gets close enough to make a target.'

Cafferty was nodding as the two men descended the stairs. He took out his phone and ordered a cab, without giving a precise destination.

'City centre,' was all he said.

Meaningless, Goodman knew. Once he was in the cab, he could order the driver anywhere — enough cash on him for a trip to Fife, or maybe even Glasgow. Cafferty shook hands with both bodyguards as they handed him his bag. It was a large brown leather holdall, and it looked laden.

The cab arrived quickly, Cafferty clambering into the back and slamming the door shut. The three men watched it move off.

'Want us to tail him?' Goodman was asked.

He shook his head slowly. 'Did you take a look in the bag, though?'

'There's a lock on it. Felt like clothes mostly, plus a laptop.'

Goodman ran his tongue over his lips as the cab disappeared from view. 'Well, good luck to him,' he said. 'By which, of course, I mean the exact bloody opposite.'

He headed back upstairs to make a call.

★ ★ ★

The flat in Quartermile had been a recent purchase — just one small brick in Cafferty's property empire. He hadn't got round to letting it yet. Place was only half furnished, though the developer had added a few nice touches, including a wicker basket of food and drink. Quartermile had been the old infirmary, its original red sandstone blocks now joined by new-build steel and glass towers. The two-bedroom flat was in one of these new additions, and not quite at the penthouse level. But it had views over the Meadows, and there were shops, cafés and pubs nearby. The university was practically next door, meaning lots of students, but that was fine with Cafferty — students wouldn't know him from any other bugger of an age they could reliably ignore.

The flat had both landline and Wi-Fi, so Cafferty plugged his laptop into a wall socket and booted it up. The password was on a Post-it note attached to one of the kitchen cupboards. He typed it in, loosened his shoulders and got busy.

Lord Minton. David Minton. There had to be something, some criminal trial, some bribe, some cover-up. He stared hard at photos of the man in various stages of his life, but no memories were stirred. The problem was, he couldn't concentrate — the Starks kept getting in the way. He called a guy he knew in Glasgow, who told him Joe was back in the city but Dennis hadn't been seen in a while, 'which is like an unexpected holiday for some of us, so feel free to keep him'. Cafferty considered getting in touch with Joe, maybe telling him to shove his nutjob son back in the kennel. Then again, by putting Chick Carpenter in hospital, Dennis was heading ever closer to a collision with Darryl Christie. If

Joe's intention had been to cosy up to Christie, Dennis was putting that in jeopardy. Dennis against Darryl — Cafferty wouldn't mind a ringside seat at that particular bout. Dennis all testosterone and big swinging punches; Darryl using brains and guile to plot his opponent's demise. How many men had Dennis brought with him? Not as many as Darryl would have. If reinforcements were called for from the west coast, well, it really *would* start to get messy.

'Good and messy,' Cafferty muttered to himself.

On the other hand, there was an outside chance that an alliance was in the offing, the Starks showing Darryl how much he needed their friendship, or how chaotic things could become if he didn't accept that helping hand. Cafferty had long known that the world of the gangster was the world of the capitalist. Markets had to be created, sustained and expanded, competition nullified. Bigger meant safer, and there was definitely shrinkage in Glasgow. The old skills of the moneylender had all but disappeared — or rather had succumbed to legitimate competition. The interest rates advertised on daytime TV weren't so dissimilar to those offered on the street, but without the threat of a hammer or a nail gun should repayments falter. A lot of the money made from protection and prostitutes had been curtailed too, thanks to the legal system stamping down harder. Drugs were still the safest bet, but bringing them into the country was always fraught.

Cafferty heard the stories from old hands and

newer ones — times were tough, meaning the Starks needed either fresh alliances or new realms to conquer. He couldn't know for sure that the missing haulier and his hidden treasure weren't a convenient smokescreen. Nor could he say as yet that either Darryl Christie or the Starks had aimed that gun at him. Which was why he turned back to the internet and started loading fresh pages about Lord Minton. If Minton had put away a Stark associate or a friend of Christie's, he might be on the road to an answer.

The view across the Meadows towards Marchmont faded as the sun dipped below the horizon. Rebus lived in Marchmont. Cafferty knew he could count on the man as an ally only so far. Rebus still had a cop's instincts, meaning he would take Cafferty down if he thought there was a halfway-decent chance of a conviction. On the other hand, war breaking out on the streets was in no one's interests. If it were to happen, the police would target both Dennis Stark *and* Darryl Christie.

And if those pieces were removed from the board, Cafferty would be the only player left.

The only player in town.

13

The back room of the Oxford Bar, the corner table by the fire.

'I'd like to convene this meeting,' Rebus announced, placing the three drinks on the table. Fox and Clarke had settled themselves, removing coats and scarves. Fox was on tonic water, Clarke the same but with the addition of two measures of gin. 'Cheers,' Rebus said, seating himself opposite them.

'Have you spoken to Page yet?' Clarke asked.

'Give me a chance,' Rebus answered, taking a sip from his pint. Then, for Fox's benefit: 'DCI Page seems to think I might be a valuable addition to the team.'

'And what's brought about this miracle?'

Clarke explained about the note Cafferty had received.

'By the way,' Rebus added, 'Big Ger thinks your haulier may be dead and buried.'

'Not possible — Compston would know.'

Rebus shrugged. 'Maybe Compston *does* know. Maybe he's not been entirely frank with you.'

'Besides,' Fox went on, 'Cafferty doesn't have anyone on the inside, does he?'

Rebus just shrugged again. Clarke was looking from one man to the other.

'What are you two talking about?'

Rebus raised an eyebrow at Fox. 'You've not said?'

140

Now it was Fox's turn to bring Clarke up to date.

'Hang on,' Rebus eventually interrupted. 'They went to the Gimlet?'

Fox nodded. 'But they were only inside a couple of minutes, meaning Davie Dunn probably wasn't there.'

'And this was after they'd given Carpenter a doing outside his own premises?' Rebus was bristling.

'Easy, John,' Clarke advised him. 'You're not CID these days.'

'Everyone keeps telling me that, but I'll be buggered if I sit around and let *my* city get turned over by a streak of piss like Dennis Stark.'

'A noble sentiment,' Clarke said, attempting levity, 'but let's try and keep a sense of perspective. Your job is to advise *us*, John. The Starks need to be left to Malcolm and his merry men.'

Rebus gave Fox a hard stare, then turned back to Clarke. 'Thing is, Compston's men were watching when Dennis Stark thumped the storage guy, and they made no move to step in or break it up. A man could have been killed, and I'm willing to bet Compston would have sat on his hands.'

'Is that right, Malcolm?' Clarke asked quietly.

'Of course it's right,' Rebus spat. 'We could have the son in custody right now, charged with assault. But that's not good enough for Compston: he wants the full set — father and son, drugs and money — so that *his* boss, our glorious Chief Constable, can look good on TV.

Wouldn't you say that's the case, DI Fox?'

The table was silent for a moment, Fox concentrating on the ice cubes in his glass.

'There's one of our lot on the inside, don't forget,' he eventually said. 'I doubt a fine for Dennis Stark would be seen as recompense for his efforts.'

'But at least the Starks would have been warned, meaning they'd slope off back to Glasgow. Peace on the streets and good luck to Hamish Wright and his ill-gotten gains.' Rebus took too swift a gulp from his pint, beer dribbling down one cheek to his chin. He swiped it away with the back of a hand.

'Have you told Doug Maxtone any of this?' Clarke asked Fox.

Fox shook his head.

'Why not?'

'Maybe because his thinking wouldn't be dissimilar from John's.'

'You're not Compston's man, Malcolm. You need to remember that.'

Fox nodded slowly.

'What do you think Malcolm should do, John?'

Rebus puffed his cheeks and exhaled. 'Take up drinking, maybe. Because sober, he's going to be replaying that beating all the sleepless night.'

'But should he take what he knows to Doug Maxtone?'

'That's got to be Malcolm's call.'

'You think Chick Carpenter will want to press charges?' Fox asked.

'He doesn't have to — we've police witnesses

to the assault.' Rebus paused. 'On the other hand, you may have a point. Could be he'll deny there *was* any assault, just like Cafferty denied he'd been shot at. These are people who don't trust us and don't trust our motives.'

'There's one further complication,' Fox added. 'Chick Carpenter is friends with Darryl Christie.'

'Then Darryl won't be happy.' Rebus paused again. 'Wait a second — and Dennis went straight from one of Christie's mates to a pub Christie used to own?'

'Yes.'

'Can't be more than six months since the Gimlet changed hands.'

'You're thinking Christie will know the new owner?' Clarke asked.

'There's only a new owner on paper,' Rebus said. 'Everybody knows Davie Dunn is fronting the place.'

'Why?'

'So it can be run down and sold off to a supermarket who might not want to buy from a known criminal.'

'It's getting closer then — some sort of confrontation. And I'm guessing we really don't want that to happen.' Clarke turned her head towards Fox. 'Meaning we maybe *do* need the Starks sent packing, despite everything.'

Fox finished his drink and got to his feet. 'My round,' he said. 'Same again?'

Rebus nodded, but Clarke demurred. When Fox had gone, she leaned across the table.

'Last thing we need is Cafferty getting involved. The two cases can't overlap.'

'Big Ger's not the one I'm worried about, Siobhan.'

'Christie?' She watched as Rebus gave a slow nod.

'Big Ger's the type to meet brute force with a bit more brute force. Darryl, on the other hand . . . I've no idea how he'll react. Could go one way or the other.'

'Lucky it's nothing to do with us then, eh? We just focus on our nice cosy stalker-cum-killer. Speaking of which, have I mentioned the desk drawer?'

'Sounds riveting,' Rebus said. 'Do tell.'

She was opening her mouth as he got to his feet.

'And while you're doing that,' he said, 'I'll be outside enjoying a well-earned cigarette.'

★   ★   ★

The taxi dropped Rebus at the top of Cafferty's street. A woman was walking her superannuated dog. It was about seven inches high and hugely interested in a lamp post. The roadway and pavement were bathed in sodium orange, the moon overhead illuminating a veil of white cloud. A quiet, orderly part of town. Rebus doubted there had been too many YES posters in the windows here during the independence campaign. The moneyed class here kept its opinions to itself, and didn't kick up a fuss unless absolutely provoked. Edinburgh had always seemed to Rebus a city that liked to keep its counsel and its secrets. He guessed that most of Cafferty's neighbours would know his reputation, not that they would ever say anything to his face. Whispers and glances and gossip shared by phone or email or in the privacy of the bedroom or dinner party. The shot fired at the detached Victorian home would have come as a shock. In the Inch maybe, or Niddrie or Sighthill, but not *here*, not in *this* Edinburgh.

As Rebus approached the house, he could see that no lights were on. The car and guards had disappeared from their posting. As he walked up the driveway, security lamps were triggered, lighting his way. There was another above the back door, but still no sign of life from within. He did a circuit of the garden and ended up at the front door, ringing the bell twice and, after a wait, squatting to peer through the letter box. Darkness within. He took out his phone and made a call, listening to the eventual ringing indoors. But no one was there to answer, so he called Cafferty's mobile instead. It rang and rang without going to any kind of answering service. Rebus hung up and sent a text instead:

Where are you?

Then he realised Cafferty might not know it was from him, so he typed in another:

It's me by the way — John.

Thought for a moment and deleted 'John', replacing it with 'Rebus'. Pressed send.

It was cold, but not quite below zero. He reckoned he could walk to his flat in fifteen, maybe twenty minutes. He had a phrase from the first *Godfather* film in his head — 'going to the mattresses'. He wondered if that was what

Cafferty was doing: hiding out somewhere while preparing for war. Well, it was time for Rebus to hit his own mattress. But as he walked back down the path, he saw a familiar figure peering through the gate.

'You again,' he told the terrier. It seemed to recognise his voice, wagging its tail as he approached. When he leaned down to stroke it, the dog rolled on to its back.

'Bit chilly for that,' Rebus said. He could feel its ribs protruding. No collar. The dog got back to its feet and waited.

'Where do you live, bud?' Rebus asked, looking up and down the street. Cafferty had seemed to think it a stray. The dog didn't look feral or maltreated, though. Just lost, maybe. Rebus began walking up the street, trying not to look back. When he did, the dog was right there, just a few steps behind. He tried shooing it away. The look on the terrier's face told him it was disappointed in him. His phone started buzzing. As he dug it out of his pocket, the dog sidled up and began sniffing his shoes and trouser legs. He had a text — but not from Cafferty.

Hell of a day! Know it's late, but fancy a drink somewhere in town? Deb

Rebus considered his options for all of five seconds, then made a mental apology to his bed for forsaking it, sent a return text, and phoned for a cab. He lit a cigarette while he was waiting. The dog was sitting on its haunches, quite content to keep him company. When the cab arrived, Rebus got in and closed the door after him.

'You've forgotten your dog,' the driver told him.

'It's not mine.'

'Fair enough, pal.' The driver started off, but halfway down the road, Rebus stopped him and told him to back up. When he slid open the door, his new friend bounded in, as if it had never doubted him.

★　★　★

It was past midnight when Siobhan Clarke slid the DVD into the player and retreated to her sofa, remote in hand. She picked up the file on Michael Tolland and skimmed it as she watched the TV interviews with the lottery winner and his wife. Tolland was effusive, grinning from ear to ear, while Ella said hardly a word. Clarke removed a photocopy of the wedding photo from the file. The bride looked soulful, as if having second thoughts. Jim Grant, the cop from Linlithgow, had sent precisely two texts since their meeting. The first had been to inform her that he'd spoken to Tolland's old school pal, who had confirmed that Tolland had seemed 'a bit jittery' at their last few get-togethers but wouldn't say what the problem was. The house had been scoured again but no note, threatening or otherwise, recovered. The second text had been to suggest they confer over 'a drink or maybe even dinner'. He had appended to this an emoji of a smiling yellow face, and another that was winking with its tongue protruding — which probably meant Clarke now owed Christine

147

Esson twenty quid. One further text had arrived — from Deborah Quant, regarding the theory that the implement used on Lord Minton could have been a crowbar rather than a hammer. Quant's reply had been a decidedly tetchy *Find me the murder weapon and I'll be able to answer*, probably composed at the end of a long day. It had been a long day for everyone, and Clarke found her eyes closing as Michael Tolland handed an oversized cheque back to the official and opened the magnum of champagne, spraying it around, not least in the direction of his unamused, newly enriched wife.

Day Four

14

Siobhan Clarke pressed the intercom half a dozen times before receiving a growled answer.

'It's Siobhan. Don't tell me you're not up yet.'

'Privilege of the consulting detective.' He buzzed her in and she climbed the stairwell to his floor. He had left the door open for her.

'I'm in the bathroom,' he called. 'Kettle's on.'

She was not alone in the kitchen. A dog was there, eating chopped-up sausages from a plate. There was the aroma of recent frying, and an unwashed pan sat in the sink.

Rebus emerged, towelling dry his hair, shirt untucked and open at the neck.

'No vegetables in your fridge,' she said. 'But good to see it's not jam-packed with booze either.'

'You applying for the post of carer?' He took the mug from her and sipped.

'Thought you were heading straight home from the Ox?'

Rebus rolled his bloodshot eyes. 'And now she's my mother.'

'It's the dog from Cafferty's street, am I right?'

'Sharp as ever.'

'And it's here because . . . ?'

'I wanted it to be a surprise.' He fixed her with a look but she shook her head.

'No way, Jose,' she said.

'Think of the exercise you'd get, not to

mention the companionship.'

'My answer's the same.'

With a sigh, Rebus led her through to the living room. 'The plot thickens,' Clarke said. 'Two used glasses, and perfume lingering amid the fug.' She walked over to the hi-fi and lifted a CD. 'Did she do a runner when you stuck this on?'

'That's the Steve Miller Band. Put on track seven while I find a tie.'

Rebus left the room and Clarke did as she was told. The song was called 'Quicksilver Girl'. The volume was turned down low, low enough for late-night conversation.

'I quite like it,' she said on Rebus's return. 'Like a laid-back Beach Boys. But there's something wrong with the speakers.'

'I know.'

'So how was Professor Quant?'

'She's not allergic to dogs.'

'Does it have a name?' Clarke said, watching as the terrier padded in from the kitchen, licking its chops.

'I thought I'd call it The Dog From Cafferty's Street.'

Clarke reached down to scratch the terrier behind its ears. 'I saw Deborah a couple of days back. We were discussing Lord Minton.'

Rebus took another slug of coffee. 'The Prof seems to like you.'

'You were talking about me last night? Doesn't exactly sound like a romantic tête-à-tête. Then again, from your music choices . . . '

'What about them?'

Clarke checked the pile of CDs. 'Van Morrison maybe, but Rory Gallagher and Tom Waits are hardly the stuff of serenades. On the other hand . . . '

'What?'

'You played CDs rather than your vinyl.'

'Meaning?'

'You didn't want to be interrupted every fifteen or twenty minutes to turn the record over.'

'We'll make a detective of you yet. So what's the plan for today?'

Clarke turned away from the hi-fi and checked the time. 'The Hermitage. Meeting the dog-walker there, the one who found the bullet.'

'Right.'

'You've forgotten, haven't you? I told you about her when you came back in after your cigarette. You said you were interested in tagging along.'

'In which case, I *am* interested. And after the Hermitage?'

'Howden Hall for the ballistics report.'

'Followed by?'

She stared at him. 'You're angling to sit in on the interview with Cafferty — that's not going to happen.'

'Why?'

'Because you're not part of the official inquiry and nor are you his lawyer. Procurator fiscal isn't going to sanction a civilian being present.'

'You could always ask . . . '

'Despite already knowing the answer?' She shook her head. 'You can listen to the recording afterwards, if that'll make you happy.'

'I'm always happy.'

'Your taste in music says otherwise.'

Rebus had donned his suit jacket and was patting his pockets, making sure he had everything. 'Can we make a detour first?'

'Where?'

'I've got the address of a vet. They said I could drop by.'

'Is this us saying a fond farewell to our new friend?'

'Your car or mine?' Rebus asked.

'Mine — if you promise he won't pee on the seats.'

'But I can smoke if I roll the window down?'

'Absolutely not.'

Rebus expelled some air. 'And she wonders why I'm not always Mr Sunshine,' he muttered, draining the mug.

⋆ ⋆ ⋆

The vet made his inspection on a stainless-steel examination table.

'No bones broken . . . teeth seem fine.' He felt at the neck, pinching and rubbing at the skin. 'Doesn't appear to be chipped, which is a pity.'

'I thought it was compulsory.'

'Not quite yet.'

'You think he's been abandoned?'

'He may just have been lost — got out of the house and found himself too far from home to retrace his steps.'

'People sometimes put up posters, don't they?'

Clarke commented.

'They do. You could do something like that yourself — a photograph on Facebook or Twitter.'

Clarke took out her phone and snapped a few pictures.

'So what happens now?' Rebus asked.

'You don't want to keep him?'

Rebus checked with Clarke and Clarke with Rebus. Both shook their heads. The vet sighed and ran his hands over the small terrier again. 'There's a database I can check,' he said. 'Just in case someone *is* looking for him. But the most likely scenario is simply that the owner was finding it hard to cope. I've seen it a lot these past few years — unemployment or maybe a benefits cut, and suddenly the family pet becomes a luxury too far. I'll contact the cat and dog home.'

'If it's a question of money . . . ' Rebus began.

'It's more that there are too many unwanted pets and not enough potential takers.'

'So they'll keep him for a while, and then . . . ?'

'He'll be put to sleep, most probably. Though I assure you, that's a measure of last resort.'

The dog was looking at Rebus as if it trusted him to make the right decision.

'Fine then,' Rebus said. 'We'll leave you to it. Hang on to him a few days, though, will you? We'll do a bit of searching.'

'Fingers crossed,' the vet said, as Rebus opened the door to leave, knowing it was best not to look back.

Outside, Clarke got busy on her phone. 'Christine's the social media hotshot. I'll get her to post the photo everywhere she can think of.'

'Better still, ask her if she wants a dog.'

'Getting soft in your old age, John?'

'Soft as nails,' Rebus said, climbing into the Astra.

★   ★   ★

The Hermitage was a woodland walk to the south of Morningside, hemmed in by Braid Hills on one side and Blackford Hill on the other. A burn ran through the gorge, crossed here and there by wooden bridges, some in better repair than others. Dog-walkers were the main clientele, along with families with wellingtoned children, plus occasional cyclists. In spring, the air carried the pungency of wild garlic, but in winter the compressed leaves on the path froze and became treacherous.

'I never come here,' Clarke said as they walked from the car. They'd had to park on the main road, just down from the Braid Hills Hotel. Clarke had been given instructions to leave the main path as soon as possible and head into the woods along a muddier, narrower route, climbing up a steepening gradient. Rebus was a few yards behind her, his breathing laboured.

'Keep up, Grandad,' she couldn't help teasing.

'You might have warned me to bring boots,' he complained; Clarke had changed into hers at the kerbside.

'Do you even own any boots?'

'That's not the point.'

The barking of a stout yellow Labrador announced their arrival.

'Mrs Jenkins?' Clarke checked.

The woman who nodded was in her sixties, hair tucked under the rim of a knitted hat, matching scarf around her neck. She wore a green Puffa jacket and faded denims tucked into green wellies.

'Detective Inspector Clarke?' she confirmed. The dog was off its lead but she was gripping it by the collar. Clarke held her ungloved palm out and the dog gave it a sniff and a lick.

'This is Godfrey,' Mrs Jenkins informed them. She released her grip, allowing the dog to bound into the woods, following some trail only it could sense.

'He'll be fine,' she said with a smile, as if the two detectives had shown qualms about her companion's well-being.

'This is where it happened?' Clarke asked.

The woman nodded. 'Just over here.' She led them a short distance. 'This is the least used of the various paths,' she informed them. 'Godfrey and I were a bit further uphill; we'd gone as far as the perimeter of the golf course. I heard the sound and knew it was a shot. My husband, Archie, used to shoot — grouse and pheasant. Horrible job plucking and cleaning them . . . '

'You didn't see anyone?'

'Sorry.' The smile this time was thinner. 'Whoever it was must have headed down the trail sharpish.'

They had stopped beside a young conifer.

Some of the bark had been dislodged, and there was splintering, either from the impact of the bullet or more likely from its subsequent removal.

'A miserable winter's afternoon,' the woman continued. 'Whoever it was probably thought they had the place to themselves.'

'There are a lot of trees here, Mrs Jenkins,' Rebus said. 'How did you happen to spot that this was the target?'

'Smell of . . . what is it? Gunpowder? Cordite? It was in the air, strongest right here, and there was even a wisp of smoke drifting upwards — I must have missed the culprit by seconds.' She looked from one detective to the other. 'The police officer said it was probably just a prank of some kind, but from your faces . . . well, I'm guessing perhaps I had a narrow escape.'

'I wouldn't go that far,' Clarke sought to reassure her. 'But there's been a shooting in the city — nothing fatal, just damage to property — and we're looking at a possible connection. You don't happen to remember seeing anyone on your walk?'

'Baby buggies, other dog-walkers, but no one who didn't look as if they belonged. I mean, no one *Arabic*.'

'Arabic?' Clarke echoed.

'Mrs Jenkins,' Rebus advised, 'has got it into her head that this may be linked to terrorism.'

'Well, these days . . . ' Mrs Jenkins' voice trailed off.

'It categorically isn't,' Clarke stressed.

'You'll forgive me, dear, but as a woman once

said: you would say that, wouldn't you?'

Godfrey was circling them, nose to the ground.

'Any room at home for another dog, Mrs Jenkins?' Rebus asked.

'I'm afraid Godfrey would eat it alive.'

Godfrey, drool hanging from his jaws, didn't appear inclined to disagree.

★   ★   ★

The forensic science lab was situated in an unassuming building just off Howden Hall Road, on the south side of the city. Security had been ramped up since an arson attack a few years back that had successfully destroyed some crucial trial evidence. Once inside, Clarke and Rebus had to wait in reception, cameras peering down at them.

'If she talks to the press . . . ' Clarke commented, not for the first time.

'I doubt even the Fourth Estate would go along with it.'

'No, but the *Fifth* might.'

'Meaning?'

'The internet. Bloggers and the like. Their creed is: print anything, just make sure you're the first.'

'And retract at leisure?'

'If at all.'

The man descending the stairs had a photographic identity card hanging around his neck from a lanyard. He was short, squat and bald, and his rolled-up sleeves marked him out as someone perennially busy.

'DI Clarke?' he said, making to shake hands. 'I'm Colin Blunt — no relation, alas.'

'To the spy?' Rebus guessed.

'The singer,' Blunt corrected him with a frown. He led them upstairs and into a bright subdivided room. There was a table in the middle, and worktops stretching along three walls.

'Not much equipment,' Clarke commented.

'Under-resourced, you might say,' Blunt offered.

He told them to sit down, and pushed a sheet of paper towards Clarke, apologising to Rebus that he'd only made one copy.

'We're just grateful you've still got a photocopier somewhere,' Rebus commented. 'Maybe you can sum up for me while DI Clarke digests all that.'

'Well, it's preliminary stuff — both bullets were pretty mashed up. The impact has a concertina effect, you see.'

'I do.'

Blunt produced a pair of spectacles and a clean handkerchief, and started polishing as he spoke. 'There's a facility we use at Gartcosh for more detailed ballistics, but we'd have to get the okay for that — it doesn't come cheap. But from the look we've taken under our own microscope, I'd say there's an eighty to ninety per cent chance the bullets were fired from the same gun. The bullets themselves are of American manufacture, for what it's worth — nine millimetre. Rifling looks similar . . . ' He broke off. 'I'm referring to the striations.'

'I know,' Rebus said. 'So how many registered

users of nine-mil pistols might there be in Scotland?'

'A handful.'

'And unregistered?'

'Who knows?'

'Not you, obviously, Mr Blunt.'

'Find us the gun and we'll tell you if it fired these bullets.'

'The more we know about the bullets, the better the chance of that happening.' Rebus paused. 'To be blunt.'

Blunt pretended to appreciate the joke, managing a weak smile.

Clarke looked up. 'Want to see?' she asked Rebus. He shook his head.

'So we've got the attack on Lord Minton,' Rebus said. 'Which involved a blow to the head — '

'Professor Quant has us looking at that,' Blunt interrupted. 'We've a database here of head injuries caused by hammers and other tools.'

'Good for you,' Rebus said, turning his attention back to Clarke. 'Then the afternoon after Minton's killed, someone discharges a firearm into a tree, and that same night a shot is fired, presumably at Cafferty's head.' He pointed a finger at Blunt. 'Which goes no further than this room, understood?'

'Understood,' Blunt spluttered.

'The gunman was doing a bit of target practice,' Clarke surmised.

'Hardly,' Rebus said. 'He fired at a tree. It's not like he placed tin cans on fence posts or pinned up the outline of a human.'

161

'Like when they go to a shooting range in the movies,' Blunt piped up. The look from Rebus silenced him.

'So what are you saying?' Clarke asked.

'I'm saying this was more like someone who just needed to know they could handle the rudiments.'

'Point and squeeze.'

'Exactly. What would the recoil be like? How far could they be from their intended target and still hit it?'

'Are you saying our guy's a beginner or a pro?'

'One or the other, certainly.'

'Great — I'll stick that in the computer and see what we get.'

'No need to be sarky.' Rebus turned his head towards Blunt. 'That's what she's being, isn't it? My ears aren't deceiving me?'

Blunt decided that a shrug was the only appropriate response. But Clarke had a question of her own for him.

'The drawer from Lord Minton's desk?'

'What drawer?' Rebus interrupted.

'You'd know if your need for a cigarette last night hadn't been so urgent.'

'Ah yes,' Blunt was saying. 'Well, again it's only preliminary . . . '

'I'll settle for that.'

'The stain is an oil of some kind, probably a lubricant. Hard to tell its age or exact make-up without specialised equipment, and again — '

'It would cost money?' Clarke nodded. 'But?'

'But we also found a few fibres from some loose-woven material, probably predominantly

162

grey in colour. Muslin, maybe.'

'Something nine inches by six, wrapped in muslin . . . ' Clarke's eyes were on Rebus. He was folding his arms slowly.

'Pistol,' he said.

'Makes sense. Minton hears a noise downstairs. Unlocks the drawer and takes out the gun. But before he can use it, he's bludgeoned.'

'Attacker pockets the gun, but hasn't used one before.'

'Or one like it, at any rate. Maybe he's a bit rusty.'

'So he reckons he'd better test it before he goes after his next victim. Probably knew Minton was a cinch compared to Cafferty — better to go at Cafferty from a safe distance. Gun must have seemed like a godsend.'

'But somehow he missed.'

'He missed,' Rebus agreed.

'So he *will* try again?'

Rebus shrugged. 'Could be Cafferty's dropped down his list.'

'No one else has come forward to say they've had the warning.'

'Maybe it's a really short list,' Rebus offered. Then, turning to Blunt: 'What do you think, Colin?'

'I try to deal with physical data rather than speculation.'

'Tell me,' Clarke asked him, 'did the evidence from the Michael Tolland murder come here?'

The scientist thought for a moment, then nodded. 'The back door, yes.'

'And?'

'And it was prised open by some sort of tool. A crowbar or the corner of a spade. No trace evidence, unfortunately.'

'Pity,' Clarke said, the corners of her mouth turning down.

Rebus laid a hand on the younger man's shoulder. 'That's precisely why you need people like us, Colin — for when your physical data just isn't there. Now tell me — because you seem like the caring, sensible sort — have you ever considered owning a lovely wee dog?'

15

Not wanting to risk being seen at a computer terminal by Compston and the others, Fox had ended up at the old Lothian and Borders Police HQ on Fettes Avenue. He showed his warrant card at reception and asked for the whereabouts of the Minton inquiry. Same floor as the old Chief Constable's lair, and not far from where Fox and his Complaints team had worked, back when the Big House had been his hunting ground and errant cops his prey. There were a few nods of recognition as he moved through the building. James Page, crossing the corridor from one room to another, spotted him.

'I'm looking for Siobhan,' Fox said, pre-empting any question Page might have.

'She's out at Howden Hall, I think.'

'Okay if I leave her a note?'

Page nodded distractedly and moved off. The room he'd just been in was now home to the Minton team, including Christine Esson and Ronnie Ogilvie. Fox nodded a greeting.

'Just trying to catch Siobhan,' he explained. 'DCI Page told me to wait. Is this her desk?'

Fox sat down in the empty chair. He waited a full half-minute, then mumbled something about doing a check and got busy at the computer. Siobhan had confided to him one night that despite hating the nickname, she used 'Shiv' as her password. Once in, Fox started checking

165

names. He had four — Simpson, Andrews, Dyson, and Rae — and he wanted to know what Police Scotland had on them.

After ten minutes, Esson asked him if he wanted tea or coffee, but he shook his head.

'Should I phone her and see how long she'll be?'

Fox shook his head again. 'Just sending her an email.'

'Using telepathy?' When Fox looked puzzled, Esson explained. 'Not very many keystrokes, DI Fox.'

For want of any lie she would be likely to accept, he just smiled and got back to work.

Rob Simpson had been part of the Stark 'family' for almost a decade, so scratch him. Callum Andrews had a criminal record stretching back to juvenile days, so Fox reckoned he couldn't be the mole. That left Jackie Dyson and Tommy Rae. Both men had seen the inside of a courtroom in the past three years, but for minor misdemeanours. As far as he could tell, both had grown up in Glasgow, leaving school at sixteen and drifting into lawlessness from there. Looked as though neither had joined the gang until a year or so ago. Fox remembered them from the beating outside the storage facility. Dyson scrawny, shaven-headed, whey-faced. Rae maybe a year or two older, with more heft to him and a scar down one cheek. A cop with scars? Well, it happened, but not often, and rarely the visible kind. A scar on your cheek came from a knife, razor or bottle. It was as if the street had given you a tattoo. No, Fox's money was on Jackie Dyson.

166

Alec Bell had said the mole had been working undercover for more than three years. Some of that would have been spent getting known, establishing a reputation, moving closer to the seat of power. Two years of graft before acceptance into the fold. Having worked surveillance himself, he was intrigued by the type of officer who could immerse himself so thoroughly. Friends and family would have to be discarded for the duration, the new identity learned by rote, old haunts shunned for fear of recognition. Fox thought back to the beating, Dyson hauling Chick Carpenter back to his feet for a headbutt, then pissing on the man's car. Meantime Tommy Rae had been content to hold Carpenter's companion at bay — so did that tip the scales back towards him? Rae content to remain on the periphery, unwilling to cause harm . . . Rae with his facial disfigurement . . . Call it seventy-thirty — seventy per cent Jackie Dyson against thirty for Rae. Fox closed down the various windows and made sure to delete his search history. His phone was buzzing, so he answered.

'Fox?' a female voice asked.

'Hello, Hastie. Do I call you Hastie or Beth?'

'If you're not already there, just to say you'll find the office empty.' All businesslike. 'Don't know when we'll be back, okay?'

'Surveillance again? A return trip to the Gimlet?'

'Bright boy. Later.' The phone went dead, and Fox got to his feet, nearly bumping into a man in a suit who was toting a box file. The man was ruddy-faced, his breathing ragged. Fox muttered an apology.

'No problem,' the man said, making his exit.

'You're honoured,' Christine Esson drawled. 'That's a rare sighting of the Charlie Sykes in its native environment.'

'He seemed busy.'

'He does a good impression. Carries that box around all day without ever feeling the need to open it.' She paused, tapping a pen against her chin. 'Do you do any impressions yourself, DI Fox?'

'Such as?'

'Man sending email.'

Fox gave a sheepish smile. 'Busted,' he said, heading for the door.

★ ★ ★

He drove to the Gimlet, unsure why. He wasn't going to get in the way, wasn't going to get close enough to be spotted by Compston's team. But maybe if there was violence, he would phone it in anonymously. Rebus had been right to castigate him, but would Rebus himself have acted differently? Fox doubted it.

The street the Gimlet sat on, an unlovely passageway between Slateford Road and Calder Road, was lined with parked cars, putting paid to his idea of finding a kerbside spot. He had a choice: reverse, or keep going? Keeping going meant passing the surveillance vehicle and maybe being spotted. But reversing would look suspicious. Biting down hard on his bottom lip, he pressed the accelerator.

He was almost level with the bar when its door

burst open, men spilling out. Dennis was first, then his gang. There was blood on Rob Simpson's white shirt, and he was holding a hand over his nose. And here came the reason — a hulk of a man in a stained T-shirt two sizes too small, his biceps bulging, arms tattooed. He was shouting the odds and swinging a baseball bat. But it was one against five, and the Stark gang were beginning to circle their prey. Fox noted that up close, Tommy Rae's scar was almost as red and angry as the tattooed man's face. Dyson's hand was going into his pocket, presumably for a knife. Fox gritted his teeth and pulled on the handbrake. Undoing his seat belt, he sounded his horn, got out and strode towards the melee.

'Hey!' he yelled. 'What's going on here?'

'Stay out of this, pal!' Dyson spat, the blade concealed in his fist.

'Not a fair fight,' Fox persisted. 'I'm calling the — '

Dyson pounced, his fist proving the perfect fit for Fox's unprepared jaw. Another swipe connected with the side of his face, and he could feel his knees buckling, the world spinning. As his vision started to blur, his last sight was of Alec Bell, hands glued to the surveillance car's steering wheel, mouth making the shapes of words that would probably not be welcome in church.

★　★　★

There was an angel peering down at him. Shrouded in white, cheeks rose-tinged.

169

'You're awake,' the angel said, turning into a nurse.

'Where am I?' Fox looked around. He was lying on a trolley in a white booth with a curtain draped across. He was still in his clothes. His face hurt and he had a blinding headache, which the strip lighting was doing its best to exacerbate.

'Royal Infirmary — A and E, to be precise. How are you feeling?'

Fox tried to sit up. It only took him ten or so seconds. His vision was still a bit blurry and his face felt swollen.

'How did I get here?'

'Your friend drove you.'

'Did he?'

'He did.'

Fox remembered Alec Bell's face. Oh, but they'd be furious with him for this. 'Just dumped me here?'

'Not a bit of it. He's in the waiting area. Doctor will want to take a look at you.'

'Why?'

'To check for concussion.'

'I'm fine.' He thought for a moment. 'Did you have a guy in here yesterday from CC Self Storage? Name of Chick Carpenter?'

'Rings a bell. He said some packing cases fell on him. What about you?'

'Believe it or not, the selfsame thing.'

'Get away. And these packing cases wore a ring of some kind?' She nodded towards his face. 'It's left an indentation. Yesterday, it was a size nine boot.'

Fox pressed a finger to the area indicated and wished he hadn't. 'Fancy that.' He winced, struggling to get to his feet, then patted his pockets to ensure nothing had been removed. 'Am I right in thinking you can't stop me leaving?'

'Only an idiot would walk out of here in your state.'

'That may well be true.' Fox smiled and gave a little bow.

'Men your age shouldn't be fighting.'

'I was trying to referee,' he told her.

'Will you take one bit of advice at least?' He paused, waiting. 'A bag of frozen peas will bring down the swelling.'

Nodding, he shuffled out of the cubicle and into the waiting area.

He had expected to see Alec Bell or another of the team, but it was the man from the bar, the one with the bat.

'What did they say?' the man asked.

'That fools rush in.'

'I don't know about that, mate. I'd say you were bloody brave.'

'What happened? After I conked out, I mean.'

'Seemed to quieten them a bit — there you were, sparked out in the road, and with traffic coming from both directions. Got to tell you, you're on free drinks for life in my place.'

'I don't drink.'

'Thank God for that — saves me a few bob. I'm Davie Dunn, by the way. I drove you here in your car. Need to get that clutch seen to.'

'Thanks for the tip.'

'I know a guy. I'll fix you up with him.'

'So they just left, did they?'

'There'd have been a few cracked skulls in here if they hadn't.'

'I thought one of them was pulling a knife.'

Dunn nodded. 'One of those thin blades from the DIY stores. But Stark gave the word and that was that.'

'Stark?' Fox asked, fishing.

'Don't be fooled, Davie — he knows fine well who Stark is.'

The voice had come from behind Fox. He turned too quickly, almost losing his balance as the world spun. Darryl Christie had emerged from the toilet and was wiping his hands dry with a handkerchief. 'This is Detective Inspector Fox, Davie. And suddenly it all makes sense. There's a surveillance operation on the Starks, yes? After the stunt they pulled yesterday with Chick Carpenter?'

'Is there?' Fox countered, dry-mouthed.

'You know one another?' Dunn was asking.

'DI Fox came to see me a couple of days back. He's been to the Gimlet, too, back in the days when I owned it.' Christie focused his attention on Fox. 'Davie here is a good friend of mine. That's why I sold him my pride and joy. The Gimlet taught me a lot of lessons — hard knocks, you might call them. So when Davie tells me the Starks have been threatening him, well . . . I listen. And that's what brought me running.' He had folded the handkerchief back into his pocket. 'Now, here's the message I want you to take back to Rebus or whoever else is

172

involved in this surveillance of yours — the Starks are going down, end of. You can save us all a lot of grief by walking away and letting me get on with it.'

'What if I'd walked away today, though?' Fox gestured towards Davie Dunn. 'What then?'

'I'm just saying, best if your lot steer clear.' Christie looked around the waiting area. 'Where are your buddies anyway? I know Police Scotland are stretched, but a one-man surveillance?' He shook his head in disbelief. 'They let you take that beating, didn't they? Is that because they didn't want the surveillance compromised? Or maybe they just liked seeing someone who used to be in Professional Standards get a doing?' Christie smiled, watching Fox try to formulate an answer. Then he patted Fox's forearm. 'Don't go straining yourself. Got all your stuff? Davie here will take you home.'

And Fox did want to go home. It didn't even bother him that both Christie and Dunn would then know where he lived. Chances were, Christie either already knew, or could find out in five minutes. So Dunn drove, while Fox sat in the passenger seat, still in pain. Christie was behind them all the way in a Range Rover Evoque.

'You've known Darryl a while, then?' Fox asked.

'Probably best we don't talk about any of that — now I know you're police.'

'Does the drinks-for-life offer still stand?'

'Of course. Thing is, once my regulars get a whiff of you, you're not going to want to linger.'

'Which might temper the enjoyment.'

173

'It might.' Dunn glanced at him. 'No offence, but you don't look like the kind of cop who'd do surveillance.'

'Oh?'

'You seem more of a pen-pusher.'

'Sorry to disappoint you.' Fox paused. 'Will they come back, do you think?'

'Stark and his posse? I suppose they might.'

'You used to drive lorries, didn't you?'

'Europe, Ireland, all over.' Dunn paused. 'How do you know that?'

'Secret of a good surveillance — know everything. You drove for Hamish Wright?'

'Haven't seen him in years.'

'I'm guessing the Starks think otherwise.'

'The Starks haven't got the brains they were born with.'

'Doesn't seem to have held them back.'

'It'll be their downfall, though. This is 2015. Stanley knives and fifty-quid drug deals? Reckon they've ever heard of Bitcoin or the darknet? They're a market stall in the age of Amazon.'

'Yet still a threat.'

'Because they're panicking.'

'Last time I saw Darryl, at his hotel, he seemed to be heading that way too.'

'Panicking, you mean? Maybe he was putting on a show for you.' Dunn glanced towards his passenger again. 'Besides, we're not talking about that, remember? Want me to drop you home and take your car to my mate's? He'd have this clutch fixed by day's end.'

Fox shook his head. As they entered Oxgangs, he had to start giving directions.

'Nice and peaceful around these parts?' Dunn enquired.

'So far,' Fox replied. 'Just here will do, thanks.'

The car drew up by the kerb, both men getting out. Fox took the keys from Dunn, who gave a wave rather than a handshake as he got into the Range Rover. Christie did a three-point turn and drove off, and Fox headed indoors. He thought about running a bath. A nice long soak. He had no messages on his phone, no missed calls. He plugged the phone in to charge and poured a big glass of tap water, gulping it down. Only then did he wander into the bathroom to check the damage in the mirror. Bruising down one side of his face. His chin hurt, and he'd obviously fallen on his arm as he hit the carriageway.

You'll live, he told himself. Not that anyone's bothered.

The doorbell went. He peered through the spyhole before opening up to Compston and Bell. Compston stormed inside without invitation, Bell fixing Fox with a look before following.

Compston stood in the centre of the living room, feet apart, arms folded. 'Nice of them to drop you home,' he growled. 'Your new friends, I mean.'

'You'd have left me lying in the road, right?' Fox retorted.

'Didn't you learn *anything* from yesterday?'

'I wasn't going to let them stab anyone.'

Compston turned his attention to Bell. 'Knives?'

'I didn't see any.'

'Jackie Dyson was getting ready to pull one out.' Fox studied both men's reaction, but they

175

were giving nothing away.

'Nevertheless,' Compston eventually said. Then: 'Did you identify yourself as the law?'

'I didn't need to — Darryl Christie knows me, remember.'

'I meant Stark and his boys.'

Fox shook his head.

'You sure?'

'I'm sure. But meantime, Christie has put two and two together — he knows there's surveillance on the Starks.' Fox raised a hand as Compston bared his teeth. 'Before you go the full Hannibal Lecter, he thinks it's locally sourced and all down to the attack at the storage unit.'

'Will he tell the Starks?'

'Why the hell should he? It gives him something over them. And incidentally, he tells me he's going to take them out of the game. Didn't sound like he was joking.'

'We'll deal with that as and when.'

'By sitting back and watching?'

Compston's face hardened. 'You used to run surveillance operations against your own kind, Fox. Like I said yesterday, I'm guessing sometimes you'd have to sit and watch.' He took a step forward, arms by his sides now. 'In fact, from what little I know of you, I'd say you enjoyed watching, and those bruises of yours tell me you'd do well to stick to what you're best at.' He paused, face inches from Fox's. 'Understood?' Without waiting for an answer, he stalked towards the front door, Alec Bell at his heels. This time, Bell kept his gaze directed at the floor. When the door had closed, Fox went back into the bathroom, intent on some paracetamol and that long soak he had promised himself.

When he emerged almost an hour later, having changed into fresh clothes, he had one missed call and one text, both from Bell. The text told him to send a message saying when would be a good time to talk.

Right now, Fox replied. Sixty seconds later, his phone rang.

'Sorry about all that,' Bell said. His voice had a bit of echo to it.

'Where are you?'

'The bogs at St Leonard's. Listen, I felt hellish, not stepping in — I just wanted you to know that. I mean, Ricky's right, of course, but all the same . . .'

'You saw the blade, didn't you?'

'He put it away sharpish.'

'Jackie Dyson, though — who also didn't hold back when it came to giving Chick Carpenter a doing.'

'So?'

'My gut feeling is, Dyson's your mole. If I'm right, doesn't it look to you like he might have gone native?'

There was silence on the line.

'Well?' Fox persisted.

'You know I can't say anything.'

'You owe me this much at least, Alec. I went to the ground and you just sat in your damned car . . .'

'Malcolm — '

'And here's the thing — I've had your back throughout, haven't I? I've not told Compston

177

you blabbed about the mole. So just tell me — it's Dyson, isn't it?'

'Maybe.'

'And could he be getting too much in character? We've both heard of it happening.'

'Our boy knows what he's doing.'

'You sure about that? How often do you talk to him?'

'Not in a while. That's how it has to work.'

'But have you noticed any change in him?'

'He has to look committed, Malcolm — that's how those guys get where they are and then stay there once they've arrived.' Fox heard the man give a sigh. 'Look, I've got to go. You should take tomorrow off, get some ice on those bruises.'

'Nice of you to show such belated concern.'

'Two final words, then, Malcolm — Fuck. You.'

The phone went dead, but then suddenly vibrated. Another incoming message, this time from Rebus:

Want a dog?

Fox shut the phone down and trekked to the fridge, in search of frozen veg.

★ ★ ★

'You coming in?' Davie Dunn asked. Christie had pulled up in front of the Gimlet. He gazed out at the pub's uninviting exterior and shook his head, but as Dunn made to get out, he grabbed him by the arm.

'Talked to your old employer recently?' he enquired.

'I'll tell you what I told Stark and his gang — I haven't set eyes on Hamish Wright in years.'

'Doesn't mean you've not spoken with him on the phone.'

'He's ancient history, Darryl.'

'You'll be history too, if you don't give me a straight answer.'

'I've not seen him, I've not spoken to him.'

'But have you heard anything about his whereabouts?'

'Nothing.'

'He has other old pals in the city, though, yes?'

'Honest to God, I wouldn't know.'

'You're absolutely sure about that?'

'On my kids' lives, Darryl.'

The two men locked eyes, Christie eventually releasing Dunn's sleeve. But as Dunn got out of the car and closed the door, Christie wound down the window and called him back. Dunn leaned in so his face filled the open window.

'Your kids are Lottie and Euan. She's sixteen, he's eleven. You split from their mum but I know the address. You swore to me on their lives, Davie. Bear that in mind . . . '

The window slid back up again, the Evoque moving off, leaving Davie Dunn standing in the roadway, his legs a little more leaden than before, his heart pounding and his mouth dry. A drink, he realised, would fix only one of these, but one out of three was a start . . .

16

Christine Esson showed Rebus and Clarke what she'd done.

'And all of it on company time, so I hope you've got my back covered.'

The terrier looked at its most appealing. A bit of the vet's arm and examination table could be seen, though Esson had managed to crop most of it out. She had provided a brief description of where the dog had been found, along with an email address.

'Whose address is it?' Rebus enquired.

'Created specially,' she informed him.

'And this is on Facebook?'

'And Twitter, and a few other places. My friends will make sure it gets noticed.'

'How many friends?'

'Around three and a half thousand.'

Rebus stared at her. 'Parties at your house must be quite something.'

'She means online friends,' Clarke explained for his benefit.

'I could set up an account for you if you like,' Esson teased him.

Rebus ignored this and instead asked Clarke how many days they should give it.

'Up to you,' she said.

'Social media usually works fast or not at all,' Esson advised.

'And meantime there's a vet in Edinburgh

getting rich at my expense,' Rebus made show of complaining.

'I don't see you spending your pension on much else,' Clarke commented.

'I still have to count the pennies.'

'All the way into the till of the Oxford Bar.' Clarke was smiling as she tried Malcolm Fox's number, but he didn't pick up.

★   ★   ★

Cafferty hadn't been answering his phone, but he had made plenty of calls, up and down the country. He'd also had quiet meetings in a bar near Quartermile, exchanging handfuls of banknotes for information or the vow to keep eyes and ears open and report back. He went out wearing a three-quarter-length brown coat (rather than his habitual black) and a cap and scarf (where usually he'd be bare-headed whatever the weather). Having not bothered to shave, he resembled the other old men on the street, especially when, having noted its near-ubiquity, he added a polythene carrier bag to the ensemble. The bag held the local paper and two tins of Scotch broth.

This disguise — fine for the streets around Greyfriars — seemed less appropriate for the bar of the G&V hotel on George IV Bridge, so as soon as he entered, he shed coat, scarf and hat and wrapped the coat around the bag. But then he had another idea. At reception, he enquired about a room. Yes, there was a vacancy. He paid by credit card and headed upstairs. The room was fine. He deposited the bundle there and went back down to the bar, checking that his guest had not yet turned up. He sat in a corner, facing the door to the street. A couple of minutes after his Bloody Mary arrived, Darryl Christie walked in. He wore a suit and open-necked shirt and seemed unconcerned by the outside world's plummeting temperature.

Christie spotted Cafferty immediately, but kept his distance as he assessed the situation. Cafferty had, as promised, come alone. The other drinkers looked to pose no threat at all. Christie gave the briefest of nods in Cafferty's direction, took out a phone and tapped in a message — presumably to a man parked outside, a man primed to intervene if his boss sensed trouble.

Finally, he approached the table. Rather than stand up, Cafferty lifted an olive from the bowl in front of him and popped it into his mouth. Christie played with his chair before sitting down, angling it so that he had at least a partial view of what might be happening behind him.

'I did say there'd be no funny business,' Cafferty reminded him.

'Maybe we have different senses of humour.' A waiter was hovering. Christie ordered a dirty martini.

'What the hell's that?' Cafferty asked, looking bemused.

'For research purposes. My barman tells me he makes the best in the city — I like to keep testing him.'

'I forgot you had a hotel.'

'No you didn't. And by the way, the drinks would have been gratis if we'd met there.'

'I thought neutral ground was best. How have you been, Darryl? You don't look like you're eating enough.' Cafferty pushed the olive bowl towards him.

'*You* look old,' Christie countered.

'That's because I am. But I'm wise, too.'

'Oh aye?'

'I know, for example, what happened at the Gimlet.'

'The Gimlet's nothing to do with me these days.'

'I know someone else runs it, but that's not quite the same thing.' Cafferty laid his drink's straw aside, along with the hunk of celery, and supped from the lip of the glass. 'Besides which, when Dennis Stark pays a visit, who else is Davie Dunn going to turn to?'

'You brought me here so you can gloat?'

'Far from it, Darryl. The way the Starks are going, they're riling the whole city — my friends as well as yours.'

'I thought your friends were all headstones.'

'Not quite.'

'So what are you saying?'

'I'm saying I'm not on Joe Stark's side.'

'Is that right?'

'In fact, there's a chance I'm on their hit list, same as you seem to be — maybe even more so.' Cafferty paused as Christie's drink arrived. There wasn't much of it, which usually, in Cafferty's experience, made it lethal. Christie took a sip. 'How does it measure up?'

But Christie just shrugged and placed the glass on the table.

'You've heard about the notes?' Cafferty asked.

'Notes?'

'One went to Lord Minton, just before he was killed.'

'Front-page news.' Christie nodded.

'Another came to me.' He had Christie's full attention now. 'I'd show it to you, but the police took it for testing.'

'You went to the cops?' Christie sounded disbelieving.

'Actually, I went to Rebus — not quite the same thing. But he passed it along. Ask him if you don't believe me. And if you're not minded to believe him, try Siobhan Clarke.'

'Okay, so you got a note.'

'I've been wondering if the Starks sent it, along with the bullet that came a few days later.'

Christie sat silently for fifteen seconds, deep in thought. 'Doesn't sound their style,' he concluded.

'Maybe.'

'How do you connect to this guy Minton?'

'He was a prosecutor. Not that he ever worked a trial involving me or one of mine, not that I can find. You ever meet him?'

'No.'

Cafferty shrugged and lifted his glass again.

'I'm still not sure why you're telling me any of this,' Christie said.

'I just thought you might be concerned for my welfare.' Cafferty waited for Christie to realise he was joking. The younger man did eventually manage half a smile. 'But the truth is,' Cafferty continued, 'I can see a time coming when you might need me and I might need you.'

'To kick the Starks out of town?'

'Something like that.'

'And what do you bring to that particular fight?' Christie stared hard at him. It was a serious question.

'Whatever you might feel you need.'

'They were going to stick a knife into Davie Dunn.'

'And Chick Carpenter ended up in hospital,' Cafferty agreed.

'With you or without you, I'm having them.'

'You know why they're here?'

'Supposedly looking for a trucker and some missing merch.'

'You're not convinced?'

'I'm convinced they're asking.' Christie had finished his drink in three swallows.

'Want another?' Cafferty asked. Christie shook his head.

'I need to be elsewhere.' He peered at Cafferty. 'Who do you really think took that shot at you?'

'I'll admit you were on the list for a while.'

'And now?'

'It's been a long time since I pissed anyone off — apart from you, obviously.'

'So if it's a grudge, they've been nurturing it?' Christie was rising to his feet and sending another text, presumably to the same destination as before. 'All those bodies you've buried down the years, all those families left wondering . . . '

'Business like ours, Darryl, it's dog-eat-dog.' Cafferty was standing now too.

'Dog-eat-dog,' Christie agreed. He looked around for their waiter.

'I've got these,' Cafferty assured him. A car was drawing up outside. Cafferty recognised the white Range Rover Evoque. 'Your carriage awaits.' He extended his hand. The two men shook. 'I'd been told you had a swagger to you these days,' Cafferty commented, releasing his grip. 'But attitude will only take you so far. When I was your age, I was getting dirty, and to be honest, I'm still that way inclined.' He paused, locking eyes with the younger man. 'Whereas you . . . '

'Yes?'

'All I can really see is a shiny fucking suit.' Cafferty shrugged and offered a thin smile. 'No offence, son.'

Christie's face grew thunderous. 'See you around,' he snarled, stalking towards the exit. Still smiling, Cafferty signalled for the bill. He signed for it, then walked towards the lift, taking out the keycard to his room, making sure it was nice and visible. He knew the white car was still outside, probably with the window nearest the hotel lowered so its occupants could get a better view. They would think they knew where to find Cafferty should they want him.

Let them think.

Let them share, if it came to that.

He stayed half an hour in the room on the second floor, using the toilet and shower, the latter only because of the quality of towels in the bathroom — better than those in his Quarter-mile flat. Descending in coat and hat, he saw that the car was long gone. He pulled the brim down low and stepped out into the evening. He had more digging to do on the internet.

And Scotch broth for his supper.

*   *   *

Malcolm Fox was sitting in his car outside his father's care home. He had swallowed half a dozen painkillers and was feeling both numb and queasy. His plan had been to visit Mitch just to sit by his bed and wait for him to ask how he'd come by the bruises.

'In the line of duty.'

Yes, that was what he'd have said — or something along those lines.

Proper police work, Dad, the kind you always say I'd be rubbish at.

But then he would have fed Mitch an obvious comeback:

Those bruises prove I was right . . .

So instead of the bedside vigil, he was staying in the car, hands resting on the steering wheel, head beginning to thrum again. He reckoned it was the caffeine in the tablets, mixed with adrenalin — the aftershock from his beating. He had been thumped before, but not for some time. Last fight he'd almost been in had been with Rebus a year or so back, until they'd realised how ridiculously it would have played out. He checked the damage in the rear-view mirror. He couldn't believe he'd been about to barge in on his father like a kid wanting sympathy for a grazed knee. After a fight one time at school, all Mitch had wanted to know was how much damage Malcolm had managed to inflict on his opponent. Sensing this, Malcolm had brought his imagination into play, until he could see that his father had stopped believing.

All fun and games, eh? he told himself now, studying his reflection. Picking up his phone, he saw that the incoming call was from Siobhan again. He was worried she'd be requesting a meet-up, and he wasn't quite ready for her sympathy. No, it was his father's sour realism he'd reached out for — and part of him still wanted it. Instead of which, he turned the key in the ignition and decided to drive himself home to his bed.

His bed — and another bag of frozen peas.

Day Five

17

It was still dark when Rebus's phone woke him. He wrestled with it while trying to switch on the bedside lamp.

'Hello?'

'John, it's Siobhan.'

'You're making a habit of this — what time is it?'

'Almost six. You need to come down to Leith.'

'What's happened?'

'Another shooting. Target wasn't so lucky this time.'

'Who?'

'Dennis Stark.'

Rebus had swung his legs out from beneath the duvet, feet touching the floor. 'Dead?' he asked.

'Dead,' Siobhan Clarke confirmed.

⋆ ⋆ ⋆

An alley off Constitution Street. The main road had been cordoned, officers in high-vis jackets detouring traffic and pedestrians. Mostly black cabs and shift workers, the rush hour still some way off. The media were there too, along with a few ghouls, who craned their necks, trying to get a better look.

Dennis Stark's body had been removed. The alley was just that: high walls, strewn rubbish and a couple of industrial-sized bins, one reinforced door providing the back entrance to an office. No CCTV, minimal street lighting. The scene of crime team were suited up and busy. A bleary-looking James Page was rubbing his gloved hands together as he gathered information from a SOCO. Rebus caught Siobhan Clarke's eye and she walked towards him, stony-faced and professional in protective overalls, hood and overshoes.

'They weren't going to let me through,' Rebus said, nodding in the direction of the cordon. 'Thought I was going to have to phone you to come get me.'

'The call came from one of the nearby flats,' Clarke informed him, sliding her face mask down to her throat. 'Three separate calls, actually, which is probably why the patrol took it seriously. Report of what sounded like a single gunshot. One of the callers was ex-army, said he knew for a fact that was what he'd heard. Calls came in at around three forty-five, and by four fifteen the body had been found.' She gestured towards the relevant spot. 'Slumped against the wall. Gunshot wound to the chest.'

'Nine mil?'

'Not sure yet.'

'Any note?'

'Same wording as before.'

Rebus puffed out his cheeks. 'Does Joe Stark know?'

'Someone was due to call Glasgow.'

'And Dennis's men?'

'We've got officers at the guest house. They'll

192

be taken in for questioning.'

'How far is the guest house from here?'

'It's on Leith Links.'

'A two-minute walk, then — and with Leith police station halfway between the two.'

'But no one on duty that time of night.'

Rebus thought for a moment. 'This is bad, Siobhan.'

'I know.'

'Lord Minton, Cafferty, and now Dennis Stark.'

'We just need to find the connection.'

'What about Compston? Does he know?'

'Haven't seen him.'

'His team are supposed to be on the Starks twenty-four/seven.'

'I know, and I'm just about to break the news to Page.' She paused. 'While I do that, I thought you could have a word with Compston.'

'Why not Malcolm?'

'He's not answering his phone.'

'Okay, leave it with me.' Rebus watched the SOCOs as they shone their torches over the ground. 'Found the bullet yet?'

'No.'

'Still in the body, maybe?'

'Entry and exit wounds, according to the doc.'

'So the bullet's here somewhere?'

'It either is or it isn't.'

'Our shooter seems a bit more confident, doesn't he? Didn't want to get too close to Cafferty, yet he's no qualms about coming face to face with Dennis Stark.'

Clarke nodded her agreement.

'And what was Stark doing here anyway?'

'Right now your guess is as good as mine.'

Page called Clarke's name. She turned away from Rebus and marched towards him, pulling the mask back up. Rebus took his phone out and called Fox's mobile and home numbers. No answer. He took one last long look at the alley before heading back towards the cordon and his car.

Traffic was light as he drove across town to Oxgangs. He rang Fox's doorbell and then banged the door with his fist a couple of times for good measure. Moments later, he heard movement, and the door cracked open a couple of inches. Fox was dressed in a pair of dark blue pyjamas, groggy from sleep.

'Don't tell me you're here to sell me a dog?' he muttered.

'What the hell happened to you?' Rebus said, noticing Fox's face.

'I tried breaking up a fight outside the Gimlet.'

'The Starks?' Rebus guessed. 'And you just waded in?'

'Can we maybe discuss this in daylight hours?' Fox was blinking his eyes into focus as he assessed his bruises with the tips of his fingers.

'You got an alibi for quarter to four?'

'What am I supposed to have done?'

'That's pretty much the exact time someone shot and killed Dennis Stark.'

'Christ,' Fox said.

'As you say,' Rebus concurred.

While Fox was washing and getting dressed, Rebus made them a cafetière of coffee. Fox walked into the kitchen knotting his tie. He had obviously been thinking.

'Cafferty and Christie, Chick Carpenter and Davie Dunn — they'll all have to be questioned.' He accepted the mug from Rebus and took a slurp. 'And what about Operation Junior?'

'That's why I'm here. No one's seen or heard from Compston and his crew — you got a number for them?'

'Should probably be Doug Maxtone actually — we tell Maxtone, he tells Compston.'

'Where's the fun in that?'

'Fun?'

'You know what I mean.'

'I suppose I do.'

'There was a note left with Dennis.'

Fox's eyes widened above the rim of his mug. 'Same message?'

'Same message.'

'So it's our guy then, rather than any of those names I mentioned.'

'They all had reason to want Dennis punished — we'll still need to talk to them.'

'Joe Stark is going to be incandescent.'

'I'd think.'

'And why didn't Dennis's men stop it happening?'

'We need to find that out.' Rebus paused. 'You discovered who the mole is yet?'

'What makes you think I'm interested?'

Rebus smiled. 'The way you reacted when Alec Bell told us. You're a born spy, Malcolm — it's why you were so well suited to Complaints. I got the notion you'd want to test yourself.'

'Well, it so happens . . . '

'Go on then, impress me.'

'Jackie Dyson's the clear favourite.'

'And he didn't step in when you were getting that kicking?'

'He's the one who doled it out.'

'Knowing you're a cop?'

Fox shook his head.

'So is the operation compromised?'

Fox shook his head again. 'I didn't identify myself at any point.' He had broken open a fresh packet of paracetamol and was readying to swallow a couple.

'Still, probably not Compston's star pupil, unless *he* doesn't know?'

'He knows.'

'So maybe I should be the one to phone him?'

Fox considered this. 'Maybe you should.' He got busy with his own phone, reeling off Compston's number for Rebus.

'One more thing,' he said. 'I woke up in hospital and the owner of the Gimlet was there, ready to thank me for stepping in. He'd brought along a mate of his . . . '

'Darryl Christie?'

'Who worked out straight away that it was no accident I was in the area.'

'And does Ricky Compston know about *that*?' Rebus watched as Fox nodded. 'Yet I'm the one everybody says is a troublemaker. Sounds as if you could teach me a thing or two.'

'Christie told me he was going to take the Starks out of the game. He said the best thing the rest of us could do was keep well out of the way.'

Rebus thought about this for a moment, then made the call, holding the phone to his ear. 'Here goes,' he said. 'Wish me luck . . . '

★ ★ ★

Having identified his only son at the mortuary, Joe Stark was in a room at Fettes, answering a few questions with his lawyer present.

That had interested Rebus — not too many parents of murder victims turned up with a solicitor in tow. But then Joe Stark was no ordinary parent. The media had upped camp from Constitution Street and were now on Fettes Avenue, their numbers swelling as the sky got lighter.

Compston had wanted to come to Fettes too, but Rebus had cautioned against it — 'unless you're winding down Operation Junior'.

His reasoning: the place would be crawling with members of the Stark crew. And sure enough, Joe's trusted lieutenants — Walter Grieve and Len Parker — were in the reception area, awaiting their boss. Rebus had even had a word with them.

'Are you members of the family?' he had asked, sounding sympathetic.

'As good as.'

'Well, I just wanted to say how sorry we all are. Hellish thing to happen to a young man, especially when he's a visitor to the city.'

'Aye, thanks.'

They had twitched in their seats, unable to work out how to react. Probably the only time they ever talked to cops was when under caution or slipping a bung beneath a pub table.

'If there's anything we can do for you gentlemen . . . ' Rebus had left them there, nodding and frowning.

Elsewhere in the building, Dennis Stark's men were being questioned or were waiting their turn. Rebus wondered if Jackie Dyson would come out of character. He doubted it. Always supposing Fox had got the right man. Fox himself was in the incident room, committing to memory the various items pinned to one wall — crime-scene photos, maps, newspaper clippings.

'Page and Siobhan are putting together a media release,' he told Rebus. 'You spoken to Cafferty?'

'Not yet.'

'Any particular reason?'

'He's like you were earlier — not answering his phone.'

'Thumping on the front door sometimes works.'

'I was there two nights back. He's done a flit.'

'Oh?'

'Self-preservation, most likely.'

'Surely he'll be in touch when he hears.'

'Who knows what he'll do — this is Cafferty we're talking about.'

Siobhan Clarke emerged from Page's office but walked straight past them without noticing, her mind elsewhere. She had paperwork in one hand and her phone in the other as she disappeared into the corridor.

'I thought she might have said something about my bruises,' Fox commented. Then, his eyes on Rebus: 'Are we doing any good here?'

'Not a lot.'

'Where are you meeting Compston?'

'St Leonard's. You coming along for the ride?'

'I suppose I might.'

'You scared I won't play nice?'

'I've often been told I'm a civilising influence.'

'Tell that to the guys who jumped you.'

'One lucky punch, that's all . . . '

18

'Well if it isn't De Niro's stunt double from
Raging Bull,' Compston announced as Fox
walked into the room, Rebus right behind him.
The mood was sombre, weeks and months of
work most likely just flushed down the toilet.

Fox was ready with a question: 'Where was the
overnight surveillance?'

'We all have to sleep sometime,' Alec Bell
complained.

'From which I take it you were the one
napping in the car?'

'Actually, it was me,' Beth Hastie piped up. 'I
needed petrol, a hot drink and the loo, so I took
twenty minutes out at an all-night garage on
Leith Walk. First I knew we had a problem was
when uniforms turned up at the guest house.'

'Wouldn't have been an issue,' Compston
added, 'if we hadn't lost Selway and Emerson,
but they were still in Glasgow keeping an eye on
the dad.'

'Chief Constable's not going to be happy with
you, Ricky,' Rebus said.

'My problem, not yours. But at least I'm not
the one failing to apprehend some nutcase serial
killer.'

'Anyway,' Fox chipped in, 'with Dennis gone, I
dare say the others will want to go back to
Glasgow.'

Compston gave him a hard stare. 'Are you off

your head? Why would they do that?' Then, to Rebus: 'Tell him.'

Rebus obliged. 'Joe's the Old Testament sort, an eye for an eye and all that. He'd raze Edinburgh to the ground to find who killed his son. DI Compston here probably relishes that prospect, because Joe's not going to hold back and that means he'll start to make mistakes. The more he does that, the easier it is to catch him in the act and put him and his boys away.'

'So you see,' Compston told Fox, 'nobody's going anywhere. And we're all going to have front-row seats. Trust me, Edinburgh doesn't know what's about to hit it.'

⋆　⋆　⋆

Cafferty's heart was pounding as he stood at the window of his Quartermile flat, looking down on to the Meadows. Students were striding and cycling down Jawbone Walk, full of confidence and vitality. He felt nothing but a sweeping dissociation — what was this other world like, the one most people seemed to inhabit? Why were they happy? He couldn't remember ever feeling carefree. Always alert to possible attack, surrounded by those he could not risk trusting, new threats piling on top of old. He had clambered his way to the top, trampling those he needed to, gouging and scratching and kicking, making a slew of enemies but ensuring, too, that those enemies would lack the strength to topple him.

Was that any sort of kingdom?

Joe Stark had done much the same in Glasgow, ruling by fearful reputation, reinforced in time by son Dennis. But Dennis had lacked his father's guile and innate canniness, and this surely had contributed to his downfall. Cafferty pressed his forehead against the tinted glass as he made the call. Darryl Christie picked up immediately.

'I was about to call *you*,' Christie announced.

'Christ, Darryl, you don't hang about, do you?'

'I knew that's what you'd be thinking.'

'It's what *everyone's* going to be thinking — especially the forces of law and order.'

'The very fact you say that tells me something interesting.'

'What?'

'You no longer have friends on the force.'

'And you do?'

'Which is why I know about the note.'

'They found a note?'

'It's not been reported yet, but yes, same as you got. So this wasn't some isolated hit — and it certainly wasn't me or mine pulling the trigger.'

'Two gangsters targeted . . . '

'Agreed — the cops are going to want to question me. And I'd be hard pressed to lie and say I'm sorry that bawbag's been eliminated. I could kiss whoever did it.'

'Joe's going to come gunning for you — maybe for me too. He won't believe it was random, and even if he did, he'd still need revenge on somebody.'

'Well he knows where to find me. You, on the other hand . . . '

'What?'

'You're hiding out, and that's bound to make you look guilty in his eyes.'

'I hope I can trust you to put him right on that score.'

Christie just laughed and hung up. Cafferty stepped away from the window and considered phoning Rebus, but ended up sitting down with his laptop instead, knowing he would have to add Dennis Stark to his search list. It was going to be a long day.

★   ★   ★

Joseph Stark stood in the alley while his men formed a line behind the cordon, scowling at the officer on duty who had refused to let them through.

'Immediate family only,' the officer had stipulated.

This hadn't bothered Joe Stark unduly — he'd wanted the place to himself anyway, to see if any trace of his son could still be found there. He remembered that Cath had wanted the name Dennis — her own father's name. So Joe had nodded away his preference for Joseph Junior. Then Cath had gone and died, leaving Joe to try running the show while bringing up the kid. His friends had told him to marry again, but he knew he wouldn't. Cath had been the woman for him. He was trying now to bring back memories of Dennis's childhood, but there were huge gaps.

First day at school? A neighbour had taken him, Joe away on business. Playing football for the youth club, Halloween dressing-up, end-of-term reports . . . What stuck in the father's mind were the summonses to the head's office. After a while, they'd realised he wasn't the kind of man to be given bad news in person. Letters after that, torn up and binned.

His own father had been handy with his trouser belt, delivering it to ears, hands, backside. Fists later on. Joe had behaved in much the same way, until Dennis grew to be a couple of inches taller than him and learned to resist. Good times too, though, surely: dinner and drinks at some fancy new place; a drive in the Jag to the seaside for ice cream; passing on knowledge about the way the world really worked.

It was the gaps that gnawed at him, however — those huge chunks of time spent away from one another. When Dennis had gone to jail, Joe had preferred not to visit. Leave the lad alone, let him learn. He knew that when he went home to Glasgow, he'd find precious few photos of the two of them together. But then what was the point of all that? What was the point of standing in a freezing alley in a strange city when your son was in a drawer at the mortuary? The formal identification had been hard, but he'd insisted on seeing the bullet hole. Small it was, in comparison to the rest of the unharmed torso. A couple of tattoos Joe couldn't remember having been told about — one a purple thistle, the other a lion rampant. He'd winced — he bore near-identical markings on his own arms. Why had the boy never said?

He crouched down, placing the palm of one hand against the wall and one on the rough ground. Then he closed his eyes, trying to feel something, *anything*. When he opened his eyes again, the world seemed unchanged. The six men were focused on him as he walked towards them: Dennis's four, plus Walter and Len. Joe Stark made silent eye contact with each one of them in turn. Len Parker gave him a handkerchief so he could wipe his hands clean. Stark nodded his thanks before handing it back, then led them away from the uniform and the locals who had come to gawp.

'Whoever did this,' he began, keeping his voice low, 'knew about the guest house. So I need you to give me names, and then we're going to have a talk with each and every one of them, see who *they* maybe spilled the beans to. Cops will be doing their own thing, but I doubt they'll be busting a gut — CID in Glasgow are probably opening the champagne as I speak. But my boy's dead and I want to know why and I need to know who. Until then, no rest, no jokes, no fun. Understood? If I'm in hell, you lot are too. Anyone want to say anything?'

There was a shuffling of feet, but then Rob Simpson cleared his throat. 'I know one of us should have been with him, but it was just something he did. Only seemed to need four hours' sleep a night, and he'd go out for a stroll. Never woke us up to go with him. He knew he could if he wanted to.'

'You all knew about this?' Joe Stark waited until Dyson, Andrews and Rae all nodded. 'Then you should have talked sense into him. Or one of you should have taken the night shift, so he wouldn't be on his own.'

They looked at the ground and shuffled uneasily.

'I hold all four of you personally responsible,' Stark went on, stabbing with his finger. 'You want me in your corner when this is done? You'll get me some answers.'

'Whatever it takes?' Jackie Dyson queried.

'Take a wild fucking guess, son,' came the ice-cold reply.

19

James Page listened as Rebus and Clarke told him their theory.

'So our killer doesn't have a gun,' Page said, 'until he takes one from Lord Minton's house? He then tests it, shoots at Cafferty and misses, and a few days later takes down Dennis Stark at point-blank range?'

'Do we know it was point blank?' Rebus asked.

'Powder burns on the deceased's jacket,' Page confirmed.

'And no bullet yet?' Clarke checked.

'No.'

'So what happened to it?'

'We don't know.' Page folded his arms. He was seated behind his desk, his phone lying in front of him. Every five or ten seconds there was another incoming text for him to ignore.

'Looks like the killer maybe took it away with him,' Rebus commented.

'Why, though?'

Rebus shrugged. 'Pity, mind — be good to verify all three bullets came from the same weapon.'

'Three?'

'The tree in the Hermitage, plus Cafferty and Stark.'

Page stared at him. 'You think there's more than one maniac out there?'

'Copycats have been known to happen.'

Page dismissed this with a scowl. 'This team

who've been keeping the Starks under observa-
tion . . . '

'Red faces all round.'

Page's nostrils flared. 'And just how did Lord
Minton get a gun in the first place?'

'Not legally,' Clarke said. 'No firearms
certificate ever issued to him.'

'But with him being a lawyer and all,' Rebus
added, 'he probably got to know one or two
people down the years who could find him what
he wanted. Thing is: why did he want it?'

'He'd been sent a threatening note,' Page
reminded him.

'He'd probably had threats in the past, though.
For some reason, this latest one got to him.'

'Because it had merit?' Page guessed. 'You
think the gun was a recent purchase?'

'I phoned his bank and managed to get a few
details,' Clarke said. 'A couple of weeks ago he
took out five hundred pounds a day on four
consecutive days. Normally he made do with
withdrawals of a hundred or two hundred twice a
week. In his wallet at time of death he had
exactly thirty-five pounds.'

Page's eyes were on Rebus. 'Would two grand
buy him a handgun?'

'Probably.'

'Why in batches of five hundred?'

'Maximum he could take from a cash machine
each day,' Clarke explained.

'We're *sure* he had a gun in his desk drawer?'

'It's feasible.'

'So who sold it to him? Is there anyone in the
city we know of?'

'We can make enquiries,' Rebus stated.

'Let's do that then.'

'Probably best not to say anything to the grieving father,' Rebus cautioned.

Page nodded his understanding and picked up his phone. 'I wonder how many of these texts are from the boss,' he said.

'We're not going public with the note to Stark, are we, sir?' Clarke asked.

'Not just yet.'

'And forensics are checking it?'

'For what it's worth.' But Page's attention was now firmly on the contents of his phone's screen. Rebus gestured to Clarke that it was time to go. Outside in the main office, she asked him about the pistol.

'You still have snitches working for you?'

'No,' he stated. 'But Darryl Christie might put the word out if we ask nicely.'

'And why would he do that?'

'Because right now he needs all the friends he can get.'

Clarke considered this, eventually nodding her agreement. 'You okay to talk to him?'

'In my consultative capacity, DI Clarke?'

'In your consultative capacity, *Mr* Rebus.'

⋆   ⋆   ⋆

Fox had listened to the interviews with Dennis Stark's associates.

Actually, that wasn't strictly true — he had skimmed three of them, but listened to the fourth in full. Jackie Dyson was good, very good, not

209

once letting the mask slip. He was belligerent, obstructive, and grudging in his answers.

'You're here as a friend of the deceased, Mr Dyson,' he was reminded at one point. 'We're just looking for anything that can help us track down his killer.'

'Then get out and look,' Dyson had snarled in response. 'Because as soon as you let me out of here, that's what I'm doing.'

Fox wondered: would Dyson want to be brought in, mission scuppered? At the very least, he would be looking to talk to Compston, just to get some pointers.

Or was he beyond all that? Was he self-sufficient and comfortable in his new skin?

Was there even an opportunity for advancement, now that Dennis was gone?

Fox looked at his phone — nothing from Siobhan or Rebus. For want of anything better to do, he decided to head back to St Leonard's. But once in his car, he opted for a quick detour first. He parked kerbside on Constitution Street and walked to the alleyway's opening. It was protected by police tape. A couple of elderly shoppers had stopped for a gawp, while the uniform on duty did his best to ignore them. He recognised Fox and lifted the tape. But having ducked beneath it, Fox paused.

'Anyone else been along?' he asked.

'Victim's father.'

'Plus entourage?'

The officer nodded. 'I only let the father through, though.'

'Bet that made you popular.' Fox smiled and

headed deeper into the alley. Forensics had picked it clean, not even a bloodstain visible. Dennis liked to go for a night-time walk, always unaccompanied — that much had been gleaned from the interviews. Fair enough, but the guest house sat on the edge of Leith Links, a much more congenial spot than this. Had he arranged some sort of meeting? There was nothing on his phone, no texts or late-night calls. Yet something or someone had brought him here. Ducking back below the tape, Fox thanked the uniform and retraced the route Dennis had most likely taken. It was a short walk past Leith police station, and yes, there were the Links, with a kids' park visible beyond the fenced-off allotments. A large wooden board was hanging from a post in the small front garden of the guest house: LABURNUM — NO VACANCIES.

The door to the guest house was yanked open from within, and Fox just had time to crouch behind a parked VW Polo as Dennis's gang emerged, Joe Stark bringing up the rear. The others carried overnight bags and backpacks. They stuffed everything into the boot of a Chrysler Voyager and got in, Jackie Dyson driving. The vehicle sped off, and five seconds later was joined by another car, driven by the unmistakable form of Alec Bell. Was the gang bound for Glasgow? They were certainly in a hurry. Looking towards the guest house again, Fox saw that the NO VACANCIES sign had been tossed to the ground.

And the front door was ajar.

He crossed the street and opened the gate,

walking up the path and calling out a greeting as he pushed the door open and stepped inside. There was a man lying on the floor of the chintzy living room. Ornaments lay smashed in the fireplace. The man's hands had been tied behind his back. He'd been seated on a dining chair, which had toppled on to its side. He was conscious, bleeding from nose and mouth. Fox knelt beside him and undid the knots.

'I'm a police officer,' he assured the trembling figure. The man was in his mid fifties, overweight and breathing hard. 'You're in shock, but are you otherwise hurt? Anything broken, or are you okay to sit up?'

'I'll be all right.'

'Should I call an ambulance?'

'I'm fine, really.' The man was sitting on the floor, rubbing his wrists.

'The men who did this, they've driven off, so don't worry.'

'What men?'

Fox stared at him. 'You might be concussed.'

'No men, no men.' The man was shaking his head.

'Maybe some boxes fell on you, eh? And tied your hands behind you while they were at it?' Fox patted the man's arm reassuringly. 'Don't fret about it. But did you tell them anything?'

'Nothing to tell.'

'Sure you're going to be all right?'

'Moira will have a fit, you know.'

'Will she?'

The man was looking at the smashed ornaments. 'Her pride and joy those were . . . '

'Let me help you to your feet. I want to check you're able to walk.'

The man accepted Fox's assistance. He wobbled a little, but regained most of his equilibrium.

'You know Dennis Stark has been killed?' Fox asked. 'I'm guessing they want to know who knew he was staying here.'

The man nodded slowly, then his eyes widened. 'They'll come back, won't they? They'll want to hear it from Moira.'

Fox considered this. 'Might be wise to pack a few things for you and Moira. Go elsewhere for a day or two.'

'Yes,' the man agreed, nodding again.

'And maybe wash the blood off, so she doesn't get a bigger shock than is already coming to her.'

'Thank you,' the man said. He insisted on seeing Fox to the door. Fox stopped on the path, picked up the sign and reinstated it.

He walked back to Constitution Street, unsure what to do next. Carnage seemed to follow the Starks. It made sense that they should be sent packing. But how? He waved a goodbye towards the officer on cordon duty and unlocked his car. There was just under a quarter of a tank of petrol, and he had a sudden craving for something sweet, so he filled up on the nearest forecourt. Entering the shop, he noted that the place closed at ten in the evening. He selected a Bounty and a Mars bar and took out his debit card.

'Where's the nearest all-night garage?' he asked the assistant.

'Used to be one not far from here, but it went

belly up — hard to compete with the super-markets.'

Fox nodded sympathetically. 'So to answer my question . . . ?'

'Canonmills, maybe.'

'Canonmills? That's a fair distance.'

The assistant just shrugged. Fox retrieved his card from the machine and got into his car. He stayed at the pump, engine off, as he chewed on the Mars bar. Then he got back out of the car and returned to the cash desk.

'Something wrong?' the assistant asked, looking distinctly wary.

'This is the only petrol station on Leith Walk, right?'

'That's right.'

'Any others nearby?'

'One, maybe two.'

'But in the middle of the night?'

'I told you, Canonmills.'

'You did,' Fox was forced to agree. He walked outside again. Why had Beth Hastie lied? Had she decided the surveillance wasn't worth her time, opted for a good night's sleep instead? He shut the driver's-side door, started the engine, and tore open the Bounty, stuffing the first segment into his mouth as he drove off the forecourt.

★   ★   ★

There were two smartly dressed and well-built doormen on the steps outside Darryl Christie's hotel — a sensible addition to the staff roster,

214

given the circumstances. Rebus stopped in front of them and nodded a greeting.

'Remember me?' he said to the one he'd spoken with in the driveway of Cafferty's house.

'I never forget a face.'

'I notice Big Ger's no longer at home. Good to see you weren't out of work for long.'

'We get around almost as much as you do.'

'I assume you've heard the news about Dennis Stark? If his crew turns up here, you better have reinforcements on speed-dial. Unless you're tooled up, of course — because trust me, after what just happened to their boss, they'll be locked and loaded.'

'Just as well we've a police force to take care of all these shady characters.'

'*Semper Vigilo* — that's our motto,' Rebus said, passing between the two men and pushing open the glass door. The same barman as before was on duty, but there was no offer of a drink, just a quick phone call to some other part of the building. The street outside the large Georgian sash windows seemed calm enough. Maybe that had always been the Edinburgh way, or at least the polite New Town way. Long gone were the days when a rabble could be roused by imprisoning someone unfairly or raising the price of bread. But he knew people would be talking, neighbours gossiping about the most recent murderous assault, shopkeepers agreeing with customers that it was both shocking and rare.

Darryl Christie walked into the room briskly, sitting down across from Rebus as if ready for only the briefest of dialogues.

'Wasn't me,' he said.

'Okay.'

'Whoever did it left a note — am I right?'

'I was under the impression we were keeping that away from the public.'

'I'm not the public, though, am I?'

'I suppose not.'

'But it means you're after the same bastard who did for Minton and tried to do for Cafferty.'

'Cafferty told you about the note? I suppose that makes sense. And you're probably right — though we're keeping an open mind. Have you heard from Joe Stark yet?'

'No.'

'Reckon those two lunks on the door will keep the bogeyman away?'

'Call them an early-warning system.'

'You're mates with their boss, then? Andrew Goodman?'

'We've done some business.'

'Any of it legit, or is that a stupid question?' Rebus saw that Christie wasn't about to answer, so gave a thin smile. 'Well,' he said, 'much as I'd like to see you put away, Darryl, I'm actually after a favour — something that could be mutually beneficial.'

Christie looked at him. 'I'm listening,' he said.

'Our thinking is, the gun was taken from Lord Minton's house by whoever killed him. He didn't have a licence for it, and it was probably a recent purchase — as in the past couple of weeks.'

Christie scratched at his chin with one

fingertip. 'Sourced locally?'

'If we're lucky.'

Christie nodded. 'Probably only two or three possible sellers. But if we need to extend the search westwards . . . ' He did the calculation. 'Add in another ten or twelve. Plus half a dozen elsewhere in Scotland.'

'If we find the gun, it helps us eliminate you from our enquiries — and might even persuade Joe not to come after you.'

Christie's face broke into a smile. 'Listen to you, Rebus — you're loving this, aren't you? One last encore before the lights go down . . . '

'You'll put the word out?'

'I'll see what I can do. Now, tell me about Joe Stark — how's he taking it?'

'How do you think?'

'He'll be wondering why Dennis went to that alley in the first place.'

'Man liked a nocturnal daunder, apparently.' Christie didn't look convinced. 'How about you?' Rebus asked. 'You taking all the necessary precautions? Not just those two bodybuilders at the door?' Christie offered a shrug as he rose to his feet. His phone buzzed. He checked the screen before answering.

'Yes, Bernard?' He listened, his eyes narrowing and coming to rest on Rebus's. 'You're okay, though?' Another pause while the caller spoke. Then: 'That's probably good advice. Don't tell anyone where you're going. And phone me again later. I owe you.'

He ended the call and turned the phone over in his hand.

217

'Owner of the guest house where the Starks were holed up,' he explained. 'They've just given him a beating, wanted to know who he'd told about them.'

'Well, we know he told you.'

'But he didn't tell them that.'

'Then you really *do* owe him.'

'They've packed their bags now, though.'

'Almost sounds like they're burning bridges.'

'Aye,' Christie agreed.

'Bernard or no Bernard, you know they'll come for you eventually.' Rebus paused to let his words sink in. Then: 'You'll phone me if you get anything?'

'Let's wait and see.' Christie turned and started making a call as he walked with purpose towards the staircase.

★   ★   ★

Fox called Alec Bell on his mobile.

'Can you talk?' he asked.

'What do you want?'

'Not that you'll be interested, but Stark and his boys roughed up the owner of the guest house before they left.'

Bell took a moment to work it out. 'You were there?'

'Happened to be passing, saw you set off in pursuit.'

'Is the guy okay?'

'Yet again, I don't see him pressing charges. This better all be worth it.'

'I'm beginning to wonder.'

'Where are you now?'

'On my way back to St Leonard's. Joe and his lads seem to be checking into a hotel at Haymarket. Beth's taken up position.'

'Is she . . . ?' Fox tried to find the right words. 'Do you trust her? I mean, is she a team player?'

'Look, she took her bollocking off Ricky. She knows she fucked up.'

'Does she?'

'What are you saying?'

'That part of town, there's no all-night garage.'

'So?'

'And the closest doesn't let anyone over the threshold after eleven, so she couldn't use their loos.'

'You saying she's lying?'

'I'm not sure what I'm saying. Maybe you could have a think, though.'

'Still got a bit of your old job stuck to the sole of your shoe, Fox?'

'I'm just wondering why she'd lie, that's all.'

The phone went dead. Fox stared at it. You did your best, he told himself, deciding to steer clear of St Leonard's for the time being and pointing the car in the direction of Fettes instead.

★ ★ ★

Rebus was in the canteen when Fox walked in. He gave a wave, and Fox, having bought a mug of tea and a sandwich, joined him.

'Want anything?' Fox asked.

'I'm fine. Been keeping your nose clean?'

'Not exactly. I decided to walk the route from

the alley back to the guest house.'

'And?'

'Joe Stark and the others were just departing, leaving behind one bruised and bloodied proprietor.'

'And?'

'And nothing.' Fox looked grim-faced. 'But we need to stamp on them eventually, don't we?'

'We do,' Rebus agreed. 'Even if it means getting them for something minor. Chief Constable won't be happy, but then it's not our job to keep a big cheery smile on his coupon.' Rebus paused. 'I get the feeling there's more. Cough up, Malcolm.'

'Beth Hastie was supposed to be on surveillance when Dennis took that walk. Her story is, she headed off for petrol and a call of nature. Only there's no all-night petrol station, meaning her story doesn't stick.'

'Maybe she did her business behind some bins and is too ladylike to admit it.' Rebus watched Fox's expression. 'You don't see her as ladylike? Okay then, she was tucked up in bed and can't say as much or she'd be consigned to one of those bins she didn't pee behind.'

'Maybe.' Fox bit into his sandwich. Tuna and sweetcorn. One kernel dropped on to the plate. He picked it up delicately and pushed it back between the two triangles of thin white bread. 'Anyway, I hope your day's been more fruitful.'

'I'm waiting for Darryl Christie to tell me who sold Lord Minton an illegal handgun. We're thinking the killer took it from him.'

'To use on Cafferty and Dennis Stark? Have

you talked with Cafferty yet?'

'The man is proving elusive.'

'Oh?'

'He's moved out of his house for the duration.'

'Isn't that suspicious in itself?'

'It's what I'd do.'

'They didn't find the bullet, did they?'

Rebus shook his head and waved again, this time towards Siobhan Clarke. She marched up to the table brandishing a sheet of paper. It was a photocopy of the note found in the alley. She slapped it down between the two men.

'Doesn't match,' she stated.

'Doesn't it?' Fox turned the note ninety degrees so it faced him.

'Howden Hall pinged it to a handwriting expert. Their best guess is, someone saw the Minton note in one of the papers or online . . . '

'And copied it?' Rebus concluded, sitting back in his chair.

'Meaning what?' Fox enquired. 'Another gunman? That hardly sounds likely. How many nine-millimetre pistols are being lugged around the city?'

'At least two?' Rebus pretended to guess.

Clarke was staring at Fox's bruised face. 'What the hell happened to you?'

'John did it when I wouldn't take the dog he was offering.'

'Seriously, though.'

'I got in a fight with one of Dennis Stark's bandits.'

'When?'

'Should I have a lawyer present before answering?'

221

Clarke turned her focus back to Rebus. 'You think it fits?'

'The two-gun theory? It fits with the bullet not being found. Couldn't be left behind or we'd have known straight away we were talking about a different gun.'

'And the note?'

'Was a fair copy. Whoever wrote it took a chance we'd not spot the differences — or else that it would take us a while to.'

'To what end?'

'To make Dennis Stark look like part of the pattern,' Fox said, realisation dawning.

'So everyone's back in the game,' Clarke added. 'Christie, Cafferty . . . ' She caught the look on Rebus's face. 'What?'

'I've asked Darryl Christie who might have sold a pistol to Lord Minton.'

'And now you're thinking it could have been Christie himself?'

'We're in danger of getting tied in knots here,' Fox complained.

'Because that's what someone wants, Malcolm,' Rebus agreed. As if on cue, his phone started vibrating. 'And here's Darryl himself.' He got up and walked over to the windows. They were large, and if not covered in grime would have given him a clear view out on to the adjacent playing fields.

'Yes, Mr Christie?' he began, pressing the phone to his ear.

'Didn't take as long as it could have,' Darryl Christie said, sounding pleased with himself.

'You've got a name for me?'

222

'He says he'll talk to you only because you're not a cop.'

'Will he do it in person?'

'At the Gimlet.'

'What time?'

'Eight tonight.'

'I'll be there. Does he have a name?'

'You can call him Roddy.'

'Then that's what I'll do.' Rebus ended the call and went back to the table. 'Eight tonight at the Gimlet.'

'Are we invited?' Clarke asked.

'Might bring back painful memories for Malcolm. Besides, our merchant of death doesn't want anyone with a warrant card.'

'Are you okay about that?'

Rebus nodded. 'But I'm happy to rendezvous with the pair of you later, if you like.'

'Oxford Bar at nine?' Clarke offered.

'Delightful,' Rebus replied.

20

It was as if the Gimlet had been vacated for their meeting, like an office with an IN USE sign placed on its door. There was a young woman behind the bar. Her bare arms were tattooed, as was her neck, and Rebus quickly lost count of her various piercings. She poured him a pint of heavy without being asked and placed it on the bar.

'First one is on Mr Dunn,' she announced. 'There won't be a second.'

'Cheers anyway,' Rebus said, hoisting the glass. There was a man seated at a table in the far corner of the large room. Sticky floor underfoot, a silent jukebox with its lights flashing, a puggy unplugged from the electrical socket. The TV on the wall above the sole occupied table was switched on and even boasted a tiny bit of volume. Sports chat, with the latest news scrolling beneath the seated presenters. Rebus wondered if its purpose was to stop the barmaid hearing anything that was said.

'Roddy?' he asked, approaching the table.

'If you like.' The man was shrunken, missing a few teeth. He could have been anywhere from mid forties to early sixties. Diet, alongside drink and smokes, had sucked the life from him. Ink stains on the back of his hands showed where ancient self-inflicted tattoos had faded. The blue veins stood out like cords. There was a packet of

Silk Cut on one corner of the table, the table itself next to a solid door that Rebus knew led to a rear courtyard, an unloved concrete space used by only the most dedicated nicotine addicts.

'Thanks for meeting me,' Rebus said as he pulled out a chair. Its cheap vinyl covering had been patched with silver insulating tape.

'Nice place, eh?' He made show of inspecting the decor. 'Your local, is it?'

The man stared at him with milky, uncertain eyes.

'Get you a refill?' Rebus persisted, gesturing towards what he took to be a rum and black. He was already wishing he'd exchanged the watery pint in front of him for a nip of whisky.

'One drink and I'm out of here, same as you.'

Rebus nodded his acceptance of this. 'New owner seems to be running the place down.' He looked around again. 'Word is, a supermarket'll buy the site. Davie Dunn fronting the deal so Darryl's name doesn't come up.' He winked, as if he were sharing gossip with an old confidant.

'Just ask your questions,' his companion muttered.

No more games, then. Rebus's face tightened, his eyes hardening. Hands on knees, he leaned in towards the man whose name was not Roddy.

'You sold a gun to Lord Minton.'

'Aye.'

'You knew who he was?'

'Not until I saw him in the papers.'

'How long after you met with him was that?'

'Less than a week.'

'Did he say why he needed a gun?'

225

'That's not how it works. He got word to me via an intermediary, I passed back the instructions. Two grand in a Lidl bag, put in the bin by the pond in Inverleith Park. Two hours later, he retrieves the same bag.'

'Containing a nine-mil pistol wrapped in muslin?'

The man nodded slowly and without emotion.

'How many bullets?'

'Seven or eight — not quite a full clip.'

Rebus studied him for a moment. 'Have you and me ever had dealings?' Roddy shook his head.

'You don't *look* familiar,' Rebus admitted.

'Biggest pat on the back I give myself — keeping under the radar as far as you lot are concerned.' His eyes met Rebus's. 'Know who you are, though. Know the sort of bastard you used to be.'

'Not so much of the past tense,' Rebus chided him.

'We done?'

'Not quite. You didn't speak to Minton? How did he find you in the first place?'

'Friend of a friend of a friend — that's how it usually works.'

'Someone he maybe put away in the past?'

'You tell me.'

Rebus wasn't sure it mattered. 'So he didn't say why he wanted a gun, but did he seem nervous?'

'I heard he was twitchy. He seemed fine when he dropped the money off, though.'

'You were watching?'

'Other side of the boating pond. Nice and casual on one of the benches. Waited till he was out of sight, then got over there pronto.'

'Did you hang around to see him come back?'

Roddy nodded slowly. 'I was curious, I suppose. He looked like a toff. Shiny shoes, expensive coat. And the way he carried himself — out of the top drawer, you could tell.'

'Far from your usual client? So what did you think when he was found dead?'

'I thought he obviously had reason to buy that gun.'

'Am I allowed to ask where you got it?'

'No.'

'What if I insist?'

'Do what the hell you like.'

Rebus allowed the silence to settle. He took another sip from the stale pint, knowing he wasn't going to touch it again after that if his life depended on it.

'Okay then,' he said eventually. 'One last thing: similar sales in the recent past.'

'It's been months.'

'How many months?'

'Seven or eight. Even then, it was a loaner.'

'So you got it back?'

Roddy nodded again. 'If it's been used, I don't want to know. But if they want to sell it back pristine, I give them a price.'

'Did Minton know that?'

A shake of the head. 'His was for keeps, right from the get-go. Are we finished here?'

'Is it worth my while trawling the records to find who you really are?'

The man tipped the dregs of his drink down his throat. 'As hobbies go, it would keep you busy — a bit like metal-detecting, but with nothing much to show for the effort.'

'Not even a few old coins?'

'Not even a rusty bottle-top, Mr Rebus.'

★   ★   ★

Cafferty had ventured to the Sainsbury's on Middle Meadow Walk, queuing behind too many students buying garlic bread and pasta salads. Back in his flat, he had eaten his own supper of cooked chicken slices, followed by a bag of green grapes, washed down with half a bottle of screw-top Valpolicella. He was beginning to wonder about the efficacy of hiding away like this. A decade or two back, he would have been scouring the streets, primed to face any situation that warranted his participation. Had the bullet spooked him? It had, though he was loath to admit the fact. Why was he still breathing? A fluke? A nasty recoil? A beginner's finger on the trigger? Or because the whole thing had been meant as warning only? Two inches from death, he reckoned he'd been. The zing of the projectile as it passed his head. The thud of impact and the sudden chalky cloud of plaster. And there he stood, numb and unprepared. The gunman could have taken aim and fired again, no problem. But he had run. Why? The obvious answer: it *had* been a warning. Or the shooter was toying with him, relishing this extended period of fear mixed with uncertainty. And what a time to pick, with Christie on edge and the Starks running amok. Perfect conditions for Cafferty to

228

make his move and reclaim his territory.

Instead of which, he cowered here, laptop open, screen awaiting his next search.

Rebus had been calling, but Cafferty hadn't answered. Rebus would know by now — know he was no longer at home. Would the investigators be trying to pin him for the murder of Dennis Stark? Unlikely — there had been another note, hadn't there? Then again, they might see the attack on Cafferty himself as part of the plan, the perpetrator trying to disguise himself as potential victim. No, Rebus would never be that stupid. But that didn't mean others wouldn't be taken in. Anything could be happening out there, and he had no means of knowing.

He had brought his passport with him from the house, and it struck him that he could simply jet off somewhere and leave the whole bloody circus behind. He'd been to Barbados, Grand Cayman, Dubai. He had old friends in all three. Warmer climes, where dirty money became clean money. Cafferty had plenty in various accounts. He could live out the remainder of his life very nicely. Then he remembered something Rebus had let slip — a lottery winner in . . . where? Linlithgow? Why had he mentioned that? He scratched at his forehead, then started a new search. His tongue felt furred from too much red wine, and he knew he'd better drink some water before he went to sleep.

Lottery winner. Linlithgow. Murder.

He clicked on the first result and started reading the news story. Michael Tolland . . . fortune, followed by double tragedy . . . wife dies, and then he's attacked by an intruder . . .

'Poor bugger,' Cafferty said. He stared at the photo of Tolland grinning next to his wife, the outsized cheque held in front of them, champagne at the ready.

'Michael Tolland,' he muttered, closing the page and clicking on the next link. Halfway down the screen, two words leapt out at him:

Acorn House.

Acorn House.

His lips formed the words silently and with slow deliberation, his eyes reduced to little more than slits. 'Is that what this is about? Holy Christ . . . '

There was still his passport, and the thought of escape. But now he had an inkling — an inkling, and the sudden need to know more.

★   ★   ★

Rebus was five minutes early getting to the Oxford Bar, but Clarke and Fox were already there. The tables were all taken, so they'd commandeered a space next to the toilets, where no one could listen in.

'You okay standing?' Fox asked.

'I still had the use of my legs last time I looked,' Rebus muttered. 'Pair of you on softies tonight?'

They both nodded, so he fetched the drinks: lime and soda, sparkling water, IPA, plus a couple of packets of crisps and some salted nuts.

'Cheers,' he said, opening one of the packs and laying it on the high circular table.

'We've already eaten,' Fox said.

'Nice, was it?'

'That tapas place on George Street.'

'Bit more salubrious than where I've just been.'

'How did it go?' Clarke enquired.

Rebus told them. He gave as good a description as he could of 'Roddy', but neither of them seemed able to place him.

'You think he's telling the truth about only selling the one gun?'

Rebus shrugged and dropped more crisps into his mouth. 'Plenty other dealers out there — doesn't have to have been local.'

'On the other hand . . . '

Rebus nodded. 'At least we'd know we were dealing with two different guns. Is Page going to go public with the copycat note?'

'I'm not sure,' Clarke admitted. 'It would put the public's mind at rest that we're not dealing with some crazed psychopath.'

'We are, though,' Fox corrected her. 'Even leaving Dennis Stark out of the equation.'

'Only other victim is Minton.'

'As far as we know.'

'Here's what I think,' Rebus interrupted. 'If it comes out that Dennis was killed by another hand, the dad is going to go even more berserk. Far as he's concerned, his son was targeted by the same person who went for Minton and Cafferty.'

'Except we're keeping Cafferty's note quiet,' Clarke interrupted.

'Thing is, right now the killer is some anonymous stranger and Joe has no idea how the victims connect. If we suddenly say, oh, Dennis was topped by someone who only wanted it to *look* like the same killer . . . '

'He'll draw up a list of likely suspects,' Clarke agreed.

'And have them dealt with,' Fox added quietly, taking a sip from his glass.

'Starting with Christie and Cafferty,' Rebus said. 'And that's when this whole thing goes nuclear.'

'I need to make sure Page understands this,' Clarke said.

'How did he react,' Fox asked, 'when you told him about the surveillance?'

'He was furious that no one had told him earlier.'

'Detective Chief Super must have been in the loop.'

Clarke nodded. 'But *he'd* been told it was to be kept under wraps.'

'By our imperial overlord?'

'The very same.'

'So you'll talk to Page?' Rebus asked.

'I'm doing it right now.' Clarke brandished her phone and headed for the door.

'And tell him about the gun,' Rebus called to her retreating figure, after which he sank another inch of his drink and scooped up a few nuts.

'So how are you, Malcolm?' he asked, chewing.

'Me?' Fox sounded taken aback by the question.

'Recovering from that hiding you took?'

'It only hurts when I laugh.'

'Can't recall seeing you laugh.'

'Exactly.'

'And things are going well with Siobhan? I'm only asking because I care.'

'We don't always see as much of each other as we'd like.' Fox paused. 'Well, as much as *I'd* like, anyway.'

'She's in love with the job, same as I was. How about you?'

'The job has its moments,' Fox was forced to concede.

'Moments aren't enough, though — everything about it should give you a buzz.'

'Is that how it was for you?'

Rebus considered this. 'The deeper into it you go, the more you find out — about yourself as well as everything else.'

'The miles you've got on the clock, you should be on *Mastermind*.'

'Pass,' Rebus said, checking his watch.

'Somewhere you need to be?'

'I'm just knackered. I'm not a young thing like you. And I'm not cut out for wallflower duties.'

'It's not like we're going to suddenly start snogging.'

'Glad to hear it,' Clarke said, standing behind Fox. She was stuffing her phone back into her shoulder bag.

'How happy was DCI Page to have his supper interrupted?' Rebus asked.

'Poor sod's still in the office. He agrees about the moratorium.'

'Is that what it is? A moratorium?'

'It's as good a word as any,' Clarke said. 'You

had any joy from Facebook and Twitter?'

'About the dog?' Rebus shook his head. 'Vet says space is at a premium in the surgery — he's all for handing Fido over to the cat and dog home tomorrow.' He paused. 'Unless some kind and sympathetic person steps into the breach.'

'I hate to say it,' Clarke commented, 'but you're barking up the wrong tree.'

'Aye,' Rebus conceded, 'and by no means for the first time in my life.'

★ ★ ★

Fox drove Clarke back to her flat, just off Broughton Street. She invited him up and they sat together on her sofa, drinking tea and listening to jazz. Eventually she rested her head against his shoulder. When the rhythm of her breathing changed, he realised she was asleep.

'Time you were in bed,' he said.

'Sorry,' she replied, opening her eyes and smiling. 'Do you mind?'

He kissed her on the lips, received a perfumed hug, and went back downstairs to his car. He took the road south through the city towards Cameron Toll, then turned right, skirting the Grange. Countless sets of traffic lights, all seemingly in cahoots — red followed by red followed by red. Greenbank Crescent at last, and then Oxgangs Avenue. There was a light on in his bungalow — the one in the hallway, set to a timer. Siobhan had laughed at him about it once — *You think a housebreaker's going to be fooled by that?*

But I've never been broken into, he said to himself. QED.

He parked on the short, steep driveway and got out, locking the car after him. He was most of the way to his door when he heard another door open and close — a car door. He turned and saw that it was Beth Hastie. She had a face like thunder. He'd seen the car parked kerbside but had thought nothing of it — someone visiting one of his neighbours. She must have laid herself flat across the front seats. Now she was shoving open his gate and striding towards him.

'Fuck is your problem?' she snarled.

'I didn't know I had one.'

'That's because you're a dickhead. Going behind my back, pouring your pish into Alec's ear.'

He realised he was studying her almost for the first time. Five-six, neither skinny nor visibly overweight. Looked like there was some muscle there — gym or maybe even a boxing club.

'Do you want to come in?' he asked into the silence.

'I wouldn't cross your threshold if you paid me.'

'Probably a no, then.'

She reached out and grabbed a fistful of his coat. 'I'm just about ready to do some *real* damage to that ugly puffed-up face of yours.'

The hand Fox placed over hers wasn't quite twice the size. He began to squeeze. She tried not to let pain show in her eyes, but eventually let go, at which point Fox did the same.

'You didn't take any comfort break at a local petrol station,' he intoned. 'Took me about five minutes to establish that. I went to Alec Bell with it because that was one way of keeping it from your boss. If you've got a different story you want to tell me, I'll happily listen.'

'I don't need to tell you a single solitary thing.'

'That's true.'

'So now you'll go crying to teacher, grass me up to Ricky?'

'Will I?'

'How else are you going to get a hard-on?'

'Whatever happened last night, Compston is going to work it out eventually — he won't need help from me or anyone else. He'll start to think about the coincidence: you leaving your post just before Dennis took his walk.' Fox paused. 'That *is* what happened? Or did you sleep through it?' He shook his head. 'No, because why lie? Being asleep is about as much of a lapse as taking a break. Want to tell me the truth, Beth?'

'You're screwing with a *team*, Fox. It's always going to be you against us — remember that.'

As if on cue, Fox heard another door open. Alec Bell must have been in the Audi with her. He too pushed open the gate, though without his colleague's pent-up sense of grievance. He was even smiling, sliding his hands into the pockets of his coat.

'I couldn't not tell her,' he announced with a shrug, eyes on Fox.

'And now the two of you are here to warn me to mind my own business?'

'We clear up our own mess, no outside help

required.' Another shrug.

Fox turned his attention back to Beth Hastie. 'I still need to know where you went, and why.'

But Alec Bell shook his head and placed a hand on Hastie's shoulder. 'We should be getting back, Beth.'

Her eyes remained fixed on Fox's. Bell's hand grew more insistent.

'Beth,' he said.

The spell seemed broken. She blinked and half turned towards him.

'Sure,' she said.

Then she twisted back towards Fox and flung her knee up into his unprotected groin. He doubled over, swallowing back a sudden urge to vomit. Pain flooded through him.

'You don't touch me,' Beth Hastie said, spitting on the ground in front of him. 'Nobody touches me.'

Alec just did, Fox would have countered, had he been able to speak. Instead of which, eyes blurred by tears, he watched Bell lead her back to the car. Then, slowly, painfully, and still stooped, he turned towards his own door and tried to find the lock with the key.

★   ★   ★

Over the wall.

Into a courtyard of some kind. Empty aluminium kegs. A barrel turned into a makeshift table. A single rickety bar stool. Two cheap overflowing ashtrays. Blocks of flats nearby. A dog barking. A starless sky.

237

The door was wooden and looked solid enough. He got to work on it with the crowbar. Locks top and bottom. Took a bit of effort. The alarm started blaring as he stepped into the narrow, low-ceilinged room. He held the first bottle in one hand, lighter in the other. Got the rag lit and tossed it high into the air. Glass shattering, the petrol spreading instantly across the linoleum floor. Second bottle for luck, aiming for the row of optics behind the bar this time. And then he was out of there, back over the wall to where his car was waiting. Two minutes since the alarm had started, neighbours probably still thinking it a mistake or malfunction, waiting for it to stop. He cruised past the front of the building, seemingly in no particular hurry as the windows of the Gimlet began to glow orange and then fiery red.

Day Six

21

'It's not every day someone offers to buy me breakfast,' Doug Maxtone said, sliding into the booth. Fox was stirring a latte in a tall glass. 'What happened to your face?'

'I tried breaking up a fight. They ended up swinging at me instead.'

'Did you report it?'

Fox shook his head and lifted the glass. Maxtone ordered a bacon roll and 'some good strong tea', then clasped his hands on the table in front of him.

'What's on your mind, Malcolm?'

The café was on Newington Road. It had been a bank or something. Fox had parked down a side street, across from a garage filled with hearses. He stared out through the window as he spoke.

'I can't do it any more, sir. Compston and his crew, I mean.'

'Has there been a falling-out?'

'They didn't do this, if that's what you mean.' Fox pointed towards his fading bruises. 'But there has been an incident — not with Compston himself, but a couple of his officers.'

'Does he know?' Fox shook his head. 'Want me to speak to him?'

'That's the last thing I want, sir. Besides which, they'll be on their way soon surely? With the son dead, some haulier and his ill-gotten gains will drop off Joe Stark's radar.'

'You might well be right. I've got a meeting with Ricky Compston this morning, as it happens. I'll be sure to put it to him.'

'You won't say anything about me, though?'

'Soul of discretion,' Maxtone assured him. Then, as his tea arrived: 'Did you hear about the pub getting torched?'

'No.'

'Some dive called the Gimlet, out Calder Road way. Insurance job, I suppose.'

'I wouldn't be too sure.' Maxtone looked up at him. 'It was owned until recently by Darryl Christie. He sold it on to a friend.'

'Well, somebody doused it in petrol last night and left not much more than a shell.'

'Sounds like a message to me.'

'From Joe Stark?'

'The man's spoiling for a fight.'

'They need to be told they're not welcome here. If you're right, and they've lost interest in the missing trucker, we can kick them back to Glasgow without upsetting the Chief Constable too much.'

Fox nodded, but without real enthusiasm. 'Joe Stark's grieving, though. That gives him good reason to hang around the investigation. If we chase him out of town, we're going to get called callous.'

'By our friends in the media? I think our skins are thick enough, don't you?'

'Yes, sir.'

The bacon roll was arriving. 'Looks good,' Maxtone said, taking a bite. 'You not eating, Malcolm?'

'Coffee does me most mornings.'

'So if you're not babysitting Compston's team, what am I going to do with you?'

'The Minton investigation could probably use another body.'

'Not the best turn of phrase,' Maxtone chided him. 'But you're right, it does seem to be growing into a monster. Want me to have a word with James Page?'

'I'd appreciate it.'

'Leave it with me.'

'And all for the price of a bacon roll,' Fox commented.

'We can always be bought, Malcolm,' Maxtone said with a wink. 'Some of us more cheaply than others . . .'

★ ★ ★

Fox sat in his car. A hearse was being valeted to within an inch of its life, two more having already left the premises at the start of another busy day. He pressed his phone to his ear and waited for an answer.

'John Rebus, Consulting Detective,' Rebus's voice sang out. 'What can I do for you this fine morning, Malcolm?'

'You at the Big House?'

'I'm in the flat, though I suppose technically that means I'm also in the office.'

'Any clients?'

'I'm a bit particular.'

'Mind if I drop by?'

'For a consultation? I don't come cheap, you know.'

'Need anything from the shops? Milk? Bread?'

'You silver-tongued devil — all right then, bring me some milk and we'll call it quits.'

★　★　★

'There was a time,' Fox said as they took their drinks through to the living room, 'when you wouldn't have let me past the front door.'

'Wasn't too long ago either,' Rebus agreed, settling in his chair. Fox made for the sofa, but then took a detour to the hi-fi instead, crouching down to flick through the albums.

'Getting pretty collectable, some of this stuff,' he commented. 'Or it would be if it was in better condition.'

'You suddenly an expert?'

'I've been known to browse eBay of an evening.' He got back to his feet and headed to the sofa, placing the mug on the carpet.

'Coffee not up to your usual high standards?' Rebus enquired.

'To be honest, I'm jangling enough as it is.'

'And why's that?'

'Remember I told you about Beth Hastie? Not being at her post when Dennis Stark left the guest house?'

'Yes.'

'Well I happened to mention to your old pal Alec Bell that her story rang false. Guess what he did next.'

'I'd imagine he told her.' Rebus lit a cigarette and leaned back in his chair, blowing smoke towards the discoloured ceiling. He had a sudden thought. 'If this is my office, am I even allowed to smoke? Government legislation and all that?'

'So then Hastie paid me a visit,' Fox ploughed on. 'She was in a right strop, too. Ended up kneeing me in the balls.'

Rebus winced in sympathy.

'Alec Bell practically had to drag her off me.'

'Not having much luck, are you?'

'No,' Fox was forced to agree. Then, after a pause: 'Can I try you with a wild theory?'

'You think Compston's team assassinated Dennis Stark?'

'Is it beyond the realms of possibility?'

'I've seen plenty in my time that would have seemed more outlandish.'

'So what do I do about it?'

'Find some cast-iron evidence. Failing which, get one of them to talk. Think you're up to accomplishing either of those?'

Fox bristled. 'You saying I'm not?'

'I'm saying you're all riled up. First Alec Bell watches you take a pasting and doesn't wade in to help, then Beth Hastie gets torn in about your gonads. You said it yourself — you're jangling. That's fine, means your juices are flowing. But you're supposed to be the rational one, the one who's always Mr Calm. Going into something because you're emotional . . . well, it's hardly playing to your strengths.'

'Are you saying I should drop it?'

'I'm saying take a step back. All you know right now is that Hastie lied to her boss, and that could be something or nothing. She could have

245

been off shagging Alec Bell or gone back to her scratcher for a kip.'

'Funny she's not around when Dennis gets whacked, though.'

'I don't disagree. But what you're saying is — she *was* around, and maybe she even did it.' Rebus paused. 'Is that right? Is that the way you're thinking? You're saying she didn't lie to Compston, she only lied to *you* in front of him because the team had to have a story to feed you.'

'Maybe.' Fox lifted the mug for want of anything else to do.

'Alec Bell and me, we're not mates,' Rebus said. 'I knew him for a short time too many years back. He's not going to confide in me.'

'He did, though — he told you there was a mole.'

'He was showing off, wanting you and me both to see how important he's become. He's not likely to do that again, not when there's a murder case at the back of it.'

'I suppose not.' Fox took a sip of coffee, trying to hide his disappointment.

'I'm not saying you shouldn't follow this up, Malcolm. Sometimes your first instinct is the right one. But you need to be careful. Ricky Compston has a mean streak — trust me, it takes one to know one. And he's surrounded himself with people who share at least some of his traits. I said you'd need cast-iron evidence, but let me put it another way: make sure it's bulletproof.'

Fox nodded slowly. 'Well, thanks for seeing

me. And for the coffee.'

'The coffee you've barely touched.'

Fox got to his feet. 'Do you need a lift to Fettes?'

'Is that where you're headed?'

'Doug Maxtone's going to get me attached to Siobhan's team.'

'Thanks for the offer, but I'll go in later.'

Fox made to leave, but paused before reaching the hall. 'You heard about the Gimlet?'

'What about it?'

'Someone torched it last night.'

'Anybody hurt?'

'I think it was after hours. A message from Joe Stark to Darryl Christie, maybe?'

'In which case his hotel might be next.'

'We always knew it would get messy. Maxtone reckons it's high time we ordered Stark and his thugs back to Glasgow.'

'He's got a point. Say hello to Siobhan for me — and bear in mind what I said.' Rebus was holding out a hand towards Fox. The two men shook. Having seen him out, Rebus went into the kitchen. His phone was charging on the worktop. He'd set it to silent. Two missed calls, both from Cafferty. He tapped callback and Cafferty answered almost immediately.

'Is this about the Gimlet?' Rebus asked.

'The Gimlet?'

'It got torched last night.'

'Nothing to do with that.'

'What then?'

'I need a favour. Can you meet me? Twenty minutes?'

'Where?'

'The G and V hotel.'

'Used to be the Missoni? Twenty minutes it is. Want to give me a clue what this is about?'

But Cafferty had already rung off.

★ ★ ★

As Rebus walked into the hotel, Cafferty waved to catch his attention. He was seated in the bar area, nursing a tall glass of tomato juice.

'This where you're holing up?' Rebus asked, sliding on to the banquette. Cafferty just tapped the side of his nose. 'Credit me with at least half a brain,' Rebus went on. 'The very fact that we're meeting here rules it out as your cave.'

'You know I'm not in the house, though?'

'Happened to be passing. Tried phoning you a couple of times too. Have you been on to Joe Stark to offer condolences?'

'He'd tell me where to stuff them.'

'What about Darryl Christie — spoken to him at all?'

Cafferty made show of checking his surroundings. 'Am I in an interview room here?'

'Whoever set light to the Gimlet had Darryl in mind.'

'Unless he did it himself for the insurance — you know he wants to sell the site?'

'I'd heard a whisper. I dare say you have an alibi for last night, just in case?'

'Why would I need one?'

'Because if Darryl didn't do it, he's obviously going to read it as a message from Joe Stark, and a dogfight between the two of them would make your year.'

'And I torched his place to ensure that came about?' Cafferty shook his head. 'Sorry to disappoint you.' He tipped the glass to his mouth.

'Any vodka in that?' Rebus asked.

'Enough to take the edge off.'

'It's early in the day, even for you.' A waiter was hovering, but Rebus waved him away. He noticed not just how tired Cafferty looked — there was something else there. The word 'haunted' sprang to mind. 'So what's this favour you need from me?' he asked, his tone a little softer.

'I don't want to get you into trouble,' Cafferty said. 'Not *this* sort of trouble. But I need to find these men.' He slid a paper drinks coaster towards Rebus. Two names written there in blue ink.

Paul Jeffries.

Dave Ritter.

Neither, at first glance, meant anything to Rebus. 'Okay,' he said, 'give me a clue.'

'They did a bit of work for me back in the eighties.'

'And they were last heard of when?'

'I bumped into Jeffries maybe fifteen years ago at a casino here in town. Just a couple of words in passing. Asked him what he was up to and he said something about driving. I had a taxi firm at the time so I said as much.' Cafferty paused. 'That was the extent of our chat.'

'Did he seem interested in the taxis?' Cafferty

shook his head. 'Another kind of driving, then — lorries, deliveries . . . ?'

'He didn't say.'

'Was he a regular at this casino?'

'He might have been — I wasn't.' Cafferty gestured towards the bar for another drink.

'And which casino was it?'

'Milligan's.'

'In Leith? Is that still there?'

'It's one of those super-pubs these days. Three floors of cheap booze.'

'Milligan's was run by Todd Dalrymple, wasn't it?'

'You've a good memory.'

'Wonder if he's still around.' Rebus scratched at the underside of his jaw. 'Right,' he said, 'description of Mr Jeffries . . . '

'Five-ten, maybe, short fair hair going grey at the temples, a gold tooth right at the front of his mouth.'

'Would he have a criminal record?'

'It's possible.'

'But nothing from when you knew him?'

'No.'

'Age?'

'By now he'd be in his mid fifties.'

'Last known address?'

'Thirty years ago he was with a bidie-in somewhere in Granton.'

'Name of bidie-in?'

'I've honestly been trying to remember.'

Rebus picked up the coaster and studied it. 'Then let's move on to Dave Ritter.'

'The two of them were old pals. I think they

were maybe at school together.'

'Where?'

'Somewhere in Fife.' Cafferty paused. 'They knew Fife pretty well.'

'Description.'

'Shorter than Paul. Maybe five-six or seven. Bit of a belly on him. Never far from a bag of chips. Longish straight hair, brown. Looked like a bad wig. He'd be the same sort of age, meaning mid fifties now. Don't remember anything about his love life. Didn't live too far from Paul either.'

Rebus waited, but Cafferty could offer only a shrug.

'That's all you've got?' he said as the fresh drink arrived and with it an unblemished coaster.

'Haven't seen Dave in nearly thirty years and didn't get round to asking Paul about him. To be honest, I probably only remembered him afterwards — he was the quiet one. It was Paul who did the talking.'

'How long did they work for you?'

'Three, four years.'

'In what capacity? Foot soldiers?'

'It's as good a phrase as any,' Cafferty conceded. 'I just thought — police computers, public registrar . . . maybe you could track them down.'

'And why would I bother doing that?'

'Because they might explain what's going on here.' Cafferty saw that Rebus didn't quite get it. 'The notes — me and Minton. Plus that care worker in Linlithgow, the one Siobhan Clarke was talking about.'

'You reckon he's part of it? And Dennis Stark too?'

251

'Stark?' Cafferty seemed genuinely confused.

'Dennis got a note. Add that to the nine-mil bullet hole . . . '

But Cafferty was shaking his head again. 'Nothing to do with him,' he muttered as if to himself. 'Joe maybe? No, not Joe either.' He regained focus, his eyes meeting Rebus's. 'That's got to be a mistake,' he said.

Rebus nodded. 'My thinking exactly. So maybe tell me *your* theory and let me be the judge.'

Cafferty ignored this. 'I had a quick look online but I didn't spot either Jeffries or Ritter. Phoned a couple of old lags, but they weren't any help.'

'What makes you think I can do better?'

'You're the straw I'm clutching at.' Cafferty managed a smile. 'That was my nickname for you — Strawman. Do you remember?'

'I remember.'

'You were giving evidence against me that one time in Glasgow, and they got you mixed up with another witness called Stroman.'

Rebus nodded. 'I really need to know what you want with those two men.'

'And I've told you.'

'Not enough for me to be convinced. Is there an angle here, something to do with Joe Stark?'

'Forget him.' Cafferty screwed up his face.

'Not easy when he's on the rampage. How long till he comes hard up against Darryl Christie?'

'Joe needs to be covering his own arse rather than kicking anyone else's.' Cafferty savoured a

252

mouthful of the Bloody Mary. 'With Dennis gone, there's bound to be some jockeying. Joe's surrounded himself with old-timers. They had reputations once, but they'd be no match for the lads on Dennis's payroll. Added to which, I can think of people in Aberdeen and elsewhere who might fancy a crack at Glasgow, now that a tin-opener's been taken to Joe's armour.'

'You've heard mutterings?'

'Didn't even need my ear trumpet.' He made eye contact with Rebus again and held it. 'You'll do this for me, John?' Pointing at the coaster Rebus was holding between thumb and forefinger.

'What do you think?'

'I think you'll have to, because otherwise those names will go on bugging you all the way to the grave.'

Rebus got to his feet. 'What did you mean, back at the start of our little chat? Something about not wanting to get me into trouble?'

'It's honestly best you don't know. Trust me — just this once. Will you do that?'

Rebus had seen much in his old foe's eyes down the years — guile, venom, darkness. But now he saw something else: uncertainty, tinged by fear. The glass was being raised again, its contents a prayed-for analgesic.

'You'll answer the phone when I call?' Rebus checked.

Cafferty nodded as he drained his drink.

22

'We should bring Beth Hastie in for questioning,' Fox told Clarke. They were in the incident room at Fettes, standing in the middle of the office, surrounded by an investigation that was all heat and no light. Clarke folded her arms, which Fox interpreted as a sign that he could continue. 'She was on surveillance outside the guest house. Her story is, she took a toilet break that just happened to coincide with Dennis Stark heading out. I don't buy it.'

'Why not?'

'She says she went to a nearby garage, but it's not open all night, and those that are don't let punters over the threshold past eleven or midnight. In any event, with Dennis murdered, shouldn't we be interviewing Compston's lot anyway? They've spent weeks tailing his every move. Might be they know something we need to know.'

'Malcolm, you've been attached to this inquiry five bloody minutes — tell me this isn't just payback of some kind.'

'It's not.' He nodded towards the door to Page's inner sanctum. 'At least take it to him, Siobhan. Not because it's me, but because it's the right thing to do.' He looked around the office. 'Unless there's some hot tip you're busy following up.'

'You know damned fine there isn't. But James

is up to his eyes — we've no idea if we should open a separate case for Dennis Stark. Soon as we do, his father's going to know there's another killer out there.'

'Well maybe I should just let you get back to finding the owner of Rebus's stray dog.' Fox waited, watching as Clarke deliberated.

'Okay then,' she said at last with a sigh, heading for the door.

'Should I . . . ?'

'Oh, you're coming too, Malcolm. This is your game plan, not mine.' As she knocked on the door, she saw Rebus enter the room from the corridor. She held up a finger to indicate that she was busy. Page called out from behind the door, and she opened it.

★ ★ ★

Rebus watched as the door closed on Clarke and Fox. He wandered over to Christine Esson's desk.

'What's up?' he asked.

'DI Fox has climbed aboard,' she explained.

'Looks like he's already making waves.'

'Choppy waters, at any rate.' She was chewing on the end of a ballpoint pen.

'How's the case?'

'You know what doldrums are?'

'Aren't they the opposite of choppy waters?' He watched her smile. 'So you're not too busy, then?'

'I've got no news about the dog, if that's what's on your mind.'

'It isn't.'

255

She leaned back in her chair to study him. 'Do I detect another favour in the offing?'

He placed a slip of paper on her desk. It detailed what little he knew about Cafferty's two names.

'I need anything you can get — police records; births, marriages and deaths; *anything*.'

She touched the note with her pen, as if reluctant to pick it up. 'How much trouble is this going to get me in?'

'None whatsoever.'

'But it's not connected to the Minton/Stark investigation?'

'It might be.'

'Care to elucidate?'

'The problem is, I can't. Not until I know a bit more about these two.' He patted the names with his finger.

'Why me?'

'Because you're IT-savvy. Me, I wouldn't know the first place to start.'

'Judging by the dates, this is going to wear out my shoe leather rather than my computer mouse. Old records, maybe not digitised yet . . . '

'Get Ronnie to help you.' Ogilvie was at a desk across the room, busy on a telephone but his eyes were on Esson and Rebus, curiosity piqued.

'And what do we say to Siobhan when she asks?'

'You're following up potential leads.' Rebus paused. 'No need to say they came from me.'

'Why doesn't that surprise me?' Finally she picked up the note and studied it. 'Leave it with me, then.'

'Magic,' Rebus said. 'When Siobhan comes out, tell her I'm in the cafeteria.'

Esson watched him as he retraced his steps, disappearing into the corridor. 'No, that's all right,' she muttered. 'I didn't want anything bringing back.' Then she turned her attention to her monitor and got to work.

Rebus was halfway down the corridor when he bumped into Detective Sergeant Charlie Sykes. A digestive biscuit was protruding from his mouth as he carried a pile of box files between offices. Rebus stopped in front of him, blocking his route. Reaching up a hand, he snapped off the visible section of biscuit and laid it on top of the uppermost box. Sykes scowled, chewing hard to try to free up his mouth.

'Still on the health kick, eh, Charlie?' Rebus enquired.

'Thought you were retired.'

'They've discovered that nothing gets done without me, which makes me almost your exact opposite.' Rebus studied the man. 'Nice suit, though — who's greasing your palm these days? Used to be Big Ger, didn't it?'

Sykes scowled. 'Everyone on the force knows who Cafferty's real friend around these parts was.'

Rebus shook his head. 'I'd better let you get on, Charlie. You'll want to keep looking like you're almost doing something useful.' He lifted the remaining sliver of biscuit and pushed it into Sykes's mouth, so that the man's curses were muffled as Rebus continued on his way.

★ ★ ★

Darryl Christie was dressed as though impervious to cold — well-tailored suit, open-necked shirt. The two men he had brought with him were swaddled in black zip-up jackets, gloves and baseball caps. West Parliament Square was the usual tourist bustle. St Giles' Cathedral loomed above Christie and his minders. Nearby stood the law courts and the City Chambers. This was the Edinburgh visitors craved, with the castle just up the hill and plenty of shops selling tartan and whisky. Joe Stark emerged from the direction of George IV Bridge. He wore a dark green raincoat and a red woollen scarf, with a white shirt and black tie beneath. Christie recognised the figures flanking him — Walter Grieve and Len Parker, both of them sporting a black tie. He gave a signal to his own men and they retreated towards the door of the Signet Library. Christie had peered through the door's glass panels earlier, noting legal types pacing to and fro, in whispered discussions with colleagues. The High Court of Justiciary was a one-minute walk away, not that Christie had ever been inside it.

Not yet.

Stark walked towards him, leaving his two old lieutenants behind. When he was a couple of feet from Christie, he nodded the curtest of greetings.

'Thanks for meeting me,' Christie said.

'Why here?'

Christie looked around. 'Nice and public,' he

ventured. 'Reckoned we'd both feel safer.'

Stark just grunted.

'I'm sorry about what happened to your son,' Christie went on, having more or less rehearsed these first few minutes. Stark glowered.

'What *did* happen to him?'

'Nothing I had any part of, I promise you. I've been keeping my distance, even though Dennis was trampling all over my territory.' Christie paused. 'That was out of respect for you, Mr Stark.'

'We're here until someone gives us a reason not to be,' Stark said. He had an old man's slightly milky blue eyes, but they contained plenty of menace still.

'You mean until someone hands you Hamish Wright?'

'It's what Wright took from us — that's what matters.'

'Plus finding whoever did for Dennis?'

'Police think it's a serial killer maybe.'

'Is that what you think?'

'Someone topped a lawyer. Not sure what that's got to do with my son.'

'They took a potshot at Cafferty, too. Did you know that? And I'm told Cafferty got a note.'

Stark's eyes narrowed a little further.

'Did Dennis know Cafferty at all?' Christie asked into the silence.

Stark shook his head.

'One more thing I need to tell you — I hear from one of my sources that the note left next to Dennis is a fake.' Christie paused to let this sink in.

'Are you fucking about with me?'

'I wouldn't dare. No bullet was recovered either, meaning the gunman almost certainly took it with him.'

'Why?'

'So it couldn't be checked against the one fired at Cafferty.'

'Different guns?' The old man nodded his understanding. 'Cops are keeping that quiet.'

'They'll have their reasons.'

'The fucker who did Dennis wanted it to look connected,' Stark mused, scratching at his cheek. 'But if it isn't . . . '

'You're looking for someone with a grudge.'

Stark peered at him. 'I'd have to put you on that list.'

'I don't doubt it. Dennis and his boys weren't very nice to my friends. Then my old pub gets torched just last night . . . '

'If you *did* put a bullet in my son, you'd have to have balls of granite to meet me like this.'

Christie offered a shrug. 'I'm telling you the truth, Mr Stark. But here's a thing — Dennis arrives in town, and almost immediately someone takes aim at Big Ger Cafferty.'

'That wasn't Dennis.'

'Big Ger may think differently.' Christie stretched out his arms. 'I'm just saying. You know he's gone AWOL?'

'What?'

'Not at his house. Not anywhere to be found, though he may be holing up in a hotel not a million miles from this very spot.'

Stark took a single step closer. 'You trying to

pit me against him, son? Cafferty's not a serious proposition these days.'

'Is that what you hear in Glasgow?' Christie smiled almost ruefully. 'Maybe he's just got better camouflage. Trust me on this — he's still in the jungle. All you have to do is ask around.'

Stark took a few seconds to digest everything he'd been told. Christie held out a hand for him to shake.

'Thank you for meeting me, sir. I meant what I said about respect.' When Stark's own hand was enveloped by the younger man's, the clasp turned into something more vice-like. Christie's eyes had darkened, his voice becoming steelier. 'But respect or not, if you have any thoughts about making a move on me or my city, best think again. There's no For Sale sign when you exit the M8.'

Stark snatched his hand away. He was rubbing it as Christie turned to go.

'Torching your pub,' Stark called out to him, 'was nothing to do with me — or with Dennis's lot. I asked them.'

Christie didn't look back. His minders fell into step beside him as he started to pass the law courts. His brow was furrowing, and he stabbed his hands into his trouser pockets for warmth.

'Everything sorted?' one of his men enquired.

'Getting there,' Christie replied after a moment's consideration, though he wasn't entirely sure he believed it.

Or Joe Stark.

★ ★ ★

Rebus sat in the Fettes canteen with tea and a ham-salad roll, his phone in his hand. His call to Milligan's Casino had been met with bemusement — nobody on duty had heard of Todd Dalrymple. But someone had laid hands on a telephone directory and a single Dalrymple T. had been found, along with an address — Argyle Crescent, in Portobello. Rebus was about to ring the number when Siobhan Clarke appeared. She got herself some coffee and a caramel wafer and pulled out the chair next to him.

'What was happening upstairs?' he asked.

'Malcolm thinks we should be interviewing Compston's team.'

'He's probably not wrong.' Rebus looked at her. 'But you're worried about his motives?'

'A little, yes.' She bit into the biscuit and started chewing.

'Is Page still going along with the plan?' Rebus asked.

'What plan?'

'Pretending the same attacker did for Minton and Dennis Stark both.'

'I'm not sure the Fiscal's office is enthusiastic — they see it as unfair on the family.'

'Thing is, family in this case means Joe Stark.'

'I know . . . ' She broke off, staring into the distance. Then: 'Any joy from the internet?'

It took Rebus a moment to work out that she meant the dog rather than the two names he'd given to Christine Esson. He shook his head.

'So what's keeping you busy today?'

'Couple of wee things,' he lied. 'Might be something or nothing.' He placed his phone on the table and lifted the tea. 'By the way, have you dismissed the possibility of a link between Minton and that Linlithgow attack?'

'Pretty much. Why do you ask?'

'Because Cafferty happened to mention it.'

'Oh?'

'The attacks on Minton, Cafferty himself and the guy in Linlithgow — he mentioned them in the same breath. And something else . . . '

'What?'

'The victim in Linlithgow . . . '

'Michael Tolland?'

Rebus nodded. 'Cafferty said something about him being a care worker.'

'He was.'

'Yes, but not knowing him, is that how you would describe him?'

'No,' she conceded.

Rebus nodded his agreement. 'You'd say 'millionaire', or 'lottery winner', right?'

'Right.'

'So why didn't Cafferty? It was like that wasn't what was important.'

Clarke thought for a moment. 'You think I should dig a little deeper?'

Rebus shrugged, but he knew the seed had been planted. 'So you're bringing in Compston and his crew, eh? Are there still tickets available?'

'I can probably get you on the guest list.' Her phone pinged, telling her she had a text. She checked her screen. 'Talk of the devil,' she said. 'Boss wants me in his office.'

'He can be a fast worker when necessary.'

She got to her feet, pushing away her coffee.

263

'You really think they'll give us anything?'

'Compston's gang?' Rebus pondered this. 'I very much doubt it.'

'Then why are we bothering?'

'Because it's the right thing to do.'

'That's pretty much word for word what Malcolm said.' Clarke smiled tiredly, gave a little wave and was gone.

Rebus turned his attention to his own phone. Should have looked in the phone book, John, he chided himself. Maybe Jeffries and Ritter were in there too . . .

'Hello?' The voice was deep and throaty. There was a dog barking somewhere behind it.

'Mr Dalrymple? My name's John Rebus. I'm calling from the police.'

'Oh aye?' Then: 'John B! Will you be quiet!'

'I was wondering if I could talk to you.'

The dog's barking had grown more insistent.

'He's wanting his walk,' Dalrymple apologised. 'I need to take him out.'

'I have a few questions about your time at Milligan's Casino,' Rebus ploughed on.

'Sorry, son, I can't hear a thing.'

'Maybe you could shut the dog in another room.'

'Give me your number and I'll phone you back. I'll only be an hour or two.'

'Where do you take him?'

'Eh?'

'John B — where do you go walking?'

'The Promenade usually.'

'I'll meet you there.'

'I'll be at the Joppa end, just down from James

Street. John B is hard to miss — twice the energy of any other dog on the beach. Just look for the doddery old bastard failing to keep up with him . . . '

23

The wind had died down and the temperature was a few degrees above freezing. The Promenade was a wide walkway which, towards Portobello, was fronted by fast-food takeaways, gaming arcades and bars. At the Joppa end, however, it was much quieter, with houses and flats facing the estuary. The tide was halfway out and the sand damp and pale yellow. There were views across to Fife, Cockenzie and Berwick Law. Plenty of dog-walkers. Rebus watched a huddle of dogs as they leapt at and past each other down near the surf. One was barking enthusiastically. It was a cross-breed with a short black coat, and seemed almost to be grinning in wonder at the world. A man a few years older than Rebus and dressed in tan cords and a Barbour jacket watched from the other side of the wall, whistling and calling out occasionally, to no effect whatsoever.

'Come here, John B! Come on, boy!'

Rebus took up a position next to Todd Dalrymple, facing the water. Dalrymple glanced at him.

'You the cop?'

'Why John B?'

'For John Bellany.'

'The painter?'

'He grew up in Port Seton. I always loved his fishing boats . . . ' Dalrymple blew his nose noisily. 'You got a dog?' He watched Rebus shake his head. 'You should. They're proven to add years to your life — if they don't give you a heart attack first.'

'They need exercise, though. I'm not really the type.'

'Good excuse to get away from the wife for an hour — and plenty of pubs accept dogs.'

'I'm suddenly warming to the notion.'

Dalrymple's eyes creased in a smile. 'So what can I do for you, officer?'

'It's a bit of a long shot. You'll know Big Ger Cafferty?'

'I know the name.'

'He used to drop by Milligan's.'

'Not too often.'

'He bumped into an old acquaintance there fifteen years or so back, guy called Paul Jeffries.'

Dalrymple started calling for John B again. Rebus got the feeling he was playing for time while he considered his response. Eventually he turned his head towards Rebus.

'I knew Paul,' he said. 'He worked for me.'

Rebus tried not to show his surprise. 'In what capacity?'

'Driver. I'd lost my licence, and he offered.'

'You knew he used to do jobs for Cafferty?'

'He told me.'

'Any idea what sort of jobs?'

'Driving. Why the sudden interest?'

'When did you last see him, Mr Dalrymple?'

'Three weeks back.'

Rebus gave a little cough as he tried to hide his surprise.

'He's in a care home — actually more of a hospice. Not much left up here.' Dalrymple tapped his forehead with a gloved finger.

'I'm sorry to hear that. He's still in the city, then?'

Dalrymple nodded. 'You've not said what's going on.'

'Does the name Dave Ritter mean anything to you?'

'Pal of Paul's, wasn't he? Remember him being mentioned.'

'You didn't meet him, though?'

'Don't think so. Did you ever go to Milligan's in its heyday?' He watched Rebus shake his head. 'Some wild nights we had. Place heaving, tables full and punters waiting their turn. Off the oil rigs and pockets full of cash, plus workers from the Chinese restaurants — those guys knew what they were up to; they'd watch a new croupier to see if they had any weaknesses. Beautiful women visited too, dressed to the nines — not too many of them on the game. Businessmen ordering champagne and expensive cigars . . . '

'I'm surprised Cafferty never tried getting his feet under the table.'

'He made overtures. But he soon realised I was no slouch.'

'I knew you ran the place — but you owned it, too?'

'Started off with loans from my family — not that they necessarily liked the business. I cleared those debts soon enough, though. Aye, it was my place all right.'

'How long did Paul Jeffries drive for you?'

'Two, three years.'

'Then what?'

Dalrymple shrugged. 'He still came by. Bit of a rough diamond, our Paul. He never divulged how he was making a crust.'

'He left or you fired him?'

'I think the job just wasn't as exciting as he'd hoped for.'

Rebus looked Dalrymple up and down. 'You're well-educated, I can tell, and you come from money. No disrespect, sir, but I'd say you wouldn't have had much in your arsenal if Cafferty had really wanted to put the moves on you.'

Dalrymple offered the thinnest of smiles. 'I had friends, officer. Quite a lot of friends. They gambled, ended up owing money. I'm talking about people of influence, politicians and the like. Maybe even a Chief Constable or two . . . '

'Making you untouchable?'

'I was able to persuade Big Ger that it would be more trouble than it was worth, should he attempt to unseat me.'

Rebus nodded his understanding. 'I don't suppose David Minton was one of your punters?'

'He came in a couple of times — always with a gorgeous young woman on his arm, as if that would stop us noticing that the fairer sex weren't his primary interest.' John B was in the water now, but unable to persuade the other dogs to follow. 'I think we might need to make an intervention,' Dalrymple said with a sigh. He led Rebus through a gap in the wall on to the sand, tugging a dog lead from the pocket of his coat.

'Can you give me the name of the care home?' Rebus was asking. 'The one Mr Jeffries is in?'

'Absolutely. But I'd be grateful for some sort of thread through the labyrinth.'

'Meaning?'

'Meaning what the hell is this all about?'

'I'm unable to say at present.'

'You almost sound as if you don't know.'

Rebus didn't like to admit that this wasn't exactly wide of the mark. John B meantime had decided to welcome his owner's new friend by shaking himself free of seawater in Rebus's vicinity.

'Probably should have warned you about that,' Dalrymple said as Rebus glared at the dog.

★   ★   ★

'Compston refused point blank,' Clarke told Fox. 'You can imagine how that went down. Give James Page his due, he got straight on to the Chief Constable.'

'And?'

'Told him it wouldn't look good if it got out to the media — police surveillance on Dennis Stark and the officers involved are refusing to cooperate with the murder inquiry.'

'Not that the news would ever leak.'

'Perish the thought,' Clarke said.

'I'm sure DCI Page said as much.'

She nodded slowly. 'So now Compston and the others are on their way here.'

'No more mayhem to report in the interim?'

'Not that I've heard.'

'What do you think Joe Stark is doing?'

'Seething.' She thought for a moment. 'And plotting. He's already given an interview to a tame Glasgow journalist. Accuses us of sitting on our hands.'

'I've not seen much evidence of that.'

They were at the bottom of the staircase now, on the ground floor of Fettes. They emerged from behind the reception desk into the waiting area. Glass walls gave a view on to Fettes Avenue. Clarke checked the time on her phone.

'By the way,' she said, 'James isn't happy about you taking part in the interviews.'

'Why not?'

'Because until this morning you were attached to Compston's team. You're just too close to it all.'

'That's precisely why I should be in the room!'

'You can listen to the recordings. Anyone tells me something you know to be a lie, you let me know.'

'That's hardly the same thing.'

'I know, Malcolm, but James is right.' She stared him out. He exhaled and slumped on to one of the seats. Clarke touched her hand to the back of his neck. 'You know he's right,' she went on.

'Don't tell me John bloody Rebus is invited, though?' Fox folded his arms, defying her to give him bad news.

'He'll be backstage, same as you. In fact, I should let him know they're on their way.'

But when she called, Rebus didn't pick up.

271

'Here they come,' Fox warned her, as two cars he recognised roared into the driveway. 'And while I'm no expert in automotive technique, I'd say they're not at their sunniest . . . '

★　★　★

Rebus had phoned Cafferty with the news, mostly because he felt smug. It had taken him only a couple of hours of old-fashioned detective work. The online world could stuff that in its pipe and vape it. But when Cafferty had asked for the address, Rebus had backed off a little.

'I need to be there when you see him,' he had demanded.

'No you don't,' Cafferty had countered. 'You know I'll track him down by myself if I have to. It'll take time, though, time that could see the mortuary filling up . . . '

Rebus dismissed the threat. 'I go with you, or I end this call right now.'

He waited, letting the silence build. He imagined Milligan's at the height of its popularity, a poker game in progress, everything in and just two players left. Fine clothes, laughter and swirling smoke, all rendered meaningless in the moment.

The phone went dead. Rebus stared at it and gave a rueful smile. His Saab was on one of the side streets off the Promenade. He smoked a cigarette as he walked in that direction, keeping the phone in his other hand. With the cigarette clamped in his mouth, stinging his eyes, he dug out his car key and unlocked the doors. Got in

272

and slid the key into the ignition. Sat there with the door open until he had finished the cigarette. He stubbed it into the ashtray and closed the door, starting the engine.

His phone started ringing. He checked who was calling. Siobhan Clarke. He let it ring. The road was a dead end, so he did a three-point turn and headed away from the beach, towards Portobello High Street, thinking maybe he should have treated himself to a fish supper. His phone rang again as he was turning right, entering the stream of traffic heading towards the city.

Bingo.

'Yes?' he said, answering.

'Fine,' Big Ger Cafferty spat. 'Let's do it your way. Give me the address and I'll meet you there.'

Rebus calculated that it would take him twenty or thirty minutes to get to the care home. 'I'll phone you back in ten with the details,' he advised. 'Make sure you're ready.'

'I've already got my coat on.'

Rebus ended the call.

He was actually only five minutes away from his destination when he sent Cafferty the text. Meadowlea was a modern single-storey building in the Grange, within tottering distance of Astley Ainsley hospital. A phone call had confirmed that Paul Jeffries was both a resident and in a bad way.

'Early-onset dementia with a host of complications — we're more what you might call a hospice than a regular residence,' Rebus was informed.

He waited in the car park for almost fifte

minutes before the black taxi chugged through the gateway, depositing a scowling Cafferty.

'You waiting for a proficiency badge or something?' Cafferty said.

'A word of thanks might be in order. But I'll settle for an explanation.'

'Here's what you get instead — you get to stand outside the room while I have a word.'

But Rebus shook his head. Cafferty made an exasperated sound and stepped past him. He tried yanking the glass door open, but it was locked tight. Rebus pressed the buzzer and waited.

'Yes?'

He leaned in towards the intercom. 'I phoned earlier. We're here to see Mr Paul Jeffries.'

'In you come, then.'

This time the door opened for Cafferty. He stood with hands clasped behind his back, looking to left and right. There were long corridors, protected by further doors. Rebus could smell disinfectant. The antechamber they were in held two chairs and one oversized pot plant. It looked to Rebus like a palm tree of some kind, its thick leaves dark green and shiny.

One of the doors opened and a staff member dressed in white gestured for them to follow her.

'This is nice,' she said. 'Paul doesn't get many visitors.' She took one look at Cafferty's face and became less certain. 'You *are* friends of his?'

'I'm just a sherpa,' Rebus explained. 'But Mr Cafferty here knew Paul some years back.'

They stopped outside a door with the name 'Paul' on it. The attendant knocked and turned the handle. It was a self-contained space with a bathroom off. A hospital-style bed against one wall, but also a fireplace with two chairs and a TV/DVD. A man was seated in one of the chairs, staring at a darts match but with the sound turned off.

'You were told he might not say anything?'

Rebus nodded and thanked the woman, ushering her out and closing the door on her offer to bring some tea. Cafferty stood in front of Paul Jeffries, then bent down so his face was at eye level.

'All right, Paul?' he said.

The room was stifling. Rebus removed his coat and took a look around. No mementoes from the resident's life. Just a few films and TV shows on DVD, and some fake flowers in a vase. There were no paintings or photos on the walls. A radio sat on a bedside cabinet, along with a jug of water and a glass.

Cafferty was waving a hand in front of the man's face. The eyes blinked without evident recognition. Cafferty clicked his fingers a few times, then clapped his hands together. The seated man flinched, but tried seeing past the blockage to where the darts match was still being played. Cafferty straightened up, picked up the remote and killed the picture.

'Paul, you prick, it's me,' he rasped.

But the blank screen was now enjoying the seated figure's attention. The man was dressed in jogging pants and top, maybe with a T-shirt beneath. Disposable clothes — cheap; easy to get on and off. There were food stains down the

275

front, and one of Jeffries' hands cupped his groin. Facially, the man was as Cafferty had described him, but older, almost drained of vigour, and his shrunken cheeks indicated that he had lost his teeth at some point and was not currently bothering with dentures. Cafferty looked at Rebus.

'Early-onset dementia,' Rebus explained.

'Maybe a slap would jolt him out of it.'

'I doubt it's a recognised medical technique.'

Cafferty too was feeling the heat. He kept his coat on, but mopped his brow with the sleeve.

'It's about Acorn House, Paul,' he told the seated figure. 'Remember Acorn House? Remember what happened? Don't think you can just sit there, you bastard!' He grabbed Jeffries by the shoulders and shook him. There was no resistance, and Rebus feared the man's neck might snap. He stepped forward and pulled Cafferty away.

'Christ's sake,' he said.

Cafferty looked as if someone had hooked him up to the mains. 'There's no way he doesn't know we're here or what this is about,' he spat. 'Fucker's just putting on a show!'

He wrestled free of Rebus and was hauling Jeffries to his feet when the door opened.

'Brought some tea anyway,' the attendant was saying. She dropped the tray when she took in the scene, her mouth opening in a silent gasp.

'It's not what you think,' Rebus said, knowing how ridiculous he sounded. The woman had fled back into the corridor, presumably to fetch the cavalry. 'We've got to go,' he told Cafferty.

'Not yet.'

'Look at him, for God's sake. That's an empty shell you're holding.'

Cafferty relented and dropped Jeffries back into his chair. But he had the man's slack-jawed attention now. Cafferty got in so close they were almost touching noses. 'Don't think you've seen the last of me, Paul. I'll be dropping by one of these nights, and we'll have our little chat then. Just the two of us.'

Rebus, coat tucked under one arm, led Cafferty out of the room and back down the corridor. They had reached the vestibule by the time the attendant hove into view from the opposite direction, bringing a good-sized male colleague with her. Rebus pulled open the front door and shoved Cafferty out, then closed it again so that the lock clicked, leaving him still inside.

By the time it dawned on Cafferty, it was too late. Rebus turned to face the two attendants, hands held up in appeasement.

'Sorry about that,' he said. 'Just a bit of rough and tumble to try and shake him out of whatever torpor he's in.'

'We have CCTV,' the male said, pointing towards the cameras on the ceiling. 'We'll be reporting this.'

'As is right and proper,' Rebus said. Cafferty started shaking the door, trying to force it open. 'But if you want me to calm that beast out there, just tell me if Mr Jeffries gets any other visitors.'

The man and woman shared a look, flinching when Cafferty's foot connected with the door.

'Mr Dalrymple's not been in for a few weeks,' the male blurted out.

'But then there's the other gentleman,' his colleague added. 'Only comes by once or twice a year. They used to be at school together, I think. Lives in Ullapool.'

'Does he have a name?' Rebus asked. 'Dave Ritter, maybe?'

'Ritter?' Nods from both heads. 'Sounds about right.'

Rebus turned and unlocked the door, blocking Cafferty from going back in. Once outside, he closed it again and started leading Cafferty towards his car.

'I've got something,' he said.

'What?'

'Calm down and I'll tell you.'

'Tell me now.'

'Get in,' Rebus said instead, unlocking the Saab. He rolled the window down and lit a cigarette.

'Give me one,' Cafferty demanded from the passenger seat.

'You don't smoke.'

'Never too late to start.' Cafferty gestured with his fingers, but Rebus showed him that the pack was empty. Cafferty cursed under his breath. 'So tell me what you got.'

'You first — what's Acorn House? And why does it ring a bell?'

Cafferty leaned back against the headrest. 'I'm going to say it just once more — you don't want to know.'

But Rebus knew now. 'It was some sort of remand home, wasn't it? I remember going once with a posse from Summerhall. Couple of kids there thought they were the pickpocket equivalent of Butch and Sundance.' He stared at Cafferty. 'That's the place we're talking about, yes?'

Cafferty was scowling at the windscreen as if ready to punch it. 'Yes,' he eventually conceded.

'Michael Tolland used to work there?' Rebus guessed. 'That's why him being a care worker clicked with you?' He nodded to himself. 'And Jeffries and his pal Ritter — they . . . what?' He paused, running his hands around the steering wheel as he thought. 'It closed down, didn't it? Acorn House? Sometime in the late eighties.' He turned to look at Cafferty. 'What is it I'm not seeing? David Minton, he'd have been an advocate back then, wouldn't he? Running for Parliament but not getting in.'

'You're seeing all the small stuff,' Cafferty said, pressing his thumbs to his temples. 'Let's go have a drink somewhere so I can start to tell you the rest . . . '

24

'I don't want this taped,' were Ricky Compston's first words as he sat down in the makeshift interview room. Fettes, having been Lothian and Borders' HQ, had always been an admin base rather than a working police station — no cells, no IRs. Siobhan Clarke had borrowed some recording equipment and set it up on the table. But now Compston was folding his arms in a show of defiance. 'I'm running a covert operation,' he went on, 'and that could be put in jeopardy by the smallest leak.'

'You're not stopping the surveillance?' James Page asked. He had slipped out of his jacket and rolled up his shirtsleeves, to show that he meant business. Paperwork was heaped in front of him, topped by crime scene photos and post-mortem shots of the victims.

'Not until the boss gives the word.' Compston turned his attention to Clarke. 'That machine goes on, I walk — don't say you weren't warned.'

'This is your idea of cooperation?' she shot back.

Compston fixed her with a stare. 'Joe Stark has just had a meeting with Darryl Christie. What happens next I can't tell you, because you've pulled my team in here, which is the last place they should be. So yes, DI Clarke, to answer your snotty little question, I'd say I'm cooperating.'

'Dennis Stark managed to get himself killed on your watch,' Clarke commented.

'Thanks, I hadn't noticed.'

'Beth Hastie had the surveillance on her own — is that standard practice?'

'Ideally she'd have had company.'

'Why didn't she?'

'Joe and his cronies had gone to Glasgow. I had to split the team. Left us a bit short.'

'But she wasn't outside the guest house when Dennis went for his stroll. His colleagues tell us it was something he often did.'

Compston nodded. 'Happened a couple of times,' he agreed.

'Yet Hastie still deserted her post? She didn't bother phoning to try and arrange cover?'

'It was the middle of the night. We were exhausted. Probably no one would have answered anyway.'

'But she didn't try,' Clarke persisted.

Compston looked from Clarke to Page and back again. 'Hell's going on here?' he demanded.

'A murder inquiry.'

'Gobby little thing, isn't she?' Compston said to Page.

'DI Clarke is a bit more than that, I think you'll find,' Page retorted.

Compston gave a theatrical sigh. 'We screwed up, and don't think we don't know it. I take full responsibility and have already told the Chief Constable as much.'

Clarke was tapping her pen lightly against a fresh pad of lined paper. 'How do you reckon Dennis Stark ended up dead?' she asked.

'A nine-mil bullet, if I'm not mistaken.'

'Did he just get unlucky, though? Goes for a stroll, ends up bumping into a stranger who shoots him? How likely is that?'

'Not very,' Compston conceded. 'One way or another, he was targeted.'

'One way or another?'

'Well, you've got this killer leaving notes next to his victims . . . '

'Actually, the victims usually receive the notes well beforehand. That was one mistake Stark's killer made.'

'Oh?'

'Not the same handwriting,' Page revealed.

'Copycat?' Compston mused.

'Someone with a grudge,' Clarke said, 'who thought they could make us think it was the same person who killed Lord Minton.'

'Which partly explains our interest in your team,' Page added. 'What would you say if I told you Detective Constable Hastie had lied to you?'

'I'd say I don't believe you.'

'She had to answer a call of nature, yes? At a nearby petrol station?'

Compston rolled his eyes. 'This is that sneaky fucker Fox, isn't it?'

'There are no all-night garages nearby,' Clarke went on.

'So?'

'And the ones that *are* open don't let customers use the loos.'

'I'm none the wiser.'

'Whoever followed Dennis Stark to that alley, they knew there was a chance he'd be out and about at that time, but they couldn't know the surveillance wasn't operational.' Clarke paused. 'Could they?'

Compston got her meaning and guffawed. 'You're saying *we* did it? After years of concerted operations to bring down the whole gang, my team suddenly decides on drastic action that'll result in anything but?' His eyes flitted between Clarke and Page. 'Do you know how ridiculous that sounds?'

'It's just a coincidence, then? Hastie does a vanishing act, Dennis goes for a walk, and the killer is waiting for him?'

'Makes a damn sight more sense than what you're suggesting.' Compston was getting to his feet. 'I've had more than enough of this. There's work waiting for me in the *real* world. I'll leave you to your unicorns and marshmallow skies.'

'We need to talk to Beth Hastie first,' Clarke stated.

'Why?'

'Because she doesn't seem to have been entirely truthful. That story she spun might have been for *your* benefit. Then again, maybe it was only meant for DI Fox. Maybe you already knew she wasn't going to be outside the guest house.'

Compston was shaking his head, but he gave another theatrical sigh. 'If Beth stays, can the rest of the team get back on duty?'

'I'd like you to wait behind,' Page said. 'We may have a couple more questions.'

'Absolute waste of time,' Compston muttered, which Clarke took as agreement.

$\star$ $\star$ $\star$

A five-minute break between interviews, just long enough for a quick coffee and confab. They'd stuck Hastie in the room and confiscated her phone so she wouldn't have a chance to be briefed by her boss. Compston was in the waiting area, having given orders to his troops and dispatched them.

'Is this getting us anywhere?' Page asked. 'I'd hate to think we're rattling their cages just for the hell of it.'

Clarke offered a shrug.

'Fox has some sort of grievance, doesn't he? That smack on the face he got . . . '

'He may have a grievance, but he also has a point. The story he was given doesn't quite chime. Besides which, it makes perfect sense for us to want to question the team who supposedly had eyes and ears on the victim.'

'Fair enough.' But Page didn't sound wholly convinced. He drained his cardboard cup. 'Let's get back, then.'

Beth Hastie did not object to a recording being made. Clarke quickly realised that this was because she had come prepared with a script.

'I got bored and went for a drive, that's the truth of it. Thought half an hour wouldn't hurt and it would help me stay awake.'

'Where did you go?'

'Down to the waterfront, along the coast a little ways, then back.'

'And this just happened to coincide with Dennis Stark leaving the guest house?'

'That's right.'

'You can see that might look like an almighty coincidence?'

'I suppose. Doesn't mean it's not what happened, though.'

'Have you owned up to DI Compston?'

'I will, soon as I get out of here.'

'You knew Dennis had trouble sleeping? That he sometimes took a night-time walk?'

Hastie shook her head. 'Nobody'd mentioned it. That was my first time on the all-nighter.'

'Nobody'd mentioned it?' Clarke sounded disbelieving, but Hastie was shaking her head again to stress the point.

'Here's the thing I keep thinking, though,' she went on. 'If I *had* been there, I'd have followed him on foot. And if I'd done that . . .'

'You'd have maybe stopped the killing from happening?' Page guessed.

She stared at him. 'No,' she said. 'What I mean is, maybe he'd have had to shoot me too. Which is why I'm actually bloody relieved I took that drive. If I hadn't, I might be on a shelf in the mortuary, right next to Dennis Stark.'

She sat back in her chair, almost shivering at the thought.

★ ★ ★

Joe Stark arrived at Fettes with one of his own men — Walter Grieve — and one of Dennis's. It had been Grieve's idea to bring Dennis's lads into the fold — last thing they needed now was bad blood. Jackie Dyson had been chosen

285

because he was the only one Joe hadn't had cause to bad-mouth or hand a slap to in the past. A relative newcomer, which, Grieve argued, meant he might be more approachable, 'if you get my drift'.

Yes, Joe knew these were delicate days. Dyson and the rest would be starting to wonder where their loyalties lay. Did they team up against the old order, or did they fall into line? He'd already given them a few quid to tide them over, promising them strengthened roles in the organisation. All the same, it didn't hurt to bring Dyson along, get to know him a bit better during the car ride, massage his ego. Then the punchline:

'If you want to see gratitude, son, I'll show it to you. You hear whispers or mutterings, you bring them to me. *That's* when you'll see me at my best.' Accompanied by a wink and a pat on the knee.

They parked in front of the main building and got out, Stark and Grieve in suits fit for a funeral, Dyson in scuffed denim and leather. As they reached the door, a couple emerged. Stark met the man's eyes but said nothing. But he watched as the pair headed towards their own car.

'That's Ricky Compston,' he told Grieve.

'Thought I knew him.'

'Who's Ricky Compston?' Dyson asked.

'Used to be Glasgow CID. Last I heard, he was being promoted to a desk at Gartcosh.' Halfway through the door, Stark stopped again. 'Gartcosh,' he muttered to himself. 'Serious and

286

Organised Crime . . . '

'Are we wondering what he's doing across this side of the country?' Walter Grieve asked, without really needing an answer.

'Bastards are after us,' Stark stated, baring his teeth. 'Heard about Dennis and think we're vulnerable.' He exited the building again and cried out to the rapidly retreating figures. 'Hey! Compston!' The woman half turned but the man did not. Stark flicked the Vs anyway and stomped inside.

The civilian on the reception desk recognised him and tried to smile.

'We're here to see Page,' Stark demanded.

'Do you have an appointment?'

'My son's been murdered — what good is a fucking appointment to me?'

The woman flushed. 'I think he's busy,' she eventually managed to say. But by then it was too late. Stark had walked around the desk and was making for the stairs beyond.

'You can't do that!' she said.

'He already has,' Dyson informed her, making to follow.

The group of three reached the first floor and asked the first person they saw where Page was.

'Next floor up.'

So that was where they went. Page was in the corridor ahead of them, talking to a woman weighed down by case notes.

'Page!' Stark snapped. 'I need to talk to you!'

'How did you get in?'

'Do we do it here, or somewhere a bit more private? Either's fine by me.'

287

Officers had appeared at the end of the corridor behind Stark and his men. They looked ready to intervene, but Page waved them away.

'My office,' he said to Stark. 'Just you and me, though.' He led the way through the incident room while the squad gawped from their desks, all except Charlie Sykes, who was busy composing a text on his phone. Grieve and Dyson looked set to linger in the outer office, but Clarke ushered them back into the corridor, closing the door on them.

'Charming,' Grieve said.

'I'm going for a piss,' Dyson told him. There was a toilet a few yards away, and he walked in. Just the two urinals and one cubicle. He unzipped and started whistling tunelessly, stopping when the door opened. The new arrival took the urinal next to him and uttered a greeting. Then the two men's eyes met.

'I know you,' Dyson said. 'Flattened you outside that pub . . . You're a *cop*?'

'What the hell are you doing here?' Malcolm Fox exclaimed, zipping himself up and taking a pace back towards the sink.

'Mr Stark has something he needs to get off his chest. Brought me along for company.'

'I saw Walter Grieve outside, but I never thought . . . '

'You seem to know all about us,' Dyson said slyly, finishing up and turning towards Fox. 'All I know about you is I almost broke your face. I'm wondering now why you didn't identify yourself as filth at the time. And also why I'm still on the street — you didn't report it?'

He moved past Fox and started washing his hands.

'Compston didn't tell you about me?' Fox asked. 'I'm Malcolm Fox. Local liaison.'

'Compston? I heard that name outside just now. It's true, then? There's a team from Gartcosh over here to put the screws on us?'

'Look, I know who you are. You're Jackie Dyson. I mean, I know that's the name you're using — '

'What the hell are you talking about?'

'I'm talking about keeping in character. I can appreciate you have to, but — '

Dyson spun around from the sink and shoved Fox so hard he went through the unlocked cubicle door.

'Am I hearing you right?' he snarled. 'You saying the cops have got someone in our team?'

Fox swallowed. 'No,' he managed to say. 'That's not what I — '

But Dyson wasn't listening. Hands still dripping, he had hauled open the door to the corridor and was gone. Fox lowered himself on to the toilet seat. His heart was racing.

It's the right guy, he said to himself. It's got to be. Alec Bell told me as much . . . He broke off, swallowing hard. *Could Alec Bell have lied?*

★ ★ ★

Ricky Compston was pummelling the steering wheel with the heel of one hand as he drove.

'All that work, all that planning . . . '

'You really think we're screwed?'

289

'Reason I've been doing minimal stake-outs is that I'm the one person Joe might have clocked. Then we walk right into him.' He shook his head, anger fighting despair. 'And we should *never* even have been there in the first place! I blame Page, and above all I blame Malcolm Arsehole Fox.'

'Person you should really be blaming is me,' Hastie said quietly. There was silence in the car for a moment. Then Compston glanced at her.

'What did you tell them back there?'

'The truth.'

'Same as you told me?'

'Not quite. I went for a longer drive than I said. Needed to clear my head.'

'Christ's sake, Beth . . . '

'So what happens now?'

'We either wrap this up pronto or pack our bags and ride into the sunset.'

'I meant to me.'

'Dereliction of duty.' Compston looked at her again. She was grim-faced but not about to protest. 'I'm assuming that's the least of it?'

'Sir?'

'You didn't actually shoot Dennis Stark?'

'No.' Accompanied by a short bark of laughter.

'And you're not covering for Alec Bell?'

'I'm not sure I . . . '

'I know you think the sun shines out of Alec's rear end, and if he told you to do something, you'd probably never think to question it.' Compston paused. 'So did he tell you to bunk off that night?'

'Absolutely not. But what about you?'

'What about me?'

'I don't suppose you've a handy alibi?'

'Fuck you, DC Hastie. End of.'

'Nice to see none of us have lost our team spirit.'

Compston had gone from slapping the steering wheel to throttling it. 'You didn't just step over the line there, you paused to take a dump on it. Far as I'm concerned, that's that — you're getting tossed back to your old duties.'

'For the record, sir, can I just say something?'

'If you must.'

'You're the worst, most useless, clueless boss I've ever had — and trust me, that puts you at the top of a really long list.'

25

They sat in Rebus's living room, Cafferty sucking on a bottle of beer. Rebus stuck to instant coffee. He wanted the clearest of heads, while Cafferty looked in a mood to move on to whisky once he'd finished his aperitif.

'Acorn House,' Rebus nudged. 'A secure environment for toerags and scumbags up to the age of — what? Sixteen?'

'They were different times. People's definition of what was acceptable . . . ' Cafferty was staring at the carpet. 'You've seen it recently: all those stories about celebrities back in the day and politicians who thought it was perfectly fine to rub shoulders with paedos.'

'Christ almighty . . . '

Cafferty met Rebus's stare. 'Not *me*! Hell's teeth, credit me with that at least!'

'Okay, you weren't fiddling with the kids at Acorn House.' Rebus paused. 'But somebody was? Michael Tolland?'

'Far as I know, Tolland was just the guy with the keys. He kept his eye on comings and goings. The place had a reputation. The kids would leg it, cars waiting for them outside. They'd be back next day wearing new clothes, money in their pockets.'

Rebus was trying to remember if there had been whispers at the time. Maybe — somewhere above his pay grade . . .

'They closed the place before it ever got to an inquiry,' Cafferty went on.

'Are we talking about something specific? Something involving your pals Jeffries and Ritter?'

'I wasn't quite the biggest player in the city back then — I'm talking 1985 — but I was making my move . . . ' The man seemed lost in memories. He sat on the edge of the sofa, legs splayed, elbows on knees, one mitt wrapped around the beer bottle. 'There was that no-man's-land, that sort of grey area where people like me got to know the movers and shakers.'

'People like David Minton?'

Cafferty shook his head. 'I never knew Minton. But he was friends with an MP called Howard Champ. Remember him?'

'I know the name. Died a few years back.'

'I only knew him vaguely. Then one night I get a phone call. There's been an incident — I think the word used was 'accident'.'

'At Acorn House?'

'In one of the bedrooms. And now there's a dead kid complicating the situation.'

Rebus found he was holding his breath as he listened.

'Something had gone wrong. A lad in his early teens had expired.'

'Howard Champ phoned you?'

'He got someone else to do it,' Cafferty corrected him. 'I'm guessing that was Tolland, though I didn't know his name back then.'

'Did he say what had happened?'

'Just that Howard Champ needed my help.'

'You went to Acorn House?'

'No way I was setting foot in that place!'

'So you sent a couple of your men — Jeffries and Ritter?'

Cafferty nodded slowly.

'And they dealt with the problem?' Rebus could hear the blood pounding in his ears as he spoke. 'How did they do that?'

'Took the body away.'

'Away where?'

'Some woods near where they'd grown up.'

Rebus thought for a moment. 'No repercussions?'

'Kids went AWOL all the time. This one had no family to speak of, just an overstretched social worker who ended up getting a holiday cruise and a new kitchen.'

'He had a name though, right, the lad who died?'

'I never heard it.'

Rebus exhaled loudly, then got to his feet, leaving the room for a minute. He returned with two glasses of malt. Cafferty took one with a nod of thanks. Rebus walked to the window and stared out at the silent, well-ordered world.

'What the hell do we do with this?' he asked.

'You tell me.'

'Tolland was there . . . you arranged the burial . . . Howard Champ was the culprit. Where does David Minton fit in?'

'I'm not sure.'

'If it's some kind of payback . . . they've waited thirty years. I don't get it.'

'Me neither.'

'And Jeffries and Ritter — they're the obvious targets, yet nothing's happened to them.'

'Agreed.'

The slight chuckle Rebus gave had no humour in it whatsoever. 'I'm completely and utterly stumped for something to say.'

'Maybe I shouldn't have told you. Could be I'm reading too much into it, seeing ghosts that aren't there . . . '

'Maybe.'

'But you don't think so?'

'The boy didn't have close family?'

'No.'

'There'll still be records somewhere, though.'

'Will there?'

'Damned if I know.' Rebus ran his hand through his hair. 'There must be people around who worked at Acorn House, or were kept there.'

'But as of right now, you've only got my word for it — and you're the only one I'm telling.' The two men's eyes met. 'I'm serious. It's not a can of worms your lot would be opening, it's a room full of snakes. Everything got kept quiet, Acorn House was shut down without a murmur. I can't think of anyone who'd thank you for shining a torch on any of it.'

'You won't talk to the police?'

'An official investigation isn't going to get anywhere.'

Rebus sipped his whisky while he gathered his thoughts. 'What did you get out of it at the time?'

'How do you mean?'

'Howard Champ — did he pay you off?'

'He offered.'

'You declined?'

'He knew he owed me — that was more important.'

Rebus nodded slowly. 'A gangster scaling the ladder — handy to have a local MP in your pocket. You never spoke about it to anyone?'

'No.'

'How about Jeffries and Ritter?'

'They knew better than to go blabbing.'

'Well someone knew — either all along, or they found out about it later. Tolland was the first to die — maybe his conscience got the better of him.'

'Who would he tell?'

Rebus shrugged. 'But with Howard Champ long deceased, the wanted list was pretty small: Tolland himself, then Minton, then you.' Rebus paused. 'Who do you think would be next?'

'Apart from Jeffries and Ritter?' Cafferty shrugged. 'Other staff, maybe, or kids who knew but kept quiet.'

'Some easier to trace than others. Minton had been a public figure . . . you too, for that matter . . . And Tolland was all over the papers when he won the lottery.'

'The money he had, why didn't they blackmail him rather than do him in?'

'Because money doesn't interest them, I suppose.' Rebus turned back towards the window and the view.

'Can you do anything with this?' Cafferty asked.

'On my own? I really don't know.'

'Will you try?'

'It's not like I've got anything else on my plate, is it?' When Rebus turned his head towards his guest, Cafferty rewarded him with a smile that mixed relief and gratitude.

'Remember,' he said after a moment, the smile fading. 'There may well be people who don't want Acorn House dusted off.'

Rebus nodded solemnly, raising the glass to his lips again.

★   ★   ★

Fox paced the corridor, his phone pressed to his ear. It was the third time he had tried Alec Bell, and this time the man decided to answer.

'What's the panic?' Bell said.

'Took your time getting back to me.'

'Big powwow with Ricky. What can I do for you, Fox?'

'You told me Jackie Dyson is your mole.'

'Did I?'

'You know you did. I need to know if you were spinning me a line.'

'Why?'

'Because I ran into him at Fettes.'

'Running into him's one thing . . . '

'He knows I'm a cop now. None of your lot seemed to have told him.'

'You talked to him?'

'So he also knows *I* know about the mole.' Fox could hear Bell sucking air through his teeth. 'Meaning that if you lied to me . . . '

'I didn't.'

'Sure about that?'

'He's not going to be too happy that anyone outside the team knows about him. Don't suppose it matters, though.'

'Why's that?'

'The meeting we just had — Joe Stark clocked the boss. Means we're on borrowed time.'

'You'll be replaced with another team?'

'Who knows.'

'And Dyson?'

'Will be considering his options. He was embedded in the gang long before Operation Junior got green-lit.'

'It really is him, isn't it?' Fox pressed. 'The mole, I mean?'

'I'm guessing the mask didn't slip . . . '

'Firmly glued on. He didn't even say sorry for knocking me out. Reckon he'd have used that blade if I hadn't intervened?'

'You said earlier you were worried he's gone native — I can assure you he hasn't. Ricky spoke to him a day or so back.'

Fox digested this. 'So that's that, then? Back to Gartcosh?'

'I wish I could say it's been fun.'

'Or even productive. You think the gang will keep looking?'

'Joe's got a bit of juggling to do. Dennis's goons were just that — who knows how they'll fit in with the old man. Joe had a meeting with Darryl Christie earlier. All seemed amicable enough. No idea what they were talking about, though. Lip-reader's what we need, next time round. Not that there'll *be* a next time. One thing that'll probably gladden your heart — Beth's been sent packing. She blew up at Ricky and that's that. Feel free to gloat.'

'Not my style.'

Alec Bell gave a loud sigh. 'Beth had it tough in her early years. Joining the police was the making of her. Never any love in her family — mum and dad drinking and fighting. She had to look after herself, her brother and her gran. That's the calibre of person you just shat on — hope the thought keeps you warm at night.'

'What about Beth, Alec? Does she keep *you* warm at night?'

The phone went dead, just as Siobhan Clarke appeared at the top of the stairs. Fox squeezed it tight in his hand and caught up with her.

'How did the interviews go?' he asked.

'Compston wouldn't let us record him. I've got notes to write up.'

'And the others?'

'We settled for the boss man and Hastie herself.'

'Did she give you anything?'

Clarke nodded. 'Whether I believe it or not is another matter. Do you want to listen?'

Fox nodded. 'And if there's anything else I can be doing . . . '

'I'll have a think.' Clarke sounded distracted. She was looking at her own phone's screen. 'Thought John wanted in on this, but he's gone silent all of a sudden.'

'Should we be worried about that?'

'Usually means trouble for somebody.' She

299

gave a fatigued smile. 'Is the day nearly over? I could use a drink.'

'I heard the Gimlet went up in smoke.'

'Fire investigators say arson.'

'Might explain why Christie and Stark met up.'

'You heard about that?' She nodded. 'I suppose it might.'

'Both of them very well-behaved, too — what does *that* tell us?'

'If I'm being honest, Malcolm, it tells *me* the square root of zero. How about you?'

'I forget the Starks aren't really your bailiwick.'

She smiled at the word. 'Only the son. And then only if he really does tie in to Lord Minton.'

'Which seems less likely now, correct? So a separate inquiry's going to have to be launched?'

'Probably — now that Joe Stark's been apprised that the note was probably a red herring.'

'That's why he stormed in here? How did he find out?'

'You've just told me he had a meeting earlier with Darryl Christie . . . '

'Christie's got someone at Fettes?'

'This is Police Scotland we're talking about, Malcolm. There'll always be someone who likes to talk.' Clarke had her phone to her ear, trying Rebus again.

'Text him instead,' Fox advised. 'Tell him we'll be at the Ox later — and we're buying.'

'It might come to that.' She looked at him. 'How are you doing anyway?'

'I'm okay.'

'Nice bit of drama at lunchtime, wasn't it? Joe Stark and his heavies barging in.'

'I missed all the action,' Fox lied. 'Pretty typical, eh?'

'Were you serious about the Ox later?'

'Only if you really want to catch John.'

'And if I don't?'

'There are other places. Some of them even serve food.'

'Sounds good to me.'

'I'll maybe bide my time till then listening to that Beth Hastie recording,' Fox said. 'Just out of interest, you understand . . . '

26

Acorn House wasn't Acorn House any more. The one-time borstal was still standing, but it had become a private health clinic, specialising in cosmetic procedures. This much Rebus gleaned from the large sign fixed to the red-brick wall. The detached Victorian house was constructed of the same material. It stood on the edge of Colinton Village, a well-heeled suburb of the city whose sign welcomed visitors to 'A Historic Conservation Village'. The main road was busy with commuters heading home, so Rebus pulled his Saab up on to the pavement, leaving just about enough room for pedestrians to get past. His phone told him Siobhan Clarke had tried calling again. He knew he couldn't speak to her, not quite yet. She was quick, and would sense something was up. He could lie to her, but she wouldn't be happy until she knew what was troubling him.

He had no intention of entering the building — what would be the point? It would have changed, and he barely recalled its interior anyway from his one and only visit. He really just wanted a sense of the place. Whatever garden had once lain in front of the house had been replaced with loose chippings, to create a car park capable of accommodating half a dozen clients and as many staff members. The houses to either side sat at a good distance. He imagined the windows covered in net curtains — maybe even the original wooden shutters, the kind that could be locked from the inside. A big, anonymous place of detention where pretty much anything could happen without society outside knowing or — very possibly — caring. Kids who had pilfered, or set fire to things, or carried out muggings and housebreakings. Kids who were quick to anger, lacking empathy and good breeding. Kids gone feral.

Problem kids.

Rebus had done a quick internet search, turning up almost nothing of value. It was as if Acorn House — existing prior to the World Wide Web — had been not consigned to history but practically erased from it.

He pulled out his phone and rang Meadowlea.

'My name's John Rebus. I was there earlier visiting Paul Jeffries — sorry again about my friend. The thing is, we weren't completely straight with you. I work for the police.'

'Yes?'

Rebus had recognised the man's voice, the same one who had spoken to him at the door.

'Sorry,' he said. 'I didn't catch your name earlier.'

'Trevor.'

'Well, Trevor, remember you were telling me about the friend who visited Mr Jeffries? I think you said they were at school together?'

'It was Zoe who mentioned that.'

'Of course it was,' Rebus apologised, 'but the name Dave Ritter rang a bell with both of you.'

'That's right.'

303

'I was just wondering when Mr Ritter last visited.'

'A couple of months back.'

'So he's not due any time soon? Does he phone ahead?'

'I think so.'

'Would you have a contact number for him?'

'I don't know.'

'Or his address in Ullapool? Would Mr Jeffries have a diary or an address book? Maybe you could take a look.'

'Is Paul in some sort of trouble?'

'I won't lie to you — it's possible. Any strange visitors? Any letters or notes he's received that seemed a bit odd? Threatening, even?'

'Nothing like that.' Trevor sounded disturbed by the thought.

'I'm sure there's nothing to worry about, but maybe you can let me know if anything does arrive. I'll give you my mobile number.' He reeled it off. 'And if you could get me the dates Dave Ritter visited, plus anything about him that might be hidden away in Mr Jeffries' room . . . '

'It's against the rules to go prying into our residents' things.'

'In which case, I might have to get a search warrant.' Rebus hardened his tone. 'Ask yourself which is going to be less stressful for your residents.'

'I'll see what I can do.'

'Thank you. And you'll call me if anything even the least bit out of the ordinary happens?'

'Promise.'

'Fine then. Thanks again.'

'But you have to give your word . . . '
'About what?'
'You'll never let that maniac friend of yours come here again.'

★　★　★

Cafferty had brought a curry back to his Quartermile apartment. He ate from the containers — lamb rogan josh, pilau rice, saag aloo, washed down with the remaining half-bottle of Valpolicella. He had half a mind to visit Paul Jeffries again — see how much of the old Paul was still in there, waiting to be awoken by the right trigger.

The right trigger.

That was another thing: he'd been thinking about a gun, wondering if he needed one. Would a gun make him feel any safer? He wasn't sure. He'd always had muscle around him in the past, but who could he trust? Andrew Goodman would lend him guys. Thing was, they wouldn't be *Cafferty's* men, not the way Dennis had soldiers and Joe his trusted cronies. Darryl Christie had not as yet found a lieutenant — he had infantry, but no one other than himself to marshal them. When his phone buzzed, he saw that it was Christie calling. Despite himself, he smiled, wiping grease from his fingers as he swallowed a final dollop of food.

It was as if they were on the same wavelength.

'Just thinking about you,' Cafferty admitted, answering.

'In a good way, I hope.'

305

'Always, Darryl. What's on your mind?'

'The police have been stringing Joe Stark along, telling him his son was part of this thing with the notes. Turns out not to be true.'

'I can see why they'd want to keep Joe in the dark.' Cafferty was sucking a finger clean. 'Once he starts to take it personally . . . '

'Well that's the stage we're entering. So if I were you, I wouldn't move too far from that hotel room of yours.'

'There is an alternative, you know.'

'You and me? We team up and take out the threat?'

'It's how wars are often fought.'

'How about I team up with Joe instead? With Dennis gone, he needs someone to replace him, no?'

'I doubt Dennis's men would warm to that scenario. You'd have to go through every single one of them, and that's not really your style.'

'Then we're left with *The Good, the Bad and the Ugly* — you, me and Joe, standing in a cemetery wondering who to aim at first.'

Cafferty smiled. 'Wasn't there buried treasure in that scene too?'

'There was.'

'And two out of three alive at the end?'

'You're thinking those are pretty good odds?'

'I prefer not to gamble these days, son. As you get older, you realise just how much you hate losing.'

'Then walk away. Keep everything you've got.'

'Sounds good.'

'It's the only sensible option, I promise you.'

Christie ended the call. Cafferty placed the phone on the worktop and picked up the wine, draining it and stifling a sour belch.

Walk away. Those had been the words, but Cafferty knew that wasn't how Christie visualised things — at the end of his version of the film, Cafferty had a noose around his neck. Either that, or he was lying cold and dead on the ground.

He squeezed his eyes shut, pinching the bridge of his nose.

'And then there's Acorn House,' he muttered to himself, bringing back the memory of the one time he wished he *had* just walked away . . .

⋆　⋆　⋆

Joe Stark stared from his hotel window at a passing parade of night-time buses. He could hear trains as they squealed to a halt every few minutes at one of the platforms in the station opposite. There were tannoyed announcements too, and occasional drunken shouts from pedestrians. His home back in Glasgow was a detached 1960s property in a quiet neighbourhood, the same house Dennis had grown up in. Joe had been thinking about the lad with mixed emotions. It wasn't that he wouldn't miss him. On the other hand, Dennis had been readying to topple him, Joe knew that for a fact. He'd been greedy, and hungry for it — Walter and Len had said as much on more than one occasion, having picked up whispers from Glasgow's pubs and clubs. It had only been a matter of time — weeks rather than months. Dennis's lads were probably gathered in one of the other bedrooms, plotting. Or maybe deciding *whether* to plot. Joe knew he couldn't look weak. He had to seem to be filled with bile and ready to wreak revenge.

But who was in the frame? Did it matter? He could strike down Cafferty or Christie or a complete bloody stranger for that matter. What counted was to take out *somebody*.

He was a good kid, Walter Grieve had said, because it was the sort of sentiment you were duty-bound to express. But one look at Walter had told Joe the man didn't really believe it — and with good reason. Because in toppling his father, Dennis and his gang would have been obliged to take Walter and Len out of the game too.

Truth was, Joe wished he could feel something other than an echoing emptiness. He'd tried to force a few private tears, but none had come. If his wife were still alive, it would be different. It would all be different. Slowly, as he continued to stare from the window, Joe Stark began replacing images of his son with those of his dear-departed Cath.

And finally his stubborn eyes began to water.

★   ★   ★

The white car was parked directly outside Rebus's flat. Having been unable to find a space on Arden Street, Rebus had left his own Saab on the next street over. As he approached the front door of the tenement, the window slid down on the driver's side of the Evoque.

'Any chance of a word?' Darryl Christie said.

'I'm busy.'

'It'll take five minutes. I can come up, if you like.'

'No way.'

'Then get in.'

The window slid closed. Christie was starting the engine as Rebus got in. He reversed out of the space and headed downhill towards the Meadows.

'Taking me somewhere nice?' Rebus enquired.

'Driving helps me think. Are you keeping busy?'

'Not bad.'

'You heard about the Gimlet?'

'A sad loss to few.'

'Maybe so, but it's where I learned the ropes. You could call that a sentimental attachment.'

'Any idea who did it?'

Christie gave him a sharp glance. 'Isn't that a question for the police? Not that any of your lot seem interested. Wonder why that is.'

'Probably reckon it's an insurance job.'

'You and me know different.' Christie paused. They were on Melville Drive, heading towards Tollcross. 'Joe Stark tells me it wasn't his doing.'

'You believe him?'

'Not sure. Here's the thing, though — Dennis is killed and my pub gets torched. Doesn't it look to you like the start of a war?'

'Only if you let it.'

'Well I know damned fine *I* didn't have anything to do with the hit on Dennis, and if his gang didn't firebomb the Gimlet . . . '

'Someone's doing a bit of stirring?'

'That's my best guess, and we both know who's holding the nice long spoon.'

Rebus gave a half-smile. 'It's an old saying, you know: 'You need a long spoon to sup with the devil.''

'I've heard it said about Fifers, too — you grew up in Fife, didn't you?'

'This isn't about me, though, is it?'

'No.'

'It's about Cafferty.'

'Oh yes.' They had turned left and were heading for Bruntsfield. Rebus realised it was a circuit. They would take the next fork and end up back in Marchmont. 'Think about it,' Christie was saying quietly. 'Cafferty pits the Stark clan against me, knowing Joe isn't strong enough to run Edinburgh by himself. The old guard and the new end up battling one another, and Cafferty watches it all happen from the sidelines.'

'You're forgetting Cafferty got a note and a bullet both.'

It was Christie's turn to smile. 'You don't see, do you? No one saw who fired that shot. Could easily be a put-up job, Cafferty painting himself as victim so nobody figures him for Dennis's unfortunate demise.'

Rebus was shaking his head. 'Look, I can't tell you what I know that you don't, but I think you're in danger of reading this whole thing wrong. Give me a few days and I can maybe prove it.'

'I'm not sure it'll wait that long.'

'I'm asking you, Darryl. You might well be right about there being other forces at work, but Cafferty's not the man.'

'Are you *his* man, though?'

'Never was, never will be.'

They were approaching Marchmont Road. 'What makes you so sure about Cafferty?' Christie asked.

'Couple of days, I might have an answer for you.'

'Nothing you can say to me right now that would put my mind at rest?'

'I think Cafferty's as nervous as you are. Which makes me grateful neither of you uses a nine-mil pistol.'

'Don't tell me Cafferty couldn't lay his hands on one if he felt the need.'

'You too, come to that.'

'And maybe a cop could too, eh?' They were entering Arden Street. Christie stopped the car in the middle of the road to let Rebus out.

'A few days,' Rebus reminded him.

'We'll see,' Darryl Christie said, moving off before Rebus had even managed to get the door fully closed.

He looked to where the Evoque had been parked. A neighbour had grabbed the space already. Cursing under his breath, Rebus dug his house keys out of his pocket.

Day Seven

27

Alec Bell and Jake Emerson were on duty in the unmarked Vauxhall Insignia, engine running so the cabin stayed above freezing. They each held a beaker of coffee, having taken over the watch only twenty minutes previously. Emerson was not Bell's favoured partner, but Beth Hastie had been banished into the wilderness. Emerson was young and a fast learner, but always ready to show off. The music he liked meant nothing to Bell, and his personal life — most of it revolving around social media — made almost less sense to the older man.

'Will Beth face a disciplinary?' he was asking now. Bell shrugged. 'Leaves us one short — will there be a new recruit? I can suggest a couple of names.'

'Way Ricky's talking, we'll all be going home sooner rather than later.' Bell craned his neck to see the front door of the modern hotel. It was part of a new development close by Haymarket station. You could hear the trains chuntering past, and every now and then a tram signalled its presence with an old-fashioned clang that Emerson had suggested had to be digitised.

'No way that's the real thing.'

The gang had moved into four rooms in the hotel — six sharing, and a single room for Joe Stark. The place had a glass front, with sliding doors leading to the reception area. There were a

315

few trendy-looking chairs and sofas there, along with a flat-screen TV tuned to Sky News. The breakfast room was on the same floor, with a bar on the mezzanine above. This much the team knew, but they had precious little else. Joe and his men had enjoyed a quiet evening — dinner at an Indian place nearby, then a couple of pints at Ryrie's. No meetings, clandestine or otherwise, and no trouble. The log from the previous six-hour shift was almost completely blank.

The Insignia was parked in a metered bay behind a taxi rank, not more than fifty feet from the hotel steps. Jake Emerson yawned noisily and tried shaking some life into himself.

'Me, I love this part of the job,' he drawled. 'It's why I joined CID in the first place.'

'We'll try to arrange for a car chase later if you like.'

'Only if we get some decent wheels.' He drummed his fingers against the dashboard. 'This thing couldn't outgun a Segway.'

'Hang on,' Bell interrupted him. 'Bit of movement. Looks like Walter Grieve's come outside for a smoke.'

Grieve was turning up the collar of his coat. He took in the scenery as he lit a cigarette, then crossed the road towards the station.

'Do I follow on foot?' Emerson asked.

'Not till I say so.' Bell watched as Grieve walked past the station entrance. 'Where's he off to?' he said. 'Maybe just stretching his legs . . . '

Yes, because Grieve was crossing the street again. He was on the pavement behind them now, sauntering back to the hotel. He passed the car, stopped to drop his cigarette on the ground, and stubbed it out. Then he turned, a *gotcha* smile on his face. He came over to the passenger-side window and rapped on it with his knuckles.

'What do I do?' Emerson asked.

But Bell was already pressing the button, the window sliding halfway open. Grieve rested both hands on it and leaned down, his face almost inside the car.

'All right, officers?' he said. 'Bit of information for you from Mr Stark. Most of us are heading back to Glasgow, there being a funeral to organise. Couple of the lads might stick around a day or so — they hear there's a castle worth seeing. Should make things a bit easier for you. Okay?'

Still beaming the same false smile, he straightened up, thumped one meaty fist on the car roof and continued on his way.

'Jesus,' Emerson muttered, his hand trembling a fraction as he lifted the coffee cup to his mouth. Bell had his phone out. He pressed it to his ear and waited for Ricky Compston to pick up.

'News?' Compston said, sounding almost painfully hopeful.

'Just a confirmation, really.'

'Confirmation of what?'

'That Operation Junior is toast.'

★   ★   ★

Albert Stout lived in the village of Gullane, in a detached Edwardian house looking on to a golf course. There were hardy souls out there already, just about visible through the morning haar, as

317

Rebus closed the door of his Saab. He had phoned ahead and Stout was waiting for him. Rebus didn't like the old bugger — as a journalist he had been devious, crooked and a thorn in the side of Lothian and Borders Police. The house was cold and smelled of damp. Mouldering piles of newsprint sat in the hall, while the staircase was mostly covered in books. The carpeting was threadbare, as was its owner. Moths had been at the saggy oatmeal cardigan, and there was a three-day growth of grey stubble on Stout's chin and cheeks.

'Well, well,' the man cackled. 'Didn't think I'd ever clap eyes on you again.'

'Sorry to disappoint you.' Rebus was ushered into a space that doubled as sitting room and office. 'Still writing your memoirs?'

'Keeps me out of mischief.' Stout gestured for Rebus to sit. The sofa was a sprawl of paperwork, so Rebus lowered himself on to an arm, while Stout took the leather-bound chair behind his work desk. 'Tell me, is young Laura still in work?'

'Laura Smith?' Rebus watched the old man nod. 'She's hanging in there.' Until his retirement, Stout had been chief crime correspondent for the *Scotsman*, a role Laura Smith now occupied.

'Good luck to her — the industry's on its last legs.'

'You've been saying that for twenty years.'

'That's often the way of it when the patient's on life support — sometimes it's kinder to switch off the machines.' Stout peered at his guest, hands clasped across his stomach. He belied his surname these days, and Rebus wondered about the weight loss. Though he'd been nicknamed The Ghoul back in the day for his ability suddenly to appear at crime scenes, he had always been overweight, belt straining at its final notch. He wasn't quite cadaverous now, but he was on his way.

'Still,' Stout mused, 'Laura's stuck at it, which speaks of tenacity if nothing else.' He broke off. 'You weren't expecting a cup of tea, I hope?'

'Don't want to put you to any trouble.'

'Well that's something we're agreed on. So what's on your mind, Inspector?' He stopped again. 'No, you must be retired by now, surely?'

'As a matter of fact, I am. But Police Scotland have offered me a bit of work, so . . . '

'Work of an archaeological nature, I'm guessing.'

'That's why I'm here, talking to a fossil.'

Stout looked ready to take offence, but changed his mind and chuckled. 'Don't let me stop you,' he said.

'I'm looking into an assessment centre called Acorn House.' Stout's mouth formed an O. 'Particularly the mid 1980s. You remember that lottery winner, the one who was killed a few weeks back? He'd worked there.'

'Had he now?' Stout's chair protested as he leaned back in it.

'And we're just checking his background, looking for anyone who might have had a grudge . . . '

Stout gave a thin smile, his eyes suddenly alive

319

and boring into Rebus's. 'I think you're doing more than that. Tell me I'm wrong.'

Rebus considered his options. 'You're not,' he eventually conceded. 'I've been hearing stuff about Acorn House, stuff that makes me think it should have been taken apart at the time and people sent to jail.'

'It did have a certain reputation.'

'How much did you know back then?'

'Rumours mostly, winks and nudges. Lawyers, MPs, public figures . . . taxis dropping them off late at night and returning to fetch them before dawn. Children — *children*, mind — in hotel rooms with men old enough to be their fathers and grandfathers . . . walked in on by unsuspecting housemaids who then felt an urgent need to unburden themselves on someone like me for the price of a drink.'

'Any names?'

'Names?'

'These public figures.'

'Plenty of names, Rebus. Plenty of interesting names.'

'Care to share a few?'

Stout studied him. 'Maybe *you* should be giving the names and I'll tell you what I think.'

Rebus shook his head. 'That doesn't work for me.'

'I don't work for you either, so do me the courtesy of answering just one question — are you here to uncover the truth, or to ensure it stays hidden?'

'How do you mean?'

'When the lottery millionaire was killed, did

the attacker maybe take something — journals or a confession?'

'I've no idea.'

'And that's not what you're worried about?'

'No.'

'How do I know you're not lying?'

'You don't.'

Stout gave him a hard stare, but Rebus didn't blink. 'Hmmm,' the old man eventually said. He unclasped his hands and pressed them to his desk. 'What happened in that place was a scandal — or should have been. But there was never any hard evidence. I twice asked my editor for money so we could set up a watch on the comings and goings, maybe grease a few palms.'

'He said no?'

'Actually, he said yes, but then his mind was changed for him.'

'Somebody had a word?'

'The proprietor at that time liked nothing better than rubbing shoulders with the great and the good. They'd invite him to dinners, pour him the best brandy and light a cigar for him. And then they'd whisper that certain things were never to be followed up.'

'Including Acorn House?'

'Especially Acorn House. Story after story found itself spiked.'

'How about other papers?'

'Same thing. You heard no end of rumours, but you couldn't print them.'

'Did none of the staff or kids ever come forward?'

'One or two,' Stout admitted. 'They talked to

me and to others, but we needed something concrete.'

'What are my chances after all these years?'

'Pretty much non-existent.'

'But there'll be people out there who were resident at Acorn House?'

'Undoubtedly. They probably won't talk, though, even though the climate these days is more sympathetic to victims. Either they'll be too scared, or they won't want to deal with the memories. Even if they *do* talk, they'd be incriminating the dead and the nearly dead, and it would be one person's word against another's.'

Rebus's eyes swept the room — so many books, magazines and newspapers, so much investigation . . . 'Did you print *anything*?'

'A satirical magazine ran a couple of pieces, no names mentioned. It would be different these days. Someone on the internet would publish, and damn the lawsuits. Besides, every kid has a phone — there'd be texts and photos. Back then, secrets could always be kept.'

'David Minton,' Rebus said suddenly, awaiting Stout's reaction.

'Lord Minton, recently deceased? What of him?'

'One of his closest friends was Howard Champ.'

Stout gave the thinnest of smiles. 'You're handing me names,' he said.

'And wanting to know what you make of them.'

'Add in the lottery millionaire and I'm seeing two men who died after being attacked in their homes, and one who succumbed to natural causes. Are you saying our lottery winner and his lordship were killed by the same person? And the link is Acorn House? So maybe one of the victims, now grown up and seething . . . ' Stout rasped his hands down his face. 'Well, well, well.'

'None of this is for general consumption,' Rebus warned.

'You'll have to forgive an old hack's instincts — I can't help myself.'

'Is there anything at all you can give me? I'm struggling here.'

Stout studied his visitor closely, and Rebus remembered what it was like to be questioned by the man — the forensic level of inquisition, each error or inconsistency dissected. 'I know you don't like me, Rebus,' he was saying now. 'The feeling is entirely mutual, I assure you. But it always did rankle that certain men could get away with . . . well, with *anything*. All down to status. All down to pecking order and privilege.'

'I'm not looking to cover anything up, Albert. Quite the opposite.'

'I can see that.' Stout sighed. 'The person you want is Patrick Spiers.'

'Why's that?'

'He was freelance — bloody-minded, but bloody good. Couldn't bring himself to work for any one organisation, liked his freedom too much. What he relished was a nice knotty investigation that would lend itself to a long-form essay — five or ten thousand words. But then the Fourth Estate started giving less space to those and more to bingo cards and celebrity gossip. Poor Patrick faded.'

'He did a story on Acorn House?'

'Yes — not that I ever saw it. He wouldn't have shown it to a rival newshound before it was published.'

'And it was never published?'

Stout shook his head.

'Where can I find him?'

Stout smiled ruefully. 'Do you have a ouija board? I was at his funeral not three weeks back . . . '

* * *

'The good news is, we're getting our desks back,' Doug Maxtone was telling Fox. Fox was climbing the stairs at Fettes, phone at his ear while he wrestled with a cardboard cup of scalding tea and a cling-film-wrapped tuna sandwich.

'They're shipping out?'

'Seems Joe Stark and his men are heading back to Glasgow — all apart from a couple.'

'Do you think we've seen the last of them?'

'Maybe they're satisfied Hamish Wright isn't in the city.'

Fox cursed silently as a splash of liquid landed on his lapel. 'Do we know who's staying put?'

'Compston gave me the names — Callum Andrews and Jackie Dyson. Said we should keep half an eye on them, just in case.'

'But not a full-blown surveillance?'

'On what grounds? Thing is, it makes war on the streets less likely.'

'Unless Joe Stark's just gone home to regroup.'

'Well anyway, when James Page gets fed up of you, your chair's waiting here.'

'Thanks for letting me know.'

Fox had reached the incident room. Esson and Ogilvie were at their desks. He nodded a greeting as he put his phone away, then started dabbing at his lapel with a handkerchief.

'Accident?' Esson asked.

'I was never much good at juggling. You keeping busy?'

'Couple of names Rebus wanted me to check. Can't say I'm making much headway.'

'Seen Siobhan?'

'In a meeting with the boss.'

'Any idea what it's about?'

Esson shook her head. Fox's phone was ringing again. He saw that it was his father's care home, so headed into the corridor for some privacy.

'Malcolm Fox,' he said, answering.

'It's about your father, Mr Fox.' The tone told him almost everything he needed to know.

'Yes?'

'He's been taken to the Infirmary.'

'What happened?'

'He just . . . he's fading, Mr Fox.'

'Fading?' But Fox knew what she meant — the body shutting down bit by bit, preparing for finality. He ended the call and walked back into the office. Esson saw the look on his face. He lifted the tea from his desk and placed it on hers.

'I have to go out. Be a shame to waste it,' he explained.

'You okay, Malcolm?'

He nodded uncertainly and turned to leave. Then he noticed he had picked up the tuna

325

sandwich. He sat it next to the tea and got going.

He had to drive all the way through town, which gave him plenty of time to think. Problem was, he felt numb, his thought processes fuzzy and incoherent, like the hum of conversation in a busy café, none of it quite intelligible. He switched the radio to Classic FM and let the music wash over him, oblivious to anything other than the need to maintain a safe distance from the vehicle in front. A different person — Rebus, or maybe even Siobhan — would have put the foot down, overtaking recklessly, impelled to make haste, but that wasn't him. He considered calling Jude but thought it could wait. He had scant news, after all, and she would only panic.

The Infirmary was a grey new-build on the south-eastern outskirts of the city. He found a parking space and walked in through the main doors. The woman at the help desk directed him to another woman at a different desk, who sent him to A&E. He remembered waking up there after Jackie Dyson had knocked him unconscious. Dyson was one of the two soldiers staying put. That was curious. If Dyson's job was to stay close to the action, surely that action had now moved to Glasgow. Away from the gang, how could he gather intelligence? Then again, maybe he was under orders from Joe Stark, and to argue would be to invite suspicion.

As Fox waited at the reception desk, a passing nurse smiled a greeting, then stopped and retraced her steps.

'You were here the other day,' she stated.

'And you were the first thing I saw when I

woke up,' he acknowledged.

'Feeling the after-effects?' she enquired. 'Of the injuries, I mean.'

'That's not why I'm here. I got a call from my dad's nursing home. He's been brought in.'

'What's the name?'

'Mitchell Fox — Mitchell or Mitch.'

She went around the desk and checked the computer screen, then announced the number of the ward.

Fox nodded his thanks. 'Does it say what's wrong with him?'

'Looks like he had a seizure of some kind.'

'That doesn't sound good.'

'They'll know more upstairs,' she said. This time her smile was that of the health professional — textbook evasive.

He returned to the main concourse and took the lift, following the signs along the corridor and pushing open the doors to the high-dependency unit. He explained who he was and why he was there, and was taken to a bed where his father lay, his face the same cement-grey colour as the building's exterior, monitors connected to him and an oxygen mask strapped across his mouth and nose. His clothes had been removed and replaced with a pale green gown. Fox looked to left and right, but there didn't seem to be any doctors around.

'Someone will be along to talk to you soon,' the nurse said, checking the monitors before moving to the next patient.

A name tag had been attached to Mitch Fox's left wrist, and there was a sensor clamped to the

327

tip of a finger. A chart at the foot of the bed told Fox nothing. He sought in vain for a vacant chair. Eventually a visitor at one of the other beds got up to leave and Fox took his chance. Seated next to the machines, registering their rhythmic beeps and subtly changing displays, he rested a hand on his father's uncovered forearm.

And waited.

28

Rebus ran into Siobhan Clarke as she emerged from the loo nearest the incident room. She was puffing out her cheeks and expelling air.

'As bad as that?' Rebus said.

'Investigation's stalled,' she explained. 'We're waiting for something to happen. And meantime the Fiscal's office wants a separate team attached to the Stark shooting.'

Rebus nodded slowly, wondering how much, if anything, he could tell her. Then he thought of something. 'Did you ever take a closer look at Michael Tolland?'

'It's ongoing.' She stared at him. 'Why?'

'I just get the feeling there's something there. Definitely no note hidden away somewhere in his house?'

'Linlithgow picked the place apart.' Her eyes were still locked on his. 'Is there something you should be telling me?'

He shook his head and followed her into the office. Ronnie Ogilvie and Christine Esson looked to be sharing a sandwich. Clarke headed to her own desk to check her messages, while Rebus stood in front of Esson's.

'I've got nothing on those two names,' she warned him.

'I've found Paul Jeffries,' he told her quietly, checking that Clarke was out of earshot. Esson glowered at him.

'When were you going to tell me?'

'I'm telling you now, so you can focus on Dave Ritter. He might be living in Ullapool. Do a check, maybe get in touch with the force up there — could be a bothy with only PC Murdoch minding the desk, but make sure they know it's urgent.' He saw the look she was still giving him. 'Okay, Christine, I'm sorry you're only hearing this now. My mind's been elsewhere.' He saw the tea on the corner of her desk. 'This going spare?'

'It's cold.'

'I'll settle for that.' Rebus took a mouthful.

'Malcolm put it there.'

'Oh?'

'He got a phone call and left in a hurry.'

'When was this?'

'Maybe three quarters of a tuna sandwich back.'

Rebus frowned in thought, then retreated to the corridor to make the call.

* * *

'Yes, John?' Fox said, answering. He kept his voice low, uncertain about the protocol regarding mobile phones. Time was, there were signs everywhere warning that they could interfere with the machines, so he kept his eye on the readouts, without noting any sudden peaks or troughs.

'Where are you, Malcolm?'

'The Infirmary — my dad's taken a turn for the worse.'

'Sorry to hear that. Is he going to be okay?'

'I've not spoken to anyone yet.'

'I'm sure it'll be fine.'

'Aye. Maybe.' Fox cleared his throat. 'Listen, Joe Stark has left town. Taking all but two of the gang with him.'

'Oh?'

'Might put your chum Cafferty's mind at rest — plus Darryl Christie.'

'It might,' Rebus seemed to agree. 'Speaking of Cafferty, which care home was your dad in again? Wasn't Meadowlea?'

'Isn't that more of a medical place? Like a hospice?' Fox saw a white coat approaching. The doctor looked only just out of her teens, but she lifted the clipboard with confidence and studied it with deep concentration. 'Got to go,' Fox told Rebus.

'Call me if you need anything.'

'Thanks.' Fox put the phone away and rose to his feet. 'I'm his son,' he told the doctor. She had finished reading the notes and acknowledged him with a nod, squeezing past to check the readouts, the drip, the oxygen. 'Is there anything you can tell me?'

'We'll be running tests later today.'

'I was told he'd had a seizure — could it be a stroke? He doesn't look like he's coming round any time soon.'

'Sometimes the body shuts down so it can repair itself.'

'But what about the other times?'

The doctor glanced at her patient's face. 'We'll know more in a short while. Your father's a good age, Mr Fox . . . '

'Meaning what?'

'You said it yourself — brain and body can just decide it's time.'

And there was that smile again, the same one the nurse in A&E had offered. He watched the doctor as she moved to the next bed. A bit of him wanted to confront her, drag her back to *this* bed. But to what end? Instead he sat back down, feeling a weight pressing upon him. It was time to phone Jude. It was time to start preparing.

★ ★ ★

Patrick Spiers didn't own a detached house in Gullane. The address Stout had given Rebus led to a 1960s high-rise in Wester Hailes. It was one of those times he was thankful his car didn't look worth stealing. On the other hand, the jazz musician Tommy Smith had grown up in this environment, so anything was possible. Maybe the kids scowling from their BMXs would grow up to be artists and musicians. Or hospital consultants. Or care workers. When Rebus gave one group an encouraging smile, however, he received only unblinking scowls in reply.

The lift was working, so Rebus took it to the sixth floor, trying not to think about what might be in the polythene carrier bag that sat in one corner, its handles tied together to create a seal.

He didn't know what he was expecting on the sixth floor of the tower block. Stout had mentioned a grown-up daughter, but he hadn't thought she lived with her father. There had never been a wife, just a string of 'significant

332

others'. The old journalist had confirmed that Spiers had succumbed to cirrhosis of the liver — 'and probably a host of other ailments besides'.

Rebus stood on the walkway. It was only partially glassed in, the glass itself scored with graffiti. But he had a view south to where snow lay on the Pentlands, just beyond the bypass. The street lights were already on, though the sun was just barely below the horizon. Long shadows at ground level. Rebus tried thinking how many hours of daylight there had been — not quite eight, maybe seven and a half. At this time of year, kids went to school in the dark and came home at twilight. He'd often wondered if crime rose in the winter — darkness changed people's mood; darkness changed everything. And under cover of darkness, anything might happen undetected.

He found himself standing outside flat 6/6. The window was curtained but there was a light on beyond the frosted-glass panel in the front door. Neighbours had added iron gates to theirs, creating a better barrier against incursion. Either Patrick Spiers had had more faith in his fellow humans, or there was nothing inside worth stealing.

The doorbell worked, so Rebus waited. A woman's voice called out from within.

'Who is it?'

'I'm with the police,' Rebus called back. 'Any chance of a word?'

He heard a chain being attached to the door before it was pulled open an inch.

'ID?' the young woman said. He could see only half her face.

'Afraid not,' he apologised. 'But I can give you a number to call.'

'And how will I know I'm talking to the police and not just some crony of yours?'

'You sound like your father's daughter all right.' Rebus gave a friendly smile. 'I don't suppose he was the trusting type either.'

'And with good reason.'

'I don't doubt it.'

'What kind of cop doesn't carry ID?'

'The kind who retired recently but is working in a civilian capacity.'

'For the police?'

'That's right.' Rebus made show of blowing on his hands and rubbing them together, but he hadn't quite gained her trust yet.

'How did you get this address?'

'Albert Stout.'

'That old sleazebag.'

'The very same.'

'He used to follow my dad around — did you know that? Just in case there was a story he could steal from him.'

'You're not endearing him to me.'

'But he's a friend of yours?'

'Not at all. I went to ask him a few questions as part of an inquiry I'm involved in, and he — ' Rebus broke off. 'It really is perishing out here.'

'You know we just buried my dad?'

'Yes, I was sorry to hear it.'

'Sorry why? Did you know him?'

'I was just hoping he could help me.'

'And that's why you're sorry?' She watched Rebus nod. 'Well that's honest, I suppose.' A few seconds later, having made her mind up, she unhooked the chain and let him in.

Rebus stood in the living-room doorway, surveying the carnage.

'Bloody hell,' he said.

'It's not as bad as it looks.'

Floor-to-ceiling box files, bulging manuscripts tied with string, and three old-fashioned manual typewriters placed around a drop-leaf table, each with a sheet of paper inserted, half a page typed. There was a venerable-looking computer too, complete with a slot for the floppy disks that sat stacked next to it. A TV set in one corner — not the latest model, but at least it wasn't black and white. The posters pinned to the walls were mostly obscured by boxes, but Rebus could make out Muhammad Ali, Bob Dylan and John Lennon.

'Your dad was old school,' Rebus commented.

'Even when it came to porn.' Spiers's daughter lifted a magazine and waved it in front of Rebus — a bare-breasted blonde with unfeasibly white teeth.

'Couple more years, you could put that on *Antiques Roadshow*.'

She looked at him and burst out laughing, covering her eyes with her free hand. She was close to tears, he could tell.

'Where do I even *begin*?' she said, dropping the porn mag to the floor.

Rebus was studying the writing on the spines of some of the box files. They seemed to be in chronological sequence. Various newspapers and magazines were mentioned, sometimes with a couple of lines about the stories Spiers had contributed and even the fee received.

'I didn't get your name,' he said as he looked.

'Molly.' He turned towards her and they shook hands. She was in her early thirties, about five and a half feet tall with curly black hair and a prominent mole on her chin. She wore a wedding band on her left hand.

'I'm John Rebus,' he said. 'Your husband's not with you, Molly?'

'You *are* a detective, then?' She played with the ring. 'We broke up a couple of months back.'

'Do you live in Edinburgh?'

'Glasgow,' she corrected him. 'Dad used to live there too.'

'How long was he in Edinburgh?'

'Best part of a decade.'

'And your mum?'

'Left me so she could go 'find herself' in India.'

'Oh aye? How's that working out?'

'Horribly, I hope.' She laughed again.

'You the only child?'

'That we know about. Dad was quite the rogue in his day.' She examined Rebus as he scanned the boxes. 'What is it you're looking for?'

'An acorn in a forest,' he muttered.

'People usually say needle, don't they? A needle in a haystack?'

'Your father wrote about a place called Acorn House,' Rebus explained.

'That rings a bell.' Rebus watched as she went to another teetering tower of box files. 'Help me with this,' she said. There were two boxes marked Acorn House, halfway down the pile. Rebus removed the top three or four, then two more, and Molly lifted the boxes in question.

'They don't weigh much,' she said.

Because they were empty, apart from a single sheet of paper in each. On the first were written words that stopped Rebus dead.

They took the lot! They took the fucking lot!

The second note consisted of a short string of numbers. 'Any ideas?' he asked Molly.

'Dates maybe?' She shrugged. Then she took another look. 'Dad has boxes of disks. Some of them have numbers . . . '

It took a further ten minutes of sifting until she plucked one disk from a box and held it up. 'This one,' she said. Rebus took it from her. It was a black plastic square with an index sticker on it. Written in pencil were numerals that matched the note. A thin brushed-metal cover could be pushed to one side, giving a glimpse of the flimsy brown circle within, the recording tape containing the data.

''Formatted for IBM PS/2 and compatibles',' Rebus recited. ''1.44 MB, High Density MFD-2HD'.'

'Cutting edge at the time, I dare say,' Molly said, folding her arms.

'Let's see what's on it, then.'

They fell at the first hurdle, however. Patrick Spiers's computer was password-protected. Molly offered some suggestions, but none proved right.

Rebus ejected the disk and cursed silently.

'Sorry,' Molly said in sympathy.

'Not your fault. But I'll have to take it with me — is that okay?'

She nodded. 'Is this you making your excuses and your getaway? You don't want to help me sift through the rest, just in case?'

'I wish I had time, Molly. But if Acorn House comes up . . . ' He handed her a business card. 'In fact, if you see *anything* you think I might be interested in . . . '

'I'll phone you,' she agreed.

As Rebus made his exit, he half turned to give her a wave, but she wasn't paying attention. She just stood there, looking suddenly tiny and exhausted, dwarfed by her father's life and times, the stories he'd written and the ones he hadn't lived to tell.

29

Rebus had called Cafferty from his flat, giving him a progress report and asking for help. Just over an hour later, his intercom buzzed. He unlocked the door and waited for the delivery. It was carried in a loose cardboard box by a young man for whom acne was proving a challenge. His head was shaved and he wore a hooded jacket under a black padded gilet.

'All right?' he said by way of greeting. Rebus showed him where to put the box, having cleared space on the table in the living room. The computer was not a make Rebus recognised. It comprised a single bulky unit with a fourteen-inch screen.

'Gold standard at one time,' the youth assured him, plugging it in. 'MS Works and Word.'

'As long as it'll play this.' Rebus handed over the floppy. The lad slotted it home and waited while the computer churned and whirred. Then he clicked the mouse.

'It's an old Word file by the look of it,' he mused. 'And not too much on it.'

'Could anything be hidden?'

'Hidden?'

'It happens,' Rebus said. 'Encryption, that sort of thing.'

'You're talking to the wrong guy.'

'Doesn't matter,' Rebus said, knowing he could hand the disk over to the forensic lab if necessary, let them explore it. For now, he had a single file of sixty-five kilobytes, which had been given the catchy title 'Doc 1'. He showed the youth out, adding a ten-pound note to whatever Cafferty had already paid. He took his time in the kitchen, opening a bottle of IPA and pouring it into a pint glass. Then he wandered through to where the computer sat waiting. Placing his drink on the table near the mouse, he lit a cigarette and took a couple of puffs, then drew his chair in closer and opened the document.

The bastards took the lot! Every note, every interview, every bit of wild speculation. Plus the few photos I had. Every scrap was gone when I got home. No sign of forced entry, just the two boxes lying open, so I'd get the message loud and clear. 'We can do this, and a lot more besides.' That's what they're telling me. So here I am, past midnight and woozy with booze, but determined to get as much down as I can remember while wondering who stole my story. There's a villain called Cafferty, apparently he's close to Howard Champ, and Champ is one of the men who uses Acorn House — and no doubt other places like it — as a personal sexual playground. But Champ has other friends too. Our esteemed David Minton for one. They control the newspapers — or rather, they know the men who own the media, and that's even better. Or maybe they got the cops to break in. Special Branch? MI5? They'll want to protect their

340

own. They don't want a scandal — awfully bad for business, don't you know. The cops, though — no way THEY want their precious Chief Constable getting found out. No, sir, that can't be allowed to happen. Did he know I was getting close? Let me tell you about how sloppy he was getting, every single fucking one of them thinking they lived in a parallel universe where they were never going to be found out.

Right, here goes . . .

Rebus read for a further hour. There were only fifteen pages, but fifteen was enough. Booze or no booze, Spiers's memory had been unimpaired. He remembered dates, names, locations. He had spoken off the record to hotel workers, taxi drivers, and even a couple of kids from Acorn House. No names, though — he hadn't put their names in print, maybe to protect them? Yes, probably.

There *was* one name, however: Bryan Holroyd. A kid who had done a bunk, so the other kids said, fed up of being hounded by Howard Champ.

Bryan Holroyd. Rebus felt the temperature in the room drop. The dead kid? The 'accident'?

When his intercom buzzed, he ignored it, but whoever was outside wasn't about to give up. He crossed to the window and looked down. Siobhan Clarke had taken a few steps back and was peering up at him. Rebus returned to the intercom and pressed the button to let her in. He turned the PC's screen off before unlocking the door, listening to her feet as she climbed the stone staircase.

'Hiya, you,' he said, ushering her inside. 'Any news of Malcolm's dad?'

'He told you?' She watched him nod. They were standing in the living room. She noted the computer and knew it was a new addition to the room — the box it had come in was sitting on the floor.

'Thought it was time to upgrade,' Rebus joked.

'What's going on?' she asked quietly.

'One of my private clients.'

'John . . . '

'What?'

She gave a sigh. 'Never mind. I'm here to deliver a bollocking — do you want to stand or would you rather sit down?'

He grabbed what little was left of his beer and made for his armchair. Clarke took the sofa.

'Ready when you are,' he told her.

'Actually, before that, let me ask you something — what are the odds that Darryl Christie has someone from our side telling him stories?'

'Telling or selling?'

'Either.'

Rebus gave a shrug. 'It's a racing certainty.'

'And if I was a punter looking for a hot tip?'

'What's happened?'

'Joe Stark arrived fuming at Fettes because he'd found out the note left with Dennis was a copycat. This after he'd had a powwow with Darryl Christie.'

Rebus nodded his understanding. 'Well,' he said, 'you could try asking Charlie Sykes how much that hand-tailored suit of his cost.'

'That's what I thought.'

'So am I in your good books now? Bollocking deferred?'

'Afraid not. I had Laura Smith on the phone. She wasn't happy.'

'She's a crime reporter — that probably comes with the territory.'

'Any idea why she'd be so annoyed with me this time, though?'

'Do tell.'

'It's because *she'd* had Albert Stout on the phone, teasing her about some huge story that's brewing and how he knows about it and she doesn't. He mentioned your name before ringing off. So Laura wanted to know why I hadn't said anything. Seems to her it's all one-way traffic between us and we're supposed to be friends.'

'It's a mistake to make friends with reporters — I've always told you that.'

'This isn't funny, John. Is it to do with that thing?' She nodded towards the computer.

'Yes,' Rebus admitted.

'And Lord Minton and Michael Tolland?'

'And Cafferty too.'

'Then it's more *my* business than yours.'

'You can't take it to Page, not yet.'

'Why not?'

'You just can't. Fob Laura Smith off with something.'

'She'll smell it.'

'Let her smell it then.' Rebus leapt from his

armchair and paced the room.

'It's eating away at you, John — you know it and I know it. Time you opened up, a trouble shared and all that.'

'Maybe. But I'm not joking about keeping it to yourself — at least for now.'

'Why?'

'Because it's basically plutonium on a floppy disk,' Rebus said.

And then he told her.

★ ★ ★

Joe Stark was back home, seated on the bed in what had been, for the first nineteen years of his life, Dennis's room. Joe remembered the announcement that he was moving into a flat with some pals. A year later, he'd bought a place of his own. Joe had never asked how much it had cost or how Dennis could afford it. He'd always seen that the boy was all right for money without going overboard. Later on, of course, with Dennis part of the company, the spoils had been shared. They had become commercial partners rather than father and son. Joe had taken counsel earlier from Walter Grieve and Len Parker, who had argued that he needed to stamp his authority on the sides of the business that Dennis had overseen. It had to be soon, too, before others stepped in to fill the vacuum.

When Joe's phone rang, he saw it was Jackie Dyson and decided to answer.

'Jackie,' he said. 'Is this you bringing me an update?'

'A straight answer's what I need, Joe.'

'Depends on the question.'

'Did you leave a couple of us here so there's less chance of us making a move against you?'

'You've got brains, son.' Stark couldn't help smiling. 'But there's another way of looking at it — you might even say I'm protecting you. Things could get ugly at home.'

'And are we still looking for Wright's stash?'

'Reckon we're ever going to find it? I think our best chance died some time back.'

'How about whoever did for Dennis?'

'Got to be down to either Christie or Cafferty, unless you've got a better idea. That's why I want you to keep an eye on them.'

'Then that's what I'll do.'

'You'll have to track Cafferty down first — Christie tells me he's not been seen.'

'No problem.'

'And if you get wind of mutterings in the ranks . . . '

'I know where my loyalties lie, Mr Stark.'

'There's going to be a bit of restructuring, Jackie. By the time you come back to Glasgow, your life's going to have changed for the better. *Majorly* for the better, if you take my meaning.'

'I can't wait.'

'Good lad.' Stark ended the call and stretched himself out on his son's mattress. There were cracks on the ceiling. As a kid, Dennis had fretted that chunks of plaster might fall off and hit him.

If they do, Joe had advised, *hit them back — they'll break before you do.*

And the pair of them had laughed.

* * *

Cafferty watched from the corner as Siobhan Clarke drove away from Arden Street in her Astra. She looked distracted, her face pale. Another time, she might have spotted him, but not today, so he started walking again, ending up at the door to Rebus's tenement and pressing the bell.

'You forget something?' Rebus's voice crackled.

'She's skedaddled,' Cafferty informed him. 'So you'll have to put up with me instead.'

The lock clicked and Cafferty pushed the door open, climbing the two flights to Rebus's flat.

'You got the computer then,' he said.

'I don't want to know where it came from.'

'Oliver says you tipped him — that was a nice gesture. What did Siobhan want?'

'Fox's dad is at death's door. She decided to tell me in person.'

'Might explain why she looked like she'd had bad news. Are her and Fox close then?' Cafferty had settled in front of the computer. The first page of the document was up on the screen. 'Juicy stuff?' he asked.

'He starts by wondering if maybe you broke into his home and stole the evidence.'

'I didn't.'

'He also says that the Chief Constable of the time, Jim Broadfoot, was up to his eyes.'

'No doubt about that. Wasn't he knighted eventually?'

'Dead now, though.'

'Yes.'

'There's a missing kid mentioned a bit further on — Bryan Holroyd. Could that be him?'

'No one ever gave me a name.'

'I'm going to see if I can source a photo.'

'Will there still be records?'

'From Acorn House? I doubt it. But the kids who went there had mostly been in trouble.'

'And the police keep everything?' Cafferty nodded his understanding. Then he looked at his watch. 'I think you deserve a drink, and I'm buying.'

'I don't feel like a drink.'

'Words I doubt you've uttered before. I did tell you it wasn't going to be pleasant.'

'You did,' Rebus conceded.

'And drink can do wonderful things to unpleasant memories.'

Rebus nodded slowly. 'Fine then.' He ejected the floppy from its slot and stuck it in his pocket.

'Probably an unnecessary precaution,' Cafferty said.

'Probably,' Rebus agreed. 'But that won't stop me making copies of it, first chance I get. And speaking of precautions . . . '

'Yes?'

'If I hear that you've been back to Meadowlea to visit Paul Jeffries without me . . . '

'I admit it's crossed my mind.'

'Staff there have my number. If they tell me you've as much as paused for breath at the end of the driveway, that's us finished.'

'Time was, a man could have some fun . . . '

'For the likes of you and me, those days are over.'

'Then what's left to look forward to?'

Rebus plucked his house keys from the table. 'We're heading there right now,' he said.

30

Fox's sister, Jude, lived in a terraced house in Saughtonhall. He'd suggested picking her up, but she'd said she would take a cab.

'Then I'll wait outside for you.'

'Because you want to pick up the tab? I've got money of my own, Malcolm.'

He'd waited in the hospital's main concourse instead, equidistant between the two entrances. Jude had come tottering through the sliding doors on three-inch heels, clad in skin-tight jeans, a shapeless T-shirt and a waist-length fur jacket. There were at least two gossamer-thin scarves wrapped around her neck, and her shoulder-length hair looked lifeless. Her face was pale, cheekbones prominent, eyeshadow over-done.

She stopped a yard or so from him and adjusted her sparkly shoulder bag. No embrace, no peck on the cheek. 'How's he doing?' she enquired.

'He hasn't regained consciousness.'

'And they're saying it's a stroke?'

'Have you been drinking, Jude?'

'Would you blame me if I had?'

'We should get you a coffee or something.'

'I'll be fine.'

'You're sure?'

'Do we take the lift or what?'

'We take the lift.'

349

'Well then.' She walked over to the wall and pressed the button. Fox had a sudden flashback — Jude as a toddler, dressed in her mother's clothes and shoes, doing a fashion parade in their parents' bedroom. Another time it had been make-up and perfume. 'You coming?'

He joined her in front of the lift. Its doors slid open, revealing an attendant in charge of an empty wheelchair.

'Kind of you,' Jude told the man, 'but I think I can walk.'

Once the wheelchair had gone, they got in and waited for the doors to close.

'Times like this,' Fox said, staring at the floor, 'I wish I'd visited Dad more often.'

Jude glared at him. 'It's not the frequency that counts, it's the intention.'

He met her eyes. 'What do you mean?'

'Dad always knew you were only there out of a sense of duty.'

'That's not true.'

But Jude wasn't listening. 'You were there because it was the thing that had to be done, and you could feel all good about yourself afterwards, because you'd *done your duty*.' Her gaze was challenging him to deny it. 'Something you felt was expected, rather than something you did out of love, like paying for your sister's cab.'

'Jesus, Jude . . .'

'Dad could see it too — how bored you were, just sitting there, trying not to look at your watch too often and too obviously.'

'You know how to kick a man when he's down, sis.'

350

She smiled, not unsympathetically. 'I do, don't I? Needed to be said, though, before the full martyr complex kicks in. That *was* where we were headed next, wasn't it?'

The bell pinged and the doors slid open, the automated voice telling them they had reached their floor. Fox led the way. The lights had been dimmed. The brightest lamp sat over the nurses' station. Mitch had been moved into a room of his own. Fox was afraid to ask why — maybe a slow death wasn't something the other patients and their visitors should have to witness. The breath caught in Jude's throat when she saw her father. She walked briskly to his bedside while Fox closed the door, giving the three of them a measure of privacy. There was a window on to the main ward, its blinds left open, the room itself unlit. Fox reached for the light switch, but Jude shook her head.

'It's fine like this,' she said, touching a hand to Mitch's forehead. Her shoulder bag had fallen to the floor, a few items spilling out — phone, lipstick, cigarette lighter. Fox crouched to pick them up.

'Just leave them,' she hissed. 'They're not what's important.'

'But they're something I can fix,' her brother said, straightening up, her things gathered in his hand.

Her face softened. 'I suppose that's true,' she said quietly. Then, half turning from the bed, she wrapped her arms around him and began to sob.

★　★　★

351

Siobhan Clarke had been sitting on her sofa for the best part of an hour, just staring at the bookshelves opposite. She sat bent forward, elbows on knees, face cupped in her hands. She'd made a mug of tea but it was as yet untouched. Acorn House — those two words kept reverberating, sometimes clashing against names like Champ and Broadfoot and Holroyd. Rebus had made her promise not to take it to James Page, not until he'd had a chance to dig a little deeper. More names: Tolland and Dalrymple, Jeffries and Ritter. Rebus had bombarded her with them, like they were dots that had to be joined together so the picture could emerge.

Tolland . . .

She still had the file Jim Grant had given her. She remembered the DVD footage, the subdued-looking wife. Ella Tolland, sad-eyed on her wedding day, her husband controlling her, his hand grasping her arm.

'It wasn't just shyness, was it, Ella?' Clarke enquired out loud. 'I think you knew. He'd said something, or else you'd always suspected.' She straightened up and looked to left and right, spotting the file on the carpet, half hidden beneath the sofa. She lifted it up and opened it, seeking the various photographs, knowing there was no way to tell for sure, just as there was no hard and fast evidence that Acorn House — whatever horrors it had contained — had anything to do with the attacks on Tolland, Minton and Cafferty.

'Proof would be nice,' she mused, knowing she was going to give Rebus another day or so. Because whatever you could say about the man, he clamped his teeth on to a case and didn't let go. 'Go get 'em, John,' she said, yawning as the photographs slid off her lap to the floor.

★ ★ ★

Fox was in bed when his phone rang. He had plugged it into a wall socket, so padded across the carpet in darkness and peered at the screen before answering.

'John?' he said. 'What's up?'

'Just thought I'd see how your dad's doing.'

'No real news. What time is it?'

'Did I wake you? It's only just gone eleven.'

'We're not all nighthawks.'

'You'll find you need less sleep as you get older.'

'Anything happening at your end? Help take my mind off my dad.'

'He'll either be fine or he won't, Malcolm. Nothing you can do except be there for him.'

'My sister doesn't think I even do that. I'm dutiful rather than loving, apparently. Look at me — at home in bed rather than keeping vigil at his bedside.'

'Your sister's at the hospital?'

'We decided to take shifts.' Fox sat on the carpet, back to the wall, knees raised. 'Do you ever see your daughter?'

'Once or twice a year.'

'If I had a grandkid . . .'

'You trying to make me feel guilty? Sammy knows she can visit any time she wants.'

'Does she know you want her to, though?

353

Seems to me we're not always good at opening up. I mean, we're fine with friends and strangers; it's our families we keep stuff from.'

'You're wishing you'd said more to your dad?'

'I said plenty, but Jude might have a point — I skated over the difficult stuff.'

'He's your father — he doesn't *need* to be told.'

'How do you mean?'

'He probably reads you better than anyone. He'll know exactly how you're feeling and what you're not saying.'

'Maybe.' Fox rubbed the back of his neck, feeling a tightness there. 'Anyway, I was asking for an update.'

'Some bad things happened in the past. They may explain the attacks on Cafferty, Minton and our Linlithgow lottery winner.'

'There *is* a connection then?'

'Connection and motive both.'

'Congratulations.'

'Bit early for that.'

'But you're making progress, showing the youngsters a thing or two.'

'It feels like the end of a long song, though — men like Cafferty and Joe Stark . . . and me too, come to that . . . we're on our last legs. Our way of doing things seems . . . I don't know.'

'Last century?'

'Aye, maybe.'

'Footwork still counts for something, John. Add it to gut instinct and you've got a formula that works.' He listened to Rebus drain the dregs from a glass, imagined him at home, one last whisky before bed. Hell, he could almost taste it, oily, copper-coloured, peat-rich.

'I should let you get back to bed,' Rebus said, after a satisfied exhalation.

'Will you pass on the news to Siobhan?'

'She'd probably rather hear it from you.'

'You're right. I'll send her a text.'

'You could even call her.'

'She might be in bed.'

'Then again, she might not — take a risk for once.'

Fox smiled tiredly. 'No promises,' he said, ending the call. Back in bed, he lay on his back, hands clasped across his chest. His eyes remained open as he stared at the ceiling. Sleep, he knew, wasn't going to come any time soon, so he got up and, grabbing his phone, headed to the kitchen, filling the kettle and switching it on. He dropped a tea bag into a mug and eased himself on to a stool. Yes, he could call Siobhan, but it was late and he really didn't have any news. Would a text wake her up? He started composing one, then deleted it. When his tea was ready, he picked up the phone again. He had no messages, no unanswered calls. He tapped the photos icon and found a picture he'd taken of Siobhan with the low winter sun behind her, so that her face was mostly in shadow.

'Don't give up the day job, Malcolm,' he muttered to himself. He opened another photo and used his finger and thumb to enlarge it on the screen. It was Hamish Wright's itemised phone bill. Most of the calls were to other mobiles. One of Compston's team had added the details in the margin: wife, insurer, client, client, garage, nephew, client, ferry company, restaurant. But there were land-line calls too: wife again, and an aunt in Dundee. Plus one 0131 number — Edinburgh. The Gifford Inn. And written next to it: *staff never heard of him, reckon a wrong number.* A wrong number on a Monday evening, one week prior to his disappearance, and lasting almost three minutes. The Gifford didn't mean anything to Fox, but he looked it up — it was on St John's Road in Corstorphine. He had driven along St John's Road hundreds of times, but then he never really paid attention to pubs — though he'd lay money on John Rebus knowing the place.

Footwork still counts for something . . . Add it to gut instinct . . .

Take a risk . . .

Take a risk . . .

Take a risk . . .

'Well, Malcolm?' he challenged himself out loud. 'What about it?'

Half an hour later, he was back in bed, hands under his head, eyes adjusting to the dark as he turned things over in his mind.

Day Eight

31

Rebus held the box out towards Christine Esson. She was seated at her computer and looked wary.

'From the baker's,' he said, placing it on the desk. She opened it and peered inside.

'Jam doughnuts,' she said.

'My way of saying sorry.'

'For what?'

'Not telling you I'd found Paul Jeffries all on my own.'

Ronnie Ogilvie approached the desk and lifted out one of the pastries, holding it in his teeth as he headed back to his own chair. Esson glowered at him, but he seemed impervious.

'The other three are yours, if you're quick,' Rebus told her.

She closed the box and slipped it into her drawer. 'Thank you,' she said. Then she noticed he was holding out a slip of paper, expecting her to take it.

'Bryan Holroyd,' he explained. 'I've not got much for you to go on — and I'm sorry about that, too. He was a teenager in the eighties, spent a bit of time at an assessment centre called Acorn House. It's been shut for years, but the fact he was there at all means he probably had a criminal record . . . '

'You think there'll be something in the archive? Doesn't stuff get expunged after a time?'

Rebus just shrugged. 'There may even be information on Acorn House — it was a remand home before they changed the wording. But whatever you do, tread softly.'

'Oh?'

'Alarm bells may sound.'

'And they'd do that because . . . ?'

'They probably won't.'

'Which doesn't answer my question.'

He gave the slip of paper a little wave. 'I brought doughnuts,' he reminded her.

After a further ten seconds of stand-off, she sighed and snatched the details from him. 'Which is more likely to trigger an alarm — online search or me traipsing to the records office?'

'Only one way to find out.' Rebus offered what he hoped was a winning smile. 'Siobhan not in yet?'

'As you can see.' Esson gestured towards the empty desk.

'Maybe she spent the night consoling Malcolm . . . '

'And why would I be doing that?'

The voice had come from the doorway. Clarke stepped into the office and lifted her laptop from her bag, placing it on her desk.

'His dad's still in hospital,' Rebus explained. 'I told him to phone you.'

'He didn't.'

'It was getting late, to be fair. Though you don't exactly look like you've had much in the way of beauty sleep.'

'Thanks for the vote of confidence.' She was

360

shrugging out of her coat and unwinding a long red woollen scarf from around her neck.

Esson had brought the box back out. 'Doughnut?' she suggested.

'Just the job,' Clarke said, plucking one out with a nod of thanks. Esson took one herself before returning the box to its drawer.

'One spare,' Rebus hinted.

'For later,' she retorted.

'I've given Bryan Holroyd's name to Christine,' Rebus explained to Clarke. 'I reckon she's got more diplomacy than me.'

Clarke nodded. 'Though if it's the same groper in charge of the archive as when I last had cause to visit, diplomacy might have to take second place to pepper spray.'

'I can handle myself,' Esson assured her. 'Just need to handle the final doughnut first.'

'Thanks for rubbing it in,' Rebus muttered, heading for the door. He was halfway there when Esson called him back.

'Yes?' he said, sounding hopeful.

'Are you not going to ask me about Dave Ritter?'

'I was surmising you didn't have anything.'

'You'd be wrong.' She paused. 'Sort of wrong, anyway. The forces of law and order in Ullapool have never had dealings with him, nor is there any record of him living in Scotland at the current time.'

'Well, thanks for sharing.'

'There *is*, however, a man called David Ratner. Known all too well by the local constabulary.'

'In Ullapool?'

'In Ullapool,' she confirmed. Now it was her turn to hand a slip of paper out for Rebus to take. He digested the details as she went on. 'Arrests for minor offences — drunk and disorderly, brawling in the street . . . '

'Might be him, then.'

'Might be.'

He stared at her. 'When were you going to tell me this?'

'It was on the tip of my tongue, until you produced yet another favour you wanted me to do.'

'What's this?' Clarke enquired, her mouth full of pastry, sprinkles of sugar on her lips.

'One of Cafferty's goons,' Rebus reminded her. 'The one we didn't manhandle in front of his carers.'

'He's living in the Highlands under an assumed name?'

'Could be.'

'You going to head up there?'

Rebus nodded thoughtfully. 'If only to protect him from Cafferty.'

'You're all heart,' Clarke said. Rebus turned back towards Esson.

'I'm all heart,' he told her. 'Official confirmation.'

With a sigh and a rolling of the eyes, Esson held the box out towards him.

★   ★   ★

It had taken Rebus only a couple of minutes with a map to work out that the quickest route to

Ullapool was the A9 to Inverness, then the A835 heading west. He filled the Saab with petrol, offered up a prayer that the old crate would survive the journey, and piled water, cigarettes and crisps on the passenger seat, along with a cut-price CD that promised him the best rock songs of the seventies and eighties.

The A9 was not a road he relished. He had driven up and down it several times a couple of years back on a previous case. Some of it was dualled, but long, winding stretches weren't, and those were where you tended to get stuck behind a convoy of lorries or venerable caravans towed by underpowered saloon cars. Inverness was 150 miles from Edinburgh, but it would take him three hours, and maybe half that again to reach his final destination.

Having witnessed Cafferty's reaction at the nursing home, he had decided to say nothing about this trip. Not until he was safely back in Edinburgh. As he crossed the Forth Road Bridge, he saw its replacement taking shape over to the west. The project was apparently on time and under budget, unlike the Edinburgh tram route. He had yet to take a tram anywhere in the city. At his age, buses were free to use, but he never took those either.

'Me and you,' he told his Saab, giving the steering wheel a reassuring pat.

North as far as Perth was dual carriageway and relatively quiet, but once past Perth the road narrowed and new average-speed cameras didn't help. He began to wish he had commandeered a patrol car and driver, with blue lights and siren.

But then he would have had to explain the purpose of the trip.

A kid was killed and I need to talk to the man who took him away and buried him . . .

The fact that David Ratner had been in trouble recently meant that he might at least be available to answer a few questions. On the other hand, how willing would he be? Rebus mulled that over as he drove. Cafferty had helped cover up a crime — possibly a murder. In the scheme of things, he should already be in custody, but that wouldn't help solve the mystery. He would clam up, and his lawyer would have him back on the street in no time. This way, as Rebus had argued to Siobhan Clarke, at least there was the possibility of closure — retribution could come later, if the Fiscal's office decided it was feasible. Rebus was a realist if nothing else. Down the years he had seen the guilty walk free and the (relatively) innocent suffer punishment. He had watched — as furiously impotent as Albert Stout or Patrick Spiers — as the rich and powerful played the system. He had come to appreciate that those with influence could be more cunning and ruthless than those with none.

'The overworld and the underworld,' he muttered to himself, pulling out to overtake an artic. Having done so, he found himself stuck behind a Megabus with a smiling cartoon character waving at him from its rear end, advertising the cheap fares. Five slow miles later, he was imagining himself beating his cheery tormentor with a stick. The CD wasn't helping either — he didn't recognise most of the tunes, and power ballads coupled with big hair had never been his thing. He changed to the radio, until the reception died as white-capped mountains began to rise either side of the road. There was snow on the verges, turned grey from exhaust fumes, but the day was overcast and a couple of degrees above zero. He hadn't entertained the possibility that the route might become difficult or impassable. How good were his tyres? When had he last checked them? He glanced towards his passenger-seat supplies.

You'll be fine, he told himself as a BMW flew past, squeezing past the bus as an approaching lorry sounded its horn in annoyance.

★ ★ ★

There was nowhere to park in Corstorphine, so Fox ended up behind the McDonald's at Drum Brae roundabout. Fringing the car park were a few stores, with a huge Tesco beyond. He reckoned the Gifford Inn would open at eleven, and it was now five to. Walking back along St John's Road, he stopped at a guitar shop and studied the window display. Jude had always wanted a guitar, but their father had never allowed it.

'Soon as I move out, I'm getting one,' she had yelled, aged fourteen.

'Leave the key on the table,' Mitch had replied.

Fox himself had surprised her a decade later by buying her one for her birthday — acoustic rather than electric, and with a teach-yourself book and CD. The guitar had sat in a corner of her room for a year or two, until he visited one day and noticed it was no longer there. Nothing had ever been said.

There were no early customers at the Gifford when he pushed open the door. It looked the sort of place that catered to a lunchtime trade. Each table boasted a laminated menu, and the daily specials were on a chalkboard next to the bar. Stripped wooden floorboards, plenty of mirrors, and gleaming brass bar taps. A man in his twenties was rearranging the bar stools.

'I'll be with you in a second,' he announced.

'No real rush — I'm not drinking anything.'

'If you're a rep, you need to phone the boss and book a slot.'

'I'm a detective.' Fox showed the man his warrant card.

'Has something happened?'

'Just checking a couple of things.'

'Sure you don't want a drink — on the house?'

'Maybe an Appletiser then.'

'No problem.' The barman checked he was happy with the stools and went around to the other side of the bar, pulling a bottle from the chiller cabinet. 'Ice?'

'No thanks.' Fox eased himself on to a stool and took out his phone, finding the photo of Hamish Wright's phone bill. He reeled off the number.

'That's us all right,' the barman agreed.

'Is it a payphone?'

'Not really.' He indicated the landline. It was between the gantry and the access hatch.

'It's for staff use only?'

The barman shrugged. 'Sometimes a regular will need a taxi or to place a bet. Usually they have their own phones, but if not . . . '

'And do they get calls too?'

'Wives looking for their husbands, you mean?' The barman smiled. 'It happens.'

'Three weeks back, a man called Hamish Wright phoned here. It was a Monday evening. Call lasted a couple of minutes.'

'I don't know anyone called Hamish Wright.'

'He lives in Inverness, runs a haulage company.'

'Still doesn't ring a bell.'

'Who else might have been on duty that night?'

'Sandra, maybe. Or Denise. Jeff's on holiday and Ben was sick around then — winter flu, also known as skiving.'

'Could you maybe ask Sandra and Denise?'

The barman nodded.

'As in — now,' Fox added.

Fox sipped his drink while the barman made the calls. The result was another shrug. 'Sandra remembers your lot phoning to ask. She told them it was probably a wrong number.'

'But she doesn't remember the call?'

'We do get more than a few phone calls, you know. When the bar's busy, you've got a lot going on . . . '

'Hamish Wright has never had a drink in here?'

'What does he look like?'

Fox took a moment on his phone to find an

internet photo of Wright. It was from an Inverness newspaper and showed him in front of one of his lorries. The barman narrowed his eyes as he studied it.

'I'd have to say he seems familiar,' he admitted. 'But that's probably because he looks much the same as most of the men we get in here.'

'Take another look,' Fox urged. But the door was opening, an elderly man shuffling in carrying a folded newspaper.

'Morning, Arthur,' the barman called out. The customer nodded a reply. 'Cold one again, eh?'

'Bitter,' the regular agreed.

The barman was placing a glass under one of the whisky optics while the customer counted out coins on to the bar. Fox turned to the new arrival. 'Does the name Hamish Wright mean anything to you?'

'Does he have two legs?' the old man enquired.

'I think so — why?'

'Because if he does, he could probably get a game for Rangers, the way they're playing.'

The barman gave a snort of laughter as he handed over the drink. Fox decided he was wasting his time. He drained his glass and headed to the Gents, passing a jukebox and a noticeboard. There was a cutting from the *Evening News* about money the bar had raised for charity, alongside cards from local businesses advertising their services. On his way back from the toilet, Fox paused again at the board and removed one of the cards. He showed it to the barman.

'CC Self Storage,' he commented.

'What of it?'

'Named after its owner, Chick Carpenter. Know him?'

'No.'

'It's in Broomhouse, not exactly on your doorstep — so why the advert?'

The barman offered a non-committal shrug.

'Does Wee Anthony not work there?' the whisky drinker called out as he seated himself at what was presumably his customary table.

Fox stared at the barman. 'Did Wee Anthony put this card up?'

'Maybe.'

'He's a regular, I'm guessing?'

Another shrug.

'And do people ever phone for him?'

'I suppose so, on rare occasions.'

'Including three weeks ago?'

'That's something you'd have to ask him yourself.'

'Then that's what I'll do,' Fox said, tucking the card into his top pocket. He dug in his trousers for change, placing a couple of pound coins on the bar.

'The drink was on the house,' the barman reminded him.

'I'm choosy about who I take freebies from,' Fox retorted, turning to leave.

★   ★   ★

He called Siobhan Clarke from the car park and asked her what she thought.

'Whose case is it, Malcolm?' she asked.

'Somebody gunned down Dennis Stark.'

369

'And where's the connection?'

'Stark was looking for Hamish Wright — what if Wright or one of his friends decided to turn the tables?'

'Okay . . .'

'Wright phoned the Gifford, a guy who drinks there works for Chick Carpenter, Carpenter got a doing by Dennis Stark . . .'

'Any number of people held a grudge against the victim. But we're looking for someone who tried to make it appear like part of a pattern.'

'To throw us off the scent, yes. Last thing they'd want is Joe Stark coming after them.'

'That's a fair point.' Clarke thought for a moment. 'Where are you now?'

'Parked outside a pet shop.'

'Thinking of taking up John's offer of a free dog?'

'Perish the thought.'

'I thought you might be at the hospital.'

'I popped in first thing. Jude told me to swap with her later on.'

'Any news?'

'No change from last night.'

'You know, nobody would blame you for taking some time off . . .'

Fox ignored this. 'I'm considering dropping in on CC Self Storage — unless you think I shouldn't.'

'There's not a whole lot you can be doing here,' she admitted. 'Though we're one down.'

'Oh?'

'Christine's gone off to the archive on an errand for John.'

'He's a one-man job-creation scheme.'
'Want to guess where he is right now?'
'Enlighten me.'
'Driving to Ullapool.'
'What's in Ullapool?'
'Last time I went, I remember fish and chips and a ferry.'
'And which of those is he interested in?'
'There's someone he needs to talk to.'
'You sound like you don't want to tell me much more.'
'One day soon, maybe.'
'But not now?' Fox was starting the ignition. 'Should I report back after the storage place?'
'Absolutely.'
'That's what I'll do then.'

32

Ullapool nestled under thick banks of bruised cloud. Rebus drove slowly along the waterfront, then uphill from the harbour. Soon enough he reached a sign thanking him for having visited, so he did a U-turn. Rows of terraced houses hid a large Tesco store from general view. A tour bus had stopped outside a pub that seemed to be serving warming drinks and hot takeaway food. Rebus pulled into a parking place and got out, stretching his spine and rolling his shoulders. He had stopped for petrol at a retail park on the outskirts of Inverness and topped up his provisions with a microwaved bridie and a bottle of Irn-Bru. He wished now that he had waited and eaten in Ullapool. Instead, he lit a cigarette and headed to the harbour. Gulls were bobbing in the water, seemingly immune to the biting wind. Rebus buttoned his coat and finished his cigarette before heading into a shop. Its wares included shrimping nets and buckets and spades — despite the season being a way off — plus newspapers and groceries. The shopkeeper seemed to size him up, realising he wasn't in the market to buy.

'I'm looking for this address.' Rebus handed across the slip of paper Christine Esson had given him.

'Did you see the Tesco?' the shopkeeper enquired.

'I did.'

'Next road on the left.' The man handed back the piece of paper. Rebus waited for more, then managed a thin smile.

'You saw the name next to the address?'

'Aye.'

'So you know why I'm here.'

'I dare say you're some kind of policeman.'

'Mr Ratner's got a bit of a rep?'

'He likes the drink more than it seems to like him.'

'How long has he lived here?'

'Six or seven years. He was dating a local lass, but that didn't come to anything. We thought he would move on, but he's still here.'

'Does he have a job?'

'I think he's on the dole. Used to do some building work, when it was offered.'

Rebus nodded his gratitude. 'Anything else?' he asked.

'You know he has a temper?'

'Yes.'

'But that's mostly after closing time. He should be fine just now.'

'And I'll probably find him at home?'

'If you don't, it won't take long to check out the nearby watering holes.'

Rebus thanked the man, bought an unneeded packet of cigarettes and walked back up the slope to his car.

'Next road on the left,' he recited as he passed the Tesco. He pulled up outside a terraced house and pushed open the knee-high metal gate. The garden was neither manicured nor a wasteland.

373

The curtains at the downstairs window were open, those upstairs closed. He looked in vain for a doorbell, then banged with his fist instead. No answer, so he thumped again. Coughing from inside. He got the feeling someone was descending from the upper floor. The door opened an inch, the eyes squinting as they adjusted to the weak daylight.

'Mr Ratner?' Rebus asked. 'David Ratner?'

'Who's asking?'

Rebus had already decided how to play it. 'An old pal of yours,' he said, shoving at the door with his shoulder. Ratner staggered backwards against the bottom two steps of the staircase. By the time he'd recovered, Rebus was inside and the door was closed.

'Hell's going on?' the man yelped, voice filled with grievance.

Rebus examined the hallway. Bare linoleum, walls that had last seen a coat of paint in the eighties, a threadbare stair carpet. The place held an aroma of single unwashed male.

'Living room,' he announced, making it sound like an order.

Cafferty's description of Dave Ritter had been sketchy, but it did fit the man in front of Rebus, the one who was wondering how best to get rid of this unwelcome guest so a courtship with cheap booze could be resumed. The good news was, Ratner/Ritter had no heft to him. He was almost as shrunken as his friend Paul Jeffries. Rebus began to wonder if the enormity of just one crime had ground both men down.

Without saying anything, the man led the way

374

into a room containing two charity-shop armchairs and a newish-looking TV. There were bottles and cans too, with empty fast-food containers providing extra ornamentation.

'Does your cleaner come tomorrow?' Rebus asked.

'Funny.' The man was testing a few of the cans, without finding a drop to drink in any.

'Do I call you Ratner or Ritter?'

The freeze was momentary, but enough to convince Rebus.

'Who sent you?'

'Big Ger.' Rebus was standing in front of the door to the hall, a door he had pushed closed. If the man in front of him wanted an exit, he was going to have to use the window.

'A name from the past. And I prefer Ratner.' He slumped into one of the armchairs.

'Here's another name from the past.' Rebus paused for effect. 'Acorn House.'

Ratner seemed to slump further, shoulders hunched. He cursed under his breath.

'Nothing to say?' Rebus prompted. 'Well that's too bad, because you're the one who's going to have to spit it out . . . '

Ratner looked at him. 'You've seen Paul?' he guessed.

'Not got much repartee these days, has he?'

'Poor bugger. At least I've still got a few brain cells. What did Cafferty tell you?'

'That you both worked for him back in the day — disposing of problems. A patch of woodland in Fife was mentioned.'

'Ancient history.'

375

'It was until recently. Things have changed.'
'Oh?'

Rebus decided to take the other chair. He pulled his cigarettes out and gestured with them. Ratner took one and allowed Rebus to light it.

'Ta,' he said.

Rebus lit one for himself and blew the smoke ceilingwards.

'Are you here to terminate me?' Ratner asked.

'I hate to break it to you, Dave, but you're not that important.'

'I never told another living soul, you know. So if someone's been blabbing, you need to look elsewhere.'

'Do you remember Michael Tolland?'

Ratner mouthed the name silently a couple of times. 'Was he the one who opened the door to us?'

Rebus nodded slowly. 'Who else was inside?'

'The MP guy . . . '

'Howard Champ?'

It was Ratner's turn to nod. 'And his pal Minton — a bloody QC. Spent his days putting folk like me and Paul away, and then headed out of an evening to bugger young boys at Acorn House. Afterwards, I cursed if I ever had to as much as drive past the place. There was talk of an inquiry at one point, but I'm guessing Minton put the lid on that and screwed it down tight.'

'Wasn't the only job you did for Big Ger, though — the only disposal, I mean?'

'There were a few, but never kids. Just that one time. I doubt a day goes by when I don't think of it. Those men climbing back into their suits, sorting their cufflinks, shaking and pale-faced, not from shame, but because they might be found out.' He shook his head slowly.

'Cafferty wasn't there?'

'God, no.'

'But it meant they owed him.'

Ratner nodded. 'I'm sure he pulled a few favours. Except from — ' He broke off, his eyes fixing on Rebus. 'Don't suppose it matters now, does it?'

'Who else was there?'

'He was just arriving as we left. Tried mumbling some excuse, but Paul and I knew what he'd come for — same thing as the rest of them.'

'Was it the Chief Constable?'

'Broadfoot, you mean? Oh, his name was mentioned — they'd thought of phoning *him* to get rid of the body, until Champ mentioned Big Ger.'

'But he wasn't actually there?'

'Guy who turned up was Todd Dalrymple.'

'From Milligan's Casino?'

'That's the one. Happily married, but that didn't mean much to some of them — Chief Constable had a wife too, didn't he?'

'Did Cafferty know?'

'About Dalrymple?' Ratner shook his head again. 'He peeled off a roll of fifties and split it between us.'

'Paul Jeffries ended up driving for him.'

'He did, yes.'

'And Dalrymple still visits him.'

Ratner's face twisted into a sour smile. 'To

make sure Paul hasn't got mouthy as well as senile.'

Rebus nodded his understanding. Silence fell over the room. Ratner rose slowly to his feet, but only to switch on the ceiling light.

'You're sure you're not here to do me in?' he asked as he sat down again. 'Because to be honest, I'm not sure I wouldn't welcome it — maybe you can tell. I was a vicious little sod back then, I admit. People can change, though . . . '

'Felt good to get it off your chest after all these years?' Rebus nodded again. 'Aye, I can see that, but to answer your question — *I'm* not going to kill you, but someone else might.'

'Oh?'

'Somebody fired a shot at Big Ger. Somebody also killed Minton and Tolland.'

'Bit of a coincidence.' Having finished the cigarette, Ratner dropped its remains into one of the empty cans. A few moments later, Rebus did the same with his.

'Acorn House seems to be the connection, wouldn't you say? Which is why we're thinking about the victim — his name was Bryan Holroyd, by the way.'

'Ah, the victim . . . ' Ratner went silent again. He rose slowly to his feet and stood by the window, his hands sliding into his trouser pockets. Eventually he turned his head towards Rebus. 'Has Cafferty worked it out then?'

'Worked what out?'

'We told him it was job done. What else were we going to do? We knew he'd go mental,

378

probably bury the pair of us with his bare hands.'

Rebus sat forward a little. 'What are you saying?'

'The kid wasn't dead. Everybody acted like he was and told us he was, and we took that at face value. Picked him up and he was all floppy, like a corpse would be. Stuffed him in the car and drove to Fife, got out and opened the boot . . . '

'And?'

'And he flew past me like a banshee! I nearly died on the spot. He was hardly dressed at all, but he was off and running.'

'You went after him?'

'We scoured that bloody forest until dawn, frozen to the marrow.'

'He got away?' Rebus's voice was a fraction above a whisper.

'No way he could have survived out there, all but naked and no shelter for miles. We kept an eye on the news, but there was never a report of a body being found. We reckoned he had lain down, covered himself with leaves and died like that, decomposing and gone for ever.'

'But supposing he didn't — he would have names, wouldn't he? Maybe not yours, but Minton and Tolland. He was probably lying there while they talked about fetching Cafferty. Those three names.'

'Is Champ dead too?' Ratner asked.

Rebus nodded. 'Natural causes, a few years back.'

'Doesn't make sense then — wouldn't the main grudge be against him? And why take so long to do something about it?'

379

'I don't know.' But Rebus knew the man had a point. 'Nor do I know what Holroyd looked like.'

'Skinny, pale, dark hair, young-looking face . . . Hardly likely to help you after all this time.' Ratner paused. 'You think it's really him?'

'It might be.'

'And you'll be telling Cafferty?'

'I have to.'

'You know he'll kill me?'

'Not if I don't tell him where to find you.'

Ratner was staring at him. 'You'd do that?'

'Maybe. But I need a statement from you — I need everything you've just told me.'

'A *statement*? So you're a cop?'

'I used to be.'

Ratner slumped back into his chair. 'That kid haunted us, you know. I think he's what did for Paul's marbles in the end. And look how great *my* life turned out . . . '

Rebus was searching his phone for the recording function. He glanced up at Ratner for a second.

'No less than you fucking deserve,' he said.

33

'Are you Anthony?' Fox asked. 'Or is it Wee Anthony?' He had parked in one of the bays in front of CC Self Storage. Chick Carpenter's Aston Martin wasn't there. The two-storey building's frontage included a loading bay, protected by a roll-down grille, plus a solid wooden door with the word RECEPTION on it. The man walking towards him had emerged from this door, obviously in response to the sound of Fox's car. He stood just under five and a half feet high, and Fox recognised him as the colleague who had watched Carpenter take a beating at the hands of Dennis Stark and Jackie Dyson.

The man had reckoned on greeting a new customer, but now he wasn't so sure. He looked right and left, as if fearing Fox might have brought back-up. Fox produced his warrant card, which did little to calm the man's nerves.

'You're not in trouble,' Fox assured him. 'Just need a quick word. How's your boss doing, by the way?'

'My boss?'

'I heard he got a thumping.'

'Did he?'

Fox smiled. 'You heard Dennis Stark got himself killed?'

'Who's Dennis Stark?'

Fox made show of folding his arms. 'This

really the way you want to play it, Anthony? You are Anthony?'

Eventually the man nodded.

'And did they manage to give you a surname at the christening, Anthony?'

'Wright.'

Fox could feel cogs beginning to turn. 'Well, Mr Wright,' he said, 'I'm Detective Inspector Malcolm Fox.'

'Whoever did him in, it had nothing to do with us,' Wright blurted out, a tremor in his voice.

'You'll appreciate we have to ask the questions, though. Here or in the office — your choice.'

'Do I need a lawyer or anything?'

Fox tried for a dumbfounded look. 'Why would you need a lawyer? This is just us having a chat.'

'I should phone Chick . . . '

'I'd rather you didn't — we'll be talking to him separately.'

'What's it got to do with me anyway?'

'You were present when your employer was attacked, yes?'

'How do you know that?'

Fox found that he was enjoying thinking on his feet. 'Dennis Stark's pals are obviously keen that we find his killer. They've been talking freely.'

'I've told you it was nothing to do with us, though.'

Fox nodded. 'You know why they were in town in the first place?'

'Looking for someone.'

'Do you know who?'

'Some guy with a haulage business.'

'His name's Hamish Wright. Same surname as you.'

Wright licked his lips, looking again to left and right, as though seeking an escape route. Fox took a step towards him.

'Do you drink at the Gifford Inn, Anthony?'

'Sometimes.'

'Three weeks back, Hamish Wright called that pub. He spoke to you.'

'Not true.'

'Staff say differently.' Fox took out his phone and got the shot of the haulier's phone bill onscreen. 'Plus there are calls here from Hamish Wright to his nephew. What would happen if I phoned that particular number?'

'Search me.'

Fox tapped the number in and waited. The phone in Wright's pocket had been set to silent, but both men could hear it as it vibrated.

'Want to answer that?' Fox said.

'What the hell is it you want?'

Fox ended the call and slid his phone back into his pocket. 'You're Hamish Wright's nephew,' he stated. 'Close to your uncle, are you?'

'What of it?'

'Why did he call you on the pub landline?'

'Can't always get a signal in there.'

Fox nodded. 'Must have been important, though. This wasn't long before he went missing.'

'He's not missing — he's away on business.'

'That's the story your aunt gave, but we both

know she's lying.' Fox paused. 'I'm assuming all this would come as news to the Stark gang. But does your employer know?'

Wright shook his head.

'Sure about that?'

'Positive.'

'You know it's not just your uncle they were looking for? He has something they think belongs to them.'

'Oh?'

'Are we back to playing games, Anthony? Do you know where Hamish is? Is he somewhere in the city?'

'Haven't a clue.'

'Because he's high on our list of suspects, as you can imagine.'

'My uncle couldn't kill anyone.'

'He worked for the Starks, peddled drugs and who knows what else around the country for them — he's not exactly Mother Teresa.'

'I don't know anything about that.'

'So you wouldn't object to me looking at your client records?'

'Soon as you get a warrant.'

'Mind you, nobody says it has to go through the books, eh?'

'Come back with a warrant and you can look all you like.' It was Wright's turn to fold his arms. He looked almost smug, which told Fox he was on the wrong trail.

'What was it he needed to talk to you about, Anthony? Did he tell you he was about to make a run for it?'

'Nothing like that — just family stuff.'

Fox was growing exasperated, his stock of ammo running low. 'Be a shame if Joe Stark *did* find out who you really are . . . ' He turned and opened his car door.

'You wouldn't do that.'

'Then tell me the truth, Anthony.' Fox looked back over his shoulder and watched as Wright's Adam's apple bobbed.

'He'll come out of hiding once this has blown over.'

'Have you talked to him? You know where he is?'

Wright shook his head. 'But that was always the plan, once he knew they were on to him. Less his family knew, the better.'

'You know it's not going to blow over, right? Not until Joe Stark knows who killed his son. Your uncle is going to be living in fear until the whole gang's put away.'

Wright nodded his understanding.

Fox made to get into the car, but then paused. 'Your dad is Hamish's brother? Have you talked it over with him?'

'He passed away last year. Maybe you saw it in the paper — Dad loved his motorbikes, so we got a dozen bikers as a cortège.'

Fox gestured towards a gleaming bike parked near the loading bay. 'Yours?' he guessed.

'And my dad's before me — he left me five in his will.'

'Lucky you,' Fox said quietly, wondering suddenly about his own father's will — did one even exist?

385

★   ★   ★

Beth Hastie watched him from her unmarked car. She had slid down low in her seat, but she doubted he would have noticed her if she'd been standing naked on the roof. Malcolm Fox was a man with things on his mind. She knew who he'd been talking to, too — the same man who had been present when Chick Carpenter had taken a beating. Why the sudden interest? After Fox had gone, the guy had approached a parked motorbike, taking out a handkerchief to polish its chrome. Hastie lifted her phone and called CC Self Storage. A woman's voice answered.

'Hello,' Hastie said. 'This is going to sound really daft, but I answered an ad from a guy selling a spare crash helmet and I've gone and lost his details. All I remember is he said he worked for you. Could that be right?'

'Must be Anthony — he's bike-daft.'

'Anthony, yes. And his surname's . . . ?'

'Wright. Anthony Wright. If you hold on, I can probably fetch him — '

But Hastie had already ended the call. She narrowed her eyes and ran her bottom lip between her teeth. Then she made another call.

'Yes?' the voice on the other end said.

'Can you talk?'

'Make it quick.'

'I'm at the self-storage place.'

'And?'

'I still think it needs to be done in daylight. But here's the thing — the employee who was there that day with Carpenter?'

386

'Yes?'

'His name's Anthony Wright.'

'Okay.'

'Any connection?'

'Could you check?'

'I'll see what I can do.'

'Make it quick.'

The phone went dead. She stared at it, then pressed her lips to the screen before putting it away and starting the engine.

34

Rebus had known ever since setting out from Edinburgh that he was going to continue north from Ullapool. His daughter Samantha lived in a house on the jagged north coast, on the Kyle of Tongue. He had phoned ahead and checked she would be home, though he'd been necessarily vague about his arrival time. The road from Ullapool was spectacular, though the sky started to darken long before he neared his destination. As he stopped his car outside the bungalow, she appeared in the doorway. Her daughter, Carrie, was almost two now. Rebus had only met her twice — once in the hospital in Inverness the day after her birth, and once in Edinburgh. She shied away from him as he tried to kiss her, and he realised he hadn't thought to bring a gift. He embraced Samantha and she led him inside to the cosy living room with its toy-strewn floor and three-piece suite.

'Is Keith not here?' Rebus asked.

'He's got some overtime.'

'That's good.' Her partner had a job as part of the team decommissioning the Dounreay nuclear reactor. 'And has he started glowing in the dark yet?'

'You asked me that last time — and the time before.'

He had taken the proffered seat while his daughter stayed standing. Carrie meantime was back amongst her toys, the adult world none of her concern. Samantha had streaks of silver in her hair, and she had lost weight.

'You look good,' he said dutifully.

'You too,' she felt obliged to respond. 'I'll just put the kettle on.'

So Rebus sat there, eyes on the child, not sure what to say or do. He was thinking of Malcolm Fox and his father, and of his own parents. There were framed photos on one wall, including one of him cradling the sleeping newborn. He felt a slight ache in his chest, which he was rubbing away with a thumb when Samantha returned.

'So you've been to Ullapool,' she said, waiting in the doorway while the kettle boiled. 'Thought you were retired.'

'Police Scotland have discovered the hard way that they can't live without me.'

'And vice versa, I dare say. How was the drive up?'

'Fine.'

'But you need to get back?'

He gave a shrug. 'I'm here now, though. I really wanted to see you.'

She nodded slowly and headed to the kitchen once more, this time returning with a tray. Tea in two floral mugs, a beaker of juice for Carrie, and a plate of digestive biscuits, one of them lightly buttered. This she handed to Carrie, who began to devour it.

'I think we used to have the same when you were young,' Rebus said. 'Digestives or Rich Tea, but with a smear of Lurpak as a treat.'

She handed him his tea and sat down on the

chair opposite. 'Everything okay with you?' she asked, unable to mask the concern on her face.

'I'm fine.'

'You sure?'

'I'm not here to deliver bad news.'

'I was a bit worried that maybe . . . '

'Nothing's wrong, cross my heart.'

'You're still drinking and smoking, though.'

'Only medicinally.'

She managed a smile and turned her attention to her daughter. 'Go and sit beside Grandad, Carrie — let him see how you've grown.'

The little girl made a show of reluctance, then crawled over to Rebus's feet and scrambled up his legs until she was in his lap.

'Don't squash me,' he teased, while Samantha took a photo on her phone.

Carrie, having rewarded Rebus with a chuckle, then became engrossed in the two toys she was clutching.

And stayed there, quite happily, while father and daughter caught up.

★ ★ ★

He decided to drive back by way of Inverness. Having been out of range for a while, his phone finally pinged to let him know he had missed a couple of calls, from Siobhan Clarke and Malcolm Fox. Stopping for petrol and coffee at the same retail park on the outskirts of Inverness, he took out his phone.

'Hey, you,' he told Clarke. 'What's up?'

'Malcolm and I were thinking of grabbing a

curry — wondered if you wanted to join us.'

'I won't be back until late.'

'We might still be there. We were thinking of the place you like.'

'Newington Spice? Well, I'll try to make it, but I'm not promising.'

'Where are you?'

'Inverness.'

'How was Ullapool?'

'I have stuff to tell you. Best said in person, though, after I've checked a couple of things.'

'I've been thinking about Tolland's wife — I'm pretty sure she knew. I feel sorry for her.'

'I thought she was dead.'

'That doesn't seem to be stopping me.'

'Each to their own. Any idea why Malcolm wanted to speak to me?'

'I haven't seen him today. He was going to take a shift at his dad's bedside.'

'Any change?'

'Not that I know of.'

'Okay, I'll maybe give him a call.'

'I'm guessing we'll be gone from the restaurant by eleven.'

'Tell them to keep me a doggy bag.'

'I will.'

He called Fox's number and waited.

'Hiya, John,' Fox said.

'How's your old man?'

'Stable.'

'You there with him now?'

'I'm actually drinking hospital coffee — prior to handing the baton back to Jude.'

'Freeing you up for curry with Siobhan?'

'She told you?'

'Doubt I can make it. I'm up north right now.'

'Where?'

'Inverness.'

'To do with Hamish Wright?'

Rebus took a moment to connect the dots. Wright: the missing haulier, who had brought the Starks to Edinburgh. 'Just passing through.'

'Thing is, his nephew works at CC Self Storage.'

'That's the place run by Darryl Christie's pal?'

'Yes. The Starks gave the owner a bit of a doing, but they didn't know his right-hand man is related to the very person they're looking for.'

'Sounds to me like you've been doing proper dogged detective work.'

'You wouldn't be far wrong.'

'So what's your next move?'

'I might try for a search warrant, see if Hamish Wright rents one of the units.'

'Even if he does . . .'

'It might not be in his name, yes. Which is why we might require a sniffer dog.'

'You've given it some thought.'

'Would you play it differently?'

'Absolutely not.' Rebus paused. 'Remember what we were talking about? Parents and kids . . . ?'

'Yes?'

'I drove to Tongue to see Sammy.'

'And it went okay?'

'It really did.'

'Then we've both had a result today.'

Rebus's phone had started vibrating, telling

him he had another call. 'Got to go,' he told Fox. But it was Cafferty's name on the screen, and Rebus wasn't ready just yet for that conversation. So instead he looked up Hamish Wright's details, and found that the petrol station was about a five-minute drive from the haulage yard.

A quick detour, he told himself, fastening his seat belt as he exited the forecourt.

The industrial estate looked like any other — anonymous corrugated structures behind either high walls or higher fences. Hamish Wright Highland Haulage wasn't hard to spot, boasting a large tartan banner above its gates and the same livery on the trucks parked up behind the razor wire. Floodlights illuminated the scene, and the gates stood open, a laden lorry crawling out. Rebus drove into the compound. A Portakabin seemed to be all the office Hamish Wright needed. The door was closed but its windows were lit. When the door opened, another driver emerged, folding a set of documents and making for his cab. He nodded a greeting at Rebus as Rebus tapped on the Portakabin door.

'What now?' a female voice barked from within. Rebus opened the door and walked in. The woman behind the desk was in her mid fifties and stubbing her latest cigarette into a brimming ashtray. There were half a dozen empty coffee takeaways in the bin next to her, and she was busy with a laptop and a stack of paperwork.

'Mrs Wright?' Rebus guessed.

'Who are you?'

'My name's Rebus. I'm with Police Scotland.'

The blood drained from her face. 'Yes?' she

said, in a voice suddenly just above a whisper.

'Just wondered if your husband had returned from his business trip.'

Her face relaxed a little and she pretended to be interested in the top sheet of paper.

'Not yet,' she said.

'No phone calls? No contact of any kind? Surely you must have an inkling of his movements?'

'What is it you want?' She peered at him above her horn-rimmed glasses.

'You look as though you're struggling,' Rebus commented.

'What business is that of yours?'

Rebus offered a shrug. 'Have you tried asking your nephew? Maybe he has some ideas.'

'Nephew?'

'In Edinburgh.' He'd been hoping for a reaction, but he was disappointed. She waved a finger to interrupt him as she took a phone call.

'Just left the yard,' she informed the caller, checking the clock on the wall. 'By seven tomorrow, yes.' She saw that Rebus wasn't about to make a move. 'Hang on a sec, will you?' she told the caller. Then, to Rebus: 'Was there anything else?'

Rebus gave another shrug. 'Nothing illegal in the lorries tonight, I hope. Not that I suppose you'll be doing much business with Joe Stark after the stunt your husband pulled . . .'

She gave him a look that would have felled lesser mortals, and turned her back on him as she picked up where she'd left off with the caller.

'Sorry, Timothy,' she cooed. 'Thought all the arseholes had clocked off for the night, but

394

there's always one more . . . '

Rebus took in the interior — desk, filing cabinets, wall planners. Having gleaned precisely nothing, he made his exit, leaving the door nicely ajar so the night air and diesel could waft in. The HGV driver was giving his vehicle a final check. Rebus crossed the tarmac towards him.

'Long trip?' he asked.

'Aberdeen, Dundee, Newcastle.'

'Could be worse, eh?'

'I suppose.'

Rebus gestured towards the office. 'How's she really coping with Hamish gone? I mean, I know she puts on a brave face . . . '

The driver puffed out his cheeks. 'She's pedalling pretty hard.'

'You think she's up to it?'

'Time will tell.'

'And Hamish? Reckon we'll see him again?'

'Are you kidding me?' He straightened up, facing Rebus. Then he drew a finger across his throat.

'Really?' Rebus's eyes widened in what he hoped looked like astonishment. 'The Starks did him in?'

'I heard he was driven away from here in a car. Two of them in the front, Hamish and another in the back. Last anyone saw of the poor sod.'

'Does *she* know?' Rebus was gesturing towards the Portakabin again.

'Everybody knows,' the driver stated. 'But nobody's saying.'

'You heard what happened to Dennis Stark?'

'Universe has a way of balancing things out.'

The driver was hauling himself up into his cab. 'Don't suppose you need a lift to Aberdeen?'

'Not right now.'

'Pity — a bit of company passes the time.'

The man closed the door, revving the engine and making a few more checks. As the lorry began trundling out of the yard, Rebus headed for his car. Wright's wife was watching from the open doorway. He stopped and began walking in her direction, but she disappeared inside, slamming the door shut.

★ ★ ★

Chick Carpenter's home was a modern two-storey detached near the zoo. Other times Darryl Christie had visited, he'd been able to hear and even smell the place — screeches and howls and dung. He remembered being taken on childhood trips, trekking up the steep slope and then back down again, or staring at glass tanks in the reptile house, or waiting with an ice-cream cone for the penguin parade to start. They had a pair of pandas these days, though he hadn't been to see them. More pandas than Tory MPs, that was the joke made in many a pub. Carpenter and his wife had turned up as pandas at the Halloween party Christie had thrown at the hotel.

Chrissie was waiting behind the door, opening it as soon as he pressed the bell. She wrapped him in an embrace, pecking both cheeks.

'You'll catch your death,' she scolded him, eyeing the black V-neck T-shirt beneath his suit. 'In you come, quick. Chick's in the den.'

'When are you going to cut your losses and run away with me?' he teased her.

'I'm old enough to be your mum.'

'You're in your prime, Chrissie — even when dressed as a panda.'

She slapped his shoulder playfully and led him to the den. It was off the huge living room, a snug space with dark red walls and oak flooring. Chick Carpenter was stretched out on the sofa, reading a golf magazine.

'Come in, Darryl, come in,' he said. 'Get the man a drink, Chrissie.'

'Just water, thanks.'

'You sure?'

'I'm driving.'

'Not quite yet above the law, eh?' Carpenter's smile became a wince as he swivelled into a seated position. The black eyes were still swollen.

'Hear you ended up with a cracked rib.'

'I'm basically wearing a corset under this shirt. Nearly had my nose broken too.'

'Sorry I've not visited sooner . . . '

Carpenter waved the apology aside. 'You've got a business to run.'

'All the same.' Darryl accepted the glass of water Chrissie was holding out to him. When she left, she slid shut the doors. 'Did they target you to get at me, do you think?'

'As a message, you mean?' Carpenter shook his head. 'They're looking for stuff Hamish Wright took from them. They'd been to another two storage places in the city. I'd had fair warning they might be paying a visit.'

'Nobody else ended up in A and E, though.'

'My own fault for getting mouthy. You know what I'm like. We'd had a day of problems with our computers and I was up for a shouting match.'

'Dennis didn't mention me at all?'

Carpenter shook his head. 'Hamish Wright is all they were interested in.' He broke off, smiling to himself.

'What's the joke?'

'Not a joke, really. It's just that Wright's nephew works for me.'

'Is that so?'

'Name's Anthony Wright — he doesn't know I know.'

'How *do* you know?'

'Wright's haulage firm is based in Inverness. Anthony's often mentioned biking there of a weekend — said he had family up that way.'

'You put two and two together?' Christie nodded thoughtfully. 'The Starks don't know this, though?'

'No.' With effort, Carpenter lifted a glass from the floor. Gin and tonic by the look of it. He sipped, his eyes on his visitor.

'I'm guessing,' Christie eventually said, 'that you'd wonder if Anthony's uncle had recently rented one of your units.'

'You'd be right. But his name's not in the records.'

'Clever money would be on an alias.'

'Which is why I made sure I was thorough. Every unit is kosher — for once.'

'Do you think Anthony might know his uncle's whereabouts?'

'He's a good lad,' Carpenter cautioned. 'I wouldn't like to see him hurt.'

'Perish the thought.' Christie drained the glass of tap water and wiped his lips with the back of his hand, his eyes fixed on Carpenter throughout. 'Here's what you're going to do for me, Chick. You're going to keep a close watch on Anthony. He drops any hints — you let me know. He suddenly needs to go off somewhere — you let me know. Is that understood?'

'Loud and clear, Darryl.' Though he had only recently put his own glass down, Carpenter's mouth sounded parched.

Christie nodded his satisfaction and rose to his feet.

'Can I just ask one thing?' Carpenter said, getting up with some effort. 'Who *did* kill Dennis Stark? Do you know?'

Christie handed the man his empty glass. 'Anyone touches me or my friends, there's a price to be paid,' he said.

As he pulled the sliding doors open and walked back through the living room, where Chrissie sat watching TV with the sound kept low, Christie knew he was taking a gamble. His parting shot would play well with Carpenter and others like him, but on the other hand, if his words got back to Joe Stark . . .

'Night, Chrissie,' he called.

'Look after yourself, pet.'

'I always do.'

35

Siobhan Clarke checked her watch again: almost half past ten.

'He's not coming,' Fox told her.

'I know.' She tore off a shred of leftover naan and began chewing it. She and Fox were the last customers left in Newington Spice. 'You heading back to the hospital?'

'I might.'

'Want some company?'

'You should really get some sleep.'

'Said the pot to the kettle.'

'Another tough day?'

'Page is getting flak for the inquiry stalling. He's been growing grumpier by the hour. I had to tell him, it's been over a week now and none of us has managed a day off. Everybody's exhausted.' She paused. 'Plus I gave a bollocking of my own.'

'Who to?'

'Charlie Sykes.'

'For being a waste of space?'

'For maybe telling tales to Darryl Christie. Charlie wasn't best pleased.'

'I'll bet.'

'I threatened to take it further unless he owned up. Told him that if I did that, he could kiss his precious pension goodbye.'

'And?'

'He's Christie's man.'

'Want me to have a word with Complaints?'

Clarke shook her head. 'It stays with us, as long as he tells Christie it's finished between them.'

A waiter was hovering. 'Gentleman, madam — was everything satisfactory?'

'Delicious,' Fox said.

'Desserts? Coffee?'

'Maybe a coffee — how about you, Siobhan?'

She nodded and started to get up. 'Back in a sec,' she said to Fox, as the waiter pointed her towards the toilets.

While she was washing her hands, she saw that a display of takeaway menus had been positioned on the window ledge next to the sink.

Pays to advertise, she said to herself, remembering that David Minton, over on the other side of town, had been the recipient of a menu from Newington Spice. As she walked past the bar, she stopped and said as much to the waiter.

'Do you really get people trekking across town?' she asked.

'We like to think we are worth a detour,' the waiter said with a smile. 'But I doubt we'd pay for someone to flyer quite that far away. Perhaps the menu was taken home after a meal.'

'Looked like it had been pushed through the door.'

The waiter just shrugged, smile still in place. By the time Clarke reached the table, Fox could see that something had changed.

'What is it?' he asked.

'Probably nothing.'

'Try me.'

'There was a menu from here in Minton's hallway. Waiter says they only flyer locally.'

'So?'

'Like I say, it's probably nothing.' But she had taken her phone out and was standing up again. 'I just need to make a call . . . '

She stepped outside, away from the piped music and the hissing of the espresso machine. Jim Grant's number was in her list of contacts. When he picked up, she apologised for calling so late.

'I'm in the pub if you fancy joining me.'

'Another time maybe. Do you remember us talking in Michael Tolland's kitchen?'

'How could I forget?'

'You said something about him eating out a lot, and using take-aways . . . '

'Yes?'

'And also something about him being rich enough to be able to order from far afield?'

'Okay.' His tone told Clarke he was wondering where she was going with this.

'How did you know that? Was it because of the menus in the kitchen drawer?'

'Must have been, I suppose.'

'You don't remember?'

'I don't, to be honest.'

'Do you think you could go back to his house for me and check?'

'In the morning, you mean?'

'Right now would be better.'

'I'm probably in no fit state to drive.'

'But you can get someone to take you?'

'Can I assume you're not offering?'

She ignored this. 'I'm interested in a restaurant called Newington Spice on the south side of Edinburgh. Just ping me a text when you've checked.'

'If it's food you're after . . . '

'Text me,' Clarke demanded, ending the call.

★ ★ ★

Rebus was halfway between Perth and Edinburgh when he got a message from Christine Esson:

Long day in the salt mines — you owe me a whole bakery. Didn't find much & drew a blank w/ Holroyd. Internet search etc. and it's like he never existed. Did get a hit on one name — David Dunn. Surprised you don't know him. Ran the Gimlet till it burned down.

Cursing under his breath, Rebus called her back.

'It's late,' she told him.

'Tell me about Davie Dunn.'

'He was in Acorn House for only a few weeks, not long before it was shut down. Shoplifting, drugs, a bit of gang activity. Cleaned up his act, though. Got a job as a van driver, passed his HGV, started on long distance. Worked for Hamish Wright Highland Haulage for a while.'

'Anything else?'

'I've got plenty of scrawls and scribbles. I'll type them up in the morning.'

'You're a star, Christine.'

'The brightest in any constellation.'

403

He ended the call and made another. Darryl Christie seemed to be driving when he picked up. Rebus could hear a stereo being muted.

'What do you want?' Christie asked with minimum politeness.

'I need to talk to Davie Dunn.'

'I'm not stopping you.'

'He's hardly likely to be at the Gimlet, though.'

'Rub it in, why don't you.'

'We both know you had the place torched, Darryl — easier that way to flog the land to a supermarket.'

'I really didn't.'

'Tell you what, then — give me a number for Davie and I'll believe you.'

'Why do you need to speak to him?'

'That's between me and him.'

'He'll tell me if I ask.'

'And you'll be denied that treat unless I speak to him first.'

'You've got a good line in patter, I can't deny it.' Then, after a pause: 'Try Brogan's.'

Rebus glanced at the time. 'Will it still be open?'

'Probably not, but there's an after-hours card game. When they unlock the door, just mention my name . . .'

★ ★ ★

Late night meant no queue at the Forth Road Bridge and a quick drive into town. Brogan's was a pub in Leith. Rebus felt like death as he parked

404

the Saab and got out. He dreaded to think how many miles he had covered. His neck felt like it was in a vice and his knees were throbbing. What was the name of that film Siobhan had wanted to take him to? *No Country for Old Men?* No denying he was old, and he doubted he would ever drive as much of the country again. From the outside, Brogan's looked deserted, but Rebus tried the thick wooden door and then banged on it with a fist.

'We're shut,' a voice barked.

'Darryl Christie said it would be fine.'

Immediately he could hear bolts being drawn back. The door was pulled open and Rebus stepped inside. The man on guard duty looked like a regular who'd been slipped a couple of free drinks as payment. He was big without being threatening. Rebus nodded a greeting.

'Back room,' the man said, sliding the bolts across once more.

Rebus headed past the shuttered bar and down a narrow passageway with pungent toilets off to one side. He could hear low voices, soft laughter. The back room was twelve feet square. One of its circular tables had been placed in a central position, and five men sat in a tight fit around it. Four more were perched on stools at the still-operational bar. There was no barman, and they seemed to be helping themselves. Rebus knew a couple of the faces, and held up his palms to show he wasn't about to cause a fuss.

'Join the queue,' one of the men at the table said, as chips were counted and readied for the next hand.

'Just need a quick word with Davie,' Rebus announced.

Davie Dunn turned round and saw the new arrival for the first time. 'Who are you?'

'His name's Rebus,' one of the others said. 'CID.'

Dunn considered for a moment, then pushed back his chair and got up. Rebus gestured towards the jacket draped over the chair.

'Might need that. And your chips as well.'

'A quick word, you said?'

'No way of telling,' Rebus admitted with a shrug.

They headed for the street, the sentry looking aggrieved at being disturbed again so soon. On the pavement, Rebus got a cigarette lit and offered one to Dunn. The man shook his head.

'Mind if we walk?' Rebus said. 'I could do with stretching my legs.'

'Hell is this all about?'

But Rebus moved off without talking. After a few moments, Dunn caught him up, the two men walking in silence for a few yards, Rebus feeling his joints loosen, glad of the exercise.

'It's about Acorn House,' he eventually admitted.

'And what's that when it's at home?'

'It's the assessment centre you were in for a few weeks in the mid eighties.'

'Ancient history.'

'It seems to have become current.'

'How do you mean?'

'Did you ever come across a lad called Bryan Holroyd?'

'No.'

'Sure about that?'

'I really don't remember much from those days.'

'Is that because you don't want to? I've heard some of the stories, and I know what went on there.'

'Oh aye?'

'Boys used by older men — men who should have known better.'

'I must have been too ugly then.'

'It never happened to you?'

Dunn was shaking his head. 'But I did hear the rumours. Mind, every place like that I ever stayed, there were always rumours — it was a way of putting the fear of God into you so you didn't step out of line.'

'Bad stuff definitely did happen at Acorn House, Davie.'

'And I'm saying I never saw anything — I was only there a month or six weeks.'

'Your name turned up in dispatches — ever meet a reporter called Patrick Spiers?'

'I remember the name.'

'He talked to you?'

'Not so much talk as pester — I told him the same thing I've just told you, but that wasn't what he wanted to hear.'

'He was trying to make a case against some very prominent men. I'm assuming he told you their names?'

'You can also assume I didn't listen.'

'How about Michael Tolland — you must remember him?'

Dunn nodded. 'He was okay. Used to dole out cigarettes and the occasional bottle of cider.'

'And he never asked for favours in return?'

They were approaching the Shore. A few stragglers from the local bars and restaurants were wending their way home, or waiting to flag down non-existent taxis. Rebus paused on the bridge, waiting for Dunn to answer, the Water of Leith dark and still below them.

'I got my life back on track, Rebus,' Dunn eventually stated. 'Got married, had a couple of kids — that's the only thing that matters to me.'

'Nobody ever threatened you? Or paid you to keep quiet?'

'No.'

'So you ended up driving HGVs.'

'That's right.'

'For Hamish Wright.'

'Yes.'

'Who's now gone AWOL, leaving behind some very irate Glasgow gangsters.'

'The same ones who tried beating me up and then torched my pub. How come you're not going out of your way to catch *them*?'

'Because right now I'm interested in Acorn House. On the other hand, if there's anything you want to tell me about Hamish Wright . . .'

'Haven't had anything to do with him in years.'

'You'll have told Darryl that, I dare say?'

'Yes.'

'Not the sort of person you'd want to lie to.'

'I don't see what this has to do with Acorn House.'

Rebus turned to face him. 'Darryl Christie told me where to find you. He's going to want to know what we talked about.'

'So?'

'So I'm about to tell you something — it's up to you how much of it you pass on to him.'

Dunn cocked his head. 'I'm listening,' he said.

'What if I were to say that someone seems intent on punishing the men who took part in the abuse at Acorn House?'

It took Dunn a few moments to digest Rebus's words. 'Is it true?' he asked.

'Might well be.'

'I heard that Tolland died when someone broke into his house.'

'Same thing happened to David Minton. He was a pal of Howard Champ, MP. You never met Champ?'

'Champ used to drop by,' Dunn stated coldly, leaning over the bridge and spitting into the water.

'I know this can't be easy, Davie, but I need to ask if there's anything you can tell me . . .'

'To catch a kid from Acorn House who's decided at last that it's Judgement Day?' Dunn's mouth twisted in a grim smile. 'Know what I say to that?'

'What?' Rebus asked, already knowing the answer.

'I'd say fucking good luck to them.'

Dunn turned and began retracing his steps, shoulders slumped, hands in pockets.

Rebus considered trying to stop him, but instead stayed where he was, the filter of his cigarette pressed between two fingers long after the cigarette itself had died. He couldn't help feeling that the man had a point, and Rebus was no longer a cop. What did it matter if Bryan Holroyd was out there, picking off his abusers and their abettors?

Yet somehow it did — it did matter. Always had, always would. Not because of any of the victims or perpetrators, but for Rebus himself. Because if none of it mattered, then neither did he. A couple of drunks walked past, their gait unsteady but smiles on their faces.

'Don't jump!' one of them called out.

'Not today,' Rebus assured the man, taking out his phone to check who was calling him at this godforsaken hour.

The answer: Cafferty, naturally.

Day Nine

36

Mid morning, Rebus met Cafferty in a café on George IV Bridge.

'Are we still keeping up the pretence that you're staying at the G and V?' he asked.

Cafferty just stirred his coffee. He had secured a large table by a window looking out across Candlemaker Row to Greyfriars Kirkyard. Rebus, arriving late, hadn't bothered joining the long queue at the counter.

'I should have got you one,' Cafferty said by way of apology, lifting the cup to his lips. 'I take it you've news?'

'The kid who died — Bryan Holroyd — didn't really die.'

Cafferty choked the mouthful of coffee down and lowered the cup back on to its saucer.

'That's why I wanted us to meet somewhere nice and public,' Rebus went on. 'Less chance of you throwing a fit.'

'What the hell do you mean, he didn't die?'

'Miraculous recovery in the boot of the car. When Dave Ritter opened it, Holroyd leapt out and ran into the woods. Ritter and Jeffries went after him but had to give up eventually. They reckoned he would freeze to death.'

'Bastards, the pair of them.'

'They were bricking it for weeks in case you found out.'

'You got this from Ritter? Where's he holed

413

up? I want a nice long word with him.'

Rebus was shaking his head. 'Not going to happen.'

'So this Holroyd kid's coming after us? After all these years?' Cafferty didn't sound convinced.

'Unless you've got a better theory.'

Cafferty was gripping the edge of the table with both hands, as though he might tip it over at any moment. His eyes flitted around the room as his thoughts tumbled, his breathing growing hoarse.

'No coronaries, please,' Rebus advised him.

'There's got to be a reckoning, John. No way I can let those two shits get away with it.'

'At least now we have a line on the person we're looking for. Only problem is, Holroyd seems to have gone off-grid — no sign of a conviction, or a National Insurance number, or taxes being paid.'

'You sure of that?'

'Christine Esson did the digging — she's thorough as any gold miner.'

'He fled the country then, and has only just come back?'

'No passport in his name.'

'Then he's changed it.'

'Which makes our job all the harder. Doesn't help that I've only the vaguest physical description, and he'll have changed a bit in thirty years. There *is* one thing, though — we've got a live one right here in Edinburgh. Or Portobello, if you want to be precise.'

'Who?'

'Todd Dalrymple — Ritter told me he was there that night.'

'But Todd always had an eye for the ladies — the man's been married three decades or more.'

'Chief Constable was married too,' Rebus said.

'Do we go talk to Dalrymple?'

'*I* certainly do, and you're invited if you think you can refrain from doing any major structural damage.' Rebus's phone was ringing: Siobhan. He got up from the table. 'Got to take this,' he said, making for the door. He pressed the phone to his ear as he passed the queue at the counter, a queue that now stretched the length of the café. 'Yes?' he said, pulling open the door and emerging on to George IV Bridge.

'We missed you last night.'

'That was always a probability. How was the grub?'

'Good as ever. But here's the thing — one of their takeaway menus was in Minton's downstairs hall.'

'And?'

'They say they don't flyer that far from the restaurant. So it's a bit odd, wouldn't you say, that there was also one in Michael Tolland's kitchen?'

'In Linlithgow?' Rebus had been wrestling a cigarette out of the packet, but her words stopped him.

'I had local CID go check,' she was saying.

'So what's your thinking?'

'If you were scoping a street out, or a particular house, and you didn't want to look suspicious . . . '

'Nobody pays much attention to someone sticking leaflets through doors.' Rebus put the cigarette packet back in his pocket. 'You might well be on to something.'

'I'm heading to Newington Spice to ask the boss a few questions. But in the meantime . . . '

'You're wondering if Cafferty got one too? Easy enough to check — he's right here with me.'

'Great.'

'Anything else?'

'Malcolm's dad's unchanged.'

'And Malcolm himself?'

'Isn't saying much of anything.'

'Oh?'

'I get the feeling he's working on his own theories. I might have to remind him he's supposed to be a team player.'

'Do I detect a hint of jealousy?'

'Your phone must be on the blink. Talk to you later.'

She ended the call. Rebus considered contacting Fox, but what would he say? So he headed back into the café instead. Cafferty had nearly finished the coffee. A couple of female students, one carrying a tray, had paused in front of the table and were sizing up the empty chairs. Cafferty's glare was deflecting them so far, and when Rebus squeezed past, they shuffled off in search of easier prey.

'Well?' Cafferty enquired.

'Takeaway menus,' Rebus said. 'You get them through the door, right?'

'Pain in the arse they are too.'

'Ever had any from Newington Spice?'

'How the hell should I know?'

'Could we go take a look?'

'Why?'

'Siobhan Clarke has a theory she wants to test to destruction.'

'A theory about Indian restaurants?'

'And the man who took that shot at you.'

Cafferty considered for a moment, then started getting to his feet. 'Pity,' he said. 'I was enjoying repelling all boarders.'

The two students were retracing their steps, trying not to look too obvious, as Cafferty and Rebus made their exit.

★   ★   ★

'So what does it mean?' Cafferty asked.

They were in Rebus's Saab, heading from Merchiston to Portobello through sluggish mid-morning traffic. Cafferty was studying the menu from Newington Spice. It had taken them only a couple of minutes sifting through the recycling bin to uncover it.

'When did it arrive?' Rebus asked.

'You're joking, aren't you — how am I supposed to know that?'

'Don't suppose it matters. Siobhan's thinking is that the gunman does a recce of each property before making his move.'

'So we're looking for a white male in his forties who doles out leaflets for a living?'

'See? Already we're hacking away at the undergrowth.'

Cafferty managed a grim smile. 'Are we headed to Dalrymple's house?'

'This time of day, we might have more luck at the beach.'

'You want witnesses around to stop me decking him?'

'I hadn't considered it.' The smile this time came from Rebus.

'I'm glad, actually — relieved is maybe the word.'

'That Bryan Holroyd lived?'

'Aye.'

'You think his 'death' put the fear of God into Howard Champ and the others?'

'Maybe. It certainly had a knock-on effect. From the moment it happened, Acorn House's days were numbered.'

'There were a lot of Acorn Houses out there though — London, Northern Ireland, all over . . . '

'You've been doing your reading?'

'Patrick Spiers had a few things to say on the subject.' Rebus glanced at his passenger. 'Any idea who might have turned his place over and lifted his files?'

'Wasn't me, if that's what you're thinking.'

'So your best guess would be . . . ?'

'Special Branch,' Cafferty stated. 'An MP, a senior lawyer and the police chief? No way they'd want any of that coming to light.'

Rebus nodded his agreement. 'And after all these years, think they'll still have an interest?'

'Those files will have been shredded — where's the evidence?'

'Bryan Holroyd is evidence.'

'Only if people stop to listen.'

'After everything that's crawled from the woodwork these past few years, I think they might.'

'Then it'll be court appearances for the likes of me and Dave Ritter, eh?'

'I'd say your own role was minimal.'

'I doubt anyone else will see it that way,' Cafferty stated grimly, as Rebus neared the Sir Harry Lauder roundabout.

They parked on James Street and headed for the Promenade, buttoning their coats against the fierce North Sea wind. There were fewer walkers and dogs than before, but Rebus spotted Todd Dalrymple by the water's edge, putting the lead back on John B.

'We'll wait here,' he told Cafferty as they stood at the sea wall.

'Is that him?' Cafferty was peering into the distance.

'That's him,' Rebus confirmed with a nod.

It was a further three or four minutes before Dalrymple was close enough to recognise Rebus. He had been happy enough on the beach, but when he saw Cafferty, it was as though a weight had descended.

'Big Ger,' he said, managing a queasy smile as he held out a hand. But Cafferty's own hands didn't emerge from their pockets, and when John B showed an interest, Cafferty pushed him away with his foot, Dalrymple reining the dog in.

'We need a word, Todd,' Rebus said.

'Here?'

419

'Back at the house.'

Dalrymple's eyes flitted between the two men. 'Is that strictly necessary?'

'Scared what your wife will think?' Cafferty sneered.

Dalrymple's lip trembled. 'No, I just . . . What do you mean?'

'It's about Acorn House,' Rebus stated.

'Acorn House?'

'We know you were there the night Bryan Holroyd was taken away.'

'Who?'

Cafferty lunged at the man, gripping him by both lapels. John B started barking, backing off but baring his teeth.

'I'll wring that dog's neck if it tries anything,' Cafferty snarled.

'It's all right, John B! Easy, boy!'

Cafferty's face was no more than an inch from Dalrymple's. 'You're going to tell us everything, you fat fuck.'

'What am I supposed to have done?'

'For starters,' Rebus broke in, 'you were witness to a huge cover-up.'

'Orchestrated by *him*,' Dalrymple protested as Cafferty's grip tightened. The dog was still barking and looking primed to pounce.

'Abetted rather than orchestrated,' Rebus said. 'But here's the thing, Todd — you might well be next on his list.'

'Whose list?'

'The man who shot at me,' Cafferty informed him.

'And killed Lord Minton and Michael

Tolland,' Rebus added. 'Which is why we need to go to your house.' He dug a hand into Cafferty's coat pocket and drew out the takeaway menu. 'To see whether you've had one of these.'

'Wh-what?' Dalrymple looked utterly lost. Cafferty released him by giving him the slightest shove. Even so, Dalrymple barely kept upright. His eyes were on the menu Rebus was holding. 'Is this some kind of joke?'

'How amused do we look right now?' Cafferty asked back.

Having given the man a moment or two to recover, Rebus gestured with his arm.

'We'll follow you,' he said.

They walked the short distance to Argyle Crescent, John B straining at the leash, keen to get home. Dalrymple unlocked the door and called out the name Margaret, but there was no response.

'She must be out,' he said, relief in his voice. He unhooked the lead from John B's collar and the dog made for its bed in a corner of the living room, eyeing the visitors warily.

'No flyers in the hall,' Rebus commented.

'We toss them straight into the recycling.'

'Which is kept where?'

'A box in the kitchen. I'll fetch it through.'

Cafferty had settled on the edge of the sofa, while Rebus stayed standing in front of the fireplace. It was a cramped room, boasting too much furniture, from the grandfather clock in one corner to the footstool Rebus had been forced to step over. There were bright paintings of harbour scenes on a couple of walls — Rebus

421

guessed they were by John Bellany. When Dalrymple arrived back with the recycling box, he placed it on the footstool and began sifting. Rebus decided to help by bending down and tipping the box up, strewing its contents across the carpet.

'Bingo,' he said, after a minute or two of crouching next to the drift of paper. He lifted up the menu from Newington Spice.

'What does it mean, though?' Dalrymple asked.

'The killer poses as someone putting flyers through doors. Gets to know the house and street, then makes his move. I don't suppose you can remember when this arrived?'

'A few days back?' Dalrymple guessed, his face turning bloodless as Rebus's words sank in.

'But you've not had a note?' Cafferty demanded.

'A note? Like the one they showed in the papers?' Dalrymple was shaking his head.

'He means like this,' Rebus broke in. He was lifting the folded piece of white notepaper. It had obviously not been noticed and had been dumped into the recycling along with everything else. He unfolded it and held it up.

Same message. Same hand.

'Fuck,' Big Ger Cafferty said.

★   ★   ★

The restaurant owner, Sanjeev Patel, was waiting for Siobhan Clarke, unlocking the door from the inside. Staff were busy in the kitchen, and Clarke could smell onions frying and a mixture of spices. The voices were loud but good-natured.

Meanwhile, a waiter was laying tablecloths and cutlery in the main room. Patel led Clarke to the bar area, where takeaway customers could wait of an evening to collect their food. He was dressed in a dark suit, white shirt and navy tie, and looked every inch the businessman, but Clarke knew he had worked his way up from a teenage kitchen porter. He was Edinburgh born and bred and, like her, supported Hibernian FC, the walls above the bar filled with autographed photos of players past and present.

'We definitely don't flyer in Linlithgow or the New Town,' he said, after she had turned down the offer of coffee.

'Is there a specific firm you use?'

Patel nodded. 'Want me to fetch you their details?'

'Please.'

He got up and went behind the counter, studying the screen of a laptop computer that sat there. He jotted a few lines on to one of the restaurant's order pads and tore off the sheet, handing it to her as he sat down again.

'You think maybe a member of their workforce . . . ?'

'This has got to stay confidential, Mr Patel,' Clarke warned him.

'Absolutely.'

She remembered the stack of menus in the loo, and mentioned them. Patel nodded.

'In the Gents too,' he said.

'So I suppose anyone could have filled their pockets?'

Patel shrugged. 'I'm not aware of them

423

suddenly disappearing.'

'You're probably not the one cleaning the toilets, though.'

'That's true — not these days. Do you want me to ask the staff?'

Clarke nodded. 'Plus if anyone suspicious has come in — maybe they took some menus but didn't stay to eat, or asked to use the toilet even though they weren't ordering food.'

'Understood.' He paused. 'Could there be another explanation?'

'I'm struggling to think of one.'

'You'll appreciate I don't want the restaurant's reputation sullied.'

'I thought there was no such thing as bad advertising.'

'It's not a theory I'm keen to test,' Patel said with a smile.

'I'll try to be diplomatic,' Clarke assured him, standing up. There was a display of menus on the table, next to a large bowl of Bombay mix. 'How often do you reprint, by the way?'

'Maybe once a year — to reflect changing prices. Last time we added online ordering — very popular with students.'

'So these menus came into effect . . . ?'

'At the start of November.'

'Only three months back? Well that's something at least.' She picked up one of the menus and studied the information on the back.

'Have you always used VampPrint?'

'For the past couple of years.'

'Got a phone number for them?'

Patel went off to the laptop again and fetched

it. Clarke thanked him and he held open the door for her. There was a shop across the road, and she headed in for some gum and a bottle of water.

'Cheaper out of the tap, love,' the woman on the till warned her.

Clarke's phone was ringing, so she pulled it from her bag: John Rebus.

'What can I do for you?' she asked, breaking the seal on the bottle as she exited the shop.

'I'm in Portobello with a man called Todd Dalrymple.' Rebus's tone told her to keep listening. 'He got one of the flyers *and* a note. Put both in the recycling so he's just finding out. Dalrymple's understandably up to high doh and I think we need to get him and his wife out of here. Which gives us the opportunity to bait a trap for our killer.'

Clarke had almost walked under a bus. She retreated to the edge of the pavement and waited for a gap in the traffic.

'You might have to start from the beginning,' she said.

'Best done face-to-face. How soon can you get here?'

'Twenty minutes?'

'I might get them to start packing in the meantime.'

Clarke could hear a woman wailing in the background. 'Mrs Dalrymple?' she guessed.

'She didn't take it terribly well. I'm not sure Cafferty would know subtlety if it stood in front of him holding up its own dictionary entry.'

'Cafferty's there?'

'Didn't I just say so?'

'Twenty minutes,' Clarke repeated, belting across the carriageway to her waiting car.

Once she had pulled out into traffic, she called Christine Esson.

'Yes, guv?' Esson said.

'Promise never to use that phrase again.'

'I'll try.'

'Is Ronnie in the office?'

'He is.'

'And are you busy?'

'I'm still trying to cough the dust out of my lungs after a day in the archives.'

'Was the groper on duty?'

'Fortunately not.'

'Well, I've got something that requires your attention.'

'Fire away.' Clarke could hear Esson summoning Ogilvie to her desk while simultaneously readying a pen and notepad. She took her eyes off the road long enough to reel off the information Sanjeev Patel had given her.

'I need you to visit both. Ask about the people who go door-to-door with leaflets, then the people who print them and look after their storage.'

'And this is because . . . ?'

'Flyers from Newington Spice were found in Lord Minton's home, plus those of Big Ger Cafferty and the victim of that attack in Linlithgow.'

'Got you,' Esson said. 'Should we split it between us?'

'That would be quicker.'

'Any description to go on?'

'Absolutely none.'

'Male? Female?'

'One or the other, certainly. Get back to me once you've finished.'

'Yes, guv,' Esson said, ending the call before Clarke could respond.

★ ★ ★

Todd and Margaret Dalrymple were upstairs filling a suitcase. Cafferty was standing by the living-room window, his back to the room. Rebus had brought Clarke indoors and she was now taking in her surroundings, including the carpet, which was still strewn with recycling.

'He won't come in daylight,' Rebus reminded Cafferty, receiving only a grunt in response. 'But feel free to make yourself a nice big target in case he does.'

He handed Clarke the note along with the takeaway menu. 'Like I say, we don't know for sure when it arrived. They put it straight in the recycling without even noticing.'

'And Cafferty got a menu too?'

Rebus nodded slowly. There was a gleam in his eyes Clarke hadn't seen in a while — alive to all manner of challenges and possibilities.

'So you went to Ullapool,' she nudged him.

Rebus kept nodding. 'And spoke to a guy called Dave Ritter. He was at Acorn House that night and was supposed to dump the body in a grave in some forest in Fife. Thing is, Bryan Holroyd wasn't dead. He'd been putting on an act. He ran for it and they couldn't find him.'

'So Holroyd's behind this?' She held up the note.

'I'd say there's a good chance.'

'And how does upstairs fit in?' She gestured towards the ceiling.

'Dalrymple was another of Acorn House's clients. Ritter told me as much, which is why Cafferty and I decided to come visit.'

'Does his wife know?'

'Like I said, Big Ger lacks a certain diplomacy . . . '

'Bit of marriage guidance needed.'

'Not our problem.'

'I'm just wondering if we need one place of safety or two.'

'I see what you mean.'

Clarke thought for a moment. 'I've got to tell Page all this.'

'Of course. But bear in mind what I said — this is our one chance at catching him. We've no idea where Holroyd is or what he looks like. All we do know is that he'll be coming here very soon.' Rebus paused. 'Which is why I'm offering myself as bait. I'm much the same age and build as Dalrymple. Enough to fool Holroyd until he gets up close.'

'And then what? He's going to have a gun, remember.'

'Firearms officers stationed outside in an unmarked car. First sign of trouble, they come running.'

Clarke pointed towards the corner of the room, where John B was asleep in his basket.

'Will Holroyd know the Dalrymples have a dog?'

'He well might. But then *I've* got access to one too, remember.'

'I don't think Page will agree to it, John — you're not a police officer.'

'You can fight my corner, though.'

'I can try — I'm just not sure I want to.'

Fresh wailing had started upstairs, penetrating the ceiling and causing John B to prick up his ears and look concerned.

'And what about him?' Clarke added, gesturing towards Cafferty.

'He doesn't want Holroyd dead, if that's what you mean.'

Cafferty turned towards them. His face looked solemn rather than angry.

'What I want,' he stated, eyes boring into Clarke's, 'is to say sorry to the man.'

Clarke met his gaze for a moment before turning her attention back to Rebus.

'I need you to take me through this one more time,' she said. 'As slowly and methodically as you can . . . '

37

Darryl Christie wasn't a huge fan of Glasgow. It *sprawled* in a way his own city didn't. And there were still traces of the old enmity between Catholic and Protestant — of course that existed in Edinburgh too, but it had never quite defined the place the way it did Glasgow. The people spoke differently here, and had a garrulousness to them that spilled over into physical swagger. They were, as they chanted on the football terraces, 'the people'. But they were not Darryl Christie's people. Edinburgh could seem tame by comparison, head always below the parapet, keeping itself to itself. In the independence referendum, Edinburgh had voted No and Glasgow Yes, the latter parading its saltired allegiance around George Square night after night, or else protesting media bias outside the BBC headquarters. The political debate had melted into a blend of carnival and stairheid rammy, so that you never knew if people were joyous or furious.

Darryl Christie had considered all the implications for his various business interests and come to the conclusion that either outcome would probably suit him just fine, so in the end he hadn't voted at all.

The place he was looking for was a restaurant off Buchanan Street. The lunchtime rush was ebbing, and as he peered through the window, he could see empty tables waiting to be cleared. Joe Stark was seated alone in one corner, his white cotton napkin tucked into his shirt collar, mopping up sauce with a hunk of bread. The other diners looked like just that, which was what had been agreed. Yes, there was a BMW outside with a couple of lookouts in the front, but that was fine too. Christie returned to the Range Rover, told his own men to stay there unless the occupants of the Beemer headed inside. Then he pushed open the door to the restaurant.

'Mr Christie?' the manager said. 'Such a pleasure. Mr Stark is waiting. Would you like to see a menu?'

'I'm fine.'

'Just a drink, then?'

'No thanks.'

Christie walked up to Joe Stark's table, pulled out a chair and sat down. Then, realising he now had his back to the room, he got up again and made to settle next to the older man on the banquette.

'I don't even let hoors get that close,' Stark warned him. 'Go sit the fuck down and I swear no one'll come up behind you with a cleaver.'

Christie did as he was told, but moved the chair until it was at a right angle to the table.

'How's the food?' he asked.

'Not bad. You know they're not releasing my son's body yet? Is that them taking the piss or what?'

'It's a murder inquiry — that's the way it goes.'

'You ready to give me a name?' Stark pushed aside his plate, but continued chewing on the wad of bread.

'A name?'

'I assume that's why you're here.'

'I still don't know who killed Dennis.'

'Then what possible use are you to me?' Stark whipped away the napkin and threw it on to the plate.

'The last time we met, I told you I respected you — do you remember that?'

'I'm getting it tattooed on my bollocks.'

Christie stared at the man. Stark was avoiding eye contact, finishing his glass of red wine and searching between his teeth with the tip of his tongue.

'This is useless,' Christie said, making to get up. But Stark reached over, gripping him by the forearm.

'Sit down, son. You've come all the way from Edinburgh. Might as well say your piece.'

Christie made show of considering his options, then eased back down on to the chair. He was about to start speaking when Stark gestured for the manager, who came bounding over.

'Double espresso for me, Jerry. And whatever my guest is having.'

'I'm fine,' Christie stated.

The manager bowed and scurried away. Another table was settling up and leaving. Christie realised that the caricatures on the walls represented Scottish pop stars, though he only recognised a few.

'Well?' Stark said, leaning back and giving the

young man his full attention.

'You were in Edinburgh looking for Hamish Wright, because he'd taken something that you felt belonged to you.'

'Aye?'

'And as part of that search, you went to CC Self Storage.'

'Dennis and his boys went to at least three of those places.'

'But what Dennis didn't know, I'm guessing, is that Wright's nephew works there.'

'Is that so?' Stark couldn't help looking suddenly more interested.

'And my thinking is, the nephew might know the whereabouts of the uncle.'

Stark gave a thin smile. 'Son, I *know* where the uncle is.'

'You do?'

'He's buried in a field somewhere outside Inverness. Dennis let Jackie Dyson have his way with him — reckoned nobody was as good at wringing the truth out of a man as Jackie. Fucker made Dennis look like Greenpeace.'

'Wright died?'

'He did, aye.' Christie watched the old man nod. He didn't look in the least concerned. 'We didn't want anyone getting wind of it — best thing was to make the cops and anyone else think we were still on the hunt.'

'So they wouldn't think you'd killed him?' It was Christie's turn to nod. 'So why tell *me*?'

Stark fixed him with a look. 'Because that's twice now you've come to me. Makes me think we might be able to help one another — now, and in the future. A sort of alliance against the jackals in Aberdeen and Dundee.'

'Are they starting to circle?'

'They smell blood, son. I can offer Dennis's crew the moon, but somebody out there's going to offer one of them Mars or Venus as a bonus. If they knew I had friends . . . well . . . ' Stark shrugged.

'How would it work?'

'Plenty of time for that later.' Stark patted Christie's leg. 'For now, you've got me interested in this nephew.'

'And you've got *me* interested — you really think we could work together?'

'Only one way to find out. Dennis was gearing up to push me aside. Everyone knew it — Len and Walter were always bending my ear about it. Either his boys will make a move on me anyway, or they'll decide they need reinforcements from outside the city. It's either you with me, or you with them. But look at me, son. I'm not going to last much longer — and when I croak, a good-sized chunk of Glasgow would be yours. *If* you take my side. On the other hand, team up with them, and you'll be surrounded by wild animals — young, hungry and stupid.'

Stark's coffee had arrived, along with an amaretto biscuit that he dunked and then held between his lips, sucking the thick black liquid from it.

'I'll have one of those too, actually,' Christie told the retreating manager. And he returned Joe Stark's smile, the two men readying to get down to business.

Anthony Wright had been in trouble a few times — speeding offences, one very minor drugs bust and a breach of the peace. Which was how Fox managed to track down his home address. It was a maisonette in Murrayburn, not a million miles from his place of work. Anthony had the upper floor. His downstairs neighbours hadn't washed their windows in a while, and the slatted blinds needed replacing. From what he could see of the upstairs dwelling, the owner was a tad more house-proud: the curtains looked new, as did the front door with its fan-shaped frosted window and brass fittings. Fox, knowing that Anthony wasn't yet home from work, peered through the letter box, discovering little — a flight of red-carpeted stairs filled his field of vision. Framed prints of motorbikes and their leather-clad riders on the walls.

He returned to his car and waited, the radio playing at low volume. It was a quiet street, though far from gentrification. He got the feeling that if he sat there much longer, an inquisitive local would emerge to check him out. One thing he had noted: no bikes on the roadway outside the maisonette, or in the flagstoned front garden. How many had Anthony said? Five? He got out of the car again and did a little circuit, establishing that the maisonette backed on to an enclosed drying green, which boasted no enclosure larger than a garden shed. There was a park beyond, really just a stretch of well-trodden grass that could accommodate a makeshift game of football, plus a graffiti-covered set of concrete ramps, presumably for use by skateboarders. On the other side of the park sat three high-rise blocks, and next to those, two rows of lock-up garages.

Buttoning up his coat, Fox started walking, sticking to the paved route so as to save his shoes getting muddied. A cheap souped-up saloon car passed him, its occupants barely out of their teens. Both front windows were down so the world outside could share their taste in what they presumably thought was music. They paid Fox no heed though. He wasn't like Rebus — he didn't *look* like a cop. A detective he'd once investigated when in Complaints had described him as resembling 'a soulless, spunkless middle manager from the most boring company on the planet'. Which was fine — he'd been called worse. It usually meant he was closing in on a result. And the fact that he didn't stand out from the crowd could be useful. As far as the kids in the car were concerned, he barely existed — if they'd thought him a threat, the car would have stopped and a scene of sorts would have ensued. Instead of which, he arrived at the lockups without incident.

There were a dozen of them, all but one with its doors locked tight. A car was jutting out from the twelfth, jacked up while a wheel was changed. The lock-up had power, and a radio had been plugged in, Radio 2 providing the soundtrack while a man in presentable blue overalls did his chores.

'Nice car,' Fox commented. The man had wiry silver hair and a stubbled face, a cigarette hanging from his mouth. 'Ford Capri, right? Don't see many these days.'

'Because they're rustbuckets. Dodgy engines, too.'

The bonnet was up, so Fox took a look. He had scant knowledge of cars, and to his eyes the engine looked much like any other.

'You in the market?' the man asked. 'Only I know there are collectors out there — I've had offers.'

'Motorbikes are more my thing,' Fox said. 'Friend of mine lives near here. He's got a nice collection.'

'Anthony?' The man nodded towards the lock-up opposite. 'That's where he keeps them.' Fox turned his head towards the graffiti-covered rollover door. There was the usual turn-handle with its central lock, but heavy-duty bolts and padlocks had also been added to either edge of the door.

'He was supposed to be showing me them,' Fox explained, 'but he's not home.'

'He's often here — takes one out for a run, brings it back, swaps to another. What's your favourite?'

'I like Moto Guzzis,' Fox said, remembering the brand from one of the prints on the staircase.

'About as reliable as my Capri,' the man snorted, flicking away the stub of his cigarette. 'The older ones, at any rate.'

'I'm surprised he doesn't keep them at that self-storage place where he works.' Fox was studying the surroundings. 'Bit more security than here.'

'This is handier, though, and he's careful — never leaves the doors open long enough for anyone to get a good look.'

Fox nodded his understanding. 'Ever meet his uncle?' he asked casually.

'Uncle?'

'Uncle Hamish — he was down here a few weeks ago from Inverness. I just thought Anthony might want to show off his collection.'

'Chubby? Fiftyish? Red hair and freckles?'

Fox thought of the photographs he'd seen. 'Sounds about right,' he said.

'Anthony didn't introduce us, but aye, he was here.' The man was wiping his hands on a rag. 'I've got to say, you don't look like one of Anthony's mates.'

'What do they look like?'

'Younger than you, for a start.'

'We drink together at the Gifford.'

The man's suspicions eased. 'He's mentioned the place — seems to like it there.'

'It's all right.'

The man gave a lopsided smile. 'I thought maybe you were a cop or something — sorry about that.'

'No problem,' Fox assured him.

'Not that you look like one, mind.'

Fox nodded slowly. 'My name's Malcolm,' he said.

'George Jones. I'd offer a handshake, but . . . ' He showed Fox his oil-stained fingers.

'No problem — I better get back and see if he's turned up. Good luck getting your Capri back on the road.'

'No chance of that,' Jones said, patting its roof. 'This isn't so much a garage as a hospice — I'm just keeping the patient comfortable until the end.'

Fox's face tightened. He offered a half-hearted wave as he turned and started to walk, pulling out his phone to call Jude. He would take over from her for an hour or two, but he knew he might well be back here later. He imagined himself calling Ricky Compston with the news — *I've got Hamish Wright and his booty. Both are here when you want them . . .*

He was almost smiling to himself as Jude answered his call.

'About bloody time you checked in,' she announced. 'Doctors want a word with us.'

'What about?'

'If you want my best guess, they're readying to pull the plug.'

'What?'

But Jude was too busy sobbing to say any more.

38

Esson and Ogilvie stood in front of Siobhan Clarke's desk as they delivered their report, the conclusion of which was that they had found nothing much of interest.

'Nothing?' Clarke felt it necessary to check.

Ogilvie stood with his hands behind his back, happy to let his partner do the talking.

'We've got a list of everyone who works for the two companies, and we'll run it to see if anyone rings alarm bells, but I'm not hugely hopeful.'

'The company that does the flyering . . . '

'Higher Flyer,' Esson reminded Clarke.

'Higher Flyer, yes — do they do any work in and around Linlithgow?'

'Strictly Edinburgh and Glasgow. They actually don't have many restaurants on their books. Mostly they do comedy shows and that sort of thing — stocking pubs and clubs with flyers. They would certainly cover the areas where Minton and Cafferty live, but it would depend on the client. Newington Spice specified the local neighbourhood.'

'Most of the people doing the flyering are students,' Ogilvie chipped in.

'Our guy would be in his forties,' Clarke commented. Her eyes drifted towards the closed door of James Page's office. 'Always supposing John's theory is correct.'

'What's he doing in there?' Esson asked, nodding towards the door.

'Trying to persuade DCI Page that a retired detective, now a civilian, should become bait for an armed serial killer.'

'Not going to happen, is it?'

Clarke stared at Esson. 'John can be quite persuasive.'

'As I've found to my cost. It would be nice now and again to go on a wild goose chase that actually had a goose at the end of it.'

'Wild or otherwise,' Ogilvie added.

Clarke pinched the bridge of her nose. 'What about VampPrint?' she asked.

'They do have a storage facility for everything they print,' Esson answered, 'but in the case of Newington Spice, all their stock went either to Higher Flyer or to the restaurant itself. That's not to say someone on the staff couldn't have helped themselves, and again we'll run all the employee names through the system.'

'One thing we do know is that no one with the surname Holroyd works for either firm,' Ogilvie stated. Esson was about to add something, but broke off as the door to Page's office opened. Rebus marched past Clarke's desk without saying anything or making eye contact. The door remained open, and a few moments later Page was standing there, indicating that Clarke should join him. She headed in, closing the door again after her. Page was back behind his desk, twisting a pen in both hands.

'At least there were no raised voices,' she commented. 'John must be disappointed, though . . .'

She saw the look on Page's face. 'You gave him the okay?'

'With the proviso that members of our team will be nearby, as well as two firearms officers. As John says, he's been on top of this throughout, putting our own efforts to shame in certain respects.'

Clarke bristled. 'I'm not sure that's entirely fair.'

'Me neither. On the other hand, we'd have known nothing about Acorn House if John hadn't told us.'

'How much *did* he tell you, sir?'

'Men in positions of authority abusing kids, the whole thing covered up, one young lad thought to be dead after some sex game or other . . . ' Page gave a pained look. 'Bloody horrible to contemplate, every single bit of it.'

'I agree.'

'And after this is over, we need to make sure something's done — the Chief has to be amenable to an inquiry of some kind.'

'An inquiry flagging up one of our own as a paedophile?'

Page gave another grimace. 'What's the alternative?'

'I'm fairly sure the Chief will present you with some.'

'Sweep everything back under the carpet, you mean? The world's changed, Siobhan. This'll get out there one way or another.'

'Well, if we need a friendly crime reporter . . . '

'Your chum Laura Smith? Maybe it'll come to that. Not that the media seemed to do much of anything last time round.'

'One or two tried.' Clarke shrugged.

Page was thoughtful, eyes on his pen as he played with it. 'I need to authorise the firearms.'

'Yes, sir. I'll let you get on with it.' She turned to leave.

'You'll be there too, of course — John more or less insisted.'

Clarke paused in the doorway, turned and nodded her acceptance, then headed back into the main office.

Rebus was there, talking with Esson and Ogilvie. His eyes met Clarke's, and he gave a wink as he grinned.

★   ★   ★

Rebus had stocked up on supplies — a couple of sandwiches, newspaper, several CDs to pass the time. But it turned out he couldn't work the hi-fi — it didn't have a CD slot, for one thing. There was a remote, and when he pressed it, music emerged from speakers in the corners of the ceiling, but it was nothing he wanted to listen to. Even the dog looked unimpressed. The terrier had been wary at first, especially after picking up the scent of another canine. The Dalrymples had taken basket and John B both, along with food and water bowls. But Rebus had found some dry stuff in a cupboard and tipped a helping into a soup bowl, placing it on the kitchen floor for the terrier. It had been quite the reunion when he had arrived at the cat and dog home.

'We've been calling him Brillo,' one of the staff

had explained, bringing the dog into the reception area. Recognising Rebus, Brillo had strained at the leash. 'You sure you only need him for a day or two?'

'That's right,' Rebus had said, avoiding the staff member's eyes.

He got up every ten minutes or so and looked out of the window. It was just before ten, and he'd been there almost four hours. The unmarked car was not quite directly outside — they didn't want to scare Holroyd away. Two officers in the car, though they hadn't been especially keen when told they might be pulling an all-nighter. Rebus took out his mobile and checked it. The officers had his number and he had theirs. First sign of anything, either they would call or he would. Esson and Ogilvie were out there somewhere too, traipsing the neighbouring streets in the guise of lovers on their way home. Esson had already sent one text to complain of impending blisters, to which Rebus had responded that she should get a piggyback from her colleague.

With no bed, Brillo had settled on the sofa, but every time Rebus moved, he looked interested, in case a walk was in the offing.

'Sorry, pal,' Rebus said, not for the first time.

He climbed the stairs and used the loo, then walked into the spare bedroom. Siobhan Clarke lay stretched out on the narrow single bed, reading a book by the light of a bedside lamp.

'I hope you put the seat down this time,' she admonished him.

'This is why I never remarried.'

444

She smiled tiredly. 'Get any pictures while you were up north?'

'No.'

'Some grandfather you are.'

'Sam took one of me and Carrie — maybe she'll email it.'

'She will if you ask her.'

Rebus nodded. 'What's the book?'

'He said, changing the subject. It's Kate Atkinson.'

'Any good?'

'Someone keeps coming back from the dead.'

'Not a bad fit for this evening, then.'

'I suppose. You really think he'll come?'

'Maybe not tonight.'

'Know the grief we're going to get if we need to keep requisitioning those gun-slingers?'

'Cheery pair, though, weren't they?'

'Rays of sunshine.' She smiled again.

'I should go downstairs.'

'I keep thinking of Little Red Riding Hood. You're the wolf dressed as Grandma.'

'I don't remember Red Riding Hood killing anyone, though.'

'Fair point. Stick the kettle on then, Grandma.'

Rebus headed to the kitchen, where Brillo was waiting, ever hopeful. He gave the dog a pat and filled the kettle. He looked at the kitchen door. It led, he knew, to a well-tended garden with the usual area of decking. There was a security light above the back door, but the bulb had given up and not been replaced. That was fine by Rebus. He opened the door and breathed the night air.

445

He couldn't quite smell or hear the sea, and there was too much light pollution for any but the brightest stars to be visible. He remembered the drive south from Tongue to Inverness, the road winding and narrow at first, and not another vehicle for tens of miles. The sky had been studded with stars, and he'd seen one owl and several deer along the route, none of which had meant very much to him — he'd still been busy with thoughts of Carrie.

Brillo had headed into the garden to do his business, so Rebus left the door ajar while he poured the tea. He took one mug upstairs, and Brillo was in the kitchen on his return, fretting over his absence.

'Here I am,' Rebus said, closing the back door and leaving it unlocked. No point complicating things unnecessarily.

★ ★ ★

Fox was in his car when Clarke rang.

'Hiya,' he said.

'Hope I didn't disturb you.'

'I'm outside the hospital,' he lied. 'Just about to head home.'

'How's Mitch?'

'Pretty bad. Jude phoned to tell me they were readying to pull the plug. She was exaggerating, but not by much. They're talking about a 'persistent vegetative state'.'

'Bit soon for that, isn't it? You sure you're okay to drive home?'

'I'll be fine. Are you at the flat?'

'I'm in the lavender-scented spare room of a Mr and Mrs Dalrymple.'

'Do Mr and Mrs Dalrymple know?'

Clarke explained the situation to him. 'John's downstairs filling the condemned man's shoes, and we've a couple of sharpshooters outside.'

'John's a civilian.'

'Try telling him that. He convinced James Page that this was the only game plan worth the name . . . Hang on, I've got a text I need to check . . . Shit, got to go.'

The phone went dead in Fox's hand. He placed it on the passenger seat and popped a fresh piece of gum into his mouth. He was parked on the road leading into the high-rise estate, halfway between Anthony Wright's home and the lock-up. There was no sign of life and the temperature was dropping. He was glad Siobhan hadn't dug too deep — this was his case and no one else's. Not just because of Compston, Bell and Hastie, but for his father, too, who had always thought him better suited to an office than the street. Yet here he was, watching and waiting.

'My score,' he said quietly to himself.

And a few scores to settle as well.

* * *

Rebus took the call from the firearms duo.

'Someone's coming. Big guy, looks like he means business.'

'You only step in when you get the word,' Rebus reminded them, ending the call. The doorbell rang and he went into the hall. Clarke was already halfway down the stairs, but he shooed her away. Only when she had disappeared from sight did he open the door.

'Hell are you up to?' he asked.

'I decided I've got the right,' Cafferty said, barging his way in.

'The right to screw this whole thing up?' Rebus snarled, slamming shut the door and pursuing Cafferty into the living room. 'Holroyd knows what you look like — he saw you through your nice big bay window, remember?'

'So?'

'So when he sees you here . . . '

'He's going to think all his Christmases have come a bit late this year.'

'Forget about it,' Rebus said. His phone was ringing. He answered. 'Very much a false alarm,' he informed the firearms officer.

'What's he doing here?' Clarke asked, joining the party.

'Says he has the right,' Rebus explained.

'You need to leave,' Clarke told Cafferty. 'You are jeopardising this inquiry.'

'I *am* this inquiry!' Cafferty spat. '*I'm* the one who's been in jeopardy.'

'Which is precisely why you can't be here. Say a shot goes off and you get hit . . . ' Clarke was shaking her head.

'I need to see him.'

'And so you will — at his trial. But that only happens if we snare him, and you being here makes that impossible. You either leave right now, or I'm pulling my team out.'

Clarke was standing only inches from him, half a foot shorter but not about to falter. Cafferty was breathing heavily, a man locked and loaded. But Rebus watched as he started to calm.

'Ballsy as ever, Siobhan. John here might not have taught you much, but he taught you that.'

'Leave now,' she reiterated. Cafferty held up his hands in a show of surrender. 'I've two detectives outside who'll make sure you don't just lurk in the vicinity. They'll want to see you get into a car or a cab. Is that understood?'

Still holding up his hands, Cafferty started retreating out of the room. Clarke got on her phone and explained things to Esson and Ogilvie. Rebus opened the door for Cafferty. Cafferty paused for a moment, glowering over Rebus's shoulder towards Clarke.

'I'll let you know the minute we have news,' Rebus said.

Cafferty nodded, without looking in the least convinced. Then he headed down the path towards the gate, where Ogilvie and Esson were waiting. Rebus closed the door again and walked into the living room. Clarke gave him a sharp look. He could only shrug a response, slumping into the chair again and waiting for Brillo to jump on to his lap.

Day Ten

39

Siobhan Clarke had fallen asleep on her bed, still in her clothes. They'd decided to quit at 6.45 a.m. She'd managed a few brief naps in the Dalrymples' guest bedroom, and had driven home with a head that felt like glue had been poured into it. Now it was just after nine and her phone was ringing. She staggered over to the wall socket where it was charging, arriving just as the call ended. She didn't recognise the number. The phone was fully charged, so she unplugged it and took it with her as she retreated to her bed. But she was awake now and knew she wouldn't get back to sleep.

'Shower,' she muttered, rising once more to her feet.

There was a café she liked just around the corner from her flat, and she headed out afterwards for the strongest coffee they could muster — a flat white with three shots of espresso. She perched on a stool by the window and watched the traffic crawl uphill towards the Leith Street roundabout. When her phone rang again, it was the same number. This time she answered. It was Sanjeev Patel from Newington Spice.

'I hope I'm not interrupting you,' he said.

'What can I do for you, Mr Patel?'

'I have been giving the matter some thought, and have spoken to my staff about the mystery, and I think I may have made progress.'

'Yes?'

'One of our regular customers often takes a batch of menus with him to distribute among his friends and acquaintances. Is it possible these may have made their way to the person you are looking for?'

'I suppose so.' Clarke stifled a yawn. 'What can you tell me about this customer?'

'His name is Jordan. That's his Christian name, I'm afraid I don't have a surname. I think he lives in Newington, but as he always collects his order, I don't have the actual address.'

'How old would he be?'

'Early twenties.'

'We're looking for someone a good bit older.'

'I see.' Patel paused. 'There's no point in sending you his photo then?'

'You have a photo?'

'The restaurant's tenth anniversary — we invited some of our regulars to join us. I was thinking I could send it to you in a text.'

'Might as well, and I appreciate you going to the trouble.'

'No trouble, Inspector. Tell me, did you gain anything from speaking to our printer and distributor?'

'Not a great deal, if I'm being honest.'

'Honesty is the best policy, I'm told. So let me say something — you sound exhausted.'

Clarke managed a smile. 'I've got caffeine on an intravenous drip.'

'Caffeine is a false god — fresh air and exercise, trust me.'

'I'll bear those in mind. Meantime, do send me that picture.'

'As soon as we finish speaking. I look forward to seeing you at Newington Spice soon — and Mr Rebus too.'

Clarke ended the call and drained her cup. She was heading to the counter for a refill when her phone alerted her to a message. It was the photo, showing a group of half a dozen men gathered around a table groaning with food. All looked like staff with one exception. Yes, Jordan was in his early to mid twenties. Close-cropped hair and small, deep-set eyes, his bare arms tattooed with what looked like Celtic symbols. Clarke used thumb and forefinger to zoom in on him. She knew him from somewhere. Then she remembered — he worked at the mortuary. She closed the photo and found Deborah Quant in her contacts list, tapping her number and holding the phone to her ear.

'I never did thank you,' Quant answered.

'For what?'

'Phoning me at that dinner so I could make my excuses.'

'Time to repay the favour then — you've got a mortuary attendant, first name Jordan. In his twenties, tattoos on his arms . . . '

'Jordan Foyle, yes.'

'Worked there long?'

'Almost a year. He was in the army before that — found it hard to adjust to Civvy Street, I think.'

'Will he be at work today?'

'No reason to think he won't — is he in trouble?'

'Probably not. I just need a word with him.'

'Well I'm headed there right now. I'll be on cadaver duty until two. After that I'm teaching a path class.'

'I'll pop in and say hello then.'

'You might have to wave from the viewing room — today's a busy one.'

'Fair enough. Catch you later.'

Clarke ended the call and tapped the phone against her teeth. She had decided against a second coffee — she was starting to jangle as it was. Walking back to her flat, she considered contacting Rebus — he might fancy the detour. Then again, the poor sod had been stuck in Argyle Crescent all night. He would almost certainly be asleep. Besides, Jordan Foyle wasn't Holroyd, not unless he had a portrait in his attic. Ex-army — she'd heard that it could be difficult for squaddies. They returned home from places like Afghanistan and never quite adjusted. Plenty passed through the police cells and prison service. She hoped Jordan Foyle was one of the luckier ones.

Five minutes later, she found herself passing the café, this time as part of the stream of slow-moving traffic. She had her window down a couple of inches, as per Sanjeev Patel's advice about fresh air — not that the rush-hour air was especially fresh. Once past the roundabout, she headed for North Bridge, signalling right on to Blair Street and down the slope to Cowgate, where the mortuary sat. It was an anonymous grey box with a few similarly anonymous black vans outside its loading bay doors. Clarke made sure she wasn't blocking any of them as she parked. The public entrance was around the other side of the building, but she opened the staff door and walked down the short corridor — the same one where she'd encountered Jordan Foyle — climbing the stairs from the storage area to the autopsy suite. The viewing room was separated from the autopsy room by a glass partition. There was a row of chairs, and she took one of these, waving to Quant, who waved back and indicated to her fellow pathologist that they had a guest.

Clarke tried not to look at the body on the metal trolley, or at the various basins filled with viscera and organs, or at the drainage channels down which liquids ran. There was a loudspeaker in the ceiling, allowing her to hear what was being said. The atmosphere was calm and professional, Quant recording her findings as the examination continued. The attendant on duty, dressed in scrubs and short green rubber boots, face masked, was not Jordan Foyle. He was a good decade older and had been with the mortuary as long as Clarke could remember. But then the door swung open and Foyle himself entered, carrying a tray of implements and a stack of disposable containers. He laid these out, his back to Clarke. When he turned again, he asked Quant if there was anything else she needed.

'That's fine, Jordan. But DI Clarke would like a word.'

She gestured towards the viewing room, and Foyle's eyes met Clarke's. He nodded slowly and made to leave. Clarke headed out to meet him.

457

He was walking down the corridor away from her, pulling off his protective gloves.

'Jordan?' she called.

Rather than stop, he broke into a run. Clarke took a second to realise what was happening, then set off after him. He was down the stairs by now, and she lost sight of him. As she emerged into the car park, he was rounding a corner of the building, shrugging off his scrubs. He began to run up High School Wynd, while Clarke faltered. On foot or in her car?

'Shit,' she said, making up her mind. She set off in pursuit but he was already at the top of the hill and heading for the Infirmary Lane steps. Clarke took out her phone and got through to the area control room, identifying herself and asking for assistance.

The steps almost defeated her and she ended up using the handrail as she heaved her way to the top, where she had a decision to make: left or right along Drummond Street? Towards the Pleasance or Nicolson Street? No sign of Foyle and no one she could ask for guidance. She swore under her breath and placed a hand to her chest, feeling her heart pounding. Her phone was ringing — a patrol car was two minutes away, its occupants wanting to know who they were looking for. Clarke started to give them a description, focusing on the tattoos and the rubber boots. Then she headed back down the steps, retracing her route to the mortuary. Quant was still in the autopsy suite. Clarke thumped on the glass and gestured that she needed a word. Quant met her in the corridor as Clarke was

458

wiping sweat from her face.

'Foyle did a runner,' she explained between breaths.

'Really?' Quant still wore her face mask and was holding her viscera-stained gloved hands out in front of her, unwilling to touch anything.

'I need his address.'

'He lives with his parents,' Quant said. 'His mother, I should say. His father passed away a month or two back.'

'The address,' Clarke repeated.

'It'll be with his personnel file. You'll need to phone the admin office.'

'Do you know their number?' Clarke had her phone out. She tapped it in as Quant recited it.

'You might want to sit down and catch your breath,' Quant cautioned. But Clarke was already walking away, waiting for someone to pick up at the other end.

By the time she reached her car, she had the address: Upper Gray Street in Newington. She called the officers in the patrol car.

'We're still on the lookout,' one of them said. Clarke gave them the address and said she would meet them there. Once on the road, she phoned Rebus. He sounded rightly groggy.

'I might have something,' she told him, explaining about Foyle.

'Can't be Holroyd.'

'I know that.'

'So what are you saying?'

'Foyle's father died a couple of months back. Interesting timing, don't you think?'

'I've had barely three hours' sleep — thinking

459

isn't top of my list of priorities.'

'He did a runner, John.'

'Could be any number of reasons for that. Bit of dope in his pocket, parking fines he's been ignoring . . .'

'Can you meet me at his house anyway? I'm nearly there.' She gave him the address. 'It's hardly any distance from yours.'

'Fine,' he said. 'You think that's where he'll be headed?'

'It's the direction he was going. And he's on foot. Have to admit, for someone in galoshes, he had a turn of speed.'

'If you've ever tried running from enemy gunfire in army-issue boots, I'd think a pair of green wellies would feel like kit from the Olympics.'

'I bow to your superior knowledge.'

'If it *is* him, you're going to have to be careful.'

'I know.' Clarke signalled off Newington Road into Salisbury Place and took a left into Upper Gray Street. She could see two uniformed officers standing in the middle of the road ahead of her. One was busy making a call, while the other looked ready to explode. They moved out of the way as Clarke squealed to a stop. She wound down her window, her phone held in her free hand.

'Bugger's got a gun,' the ruddy-faced officer said.

'You let him take your car?'

'He was running out of the house as we got here. Changed his shoes and with a backpack over one shoulder. Then the gun came out, could

460

have been fake but impossible to tell.'

'You hearing this?' Clarke said into her phone.

'I'm on my way,' Rebus replied.

★   ★   ★

Denise Foyle sat at the kitchen table with a mug of sweetened tea. There was a laptop on the table, with a printer on the floor beneath. She made a bit of money as an eBay trader, as she had explained to Siobhan Clarke.

'But I just don't understand,' she was repeating for the sixth or seventh time. 'I can't get my head round what you're telling me.'

She was in her late forties, with dyed ash-blonde hair. She wore jewellery round her neck and on her wrists, plus a pair of large earrings that resembled peacock feathers. Though she worked from home, her make-up was immaculate, as were her painted and manicured nails.

Clarke was perched on the edge of a chair opposite while Rebus stood with his back to the sink. He hadn't shaved and was in the same clothes as the previous day.

'Where did he get a gun?' Denise Foyle was asking.

'We have a theory,' Clarke told her. 'But right now, our main concern is to bring Jordan in safely.'

'Safely?'

'He's carrying a firearm, Mrs Foyle. And he brandished it at two unarmed officers. That means we have to take this very seriously. Our own armed response team has been put on alert.'

She paused meaningfully. 'We don't want anything to happen to him, so it would be helpful if you could answer a few questions. Do you have any idea where he might go?'

'He has friends.'

'Details would be good.'

'I've probably got a few phone numbers.'

Clarke nodded her satisfaction. 'Also, a recent photo of Jordan. We've got one, but it's not the greatest quality.'

'There'll be some on here from Christmas.' Foyle pointed to her laptop. 'Not that it was very festive . . . '

'Your husband passed away?' Rebus asked. She turned her head towards him.

'At the beginning of December,' she explained. 'We'd driven out to Chesser Avenue. We always get a tree from the same charity, Bethany Trust. They have a site there. Mark had just stopped the engine when he slumped forward.' Her eyes were filling with tears. 'There'd been a few warning signs — he'd been to the doctor with chest pains, apparently. Again, I only found out after . . . '

'Would you have a photo somewhere?'

'On the mantelpiece.'

'Do you mind if I . . . ?'

She shook her head and Rebus exited the kitchen, turning right into the living room. There were half a dozen condolence cards still displayed on the mantelpiece, along with a selection of photos of the deceased. The most recent showed a man in his mid forties with salt-and-pepper hair and a smile that didn't quite reach his eyes, not even in a much earlier photo taken on his wedding day. Rebus focused on this picture, since it was the one that showed Mark Foyle at his youngest. He lifted it up and studied the face, though he was not sure what he was seeking. He photographed it with his own camera. When he'd left Ullapool, he had taken Dave Ritter's mobile number with him. Now he added the photo to a text — *Long shot, but could this be the same kid?* — and sent it.

On a corner unit sat further framed family photos, mostly of Jordan Foyle — at primary and secondary schools, then as a teenage army recruit. He had his arms folded and was grinning fit to burst. A later snap had been taken by one of his comrades and showed him in the desert somewhere, his convoy having come to a halt, a fellow soldier holding him in a playful headlock. Rebus wandered back through to the kitchen. Denise Foyle was blowing her nose into a square of kitchen towel, Clarke handing her another so she could dab her eyes.

'Jordan and his dad had a difficult relationship,' Clarke explained to Rebus. 'Mark wasn't exactly touchy-feely modern-father material.'

'How did you meet your husband, Mrs Foyle?' Rebus asked.

'At a nightclub, like you do.'

'Here in Edinburgh?'

She shook her head. 'Glasgow — he was living there at the time.'

'Doing what?'

'Car mechanic.'

'But he was from Edinburgh?'

She shook her head. 'He grew up in Glasgow.'

463

'So he had family there?'

'I got the feeling there'd been a falling-out. He never spoke about them.'

'Never?'

She shook her head again. 'Not one of them came to the wedding.'

'You never met them?'

'His parents were already dead, I think.'

'He had school friends though?'

'Not by the time I met him.' She paused. 'What are you getting at? What does this have to do with Jordan?'

'Why did you move through here?'

'I lived here. Worked as a secretary. Mark wasn't keen, but I talked him round.' She broke off again. 'Maybe I shouldn't have. I don't think he ever really settled.'

'Would you mind if I took a look at Jordan's room?' Rebus asked.

She shook her head slowly as she dabbed at her eyes.

Rebus headed upstairs. Jordan Foyle's bedroom bore a poster of a supermodel from yesteryear on its door. Inside, the bed was messy, clothes spewing from a chest of drawers and a narrow wardrobe. Photos from his army days stuck to the walls, plus more pictures of large-breasted women. There probably should have been a laptop of some kind, but it was missing. In amongst the clothes spilling from the wardrobe, Rebus spotted a rectangle of muslin, stained with oil. And beneath the bed, a small pile of menus from Newington Spice. Back downstairs, Denise Foyle was telling Clarke why her son had left the army.

464

'Afghanistan destroyed him. I'll probably never know what he saw there, but he came back looking like a ghost. Used to wake up screaming in the night, or I'd hear him sobbing in the bathroom at three in the morning. I don't know if they offered him counselling, but he certainly never got any, and if I tried suggesting it, he would jump down my throat. But he looked like he was coming out the other side. He'd got himself a job, and even an on-off girlfriend — '

'We'll need her number too,' Clarke interrupted.

'But then when Mark died . . . I mean, they'd never been close. Quite the opposite. But something happened. Don't ask me what.'

The front doorbell sounded. Rebus went to answer, and found the two officers from the patrol car standing there.

'He dumped it,' one of them stated.

'Where?'

'Cameron Toll car park. Took the bloody keys with him, though.'

'It's going to be fun writing up your report, isn't it?' Rebus allowed a smile to flit across his face. 'We'll have a recent photo of him in a few minutes. Need to get it distributed along with his description. You better get busy with that, since you two are the only ones who know how he's dressed.'

'Shouldn't we be getting checked over?' the other uniform enquired.

Rebus narrowed his eyes. 'For what?'

'Post-traumatic stress — we had a gun pulled on us.'

'By a lad who served at least one tour of duty

465

in a war zone,' Rebus retorted. 'Anyone should be getting looked at, it's him.'

And he slammed the door shut on the pair of them.

40

'You look like hell,' Jude said when Fox found her sucking on a cigarette in the hospital grounds.

'Well, if we're being frank with one another . . . '

She looked down at her unwashed clothes. 'Okay, it was a low blow. I'm sorry.' She tried not to shiver.

'Want my coat?' Fox was already shrugging out of it.

'Very noble of you.' She allowed him to place it over her shoulders.

'Just don't get ash on it.'

This almost merited a smile, until she remembered why they were there. 'So, do we sign the death warrant or not?'

'It's a Do Not Resuscitate agreement . . . '

'I *know* what it is, Malcolm! But this is our dad we're talking about — the only one we get. And if we put our names on that form, we lose him.'

'You don't think he's already lost?'

'Miracles can happen.'

'I've not seen too many recently.'

'I spent half the night on the internet reading up on them. Patients waking from a coma after years, suddenly ravenous and asking what's for breakfast. It *happens*, Malcolm.' She drew on the cigarette again.

'They've run every test, Jude.'

'Not *every* test — I looked that up too. All I'm

saying is . . . ' She started coughing, head bowed. The coughing stopped, but her shoulders still shuddered, and Fox realised she was sobbing. He grabbed her in an embrace. Her scalp was oily, her hair needing a wash, but he planted a kiss on the crown of her head.

'We'll go in when you're ready,' he said. 'And not before.'

'We'll be out here till we freeze then.'

But he knew she didn't mean it.

⋆ ⋆ ⋆

It was a manhunt now. Photos of Jordan Foyle had been distributed to the media, who were clamouring for more information. All they'd been told was that he was armed and potentially dangerous. The story of the hijacked patrol car had got out, however, and the Chief Constable had been on the phone demanding answers. James Page wanted answers too, and didn't seem even half satisfied at the end of the briefing by Clarke and Rebus.

'You think Mark Foyle was Bryan Holroyd, is that what I'm hearing? But you've no actual evidence?'

'It makes sense,' Rebus argued. 'Father dies, son decides to avenge him for the hurt he endured.'

'The son who never had the closest relation-ship with his father? Did the family even *know* about the abuse Bryan Holroyd suffered?'

Clarke and Rebus shared a look.

'Wife seems in the dark,' Clarke eventually conceded.

'But you're saying somehow the son knew?'

'The restaurant menus, the muslin from Minton's desk drawer. This is our guy,' Rebus stressed.

'My point is, there could be a dozen other reasons why he's set out on this particular path.'

'I don't think so.'

Page sat in thoughtful silence, sizing up Rebus and Clarke. 'I had to tell the Chief about your involvement, John. Needless to say, that's a rocket waiting for me when the dust settles.'

'Sorry to hear that.'

Page sighed. 'One thing's clear — Portobello is a bust.'

'Are you sure?'

Page gave Rebus a hard look. 'He's on the run, John. What would a good soldier do?'

'Abort the mission,' Rebus admitted.

'Plus, those two firearms officers have already been redeployed. Everyone's on their toes — checking trains, buses, routes out of the city. Even the airport. Does he have money?'

'Debit and credit cards,' Clarke said. 'We're asking his bank to alert us to any new transactions. Same goes for his mobile phone provider. His mum thinks his passport is gone, along with a laptop and maybe some clothes.'

'Are we interviewing her formally?'

'She's in an interview room at St Leonard's. Jordan's girlfriend is being fetched there too. I've put Esson and Ogilvie on it. They'll also check social media sites, see if he's talking to anyone.'

'Are Christine and Ronnie compos mentis?'

'We're all tired, sir,' Clarke said with a smile.

469

'You should get some rest then. We've got half the force out looking for the target. Not much else to be done until he's brought in.'

'Yes, sir,' Clarke said, turning to go. But Rebus was standing his ground.

'About tonight . . . '

'I said no, John. Can I make myself any clearer?' Page peered up at him.

'Fair enough,' Rebus said, making to follow Clarke. Page probably thought he was stuffing his hands into the pockets of his jacket to show how fed up he felt. But he was actually checking.

Yes, he still had the keys to Argyle Crescent . . .

★   ★   ★

Anthony Wright had his key out and was about to put it in the lock when he saw that his front door had actually been forced open and then pulled closed again.

'Bollocks,' he said. A break-in was all he needed after the past week or two. He pushed at the door and listened to the silence. He had a decision to make — stomp upstairs in the hope of scaring anyone who might be there, or move on tiptoe so as to surprise them? Having opted for the latter, he took the steps quietly, eyes alert in case a figure should suddenly loom in front of him. He paused in the narrow upstairs hall and listened again. What would they have taken? His laptop and CD player for definite. He didn't have insurance, but someone at the Gifford would sort him out with replacements. Then he remembered the keys to his motorbikes, kept in a drawer in the kitchen, along with others for the garage's various locks. When he thought of what else was in the garage, his stomach flipped. He placed his crash helmet on the floor and padded towards the open door of his living room.

Where a man and a woman waited.

The man sat in the only armchair, legs spread, a pistol of some kind resting against his crotch. The woman stood to one side of the doorway, and hauled him into the centre of the room.

'You'll be Anthony then?' the man said.

'I know you.' Wright's eyes narrowed as he tried to remember.

'Let me give you a clue.' The man jabbed his head forward, miming a butt.

'Dennis Stark — you were with him that day. Nearly broke my boss's nose.'

The man nodded. 'Might have saved us all a lot of grief if I'd known then who you are.'

'Who am I?'

'You're Hamish Wright's nephew. I just looked at the photos from your dad's funeral — it was all over the papers — and there was Uncle Hamish. Explains why he told me the stuff was in the self-storage. I ninety per cent believed him, and it turns out he was telling about ninety per cent of the truth — isn't that right?'

'I don't know what you're talking about.'

'I'm talking about these.' The man dug in his pocket, producing key after key, tossing them on to the carpet at Wright's feet. 'Four motorbikes, Anthony. Plus the one you rocked up here on. Keys to padlocks, too. So now I need to know where you keep the bikes.' He paused. 'Your uncle wasn't easy to break, but I broke him. And then he snuffed it. Sometimes pain can do that. The body just decides it's had enough. I can do the same to you, Anthony. Or we can make it nice and straightforward.'

'I'm honestly telling you — '

Before he'd ended the sentence, they were on him. Packing tape binding his legs at the ankles, and his hands behind his back. The man held him down, a knee on his throat, almost crushing his windpipe, and a hand clamped over his mouth, removed only to be replaced by more of the silver tape, which was wound around his head a couple of times.

They stood over him when they were finished, while he wriggled on the floor. The man aimed a kick at his midriff, causing him to groan, eyes screwed shut in pain. The woman had yet to speak. She left the room and returned with items from his kitchen drawers — knives, scissors, kebab skewers.

'Nice,' the man said, appraising the haul as she laid them out on the floor. He lifted her face towards his and kissed her on the lips. Wright wanted to tell them they were crazy, but all he could do was moan behind the gag. And now the man was crouching in front of him, and the barrel of the gun was pressing into his forehead, so that he felt compelled to screw his eyes shut again.

'I killed Dennis, you know,' the man drawled. 'It wasn't just that I hated his guts. I had to focus everyone's minds elsewhere. Plus he was talking about paying your place of work another visit, and since that was where I'd been told the stuff was stashed . . . ' He paused and scratched one cheek thoughtfully. 'But now Joe's back in Glasgow, meaning I can get my hands on it without anyone knowing.' He glanced around and snatched up the padlock keys in his free hand. 'A garage would be the obvious answer. Nod if I'm warm.'

Wright shook his head and felt a fresh blast of pain as the barrel of the pistol connected with his left temple, slicing it open. With the keys clamped between his teeth, the man picked up one of the knives and pushed it with slow deliberation three quarters of an inch into his victim's shoulder. Behind the gag, Anthony Wright tried to scream.

41

Malcolm Fox was back at the same spot, on the road leading to the lock-ups. Jude had sent him half a dozen texts telling him how callous he was. They'd been at Mitch's bedside when he'd told her he had to go out for a while.

'How long?'

'A few hours.'

'*A few hours?*' Because they'd been told by the consultant that their father might only have a few hours.

A few hours.

A few days.

Maybe a week.

This before they'd signed the forms, Jude sobbing all the while. The consultant had asked her if she wanted a sedative, but she'd shaken her head. Her texts were now arriving like blows every twenty minutes or so. Fox sat with his hands resting on the steering wheel, Classic FM at just audible volume on the stereo. A kid on a BMX had ridden past four times, eyeing him inquisitively without stopping. George Jones — the man with the Capri — had worked on it again, reversing it back inside and locking the garage door only quarter of an hour back, after which, rubbing oil from his hands with a rag, he had headed on foot towards one of the tower blocks. Fox popped a mint into his mouth and sucked on it, hoping it might clear his head. He dropped the packet on the floor and was reaching down to retrieve it when a car passed him. He watched as it crawled towards the lock-ups, coming to a stop between the two rows. Both front doors opened. Female driver, male passenger. In the gathering gloom, he couldn't make out their faces. The man walked down one line of garages and up the other, not pausing until he finally reached the one owned by Anthony Wright.

'Well now,' Fox murmured. He got out of his own car, closing its door quietly, and made his approach on foot, trying to look like a worker slouching homewards. He could hear a metal door shuddering open. Both figures had moved out of his sight line, so he speeded up. When he was close enough to make out the car's number plate, he decided to commit it to memory, but quickly realised he already knew it.

One of the cars from Operation Junior.

He cursed beneath his breath and steadied his pace. A light had gone on inside the lock-up. As Fox approached, he could see that the motorbikes were draped with polythene dust sheets. The two figures, however, were standing by the rear wall, intent on the contents of what looked like a packing crate. Even from behind, he recognised Beth Hastie. When the man half turned, he saw it was Jackie Dyson. Dyson planted a kiss on Hastie's cheek, stopping Fox in his tracks. Too late, though — Dyson had spotted him out of the corner of his eye. He spun around, pointing the pistol at Fox's chest.

'Don't be shy then,' he said. 'In you come.'

'Fuck's he doing here?' Beth Hastie spat.

'It all makes sense,' Fox said, holding up his hands as he took a few steps forward.

'Is that right?'

'Hastie covered for you while you followed Dennis that night to the alley. How long have you two been an item?'

'What are we going to do with him?' Hastie was asking Dyson.

'I'll need to think. Meantime, fetch the roll of tape from the car.'

Hastie did as she was told, giving Fox a cold stare as she passed him.

'So it's true what they say,' Fox commented to Dyson. 'Undercover cops do get turned. I fail to see how you're going to get away with it, though.'

'Is that right?'

'I'm hardly the brightest, and I worked it out.'

'Seems to me you worked out hee fucking haw until we were standing right in front of you.' Hastie had returned with the tape. 'Hands behind your back,' Dyson ordered. Fox did as he was told, his eyes on the man as he spoke.

'That note you left next to Dennis was hardly proof of smart thinking — it didn't have us fooled more than half a day.'

'Muddied the water, though, didn't it? Less chance of Joe cottoning on. Just like torching that pub, giving Darryl Christie something to chew over so he didn't get too interested in Wright's stash.' Dyson examined Hastie's handiwork. 'Do his ankles next,' he commanded her.

'How long have you had the gun?' Fox was asking.

Dyson gave a cold smile. 'Insurance in case the Starks ever rumbled me. When Compston told me there was another nine mil doing the rounds, well, it seemed like kismet.'

Fox felt the tape being wrapped around the hems of his trousers. He tried flexing his wrists, but she'd done a good job, leaving almost no play at all.

'Now take the covering off one of those bikes,' Dyson was saying. 'We're going to wrap you up nice and neat like a mummy, Fox.'

The bike, when revealed, was a gleaming red model, streamlined and built for speed. Dyson muttered his appreciation while the sheet was laid out on the ground. Hastie gave Fox a shove and he could do nothing other than topple on to it. She crouched and wound the tape around his mouth. Then, with her lover's help, she started covering Fox in his makeshift shroud. As more tape was applied, he realised he would suffocate unless they left a gap somewhere.

And a gap didn't seem to be part of their plan.

He began to strain against his bonds, his cries for help muffled. Dyson was grinning as he finished the job. The covering was translucent, and Fox watched as the pair clambered to their feet again. They got to work emptying the crate of its contents, transferring everything to the back of their vehicle. Fox was trying not to panic, trying to keep his breathing shallow. There was a bit of give at his wrists, but not as yet enough. He was working his lips and jaw too, trying to break the seal on the tape, rubbing his face against the thin plastic sheeting but failing to find an edge that might help shift the gag.

Despite himself, his breathing was growing ragged, adrenalin surging through his body.

Yet all the time he watched.

To and fro they went until they were satisfied. Then they paused for a moment to embrace and kiss, only a few feet away from his prone, writhing figure. Dyson squeezed Hastie's hand and she headed outside, Dyson pausing for a moment, his eyes on Fox. Then he switched off the ceiling light and started to leave. Fox's makeshift shroud was beginning to steam up, but he could make out Dyson's figure silhouetted against the night as he stretched up to grab the door and pull it down, locking Fox in his tomb.

Sudden movement.

A woman's shriek.

Someone had come up behind Dyson and hit him with something. Fox thought he could make out a hammer. The pistol clattered to the ground and another figure picked it up. The attacker was delivering a second blow, and then a third and a fourth. Dyson fell to his knees, then on to his front, face against tarmac. Fox had the impression that a second shriek was coming from a distance — Beth Hastie was making a run for it. He found that he was almost holding his breath, the blood pounding in his ears. And now Dyson — unconscious at the very least — was being dragged along the ground by his feet, disappearing from view. Fox got the feeling he was being lifted into the boot of his car. He heard the boot lid slam in confirmation. And now there was a shadowy figure standing at the threshold to the lock-up, as if taking stock. It moved forward into the gloom and knelt in front of Fox, for all the world as if it might be about to pray. But then there was a glint of steel and a knife began to slice through the covering. The figure prised the polythene apart, exposing Fox's face.

Darryl Christie.

He looked Fox up and down, then got his fingernails under the tape and pulled it free of his mouth. Fox took in gulps of air, feeling he might be sick at any moment.

'Dyson killed Dennis,' he blurted out. And was rewarded with a slow nod.

'Anthony told us. They trussed *him* up too.'

The second figure was waiting a couple of yards away, and Fox realised it was Joe Stark.

'Joe's a traditionalist,' Christie explained. 'No shooters needed — just a nice big claw hammer. I find that admirable.'

'We need to go,' Stark growled.

Christie got back to his feet, brushing dust from the knees of his trousers. 'I'll call it in,' he told Fox. 'The cavalry'll come for you soon.'

'Hastie . . . ?'

'She's running like her life depends on it. Which it probably does. She might actually never *stop* running.' He began to walk away, pausing only to admire the red motorbike. Then he got into the car and started reversing out of Fox's field of vision. Joe Stark hadn't got into the passenger seat — presumably the car they had come in was nearby. A small pool of liquid shone in the moonlight, all that remained of Jackie

Dyson. Fox wondered if he would ever come to learn his real name, the name of the man he had been before he'd been sent into the underworld as a mole.

He didn't suppose it mattered.

★ ★ ★

The first youth appeared a few minutes later, hood pulled low over his head, a scarf masking the lower half of his face. He studied the prone figure and listened as Fox asked for help. But, saying nothing, all he did was wheel away the red motorcycle. A couple of minutes after that, more hooded figures arrived and took the rest of the haul, leaving Fox to wait for the patrol car with its flashing lights. Siobhan Clarke was there too, helping to cut him free and listening to his story.

'We better check Anthony's okay,' he said, rubbing the circulation back into his hands.

'We'll do that.'

His phone had fallen from his pocket and she picked it up, handing it to him. 'You've got a text,' she said.

He looked at the screen. At the two words written there.

He's gone.

42

Rebus sat in the living room. It was lit by a single standard lamp in the opposite corner. The curtains were open a few inches and the back door was unlocked. Brillo was curled at his feet as he held the phone to his ear, waiting for it to be answered. He had already had one text from Dave Ritter to the effect that he couldn't say for sure the photo had been of Bryan Holroyd, plus a long call from Deborah Quant expressing her disbelief that the killer had been under her nose the whole time.

'It's often the way, Deb,' Rebus had told her, thinking of how the Acorn House abusers had carried on with their lives undetected.

The ringing tone stopped, replaced by Malcolm Fox's voice.

'Not really a good time, John.'

'Siobhan just told me. Sorry about your father.'

'I'm at the hospital right now.'

'How's Jude?'

'Weirdly calm.'

'And you?'

'Most of me's still lying cocooned in that lock-up.'

'It was Jackie Dyson then?'

'With a little help from his lover. We need to bring in Christie and Stark.'

'It'll happen. Though I don't suppose we'll ever find a body or the car they took it away in.'

'It was still murder.'

'You sure he was dead?'

'He had to be.'

'I know what a good advocate would do with that in court.'

'Nevertheless.'

'Chief Constable's not going to want it getting out — undercover officer goes feral, kills two.'

'Nevertheless,' Fox repeated. Then: 'I would have died back there if Christie hadn't come to my rescue. I was stupid not to take backup.'

'Welcome to my world — it's taken you long enough.'

'I really don't know if I can do this.'

'Go easy on yourself, Malcolm — your dad's just died. Of course you're feeling low. You need to focus on the funeral now. Give it a week or two before you decide to chuck in a job you're just starting to get good at.'

'Aye, maybe.' Fox expelled air loudly. 'Are you at home?'

'Where else?'

'Finally got a suspect for the Minton murder, I hear.'

'City's locked down tight. He won't be going anywhere.' Rebus paused. 'I better let you go — sorry again about your dad.'

'Thanks.'

'Anything I can do, you only have to say. We'll have a bit of a wake, see how you're feeling by then.' Rebus turned his head towards the open doorway. Jordan Foyle was standing there, a crowbar in his hand. 'Talk to you later,' Rebus said, ending the call. Brillo had woken up and

482

was taking an interest in the new arrival.

'You're not Dalrymple,' Foyle said, taking a couple of steps into the room. He was wearing a thin cotton camouflage jacket over a hooded sweatshirt.

'Not brought the gun?' Rebus commented.

'Who are you?' Foyle was standing in front of him, half brandishing the crowbar. Rebus rested his hands on the arms of his chair, presenting no threat whatsoever. 'Haven't I seen you at the mortuary? You're the guy Professor Quant goes out with.'

Rebus acknowledged the fact with a slight bow of the head. 'My name's John Rebus. I've been looking into Acorn House. Your father changed his name from Bryan Holroyd, didn't he?'

Foyle's eyes widened slightly. 'How do you know?'

'More to the point, son, how do *you*?'

'Where's Dalrymple?'

'It's finished, Jordan. What we need now is an inquiry into Acorn House. For that to happen, we need at least one of the abusers able to testify — meaning alive. You were in Afghanistan, weren't you? I served in Northern Ireland during the Troubles. It never quite goes away — you change and you stay changed. I'm not saying I know what you've been through . . . ' Rebus broke off. 'Look, why don't you sit yourself down? You seem about ready to keel over. It's a cold night to be on the run, but you're safe enough here. There's a sandwich on the kitchen table and a couple of cans of Irn-Bru. Feel free to help yourself.'

'Who are you?'

'I used to be a cop. I've known Big Ger Cafferty for years. He wanted me to help find whoever fired that shot.'

'Can't believe I missed.'

'Minton got the gun on the black market — sighting's probably wonky. Fact he bought it at all means he took your note seriously. Cafferty's a bit more used to threats, so he dismissed it at first. Did Michael Tolland get one too?' Rebus watched the young man nod. 'Must have tossed it then, because we never found it. Took the inquiry a while to link the cases because of that.'

'You know I'm still going to have to kill you?'

'No you're not. You're going to take the weight off your feet and tell me the whole story. Unless you want a drink first.'

The young man stood there, Rebus allowing the silence to linger as calculations were made. 'I need to fetch my backpack,' Foyle said eventually.

'Where is it?'

'The garden.'

'Is the gun in it?'

Foyle nodded. 'But that's not what I need.'

'What then?'

'It's not my story you need to hear — it's my dad's.'

'And that's in the backpack?' Rebus watched the young man nod. 'On you go then,' he said.

'You're coming with me — so you don't try calling anybody. In fact, give me your phone.' Foyle stretched out his free hand and Rebus placed the phone in it. Then he rose slowly to his feet and preceded Foyle into the kitchen and the garden beyond. With the backpack retrieved, they headed back indoors, Rebus suggesting that Foyle could maybe dispense with the crowbar.

'I don't think so,' Foyle said.

'There are armed officers all across the city, Jordan. They see you brandishing anything more solid than a white hankie, they're going to take you down. There were even a couple of them here last night, lying in wait.'

Foyle couldn't help himself. He swivelled towards the window, peering through the gap in the curtains.

'They're not there now,' Rebus assured him. 'Nobody thought you'd be coming. Nobody but me. That's why I left the door unlocked.'

After a further check of the street outside, Foyle settled on the edge of the sofa. As he undid the backpack's straps, he studied Brillo.

'Your dog?' he asked.

'Sort of.'

'I was never allowed a pet. Dad wouldn't let me.'

'I spoke with your mother — he seems to have been a piece of work.'

'That's why he wrote the journal — a sort of apology, I suppose.'

'Your mum doesn't know about it?'

Foyle shook his head. 'He handed it to me one night, told me to keep it to myself. He knew he was ill by then . . . ' He broke off. 'Easier if you see for yourself.' He got up off the sofa and crossed the room towards Rebus, handing over a moleskin notebook, held closed by an elasticated cloth band. 'I'll maybe go get that sandwich,' the young man said, leaving the room.

Rebus unhooked the band and began to read.

The first thing I need you to know, Jordan, is that I wasn't born Mark Foyle. Mark was a lad I got to know when I was sleeping rough in London. He was an addict and one winter he just passed away. Similar age to me and he still had a National Insurance card, so it was easy enough to take his identity. Up till then I'd been Bryan Holroyd. That's the name I was born with. My real birthday's exactly a month before you think it is. Not that I'll be having any more birthdays. I've not said anything to your mum but I've been seeing doctors and it doesn't look good — there's an operation I could have but I don't want it. When it's time, it's time. I've cheated death once, and once was probably enough. I was hanging around in a café before one of the consultations, thinking the usual morbid thoughts, when the song came on. At first I couldn't think where I'd heard it, then I remembered. I opened Shazam on my phone and got a match — 'Even Dogs in the Wild'. It's by a group called the Associates. Turns out they're Scottish. It had been playing that night, as they drove me out to a forest in Fife to bury me. It all came flooding back then, and I felt suddenly really shitty about the way I'd treated you. I couldn't bring myself to love you. I just couldn't. Maybe after reading this you'll understand why . . .

Rebus broke off and watched as Jordan Foyle resumed his perch, the club sandwich in one hand and an open can in the other. The young man chewed, saying nothing, his eyes on Rebus's. Rebus lowered his own eyes and took up the story again.

For a while I was worried I must be gay. I mean, I didn't feel gay, but I'd had sex with a man, so did that make me gay? When Denise showed an interest, I tried putting her off, but you know your mum — she's nothing if not persistent! And later on, when I would wake up sobbing, she'd calm me down. She knew there was something I wasn't telling her, but she said I'd confide in her when I was good and ready. That day's never come. Maybe you'll show her this and maybe you won't — your decision. She was the love of my life — she probably saved my life — and that's the truth. Then she got pregnant and out you popped. And I was cold towards you from the start. I wanted to shut you away from the world, from all the predators out there. I even feared I might turn out to be one myself. So I pushed you away and I know that hurt you — it won't be any consolation that it hurt me too . . .

'First few pages are mostly family,' Jordan Foyle stated, slurping from the can. 'Bit that might interest you is further on.'

Rebus turned some pages until he saw names he recognised and started to read again.

They'd been drinking and doing drugs, and forcing them on me too. Anything to deaden the thoughts and feelings. These were men with gross appetites and nothing to stop them indulging those appetites to the full. Me and the other kids weren't going to be listened to. We were the dregs. David was David Minton, a bigwig lawyer — for years I felt queasy if I ever saw him in a newspaper or on TV. His pal was an MP called Howard Champ. Jimmy was James Broadfoot, and believe it or not, he was Chief Constable in the city. See? These are the kind of men they were — powerful and full of themselves. Todd Dalrymple mostly liked to watch, or just hang out with these bastards. I think he owned a casino in the city. Mickey Tolland worked at Acorn House — everyone based there knew what went on, but he was the one doing the organising. And guess what? He won the bloody lottery a few years back — I had to switch the news off when they showed his stupid grinning face. Married, too. Happy as a pig in shit. Pricks and bastards, the lot of them.

It was Champ who throttled me. That was his thing. But instead of going along with it, I keeled over and pretended I was convulsing. Then I went stock still and held *my breath. Thought I was going to be rumbled when someone checked my pulse, but they were so out of it and panicky, they obviously didn't do it right. A man called Cafferty was mentioned. He'd sort it out. By which they meant get rid of my body. So these two men arrived. By that time, I'd been wrapped up in the sheet I was lying on, which was fine by me — I could breathe a bit without them noticing. They threw me into the boot of their car and that was that. Their names were Paul and Dave, but that's all I know. And they had the radio on. No, actually it was a tape, because one of them ejected it — he didn't like the song. The same song I heard in that café — 'Even Dogs in the Wild'. I listened to it and couldn't believe the words. It was almost as if they'd been written for me. I decided there and then to buy this diary and write in it, something for you to have while I'm still alive.*

Rebus looked up again. Lured by the sandwich, Brillo was sitting on the floor at Foyle's feet. Foyle was feeding him morsels of chicken and bacon and rubbing his coat at the same time.

'Did you talk to him?' Rebus asked.

'He only gave it to me the night before he died. But that morning, I gave him a hug in the upstairs hall. We weren't great at talking. And all because of what happened in that place. His life ruined, my relationship with him ruined

— because of those fuckers.' Foyle nodded towards the book. 'He ran for his life and lay shivering in those woods all night, covered with leaves and whatever else he could scoop up. Then he stole clothes and money from a house and got as far away as he could. London for a while, then Glasgow — that's where he met Mum.' He paused. 'Did you mean what you said about an inquiry?'

'Yes.'

'Would it do any good?'

'It might take down a few reputations.'

'And meanwhile I'll be doing time for murder?'

'You'll plead diminished responsibility. Throw post-traumatic stress into the mix and you should be fine.'

'Meaning?'

'You'll serve a few years, but not many.'

'*If* I turn myself in.'

'What else are you going to do — run away to London?'

'That man Cafferty — he'll put a price on my head.'

'No he won't. He wanted your dad found so he could say sorry to him. My guess is, the same apology's coming to you.'

'Even though I tried to kill him?'

'Even so,' Rebus confirmed.

Foyle turned his head towards the backpack sitting next to him on the sofa. 'I was seriously thinking about blowing my brains out — after I'd settled with Dalrymple.'

'You shouldn't do that,' Rebus said quietly.

Then: 'Any chance I can have my phone back?'

Foyle's eyes narrowed. 'Why?'

'I want to see if I can get on the internet. There's a song I really need to hear.'

Foyle considered for a moment, then handed the phone over. But before he did anything, Rebus skipped to the end of the journal, reading Bryan Holroyd's last words.

I never did love you, son. I wouldn't let myself, and that goes with me to my grave. I wish I could change the past, but I can't. All I can offer you is this story. I've been so proud of you, and I hated what your time as a squaddie did to you. We're none of us machines, Jordan, though sometimes that's the way the world treats us. Look after your mum and look after yourself. And don't go getting any more of those bloody tattoos.

Silent tears were running down Jordan Foyle's cheeks as he lifted Brillo up, burying his face in his fur.

Epilogue

The mourners at Mortonhall Crematorium just about filled the smaller of the two chapels. Fox and his sister shared the front pew, with staff and residents from Mitch Fox's care home in the others and Rebus and Clarke by themselves at the back. The order of service had a photo of the deceased on the front, smiling at whoever had been holding the camera and probably taken two or three decades back.

'He looks like Malcolm,' Rebus observed to Clarke.

'Apparently Jude takes after their mum,' Clarke whispered back.

The service was brief, just the two hymns and some biographical details from the minister, along with a prayer. Neither Fox nor his sister got up to speak. Everyone stood as the minister led them back out into the sunshine, where a few wreaths lay. Rebus shook Jude's hand and introduced himself as 'a friend of Malcolm's'. Another handshake from Fox himself.

'Are you coming to the hotel?' Fox asked.

Rebus shook his head. 'Things to do — you know what it's like.'

'I'm coming,' Clarke interrupted, giving Fox a hug and a kiss on the cheek.

'We're rendezvousing at the Ox later, though?' Fox checked.

'Try and stop me,' Rebus said, digging into his

pocket for his cigarettes before heading for the car park. The day was bright, the sun low, casting long shadows. He'd had to scrape ice from the Saab using the edge of a credit card, a move he regretted when the card snapped in two. He would call into his bank on the way home and let them know. Or maybe it could wait until tomorrow.

There was a figure in black standing by the car — Cafferty, in a three-quarter-length coat, its collar turned up.

'I still want to speak to the lad,' he said.

'He already knows what you'll say.'

'Even so.'

Rebus offered a shrug and tapped on the car window. Brillo was seated inside, waiting impatiently. 'I've asked Page and he's said no. You can always visit Jordan in jail.'

'If I live that long.' Cafferty looked towards the small crowd outside the crematorium. Fresh mourners were arriving for the next session, mostly in cars, a few on foot. 'I hate these places,' he muttered with a shiver.

'Don't we all?'

'It's in my will that I'm to be buried rather than burned.'

'In consecrated ground?' Rebus took one last puff of his cigarette before grinding the stub under his heel.

'I'm prepared to repent my sins at the last.'

'Better start now — it's going to take a while.'

The two men shared a smile. Cafferty examined the tips of his shoes. 'Christie's teamed up with Joe Stark,' he said.

'So I hear.'

'Means he might end up running Glasgow.'

'If we don't put him away as an accessory to murder.'

'Good luck with that. Is it true Holroyd left a diary?' He watched as Rebus nodded. 'Naming names?'

'Including yours.'

'You think the inquiry will get off the ground?'

'I dare say some will want it strangled at birth.' Rebus had taken out his car keys. 'Can I give you a lift?'

Cafferty shook his head and gestured towards the window. 'You keeping the dog?'

'Maybe.'

'Might be a good move, now you're retired — nice long walks in the fresh air. I find I like walking too.'

'Now that there's no one with a gun out there looking for you?'

'Every car that passes, though . . . I always wonder if this'll be the time it stops and Darryl Christie invites me to step in.'

'If we get him to trial, will you testify?'

'Absolutely.' Cafferty paused. 'But for the defence rather than your lot.' He gave the briefest of waves as he turned to go.

'You still reckon you have the beating of him, don't you?' Rebus called out. Cafferty paused without looking back and held up a single index finger. Rebus knew what the gesture meant.

One last good fight left in me . . .

He didn't doubt it for a minute.

Opening the Saab and getting in, Rebus gave

Brillo's coat a rub before starting the engine. He watched as Cafferty's figure receded, then lifted a CD from the passenger seat and slotted it home. It had arrived first thing, mail order. The album was called *The Affectionate Punch*. He skipped through it to track seven and listened as Billy Mackenzie started to sing about a boy, a boy frightened, neglected, abandoned. Sons and fathers, he thought: Malcolm and Mitch Fox, Dennis and Joe Stark, Jordan Foyle and Bryan Holroyd. His phone alerted him to a text. It was from Samantha. She had sent the photo he'd asked for, the one of him and Carrie. He studied it for a moment before showing it to a quizzical Brillo; then, having turned up the volume on the stereo, he reversed out of the parking space and headed back into the city.

We do hope that you have enjoyed reading this large print book.

Did you know that all of our titles are available for purchase?

We publish a wide range of high quality large print books including:
Romances, Mysteries, Classics
General Fiction
Non Fiction and Westerns

Special interest titles available in large print are:
The Little Oxford Dictionary
Music Book
Song Book
Hymn Book
Service Book

Also available from us courtesy of Oxford University Press:
Young Readers' Dictionary
(large print edition)
Young Readers' Thesaurus
(large print edition)

For further information or a free brochure, please contact us at:
Ulverscroft Large Print Books Ltd.,
The Green, Bradgate Road, Anstey,
Leicester, LE7 7FU, England.
Tel: (00 44) 0116 236 4325
Fax: (00 44) 0116 234 0205

SAINTS OF THE SHADOW BIBLE

Ian Rankin

John Rebus is back on the force, albeit with a big demotion and an even larger chip on his shoulder. A new law has been passed allowing the Scottish police to re-prosecute old crimes and a thirty-year-old case is being reopened, with Rebus and his team from back then suspected of corruption and worse. Known as 'the Saints', his colleagues swore a bond of mutual loyalty on something called the Shadow Bible. But with Malcolm Fox as the investigating officer — and determined to use Rebus for his own ends — the crimes of the past may not stay hidden much longer. With political turmoil threatening to envelop Scotland, who really are the saints, and who the sinners? And can one ever become the other?

THE NAMING OF THE DEAD

Ian Rankin

July 2005, and the G8 leaders have gathered in Scotland. With daily marches, demonstrations and scuffles, the police are at full stretch. Detective Inspector John Rebus, however, has been sidelined . . . until the apparent suicide of an MP coincides with clues that a serial killer may be on the loose. The authorities are keen to hush up both, for fear of overshadowing a meeting of global importance — but Rebus has never been one to stick to the rules. And when his colleague Siobhan Clarke finds herself hunting down the identity of the riot cop who assaulted her mother, it looks as though both Rebus and Clarke may be pitted against both sides in the conflict.